Another Christmas Without You

LARA KETTER

This is a work of fiction. All characters, organizations, businesses and events portrayed in this novel are either products of the author's imagination or are used fictitiously.

Cover design by Lara Ketter on Canva.com.

My first novel is dedicated to you, the reader.

Table of Contents

Lara Ketter
ANOTHER CHRISTMAS WITHOUT YOU

A NOTE FROM THE AUTHOR

Dear Reader,

I've dreamed of writing a novel for several years now, but the thought of it was intimidating. Novel writing is an entirely different beast from the type of writing I've done – columns, blogs, newspaper articles, memoirs – and I didn't know if I was up to the task. But when the idea for this novel came to me, I knew I had to do it.

Another Christmas Without You draws inspiration from the Legend of Waconda, the tragic yet moving story of a Native American princess named Waconda. You'll read about the princess, the spring that came to bear her name and Waconda Lake, but I want you to know that what you're about to read is historically accurate based on research I personally conducted. Waconda Lake is 25 miles from my home.

The book is unusual in that I've incorporated the Legend of Waconda into the theme, but it's also somewhat of a cliché because my dream was to write a novel that included a coffee shop at Christmastime with a handsome stranger. But make no mistake ... this is not your cookie cutter Christmas story.

When the story idea came to me I knew immediately that I wanted the town to be called Waconda because a town by that name was founded when the area was settled. The town didn't survive, so I decided that I would use the real town of Glen Elder as the inspiration for Waconda.

As a Kansas native and prolific reader, I've dreamed of writing contemporary novels set in Kansas. They say to write what you know. Well, I know Kansas!

I hope you enjoy reading this book as much as I enjoyed writing it.

With warm regards,
Lara Ketter

PROLOGUE

When I was a small child, hair damp from a bubble bath and cotton nightgown carelessly pulled over my head and lanky arms, I'd snuggle under my pink chenille bedspread, Bedtime Bear hugged tightly to my chest, and I'd sigh in contentment as Dad told me the story of a beautiful Native American princess named Waconda who lived in our valley many moons before. My bedroom was shadowed in the faint glow cast from a single nightlight, and Dad would stretch out his long limbs beside me, his huge feet hanging over the edge of my tiny twin mattress. As Dad recounted the tale, he transformed from a simple farmer into a master storyteller, his face lively and his hands animated. I closed my eyes and pictured every nuance, every detail of the Legend of Waconda splashed in vivid hues across my mind, the story I never tired of hearing … the story I begged him to tell me over and over and over again.

Waconda was the daughter of Chief Mansotan of the Cheyenne tribe, and her beauty and intelligence were known throughout the land. Because of this Waconda was desired by young chiefs and warriors who sought her hand in marriage and wooed her father with gifts of ponies, colorful beads and buffalo robes. Chief Mansotan sent away the suitors because he'd promised Waconda she could pick her own mate. She chose Chillotan, a brave warrior who was skillful, strong and won her heart.

In the valley where the Cheyenne lived there was a natural spring whose water was revered by the Native Americans for its healing properties. Waconda was taught that the Great Spirit, who gave to the world all its beauty and delights, was present in the waters of the spring, and with bowed head and heart she worshipped at that liquid shrine as devoutly as any Christian.

After Waconda chose Chillotan to be her mate, but before they were married, the Sioux from the north invaded the hunting grounds of the Cheyenne, and all of the warriors from the village joined the fight, including Chillotan. Waconda promised Chillotan that at every sunset she would walk to the spring, make an offering to the Great Spirit and pray for the success of her tribe and the return of her lover.

Days passed and news from the north was devastating as the Cheyenne were driven from their hunting grounds by the Sioux. Waconda was faithful to her word, visiting the spring every sunset to pray. When the war ended word arrived that Chillotan had been killed in the battle. That evening Waconda left the village and as usual went to the spring, but this time she did not return. It was said that in her distress and grief she threw herself into the spring to join Chillotan in the Great Beyond. The natives believed the Spirit of Waconda resided in the waters, and thus the Legend of Waconda was born.

It seems a sad and tragic story to share with a child, but I was fascinated with the kind of love that could drive a person insane with its loss. I was so enamored with Waconda that I often asked Dad to tell me her story, and then I'd lie in the dark and wonder if I'd ever love someone that deeply.

I did. With all my heart.

Then, like Waconda, I lost my lover in tragedy. Sorrow, grief and anger crowded my heart and threatened to cease its beating. I didn't care if my heart shriveled up or exploded into a thousand tiny pieces. Like Waconda, I was insane with loss and ready to fling myself into the spring to join my love in the Great Beyond. I'm not sure what kept me from doing it.

For years afterward I dreamt of Waconda and the spring she revered. In my dream she was suspended in midair over the silent water as if in flight, arms out at her sides like the wings of an airplane. Her lustrous hair, the color of a raven, flowed in a gentle breeze, and she smiled right before she fell into the spring, its waters icy cold. She didn't flail about or fight to save herself, and her bronze eyes remained open, exuding peace as she floated gently downward. When she reached the bottom, her hands fell together over her heart and her eyes closed one last time.

As I gazed at Waconda I would slowly come to the realization that I was in the water next to her, and this sent me into a panic as my lungs begged for oxygen. I fought to push off the bottom of the spring toward the surface, but my legs wouldn't move because they were frozen solid. I flailed wildly about, straining with my arms to gain momentum upward as I gulped ice-cold water into my lungs, but my arms were leaden and chilled to the bone. As the futility of the situation settled into my heart I realized I was going to die.

This is the moment I'd wake drenched in sweat and hyperventilating, gasping for air then drawing huge breaths into my lungs. *It was just a dream, it was just a dream*, I'd repeat like a mantra until I was fully awake and aware of the fact that I was in my warm, cozy bed and not frozen at the bottom of Waconda Springs.

It's fascinating how human beings can compartmentalize in order to survive. Tragedies too difficult to bear are often filed and locked away, yet the horrifying memories and painful feelings are always right there, just under the surface. We choose to forget, and we wear the facade of control, but we're not in control. One person or event can pull away the veil, leaving us exposed and raw.

Ten years ago, I suffered a tragedy that rocked me to my core. Months later, in order to survive, I buried this awful day and moved on. It was either that or waste away in my childhood bedroom which, I can tell you, was quite tempting but not realistic.

The pain, anger and resentment were buried as well, and to keep them hidden I stayed busy. Forgiveness wasn't even on the radar; I would no sooner forgive than cut off my right hand. When memories surfaced I pushed them down; when feelings chased me, I took up running; when loneliness threatened I hugged a friend.

My strategy for survival was working: I was coping; I was dealing; I was getting by.

That was all about to end.

I can tell you this much: I was in no way prepared for what was to come.

THURSDAY, DECEMBER 14, 2017

Chapter 1

When my phone's alarm went off at 5 am I had no way of knowing that in a few hours I would meet both my past and my future in one person.

I rolled over and grabbed the phone off the nightstand, tapped the STOP button to blessedly end the alarm's annoying tune and dropped it onto the white plush comforter. Groaning, I fell back into the softness of my pillow-top mattress and pledged that today would be the day I actually changed the alarm to a pleasant tune.

I rubbed my eyes, ran fingers through my tangled hair and fantasized about sleeping until noon. Lord, I was tired. I rolled onto my side, pulled the comforter under my chin and wondered if I could stay in bed all day and ignore my caffeine-dependent customers. They could make their own coffee, right? In their own homes? Maybe eat some heart-healthy oatmeal instead of the sugar-laden confectionary delights I sold them?

It was an argument I had with myself every morning at 5 am, and ultimately my need for income always won out over my need for sleep. This day was no different. As one of my favorite sayings goes, *First I drink the coffee, then I do the things.*

I sighed, sat up and turned on the bedside lamp, squinting as my eyes adjusted to the sudden source of light. I stretched out my legs and assessed the damage from my two-mile jog the day before: my right hip was a little tight and my left calf muscle was sore but, overall, not bad for a woman who would celebrate her 37th birthday the next day.

Sleep had eluded me again — I fought demons in nightmares, changed sleep positions what seemed like every five minutes and checked the clock multiple times to see if I'd dozed at all. When was the last time I'd slept through the night? I couldn't remember.

I forced myself to leave the warm cocoon of my bed and flinched when my bare feet touched the chilly hardwood floor. I stood, reached my arms toward the ceiling and bent over to touch my toes, which I was proud to say I could still do. I rubbed my right elbow and upper arm in an attempt to work out the kinks that I knew would never work out.

I shuffled to the small bathroom where I glared at the dark circles under my eyes, then brushed the knots out of my long, unremarkably brown hair and pulled it into a messy bun on top of my head, securing it with a ponytail and several bobby pins. The cold water I splashed on my face was all I could manage since I didn't have time to wait ten minutes for the hot water to reach the sink. I grabbed the hand towel and dabbed at my face, then smoothed on a thick layer of moisturizer.

In the living room I grabbed the remote and turned on the television to see if the world had imploded while I was trying to sleep. My favorite meteorologist, a handsome, clean-cut guy I'd nicknamed Cutie Boy Ross, gestured to a weather map of Kansas that filled the screen behind him. "If you're dreaming of a White Christmas, it's on the way to the sunflower state. An arctic air mass will drop into the U.S. from Canada tomorrow, and the system will dump up to three feet of snow across Kansas beginning early Saturday morning." He smiled at the camera as computer-generated snowflakes floated across the map. "Snow prediction is highly volatile and it's difficult to tell how long the front will remain stagnant, but we expect it to pull out of the area late on Sunday and to see some sun by Monday morning."

Ross smiled at his viewers, and if any teenage girls had been awake at that ungodly hour they would have sighed and clutched their chests. Ross continued: "Temperatures aren't expected to climb above freezing for several weeks and this means the snow will hang around through Christmas." He clapped his hands and grinned in delight. "Get out those sleds, kids, and find a big hill ... snow is on the way!"

In the closet I halfway listened to the news and donned my standard work fare — skinny jeans, an oversized white V-neck T-shirt and navy blue bandana that I rolled into a headband to keep the hair out of my eyes and the customers' food and drinks. I tied the bandana at the base of my neck as I walked back into the bathroom.

Makeup for work was simple and fast. Foundation melted under the steam of an espresso machine, so I skipped the base makeup, brushed on neutral eye shadow, lined my eyes and then applied black mascara, rosy blush and pink lip gloss. I noticed a pimple forming on my chin and, after close examination, once again marveled that a woman my age could still sprout acne. I glared at the dark circles again, one of the myriad side effects of sleeping like a newborn baby. I find it ironic that when people sleep well they say they slept like a baby — any baby I've ever known wakes up several times during the night crying for one reason or another. I'd rather sleep like a teenager, oblivious to the outside world and unconscious until at least noon.

I walked over to my bed and laughed at the chaos: it looked like two raccoons had been trapped and tried to battle their way out. I picked up my phone and slipped it into my back jeans pocket as I tugged the sheet and comforter into position, then I tucked the sheet in tightly at the bottom of the mattress, fluffed the pillows and readied the bed for another go at sleep that night.

I stopped at the nightstand and reached into the heart-shaped ceramic dish that held my only jewelry — diamond earrings and a pendant necklace with a blue sapphire stone at its center surrounded by five delicate diamonds in the shape of a flower. I inserted the earrings and secured the necklace at the base of my neck, then lifted the pendant to my lips for several seconds as my eyes closed in a silent prayer. With a deep sigh I walked into the closet where I grabbed socks and a pair of red Skechers from my ridiculously large collection of athletic shoes. Did my shoes mate and have families while I was at work?

Satisfied that the world had survived another night, I turned off the TV and walked to the door that served as both my front and back entrance — in fact, the only entrance and exit unless I jumped out of a window. Sitting on the small blue bench I'd found at a yard sale the summer before, I pulled on my socks and shoes. I stood and slipped into my heavy gray coat, grabbed a set of keys off the hook by the door and headed out to work.

Here's the advantage to living above your place of business: the commute is a piece of cake. I ran down the stairs, taking care not to slip on the ice that usually formed during the night when winter set in. Once I reached the back door on the ground level I unlocked the dead bolt with one key, the doorknob with another key and grinned at the Bree Brews It Coffeehouse & Cafe sign painted in white block letters on the bright red door.

I stepped inside and flipped on the four switches by the back door. As the large space filled with light, I sighed in satisfaction. I really love my coffee shop.

If I'd made such a statement in grade school some young punk would have laughed in my face. "If you love it so much, why don't you marry it?" Back then I would have stomped off in embarrassment but today I'd just smile and say, "Good idea. I think I'll marry my coffee shop!"

I shut the door, shrugged out of my coat and hung it on a rack in the corner. My key ring was relegated to its usual spot over an old nail in the limestone wall. I shivered and turned the heat up to 70. Grabbing an apron, I slipped it over my head and tied it at the waist, then I scrubbed my hands with soap for twenty seconds per the directions of the esteemed Kansas Department of Health. At the prep sink I filled two large pitchers with water which I carried one at a time to the self-serve coffee bar at the front of the building.

I opened the lids of the double coffee brewers and my right elbow cried in protest when I lifted the pitchers and filled the water reservoirs. I wondered what I'd do when my elbow finally gave out on me. I scooped generous amounts of ground coffee beans into the filters, one a dark roast and the other a breakfast blend. After I slipped the filter baskets into place I turned both sides of the machine to ON, held my breath and listened as it whirred to life. I crossed my fingers and studied the cantankerous old machine until I was certain the coffee was, indeed, brewing. I exhaled in relief. Three months earlier the old broad had refused to brew the coffee, and the catastrophe was dubbed The Great Coffee Debacle by my regulars who think they're all comedians. The non-caffeinated masses were not happy, and they teased me mercilessly for months. I gently patted the side of the massive machine. "Good girl."

I made my way to the refrigerator where I pulled out a stainless steel server filled with milk and a bowl of half-and-half containers which I carried to the coffee bar and set in their usual spots. I examined the supply of white ceramic coffee cups, to-go cups and lids, packets of sugar, creamer and coffee stirrers, and then I reached under the counter for more coffee cups. Satisfied that the self-serve coffee bar was ready for action, I turned to my other early-morning tasks. I glanced at the clock and saw that it was 5:40. Jim would be here soon.

I walked back to the granite island behind the front counter and checked to see that the espresso machine was filled with water, the only prep work necessary since I kept it immaculately clean. In the kitchen at the back of the building I emptied the dishwasher and carried a tray full of white ceramic coffee cups to the island, stacking them next to the espresso machine.

In the supply closet I grabbed a package of to-go cups and lids, set them on the island near the espresso machine and poured coffee beans into the grinder. I filled the hot water dispenser that was used to make cocoa, and I turned on the iced tea maker/dispenser I'd prepped the day before. It continued to astonish me that customers actually ordered iced tea in the middle of winter, but they did. I was ready for the drinkers of the world … or at least the Waconda Lake area.

I heard pounding on the back door, a sure sign that Jim had arrived. I looked at the clock — 5:45 and on time as usual. I hurried to the back, opened the door and found him balancing four boxes in his ample hands.

"Good morning!" Jim charged through the door to the island where he ceremoniously set the boxes down. His black Sweet Eats Bakery T-shirt was strained at its seams and his ample belly did its best to stay concealed. "There you go, my lady." He grinned and struck a Price is Right model pose to show off the large white bakery boxes.

I looked down at him and shook my head. "Still refusing to wear a coat, huh?"

"Why? Is it cold outside?"

"I guess not for studs like you." I lifted the top box, set it on the counter and, as I opened its lid, the tantalizing aroma of fresh glazed doughnuts hit my nostrils. "They look and smell amazing, as usual." I couldn't resist; I lifted one from the container and bit into the soft dough, sighing as the sweet pastry and gooey glaze melted together in my mouth. "Tastes even better!"

Jim laughed and set his order book on the counter, pulled a pen out of his jeans pocket and grinned. "You're looking more beautiful than ever. Are you doing something new with your hair?" He was an unapologetic flirt.

I slapped his arm. "I can't believe you noticed. I just had some highlights put in."

"Well, a smart man pays attention." He winked and leaned against the counter. "You really should model, you know. I could sell a lot more doughnuts if you'd let me put your picture on the side of my truck."

I smiled as I shoved another bite in my mouth. "You certainly have a way of making me feel good about myself at six in the morning … even if it involves doughnuts."

"Offer always stands. Put a pretty woman with any product and sales skyrocket. It's good business, pure and simple."

I finished off the doughnut and wiped my hands on my apron. "I'll keep that in mind if I ever get sick of peddling coffee."

He chuckled and picked up his order book. "I'll hold you to it." Pleasantries over, Jim turned serious. "Okay. I need to double check your order for tomorrow."

I nodded. "The birthday cupcakes."

"Yep." He thumbed through his order book until he reached the right page. "You ordered 200 cupcakes, correct? We just need to double check before we bake them this afternoon."

"That's right."

Jim smiled and shook his head. "You certainly do spoil your customers with free cupcakes on your birthday."

"It's part of my master plan to keep them buying coffee."

"Well, it must be working." Jim studied his order pad. "Okay. I've got down 200 chocolate fudge cupcakes with hot pink buttercream frosting and silver sprinkles?"

"Yep."

He looked up and grinned. "We'll get 'er done and deliver in the morning along with your usual Friday order."

I shook my head. "Since most of my customers will eat a free cupcake tomorrow I won't need as many doughnuts and pastries."

Jim held his pen over the order book. "Okay. How many are you thinking then?"

I crossed my arms and considered for a moment. "Why don't you just bring half of my normal Friday order."

Jim scribbled in his order pad. "Okey dokey. Sounds like a plan." He turned to leave but stopped and studied me. "So which birthday will this one be?"

"Thirty-seven." I marveled that I was just three years shy of 40.

Jim tapped his chest. "You're just a bit younger than me, then. I'll be forty in May."

"It's weird getting older, isn't it?"

He frowned. "I always say it beats the alternative. I'd rather be looking at the grass than the roots." He pointed at me. "It's just a number."

I laughed at his logic. "You're right. I'll try to remember that."

"By the way, I'm taking next week off, so Justin will be running my delivery route."

I leaned against the counter. "Are you flying up to Canada again?"

"Yep. Same old trip. My brother and a group of friends are heading up to British Columbia to fly fish." He slipped the order pad into a back pocket and crossed his thick arms. "I'm not much of a fisherman but it's beautiful up there. The guys reel 'em in and I cook 'em. Delicious! And the beer is great."

"Will you be back for Christmas?"

"Yep. We fly home on the twenty-third." He saluted me and turned to go. "Always a pleasure, Miss Bree. I'm off. See you in the morning." With a slam of the door he was gone.

I carried the boxes of baked goods to the front counter where I set them down and slid open the glass doors of the bakery display case. I pulled out four large trays that held the confectionary delights, as I liked to call them, and set aside three glazed doughnuts and two banana nut muffins left over from the day before. I carried the empty trays back to the kitchen where I washed and dried them, then returned to the front counter and arranged glazed doughnuts, chocolate-filled doughnuts, long johns, blueberry, banana and chocolate chip muffins, plain and blueberry bagels and croissants into even rows. I slid these into the display case and closed the doors.

At the dark walnut console table near the front door I turned on the shop's satellite radio and jumped when "Ice Ice Baby" blasted from the speakers, clear evidence that "90s on 9" was tuned in. I turned down the volume and smiled; the song was fitting for such a frigid day, but I was craving Christmas music, so I turned to the "Holiday Traditions" channel and grinned when Bing Crosby's "White Christmas" filled the old limestone building.

In desperate need of caffeine, I walked to the self-serve coffee bar where I grabbed an extra-large ceramic mug that read "Life Happens. Coffee Helps." from my extensive collection and filled it with dark roast coffee, added sugar and milk, stirred it twice and sighed as the rich liquid slid down my throat. I relished this quiet time before my customers rolled in; the smell of coffee and bakery confections swirled together in the air and became its own intoxicating aroma. I gulped the coffee like it was my last drink before I was led to the electric chair.

I walked to the front door and unlocked it, then turned the CLOSED sign to OPEN. I picked up the sidewalk sign that was leaning against the wall inside the door and carried it over to the front counter. I erased yesterday's lunch special and wrote in white chalk on both sides: TODAY'S LUNCH SPECIAL: Sloppy Joe, Potato Salad, Homemade Cookie - $6.99. CHERRY PIE. PUMPKIN PIE. I drew holly and berries with green and red chalk, carried the sign outside and set it up on the sidewalk.

I shivered in the brisk morning air and gazed across the street at the Town Square decorated for Christmas: strings of bright lights, greenery and red bows cheered up the dreary winter landscape. The largest evergreen in the park was circled in multi-colored lights with a flashing star on top. An inflatable Santa Claus driving a motorcycle winked back at me, and the plastic manger scene on the corner was missing its donkey, most likely the result of a teenage prank. It would show up eventually.

The electronic sign on the bank announced that the temperature was 26 degrees. The air smelled cold, if cold has a smell, and my breath turned to fog. The bare tree limbs and grass in the park begged for a covering of white, and I hoped Cutie Boy Ross was right about snow this weekend. Winter was in need of a makeover.

I pushed open the front door and walked inside followed by Rich and Dave, who made a beeline for the coffee bar and helped themselves.

Rich spoke first. "Morning, Bree."

Dave mumbled his greeting. "Morning, Bree."

I leaned against the limestone wall by the coffee bar. "Good morning, guys. What's the news today?"

Rich grabbed a coffee cup and filled it with the dark roast. He liked it black, no frills. "Snow's coming. Get out your long johns!"

I laughed. "Oh, they're out; I layer up when I go for a run. Yeah, I heard on the news this morning that snow is definitely coming."

"Did Cutie Boy Ross tell you that?" Rich grinned and gulped at his coffee.

I shook my head and chuckled. "I will always regret telling you my nickname for the weatherman."

He nodded in agreement. "You really should know better than to reveal your secrets around here."

"Don't plan on going anywhere this weekend." Dave issued his warning sober-faced. He dropped two dollar bills into the change basket and fished out change. "They say we could get up to three feet."

I crossed my arms. "I thought snow was the hardest weather to predict."

Dave rolled his eyes and filled his cup with the breakfast blend, then added three packets of sugar and two creamers. He stirred it slowly. "That's what the weathermen say so they don't get caught with their pants down. They're just covering their…"

Rich interrupted. "Watch your language. We have a lady present."

Dave looked around the coffee shop as if searching for something. "Where?"

I playfully slapped him on the shoulder. "Watch yourself, now."

Rich slurped his coffee and sat down at one of the tables I bought at an auction and refinished myself. "With this drought we're in the wheat could really use a drink."

Dave joined him with his coffee, sank into a chair and pointed outside. "Rain or snow, we'll take it however we can get it. We're not picky."

"Well, I'm dreaming of a white Christmas." I sipped at the strong coffee and noticed my cup was almost empty.

"So, you're one of those, huh?" Dave was smiling. "Just like my wife — a romantic at heart." His eyes softened and he gazed out the window. "Her favorite movie is 'White Christmas'."

I refilled my cup and added hazelnut creamer. "I love that one too." I sat down and swallowed some of the hot liquid. "We don't get snow like we used to. I was just thinking about how the kids around here barely know what snow is — let alone how to play in it. Do they even know how to build a snowman or sled down a hill?"

Rich nodded in agreement. "I know what you mean. When we were kids it would snow six, eight feet, easy. We'd have snowball fights and build snowmen and make snow tunnels. God, it was fun." He smiled at the memory.

Dave leaned his elbows on the table. "We played Duck-Duck-Goose and made snow angels."

My eyebrows shot up. "You made snow angels? I can't imagine."

"I was young and sweet once, young lady, until life kicked me in the…"

Rich interrupted again. "Watch yourself, Dave."

"I know, I know. There's a lady present." He sauntered over to the coffee bar and refilled his cup.

"It's okay, Dave. I've never considered myself a lady."

Rich placed his hand on my arm and gently squeezed. "You are definitely a lady. And without you we'd be making our own coffee every morning. You're an angel."

"Yeah, a coffee angel." Dave sat back down and grinned.

"Well, don't tell anyone, but you guys are my favorite customers."

The men high-fived and Dave squinted at me. "Will you put our picture on the wall? Customers of the Month. Better yet, Customers of the Year!"

"I said it was a secret so don't go opening your big mouth." I pointed at Dave who pulled an imaginary key out of his pocket and locked his lips together.

The bell over the front door rang and Brice stepped inside. Thrilled to see him, I jumped to my feet and he walked straight over, grabbed me in a bear hug and lifted me clear off the ground, one of the few men who actually could. "Morning, Sis."

I managed to return his greeting even though it was hard to draw breath while being squeezed so tightly by my big brother. He set me down, and as he ran fingers through his messy dark hair I noticed that Brice's brown eyes were bloodshot, a coating of stubble shaded his face and the white T-shirt under his coat was as wrinkled as a Shar Pei puppy. He looked like hell on a bad day. "God, I need an espresso. A double."

I made my way to the espresso machine behind the front counter as a group of regulars walked in and gathered at the coffee bar. Brice followed me, and I smiled in sympathy. "You look exhausted. Rough night?"

He leaned on the counter and dropped his head. "Lord, yes. Nate had a nightmare and couldn't get back to sleep so I let him get in bed with us and that was a huge mistake! He kicked me all night. That kid is a wild sleeper. I already feel sorry for his future wife."

I laughed as a picture formed in my mind of Brice's five-year-old son kicking the daylights out of him. "I bet he slept okay."

Brice nodded. "Oh yeah. He was out like a light when I finally gave up and came here. I left Caitlin a note that I'd bring her a latte."

I pulled the porta filter out of the espresso machine, wiped it down with a clean white towel and then held it under the automatic coffee grinder, watching as it filled with ground coffee in a dark, rich color. I leveled it off, tamped the grounds evenly, cleaned the rim and slid the filter into the espresso machine until it locked. I flushed the water in the machine, set a cup under the dispenser, turned on the machine and watched as the espresso was extracted into the cup. When it was almost full I turned off the machine and handed it to Brice who drank it greedily.

"One double espresso for you and I'll get Caitlin's drink going. Do you think she wants her usual cinnamon vanilla latte?"

Brice looked up from his drink. "You know it. She'd probably send me back if I brought her a plain latte."

I laughed. "Well, I don't want you to get in trouble with your sweet wife."

Brice shook his head. "She's not so sweet until she has her coffee."

"I can relate." I repeated the process, and as espresso flowed into the to-go cup, I poured whole milk into a stainless steel steaming pitcher, lowered in the steam wand, opened the valve to full power and watched as the milk turned hot and foamy. When the foam was a consistency I was happy with, I turned off the steam valve and swirled the pitcher to combine the foam on top with the milk on the bottom. I turned off the espresso machine, stirred in pure vanilla and poured the steamed milk into the dark coffee, creating a heart design. To finish the drink, I sprinkled cinnamon on top. I snapped on a lid and handed the drink to Brice who gave me his cup, now empty.

"Could you get me another, this one to go? And make it an Americano — but strong."

I laughed. "Your wish is my command, sir, but be careful driving home." Brice nodded tiredly as I ground coffee beans for his Americano, extracted the espresso and added hot water. I popped on a lid and handed him the drink. "How about some doughnuts or muffins?"

He nodded toward the display case. "What do you have left from yesterday?"

"Three glazed doughnuts and two banana nut muffins."

"I'll take 'em and throw in another glazed and two blueberry muffins."

"You got it." I filled a white to-go box with his order and handed it to him. "It's on the house, as usual, since you're my favorite brother."

"That's so kind of you considering I'm your only brother." He set the drinks on top of the box and turned to go but stopped suddenly and came around the counter to where I was standing. "Hey. Have you heard from Ice-T? She hasn't called Caitlin or me for at least three days."

My good mood soured. "Yeah, I haven't heard from her, either. It's been nice."

Brice frowned. "Now, Bree, this is Mother you're talking about."

"What she does and who she does it with is really none of my concern." I grabbed a rag and wiped down the clean counter.

His voice was tender. "I know that, but she was so excited about this Alaskan cruise with Hank, and I worry about her. Two weeks is a long time to be gone."

"Brice, you know Mother can hold her own with anyone. Hank better not cross her, or she'll run him right off the ship. Make him walk the plank or something."

Brice chuckled. "Have you heard the radio ads for his used car dealership? They're hilarious."

I snorted. "You mean the ads that run every five minutes? Why do you think I switched to satellite radio?"

"I love how he says, 'Come on down to Castillo Cars — where the customer is king and Honest Hank will give you one whale of a deal.'"

I stared at him. "You have that memorized?"

"I've only heard it a hundred times. Unlike the aristocracy, we peasants can't afford satellite radio."

I glanced around to make sure no one was listening and then leaned toward Brice. "Before she left Mother said she thought Hank was going to 'pop the question' during the cruise."

He smiled warmly. "You know, he's not that bad of a guy. It might be good if the ol' Ice Queen got remarried."

"I really don't care one way or the other." And I didn't, but then the thought hit me that a union between the two was not without its advantages. "The only good thing to come out of her marrying Hank is that she'd probably move to his mansion in Beloit and you could sweet-talk Caitlin into finally moving out to the farm."

He shook his head. "I'll believe it when I see it."

I pointed to the food and drinks in his hands. "You'd better get out of here. I'm sure Caitlin is waiting at the door for her latte."

"Yeah, I'm going, but if you hear from Mother will you tell her to call me? I just want to know that she's still alive and hasn't fallen off the ship into the icy water."

I snickered. "That would be a funny way for her to go, wouldn't it?" Brice just stared at me as I explained. "Ice-T? Ice? Icy water? It would be fitting."

"Whatever, Bree." Brice hurried to the door, juggling two coffees and the box of goodies. "See you later."

I called after him. "Tell Caitlin and the boys hello. Enjoy the confectionary delights!" Brice walked out into the cold morning and disappeared from sight.

Conversation and laughter bounced off the walls as my early-morning coffee drinkers speculated on the coming snow, shared tidbits of gossip and teased each other. I walked among the tables taking orders for baked goods, and back at the display case I picked up the plastic tongs and placed four doughnuts, five muffins, two bagels and three croissants on a tray. At the refrigerator I grabbed two packets of cream cheese, picked up a stack of small plates and returned to the front where I handed out the goodies and collected money.

"Bree?" Doris Waverly grabbed my arm as I passed by her chair.

"Morning, Doris. How's the blueberry muffin?"

"Delicious as always." Doris turned to look at the woman sitting next to her. "Honey, I want you to meet my sister, Gloria, from Topeka."

Gloria was definitely Doris's sister. Something around the mouth and nose was similar, and their light aqua eyes peered curiously from behind wire-rimmed glasses. Their silver hair was cropped short in identical styles, and I wondered how much hair product was required to achieve such volume. The only noticeable difference between the two was their sizes: Gloria was twice as wide as her petite sister.

Doris was still talking. "Gloria is retired like me. She and her husband are on their way to Colorado for Christmas. Their son and grandchildren live there."

I smiled at Gloria. "Welcome to Waconda. Is this your first time here?"

"Yes. It's so quaint, what with The Square and all." She pointed out the window. "It looks like a Hallmark movie."

I nodded. "I've often thought the same thing."

"And your coffee shop." Gloria gestured excitedly around the room. "It's so lovely. The Christmas decorations are adorable. Those must be your Santa figurines and ornaments."

"Guilty as charged." I looked at the ladder shelf filled with — I counted when I set them up — 23 Santa figurines, and the eight-foot Christmas tree in the front corner by the windows, weighed down with clear twinkle lights, red paper raffia and a dizzying array of Santa Claus ornaments. "I guess it's pretty obvious I love Santa."

Gloria giggled. "So do I, honey. You should see my collection." She pointed at the ladder shelf. "I love that beach Santa holding the surfboard."

I glanced at the eclectic assortment of Santas standing guard over the store. "That's one of my favorites too. I was excited when I found the farmer Santa holding a toy tractor; I bought it at an estate auction."

I bent down and looked Gloria in the eye. "I'll let you in on a little Santa secret, between collectors. Have you ever noticed that Santa figurines are always holding something?"

Gloria's stared at me in wonder. "Really?"

I nodded. "It's rare to find a Santa that isn't holding at least one thing like a present or a lantern. I've decided it's a law that all inanimate Santas are required to hold something."

"That's funny." Gloria inspected the Santa figurines more closely. "Well, I'll be darned if you're not right. I never noticed that, but now I definitely will."

"You won't be able to help yourself."

She grabbed my hand and shook it. "Well, it's just beautiful in here with the greenery and the twinkle lights and all of the red bows. The smell is absolutely heavenly."

I smiled warmly. "Thanks. It's nice of you to notice. When my Aunt Judy walked in after I decorated she said it looked like Christmas threw up in here, but in a tasteful way, of course."

Doris laughed. "That sounds like Judy."

"The one and only." I turned to Gloria. "You have a great Christmas in Colorado."

She nodded. "I certainly will. And I'll be back!"

Chapter 2

I was at the espresso machine making a caramel macchiato when Aunt Judy rushed through the back door at 7:08 am, donned an apron and joined me at the front counter.

"How's it going, Bree?" She grabbed me in one of her famous bear hugs and pulled a chocolate chip muffin from the display case before planting herself on a stool behind the cash register.

I did a double take of her red and green leggings, oversized Santa Claus sweater and Christmas tree earrings. I shook my head and grinned. "It's all good." I regaled her with Brice's sleepless night and his double espresso order.

Aunt Judy chuckled. "That boy must be levitating by now."

"No doubt." I passed the macchiato to a young woman waiting at the front counter who handed me four one-dollar bills. I stuffed the money in the cash register and smiled widely. "Thanks and enjoy." She walked to a table and sat down by herself.

Aunt Judy popped a bite of muffin into her mouth and pointed to the espresso machine. "Would you make me an Americano, honey?"

"Sure." I looked down at Aunt Judy. "I like your haircut."

"Really?" She ran her free hand through the blonde strands and doubt filled her plump face. "Did she take off too much? I said 'bob' but it feels more like a 'pixie'."

I shook my head as I ground coffee and turned on the espresso machine. "No, pixie is really short. That's definitely a bob, although a short one. It looks good on you." I topped off the espresso with hot water and handed the cup to Aunt Judy. "What's Uncle Joe up to?"

She rolled her eyes and sipped at her drink. "He was online shopping for new campers when I left. I swear, since that man retired he does nothing but sit around on his computer. He knows we can't afford a new camper. And what's wrong with the one we already have? Worked just fine this past summer, and we camped at the lake almost every weekend."

"He's just bored." I patted her back. "He'll be more active when the weather warms up. I've never met a man who loved to fish more than Uncle Joe."

"Lord, that's the truth. But I'm afraid until spring I'll have him underfoot most days — unless he's ice fishing, of course." Aunt Judy finished her muffin, threw the wrapper into the trash and pulled a chocolate-filled doughnut from the display case. She saw me watching her. "What are you looking at, Flagpole? It takes work to keep up my 'pleasantly plump' appearance."

I laughed and turned to wipe down the espresso machine.

The bell over the front door rang and Aunt Judy set down her doughnut and dialed up the charm for the woman who walked to the front counter. "Why hello there, Celia. How are you today?" As Aunt Judy asked a slew of questions about Celia's health, her husband's health, her children's health and her grandchildren's health — she was overly preoccupied with everyone's health — I whipped up Celia's order for a gingerbread latte.

Aunt Judy tucked the payment into the cash register and handed Celia her drink and a blueberry muffin. "You know this drink comes with a warning, right?"

Celia's brow furrowed. "What do you mean?"

I jumped in. "We had an incident yesterday with one of our Christmas specialty drinks. A woman chugged a peppermint mocha latte, and the sugar rush overwhelmed her frail system. She practically fainted." I leaned toward Celia. "We called her daughter, and she rushed over and raced her mother to the doctor. She was fine but her daughter asked me not to serve her mother any more sugary drinks, even if she begged."

Celia nodded her head. "Isabel Compton. Poor thing. I heard about that, but I've had this one before. You ladies should know I like to live dangerously. Besides, it's heaven in a cup!" Celia smiled and joined a table full of other grandmothers.

The next customer ordered an apple pie spice latte, and I was adding the spice mixture to the drink when my cell phone rang. I popped a lid on the to-go cup, handed it to the customer and pulled the phone out of my back pocket. I frowned when I saw who the caller was. Mother.

Remembering Brice's earlier request I reluctantly answered the phone. "Hello, Mother."

"Breanne? Is that you? It's your mother."

"I know who it is. Your name shows up on my phone whenever you call." I could never seem to get this concept through her head.

"I'm just calling to let you know that we're in Juneau and doing fine. The glaciers are magnificent. You should see this place. It's unbelievable!"

I sighed and leaned against the counter. "I'm glad you're having a good time." The lie slipped out easily. "How's Hank?" I was strangely intrigued by the brackish used car salesman who ordered pineapple juice whenever Mother brought him into the coffee shop.

"Oh, he's great." She lowered her voice and whispered. "He hasn't popped the question yet, but he still has plenty of time … probably planning something elaborate for later in the cruise. I'll call you the minute he asks me to marry him."

Like I care, I wanted to say, but of course I didn't. I stared at the floor, noticing a spot in the hardwood that needed attention.

Mother babbled on at regular volume. "We met a lovely couple from Vancouver who sat next to us at the all-you-care-to-eat seafood buffet. I thought it was interesting how they changed the name from all-you-CAN-eat buffet to all-you-CARE-TO-eat buffet. Did you notice the difference? They were smart to do that because it really is best to just eat all you care to rather than shoving it in until you pop. Of course, Hank ate until he was sick and then…"

The bell over the front door rang and I glanced up as the best-looking man I'd ever seen walked into my coffee shop.

My heart jumped into my throat, my eyes grew huge in my head and I mumbled into the phone. "Sorry, Mother. Gotta go." I abruptly tapped the END CALL button while she was still talking, tucked the phone into my back pocket and set about looking busy: I wiped the front counter and pretended to check the inventory in the display case, acutely aware of the remarkable man in a black leather coat surveying the room.

Aunt Judy grabbed my arm. "The man who just came in. Have you ever seen him?"

I shook my head. "No." I would definitely remember a guy like that.

Aunt Judy's mouth fell open. She pointed and I slapped her finger down before he noticed. "He looks like he walked off the cover of a romance novel." Her grip on my arm tightened and her voice raised in pitch. "Oh my Lord, a cleft chin. I bet when he smiles he has dimples." She was stunned. I thought she might swoon herself onto the floor.

Mr. Gorgeous glanced around the room, and when he noticed me his vivid blue eyes registered surprise. The hint of a smile tugged at the corners of his mouth, and I sensed an inward shyness that belied the confident pose. His raven hair was brushed back and tucked behind well-proportioned ears with neatly-trimmed sideburns. His skin was the shade of a rich summer tan, and a cleanly-shaven jaw was smooth and pronounced. I noticed that his nose was slightly crooked in the middle but, strangely, this only added to his incredible looks. Gorgeous cerulean eyes were hooded with laugh lines in the corners, and he exuded charm and elegance. I could smell the culture and breeding oozing out of him. I had never in my life seen such a striking man, and in my state of shock I was worried I'd forget how to verbalize the English language.

Our visitor walked to the front counter and looked up at the menu. I stuck my hands in the pockets of my apron and mentally donned a mask of cool detachment.

Aunt Judy launched into her professional mode. "Good morning, sir. How are you today?"

"Very well, thank you." He smiled with even, white teeth, which produced dimples in both cheeks. Aunt Judy turned around, winked and mouthed, *I told you so*. I glanced at his beautiful face and my own dimple-free cheeks blushed with warmth.

She turned back to the front counter. "What can we get for you?"

"I'm not sure. What do you suggest?"

Aunt Judy ran through her new-customer gamut. "The coffee bar is over there." She gestured to the south wall. "It's self-serve with two popular coffee blends. That's for people who like regular ol' coffee." He glanced toward the coffee bar and back at Judy.

"And then right here we can make you any of our specialty espresso drinks that are listed on the menu." She pointed up at the chalkboard sign hanging overhead. "Bree here, that's the owner, makes those." She turned her plump index finger toward me even though I was the only other person behind the counter. "We also have doughnuts and pastries. Oh, and I almost forgot, for the month of December we're offering gingerbread and peppermint mocha lattes. People love them but they come with a warning because of all the sugar." She gave him one of her sweet, grandmotherly smiles.

Mr. Gorgeous smiled back. "You're very helpful. Thank you." He looked up at the menu again. "I think I'll have a honey cinnamon cappuccino and a blueberry muffin."

Aunt Judy nodded in agreement. "Good choice. Will that be for here or to go?"

"For here, please."

She turned to me. "Bree, the gentleman would like a honey cinnamon cappuccino." She winked twice and moved to the display case where she grabbed the tongs and placed a blueberry muffin on a white ceramic plate. As I made the "gentleman" his cappuccino, I wondered at Aunt Judy's sudden formality. She was flummoxed by his good looks, no doubt, and I had to admit that I wasn't far behind. But in spite of his extraordinary features he was just a man, like any other, and for the past decade I'd been ignoring men with great success. This would be no different.

By the time his cappuccino was ready I was once again calm and composed, but when I handed over the drink our fingers touched, and I felt the warmth of his skin on mine. I automatically pulled away. "Enjoy." I swallowed and glanced up, surprised to see him staring straight at me.

His blue eyes bored into mine and his smile was tender. "Thank you. I'm sure you're a fabulous barista."

I shook my head vigorously. "Actually, I don't consider myself a barista."

His brow furrowed. "Why is that?"

"Well, I have no formal training. The espresso machine does all of the work."

He sipped at the cappuccino and nodded with pleasure. "This is delicious, and you're definitely a barista. I should know. I've had a lot of espressos in a lot of places."

My heart swelled. "Thank you. That's very kind."

Aunt Judy rang up his total on the cash register; he paid with a ten-dollar bill, told her to keep the change and carried his coffee and muffin to a small round table next to the Christmas tree by the front window.

When he was out of earshot Aunt Judy grabbed my wrist, pulled me down to her level and whispered, much too loudly. "Lordy, what a fine-looking man. I caught a whiff of his cologne and almost fainted. Do you see those clothes? He may be wearing jeans but they're not from Target. That coat must be real leather." She clucked her tongue and shook her head. "I'm not sure this town can handle him. I wonder what he's doing here."

I was equally curious but didn't admit it. "He's probably just passing through." I thought of my sign along Highway 24 that urged drivers to take the half-mile detour into town for "Specialty Coffee Drinks, Confectionary Delights and Daily Lunch Specials. You're Just Minutes Away From a Hot and Delicious Cup of Coffee!"

Our new customer perfectly fit the cliché of the "handsome stranger." I watched him for a few minutes; he was staring out the window in deep thought, sipping his cappuccino and ignoring the blueberry muffin.

Chapter 3

I spent the next hour planted in front of the espresso machine filling orders, leaving only to grab more to-go cups from the supply closet.

Aunt Judy tapped me on the shoulder. "We're caught up, honey."

"Thank goodness. I need to sit down." I pulled up a stool, sank down and noticed that Mr. Gorgeous was in the same spot, still gazing out the window.

"Was that Trudy on the phone earlier?"

I nodded. "Yes."

"How's the Alaskan cruise going?"

I opened the display case and pulled out a chocolate chip muffin. "She said it's great. They're in Juneau."

Aunt Judy put her hands on her ample hips. "Did Hank ask her to marry him yet?"

My eyebrows shot up. "She told you about that?"

"Well, she is my sister. We do talk, you know."

I pulled apart the muffin, popped a bite into my mouth and chewed deliberately. "No, he hasn't asked her, but she's convinced he will."

Aunt Judy leaned toward me and squeezed my arm. "It might be good for her to marry him, Bree. Would it upset you if she did?"

I chewed on another bite of muffin. "I don't care what she does."

"Really?" Her voice was caring and tender. It was impossible to hide my feelings from her.

I stared into her piercing green eyes, so much like Mother's, but filled with love and warmth instead of judgment and ice. Aunt Judy would rather hug her enemy than punch him. "Why can't she be more like you?"

Aunt Judy sighed. "We've talked about this before, Bree. She's always been cool and unemotional. As a little girl she was practical and all business. Our mother didn't know what to do with her."

I ate the last of the muffin and wiped the crumbs off my apron. "She just makes it so hard to give a damn about what she's doing. Does she think I actually care if she marries Hank?"

Aunt Judy nodded. "Believe me, honey, I know. When you and Brice started calling her Ice-T in high school I laughed so hard I fell out of my chair. But it also made me sad."

I studied my fingernails, chipped and cracked from washing dishes. "If the shoe fits, wear it."

"Listen, I know it's been hard for you with Trudy the way she is and your dad's accident and all, but I'm real proud of the way you've handled it." She reached over and patted my knee. "You've been through so much, Bree. My God, any other person would have completely given up in your situation. When you came home after the…"

I sat up straight and cut her off. "You know I don't like to talk about that." I fiddled with the sapphire and diamond pendant hanging at my throat.

Aunt Judy noticed. "I'm sorry. I know." She touched my cheek. "Just remember that I'm always here for you."

A tear formed and threatened to spill. I wiped it away and hugged her quickly.

She changed the subject. "We're not as busy now so I'd better get into the kitchen and start on the sloppy joe meat. Just yell if you need me."

I nodded. "I'll clean up in front and then come help with the lunch prep." She hurried off toward the back, her ample behind jiggling like Jell-O. She could give Mrs. Claus a run for her money.

To calm myself I made a double espresso and drained it in record time. I walked to the coffee bar and picked up the black plastic tub that was filled with dirty coffee cups and plates. I was keenly aware that Mr. Gorgeous was still sitting by the Christmas tree, staring out the window at who-knows-what. Most people distracted themselves by scrolling through their phones, but not this guy. I noticed the blueberry muffin had been eaten and wondered if he needed another cappuccino. I was about to offer him a free refill when the front door opened and a young man I'd never seen peered inside.

He spotted me. "Do you still have coffee?"

"Yes, we do. What would you like?" He walked in and met me at the front counter.

"I could sure use an espresso today. Make it an Americano."

I set the tub of dirty dishes on the island. "Is this to go?"

"Yes, ma'am. I'm hauling for Waconda Grain and it sure is cold."

I inspected his shaggy beard and the dirt under his fingernails. "You must be new. I haven't seen you around." He was slightly shorter than me with red hair and freckles. He didn't look a day over 20.

"Yep. Just bought a semi and found work here. I'm from Hastings, Nebraska. The name's Garrett."

"Garrett. Welcome to Waconda. I'm Bree, and this is my coffeehouse. I shop in Hastings sometimes. Nice town." I turned to the espresso machine. "I'll have your drink ready in a minute. We have a few confectionary delights left if you need something to eat. Take a look."

I made an espresso and filled a to-go cup half full, added hot water to the top and pushed on a lid. "Anything else?"

He pointed at the display case. "I'll take the last two glazed doughnuts."

As I dropped the pastries into a small paper bag using the plastic tongs, Garrett studied me from top to bottom, a silly grin on his face. "You sure are tall, Ma'am. How tall are you?"

I stopped what I was doing and pointed at him. "Did you just ask about my height?"

His cheeks turned slightly red. "I'm sorry if I offended you. I didn't mean anything by it."

"You didn't offend me at all, but you might be sorry you asked."

I bent down and pulled a hand bell from under the counter and rang it vigorously to catch everyone's attention. The mid-morning coffee drinkers — a large table of retired women, a smaller table of home-from-college locals, plus Mr. Gorgeous by the window — looked up in unison. The locals knew what was coming, and our tall, dark and handsome stranger regarded me with acute interest.

Aunt Judy ran up from the kitchen, grinning from ear to ear. Garrett's face was twisted in confusion.

I cupped my hands in the shape of a megaphone. "This is Garrett's first time in my coffee shop, and he wants to know how tall I am."

The regulars hooted and clapped as I handed Garrett a business card from the basket next to the bell.

It read:

Hi.

My name is Bree Somers.

Yes, I know I'm tall — 6'1" in fact.

Yes, I played volleyball in college.

Yes, the weather is nice up here.

Thanks for asking.

Take care and have a nice day.

The other side of the card listed our business hours and phone number.

Garrett clearly wished the earth would open up and swallow him whole. "You're right, Ma'am … I'm sorry I asked."

I walked around to the front of the counter and placed my hand on his shoulder. "No worries, Garrett. Your order's on me. No charge."

"What?" He looked even more confused.

"That's the deal. You're new here, you ask how tall I am, I give you a hard time for my own amusement and then I don't charge you a dime. Do you forgive me?"

Realization lit up his face and he grinned. "That's really nice of you. Thanks."

I slapped him on the back. "You're a good sport, Garrett. Come back now."

"I will. I'd better get going." He shuffled out the door, smiling all the way.

Aunt Judy beamed at me. "Do you ever get tired of that bit?"

I chuckled. "Never. We've got to keep things exciting around here, don't you think? Plus, you know I'm partial to redheads."

"Oh honey." Her eyes filled with tears and she wrapped her arms around my waist. "Whatever makes you happy. I love seeing you smile." She let go and walked back to the kitchen, wiping the tears from her cheeks.

I caught movement out of the corner of my eye and looked up to see Mr. Gorgeous stand and pull on his coat. He glanced my way, waved a friendly goodbye and stepped out into the crisp late-morning air. I walked to his vacated table and picked up the empty cup and plate.

It had been years since I'd thought of a man as anything other than a friend, a brother, a father, an acquaintance. I knew nothing about this man and yet I was intrigued by his appearance in my coffee shop. My curiosity surprised me: I wondered what he was doing in Waconda, Kansas, of all places, and if I'd ever see him again.

Chapter 4

Aunt Judy carried a large roaster filled with sloppy joe meat to the spacious granite island behind the front counter and plugged it in. Wordlessly we prepared for the lunch crowd, setting out bakery buns, plates and cutlery, and I grabbed a box of individually-wrapped chocolate chip cookies and set them next to the buns.

I had an idea. "Let's just leave the potato salad in the refrigerator and pull it out as we need it. I had to turn on the charm to win over Alice the Health Inspector and I'm not about to tick her off with room-temperature potato salad."

Aunt Judy agreed, planting hands on her plump hips. "I think that woman installed a secret camera in here somewhere. How else does she know when to show up and catch us doing something wrong?"

I laughed. "I wouldn't put it past her."

As the lunch orders rolled in Aunt Judy and I were a well-oiled machine: she put together the sloppy Joe dinners and I grilled paninis, assembled sub sandwiches and created fresh chopped salads. We sold the rest of the cherry pie and all but two slices of the pumpkin. I made a mental note to call Peggy the Pie Lady and place an order. A few customers ordered specialty coffee drinks with their lunches and we were busy but not frantic. I ran up front to pour myself a cup of black coffee and sipped it between filling orders.

The bell over the front door rang regularly as customers came and went. I was finishing an order for a chicken salad sandwich when I heard them before I saw them.

"Aunt Bree! Aunt Bree!" Angels in heaven couldn't have sounded any sweeter.

I set the sandwich on a plate, added a bag of chips and pushed it across the counter to Aunt Judy just in time to kneel down as my two brown-haired, five-year-old nephews charged behind the front counter and threw their compact little bodies at mine. We were a tangle of arms and heads, but I managed to hug Nate and Matt separately and kiss them on the tops of their heads.

"How was school today?" They were vibrating with excitement.

"That's what we want to tell you about." Nate grabbed my hands in his chubby ones.

Matt interrupted. "Yeah! We're going to sing Chrissas songs…"

"In front of people!" Nate refused to be left out.

Matt tapped his finger on my shoulder. "And we want you to come."

They both smiled sweetly, displaying crooked teeth that would someday need the attention of an orthodontist but made them even more endearing at this age.

"Are you going to be in a Christmas program at school?"

They yelled in unison. "YES!"

Matt snuggled into my side. "Will you come, Aunt Bree?"

Nate squeezed my hands even harder. "Please?"

For ten agonizing seconds I pretended to consider the invitation, and their brows furrowed in concentration awaiting my answer. "Of course I'll be there, you silly little monkeys." I tickled their tummies and they squealed in laughter. I looked up as Caitlin appeared.

Matt ran to her. "Mom! Aunt Bree said she'll come to our Chrissas concert."

Nate smiled and then turned serious. "But you need to sit in the front row so you can see us. We're not going to tell you what we're dressing up as. It's a secret."

"I bet I could tickle it out of you." I lunged for the boys and they both screamed and raced toward the back of the building.

I straightened up and Caitlin put an arm around my waist, leaning in for a hug. "Now I'll never calm them down. Thanks a lot."

I hugged her in return. "I think the Mother of the Year can handle them just fine."

"Very funny. Mother of the Year? I barely get them to kindergarten on time, and we live in town. Imagine how bad it would be if we lived on the farm."

"Excuses, excuses. Don't forget there are school buses, my dear."

Caitlin rolled her eyes. "Whatever."

"I may have riled them up, but I know how to calm them down." I called for the boys and they came running but stopped just out of my reach, afraid I'd tickle them. "Why don't you guys ask your Great Aunt Judy for a cookie." They raced to the other side of the island and I patted myself on the back. "I've still got it."

Caitlin called after them. "Don't forget to say please and thank you."

Within seconds Aunt Judy was fussing over the boys, asking them questions about kindergarten and handing them each a chocolate chip cookie which kept them quiet for a few minutes.

Caitlin pulled me aside, her blue eyes intense and focused on mine. She tucked a strand of long blonde hair behind her ear. "I know it won't be easy for you to attend their school Christmas concert, but I couldn't stop them from asking you. They had their hearts set on it." Her voice was strained.

I patted her shoulder. "You're sweet to be concerned, but of course I want to go. It'll be fine." She still looked doubtful. "Besides, it's their first school Christmas program. I wouldn't want to disappoint the little guys."

"Are you sure?" Caitlin's distress was sincere. "It might bring back some difficult emotions, and I don't want to be responsible for upsetting you."

I smiled and grabbed her hands. "No, really. It's all good. No worries."

She sighed and grinned. "And it's not actually called a 'Christmas' program anymore. It's a 'Holiday' program, whatever the hell that is."

I laughed. "We must be politically correct, even out here in the boondocks." I walked back to the island to help Aunt Judy with the lunch orders. Caitlin followed and I turned to her. "Do you guys want the sloppy joe special?"

"Of course we do. The boys are always starving when they get out of school, but I'm still glad kindergarten is just half days."

I grabbed three plates and placed buns on each one. "When I was teaching I thought a half day for kindergarten was plenty long."

Caitlin leaned against the island. "Would you give the boys chips instead of potato salad?"

I nodded, knowing full well that Nate and Matt couldn't stand the taste of potato salad. "Anything for my boys." I scooped sloppy Joe meat onto the buns and added bags of potato chips.

"Lunch is ready!" I yelled to the back of the building where the boys were tying Bree Brews It aprons on each other.

When Caitlin saw them she laughed. "Looks like you've got some new employees, Bree."

The boys ran to us, beaming with pride, and I clapped my hands in glee. "Do you care if I take their picture and post it on my page?"

"Only if you promise to text me the photo."

"Agreed!" I pulled my phone out of a back pocket as Caitlin fussed over the boys' hair, much to their annoyance. "Okay, Mom of the Year, that's enough. They look great." Caitlin stepped to the side, and I held my phone up and told the boys to smile. I snapped several photos of Nate and Matt with their arms around each other, cheesy smiles on their faces. "Caitlin, let's get one of you with the boys and I'll send it to Brice. I won't post it on my page."

"Do you promise?" She knelt down between Nate and Matt and smiled at me.

"Of course. Okay, guys. Smile." I snapped a photo. "Now give your mom a big kiss." Nate and Matt turned to Caitlin and plastered kisses on her cheeks. Happiness transformed her face. I took several photos in succession, and when I was done the boys ran over to see themselves on the screen. I held up the phone for Caitlin so she could see the photos of her and the boys. "These are the money shots."

Caitlin crossed her hands over her heart. "Those are precious. Send them to me ASAP. Brice too."

"Will do." I motioned for her to follow and we carried their meals to an empty table in front. The boys sat down and dived into their sandwiches. Kindergarten must have been exhausting work. Caitlin walked behind the counter and returned with containers of orange juice for the boys and bottled water for herself.

I turned to Nate and Matt. "I need to get back to work but you know what it means when you wear an apron in here."

They glanced up at me, sloppy joe sauce lining their mouths. "What?" It always gave me goosebumps when their twin minds melded, and they talked in perfect unison. I was reminded of the Wonder Twins from the Super Friends comic of my childhood. They would bump fists and command their twin power to activate. I made a mental note to show them some of the old clips on YouTube.

I pointed at each of them. "It means that when you're done eating you have to do all of the dishes."

They stared at me like I'd grown a second head.

Matt spoke up. "Are you serious? ALL of them?"

Nate looked equally baffled. I winked at Caitlin who suppressed a laugh.

"Yep, ALL of them." I paused for several seconds as the boys sat with shocked looks on their faces, sloppy joes held in midair. Finally, I released them from their torture. "Gotcha!"

Nate and Matt glanced at each other and then back at me, realization crossing their cherubic faces. Nate pointed at me. "You got us good, Aunt Bree."

Matt bit into the sandwich and talked with his mouth full. "Yeah, but we'll get you back, though." Caitlin told Matt not to talk with food in his mouth.

"Good luck, boys. It's not easy to pull one over on your Aunt Bree." I patted their heads and walked behind the counter to help Aunt Judy with the lunch orders.

She was scooping a serving of potato salad onto a plate when I returned. "Those boys really love you, honey."

"I love them more."

She carried the plate to the front counter and handed it to a customer. She turned to me. "Rex is waiting on his ham and cheese panini."

I saluted. "Yes, Ma'am." I heated up the panini press and pulled packages of honey ham and Swiss cheese out of the refrigerator, grabbed a loaf of Italian bread, a bottle of olive oil and set about making a panini for Rex, one of our regulars. As the sandwich grilled I shook my head. "He knows we sell other food, right?"

Aunt Judy laughed. "If I ate one of those every day like he does I'd be sick of it, but the man loves his ham and cheese paninis, bless his heart."

"I guess whatever floats his boat. As long as he pays I'll make him one every day until the Apocalypse."

When the sandwich was crispy on the outside and gooey on the inside I used a spatula to lift it onto a plate, and I added a bag of potato chips and a chocolate chip cookie. "Did you already give him his iced tea?"

Aunt Judy nodded. "Yep."

I carried his lunch to the front and walked to the small table where Rex was sitting alone, reading a book. When I set the plate down he peeked at me over his reading glasses and smiled. "Thanks, Miss Bree."

"You're welcome, Mr. Rex." I crossed my arms. "What are you reading today?"

He held up the book so I could see the cover. On it, a shirtless man with bulging muscles wearing a pirate's hat was carrying what appeared to be a damsel in distress, her pink gown ripped in just the right spot to reveal most of her ample bosoms. "This one's called Love's Endless Bounty. It came in this morning."

The world is full of contradictions, and Rex was one of them. The retired mailman, a 76-year-old bachelor, read romance novels. He was a voracious reader and often started and finished a book in the same day. The town's librarian was challenged with keeping him supplied in reading material. Funny thing was, none of the old timers remember Rex ever dating anyone. He was always a loner. I smiled and pointed to the book. "Looks like a good one."

He grinned and nibbled at his sandwich, then resumed reading.

I felt a tug on my shirt and turned around. It was Nate. "We're going home, Aunt Bree." The boys pulled on their coats, hats and gloves.

I bent down for hugs and kissed their cheeks. Before I let them go I shared news that every child loves to hear. "I heard this morning that it might snow Saturday." Their eyes grew huge at this bit of information. "If it does we can play in the snow when I come over on Sunday."

Nate and Matt jumped up and down with excitement and then ran to the front window where they peered into the sky, willing it to start snowing immediately. I laughed. "Saturday, boys. That's two days from now." They ignored me and muttered between themselves. I knew they were making plans for some monumental snow adventures.

Caitlin slipped into her coat and joined me. "Don't forget supper tomorrow night at the bar. The Birthday Girl gets steak and a bottle of wine."

I leaned down for a hug. "I'll be there. If you have time, bring the boys by for cupcakes tomorrow. I'll save you some."

"Will do. Thanks for lunch."

I called to the boys. "See you later."

"Bye, Aunt Bree." They yelled in perfect unison.

"Tell her 'thank you' for lunch." Caitlin was such a mom.

"Thanks for lunch."

"Thank you."

"You're welcome." They ran out the door and down the sidewalk, Caitlin on their heels.

The lunch crowd was brisk for a Thursday, and when the last customer finally left Aunt Judy and I grabbed a short break and then delved into the clean-up. At 2 pm I carried the sidewalk sign inside, turned the OPEN sign to CLOSED, locked the front door and shut off the satellite radio. I sighed and leaned on the counter.

Aunt Judy said goodbye and rushed out the back door carrying a boxed sloppy Joe special with two sandwiches and a slice of pumpkin pie for Uncle Joe's late lunch.

I walked to the front window and stared outside, surprised that our good-looking cappuccino drinker was still on my mind. I'd meditated enough to know that thoughts couldn't be willed away — it was best to let them come and go as they pleased. This one had arrived and was in no hurry to leave.

I sat down where he sat that morning and wondered about my interest in a stranger off the street. Sure, he was good looking, but I'd seen impressive men before. No, this was something intangible, something I couldn't touch even if he was standing right in front of me.

He'd rattled me, that's for sure, and I wasn't used to being rattled. I looked out the window. What had Mr. Gorgeous been thinking as he sat here staring at nothing?

Chapter 5

I locked the back door of the coffeehouse and skipped up the stairs to my apartment where I changed into old faded jeans and cowgirl boots, grabbed a coat that was new in 1999, ran back down the stairs and hopped in my white and gray 1995 Ford F-150, Dad's old work pickup. I backed up, pulled out of the alley onto Main Street and drove past the town square west toward the dam. Small, tidy houses lined both sides of the road, and most were draped in a dizzying array of Christmas lights and yard decorations that would thrill the children of Waconda when the sun went down and the automatic timers kicked on.

Several blocks later the land rose steeply, and I pushed down on the accelerator to climb the hill. When I reached the top of the dam I paused at the STOP sign and turned left toward the farm.

I admired the ornate new homes that overlooked Lake Waconda, built by the wealthy families of town during the past decade; I drove across the three-mile-long dam and glanced at the icy water of the lake, austere in its wintertime beauty. With the temperature hovering around 25 degrees, the lake was icy along its edges but still flowing at its center. A group of Black-Throated Loons swam in the open water, and I marveled at the design of feathers that could withstand such temperatures without their small bodies freezing. Overhead, two white jet trails crossed in the sky, forming a perfect X.

From a young age I've been mesmerized by the vast openness of the Kansas landscape and a sky that goes on forever, changing color with the moods of the seasons. As a child I studied the ripening wheat and thrilled at the site of Dad pulling the combine out of the shed on the first day of harvest. I explored the creeks, climbed the cottonwood and oak trees, and walked for miles through meadows filled with sweet-smelling hay. I traveled the fence lines watching closely for Meadowlarks and listened carefully when they sang their distinctive tune, whistling a response but failing miserably.

I love Kansas in the summer when you could melt from the heat, so you slip on a bikini and head for the lake, a case of beer and summer sausage in the cooler. I love Kansas in the fall when the landscape turns a dozen hues of orange, the wheat comes up in tidy rows that flow with the terraces in the fields and I pull on my favorite old sweater with a hole in the sleeve. I love Kansas in the winter when the fertile land sleeps, a covering of snow creates shadows that reveal the gentle flow of the terrain and I cuddle up with a fuzzy blanket and a good book. I love Kansas in the spring when the earth wakes up and flowers bloom and gardens are planted, and I throw my coat in the closet and pull out a jacket instead.

I'm a Flatlander, a Midwesterner, a Prairie Girl.

Past the dam I drove for two miles and turned east onto a rock road as straight as a toothpick. As I accelerated, clouds of dust kicked up behind me and I braked for a ringneck pheasant crossing the road. Three miles later I pulled into a driveway with a limestone sign that read: Somers Family Farms. I parked in front of an enormous gray machine shed next to Brice's much-newer Ford F-150 in cherry red. The massive blue doors of the building were closed tightly against the icy winter air.

I hopped out of the pickup, slammed the door shut and ran over to the building, quickly ducking inside to escape the cold. My old pickup's heater put out little in the way of actual heat, and I was chilled to the bone. I'd barely made it inside when two ink-black Labrador retrievers ran over and fought for my attention.

"Hello there, boys." I knelt down and scratched the dogs' smooth heads as they licked my face, hands and each other. I laughed. "It's good to see you too." Greeting the dogs this way reminded me of that morning with Nate and Matt, but I'd never tell Caitlin I'd compared her boys to dogs.

"Forrest and Gump are happy to see you." Brice walked up, wiping his hands on an old blue rag. "Typical boys. A pretty girl walks in and they lose their minds."

"What can I say? I'm hard to resist." Forrest licked my hand and Gump added several strokes to my right ear. "Finally winterizing the sprayer?"

"Yeah. Now that it's below freezing I thought it was time. I think I'm done spraying for a while."

I rose and tapped Brice on his head. "You're a smart man, B.S."

He smiled and playfully kicked my shin. "I have my moments, B.S."

I looked around the shop. "You didn't bring the boys with you?"

"No, I'm still exhausted from last night and didn't plan on being here long." He threw the rag onto the work bench and crossed his arms.

"I almost forgot ... Mother called this morning."

Brice smiled. "Yeah, she called me too. She sounded good."

"Did she tell you they're in Juneau? I guess Hank hasn't popped the question yet." I emphasized 'popped the question' with air quotes.

"I know, but he'll get around to it."

"I wouldn't bet on it."

"I would."

"How are you so sure?" I studied his face, but it was void of clues.

"I have a feeling."

"You have a feeling?" I stepped closer and stared him in the eye. "You know something."

"No, I don't."

"Yes, you do." I moved until I could see the white flecks in his pupils. "Now I see it. Your right eye is doing that funny twitching thing it does when you're lying."

His brows furrowed. "Would you let it go?"

"This is not Frozen. I will not let it go."

Brice was quiet for a moment. "Hank called the day before they left."

I waited for more, but he was silent. "And?"

Brice rested his hands on his head. "He said he loves Trudy and asked permission to marry her."

I was stunned. "And you're just telling me this now?"

"He asked me not to say anything to anyone."

"Oh." I stepped back and crossed my arms. We were quiet for several minutes. Forrest and Gump, sensing the tension, sat on their haunches and looked back and forth between us.

"I told him that whatever Mother wanted was fine with me. He said he was going to ask her during the cruise."

"Wow. Ice-T was right about an Alaskan engagement."

Brice leaned to within an inch of my face. "Listen, he's not that bad of a guy. He said he loves her." He stared out the window. "And once Mother moves out of the farmhouse I think I can convince Caitlin to move out here and then the boys can grow up on the farm like we did."

I nodded weakly. "I know you're right."

He thought of another benefit. "And remember, if she's in Beloit that means she's not in Waconda. You'd see a lot less of her."

I smiled. "You always know how to cheer me up."

"Trust me, it's all going to work out." He glanced at the clock on the wall. "I need to run over and check the cows in the south pasture. It's about time to bring them home for the winter."

I looked down at the dogs. "I was thinking of taking Forrest and Gump down to the creek. I could use the fresh air and a bit of exercise. But only after I warm up a bit." Hearing their names and the word 'creek,' both dogs' entire back ends wagged wildly.

"It looks like they'll love it." He patted his dogs on their wagging rumps. "Turn off the heater in here when you leave and since Mother's gone, lock the boys in their pen before you go. They become nomads when no one's around."

I chuckled and patted Forrest and Gump on their solid heads. "Don't I know it."

"Remember last year when Mother went to Branson and they wandered off and were found two counties over? We're still not sure if they walked or hitched a ride." Brice burst into laughter.

"Don't worry. I'll feed them and then lock them in the pen before I leave."

"Thanks." He headed outside to his pickup. "I need to get going before it gets dark." He hopped in the truck, backed into the driveway and sped off.

I walked over to the large space heater in the corner and warmed my hands for five minutes while Forrest and Gump crowded around me, vying for attention. I could tell they were itching to get outside, so I finally turned off the heater and the three of us headed out into the frosty air.

I pulled on gloves and a stocking hat from my coat pocket. The dogs streaked past me toward the creek, and I walked by the enormous white two-story farmhouse with its blue shutters, the massive front porch filled with white wicker furniture. I pictured Brice and Caitlin sitting on the porch while the boys raced around the yard with their dogs.

I followed Forrest and Gump past the farm and into a milo field; stalks about a foot high stood in rows except where the combine, tractor and grain cart had driven over them during fall harvest. The field was full of birds eating grain out of the heads of milo that had escaped the combine, and Forrest and Gump zigzagged back and forth, jumping to catch a bird but missing every time.

I picked up two milo stalks and called to the dogs. "Come here, boys! Forrest! Gump!" The brothers ceased hunting birds and ran up to me. They immediately noticed the sticks. Their ears perked up and they grew excited with anticipation. "Go get it, Forrest!" I threw the first milo stalk and Forrest raced off to fetch it. Gump looked up and seemed to ask, "Me too?"

"I haven't forgotten you, Gump. Go get it!" I threw the second milo stalk in the opposite direction and Gump ran after it. Within seconds both dogs were nuzzling their noses into my thighs to "hand me" the milo stalks. "Drop them." They did so on cue. I picked up the slightly wet milo stalks and repeated the game until I was tired of throwing. They would never grow tired of fetching. In fact, I think they'd fetch all night if I let them. "Let's go to the creek." Forrest and Gump knew what the creek was and tore off in that direction.

I followed, thinking about Dad, which came naturally out here on the farm. The memories flooded through me when I visited his favorite place on earth. I sat down on a fallen tree branch and watched the dogs play together in the creek that was more dirt than water. A small patch of ice confused Forrest and Gump. They pawed at it, licked it and finally gave up and ran off to scare sparrows out of the brush.

I wished Dad was sitting beside me on this tree branch like he used to. It was our spot, a special place where we'd talk about life and commune with nature. I missed him so much. I looked up into the branches of the massive oak tree dominating this part of the creek and spotted a bright red male cardinal and its mate, a brown female with highlights of red on its crown and lower wings. The female was preening herself, and the male sang his distinctive tune. I once read that when you spot a cardinal it's a loved one visiting from heaven. I'm not sure I believed that, but the two cardinals' presence was somehow comforting.

I wondered what Dad would think of the Ice Queen getting remarried. I shook my head and tears spilled down my cheeks. It had been five years since Dad died, and it still hurt like the day it happened. Grief was like that … you forged ahead and smiled on the outside while drowning on the inside.

The chilly breeze was light as a feather, and it played a somber melody as it snaked through the bare branches of the cottonwood trees lining the creek. I heard a loud rustle and saw two sparrows fly out of the thicket. Forrest and Gump took off on a chase they wouldn't win.

Dad was always there when I needed him. I choked on a sob and thought back ten years to my childhood bedroom and the grief that almost killed me. After several months of wallowing in self-pity, Dad marched into my room. "Bree, I love you, but you cannot spend the rest of your life in bed. Get up and put on some clothes." He drove me into Waconda and parked in front of the old Rogers Variety Store that had been empty for years. "How about we buy it, remodel it and start a business you can run? What do you say?" And then he leaned over and hugged me. "You have to get on with your life, honey." That's what he told me. I shivered at the memory.

He saved my life that day.

More tears rolled down my cheeks, and they became so cold I couldn't feel them anymore. After I was running my coffee shop and could envision a future in Waconda, I thanked Dad for saving my life. He squeezed my arms and said that I was under contract to live it. "And that's an order." I hope he knows I'm trying. Every day. For him.

The sun was setting when I called to the dogs, and we trekked back toward the farm. A spectacular sunset was taking shape and I stopped to admire the hues of pink, peach and coral blending together and streaking the western horizon. God's painting is what Dad would call it. He said you could travel anywhere in the world and you wouldn't find a more beautiful sunset than here on the plains of Kansas. I breathed a silent thank you and then turned toward the farm, Forrest and Gump dashing past me as they raced with wild abandon.

My phone chimed and I pulled it out of my back pocket and read the message. "REMINDER: Decorate for Birthday Party." I thanked the phone for reminding me that I still needed to hang streamers and blow up balloons for my 37th birthday party at the coffeehouse tomorrow. I decided to tackle the chore immediately when I returned to town.

I ran through the events of the day and an image of Mr. Gorgeous filled the screen in my mind. Why was I thinking about him again?

And more importantly, what was his name?

FRIDAY, DECEMBER 15, 2017

Chapter 6

I was pouring foamed milk into an espresso when Aunt Judy, tying her apron after arriving at work, sidled up next to me and whispered in my ear. "His name is Maxim Hall."

"Huh?" I turned off the machine and reached for the cocoa powder. The name sounded familiar and my mind sorted through everyone I'd ever known, coming up dry as I measured out two generous spoonsful of cocoa into the cup of latte. "What in the world are you talking about?" I stirred and watched as the powder melted into the coffee and transformed into a drink that God himself would have given five stars.

Aunt Judy sighed, tugged at her candy cane leggings and adjusted today's red sweater that read, I'm On Santa's Naughty List. "The looker who was in here yesterday? Easy on the eyes? The city hot shot who ordered a cappuccino and called you a barista? That's his name. Maxim Hall. He's a famous writer."

"Really." It was a statement, not a question. The name hit a note of recognition in my brain, and I was more interested than I should have been. "How do you know that?" I popped a lid on the mocha latte and handed it to Tyler, a teenage boy whose droopy eyes and deep yawn proved he needed the caffeine in a desperate way. I punched the amount into the cash register and collected his money.

"Don't forget to grab a free cupcake on the way out. Hannah will help you." I pointed to a table by the coffee bar where Hannah, home from college for Christmas break, was manning the birthday cupcake stand.

Tyler inhaled a drink of coffee, gazed at Hannah and showed some actual signs of life. "Thanks."

"You're welcome, Tyler. And sign up for the drawing. I'm giving away ten specialty coffee drinks. Have a great day."

"You too." He stopped at the cupcake table on his way out, flirting with Hannah before leaving.

Aunt Judy looked impatient; she was in prime storytelling mode, and her chest puffed out with the information she was holding in. I was worried she might explode. She continued hurriedly. "Last night Evelyn called and said a man had been in the City Office asking about Waconda Springs."

She had my attention. "Go on." I cleaned the espresso machine and wiped down the counter.

"He said his name is Maxim Hall and that he's here from New York City doing research for his next novel. He asked for information about Waconda Springs and you'll never guess what she told him."

"I'm sure I won't."

Aunt Judy winked. "Go ahead. Guess."

I sighed and crossed my arms. "She told him that when her husband died three years ago she swore a vow of chastity but seeing him she'd changed her mind. And then she threw herself at him."

Aunt Judy put her hands on her ample hips and leaned forward. "You are a sarcastic thing, aren't you? And ornery too. If I had a dollar for every time you gave me a smart answer I'd be rich, and you'd be missing the best employee you've ever had."

"If I'm so awful maybe you should get your old job back at the City Office and you could gossip with Evelyn all day."

Aunt Judy groaned. "Why do you think I retired? That woman drove me nuts."

"I remember. You complained about her all the time."

"Yeah, but retirement wasn't much better. I was bored as a gourd at home."

"And I rescued you by offering you a job here."

"Yes, honey, where would I be without you?"

I grinned. "Bored as a gourd at home, tripping over Uncle Joe and sewing seat covers for the new camper?"

Aunt Judy laughed and pinched my arm. She scrutinized me from head to toe and suddenly a great realization flooded her face. "Oh, Bree, I've been jabbering on and haven't told you happy birthday yet." She hugged me fiercely. "Happy birthday, honey! I'm sorry I didn't say it the moment I came in, but I was so excited to tell you about Maxim Hall."

I threw my arms up in the air. "What gave it away that it's my birthday? The pink pointy birthday hat I'm wearing that somehow makes me look even taller than usual, or was it the dozens of pink cupcakes filling up every counter in the store?"

She smiled and surveyed the room. "Give me one of those hats." She poked me in the chest. "I've never forgotten your birthday in your entire life, and you know it. I even brought you a gift."

I placed a birthday hat on her head and secured the elastic string under her chin. "That was sweet of you, but you know you didn't have to."

"I know that, but I couldn't resist." She frowned. "Why are these hats always so damn uncomfortable? It's cutting into my three chins."

I dove in for the kill. "Maybe if you'd narrow it down to one chin it wouldn't hurt so much." My God, she was right: I really was sarcastic and ornery. Oh well, too late to change now.

She ignored my remark. "I'm just going to wear it without the band." She pulled off the elastic string and set the hat on her head where it threatened to fall off at any minute yet somehow didn't. "Anyway, back to Maxim Hall. Like I was saying, he asked Evelyn for information on Waconda Springs and she directed him to the expert in town."

I suddenly knew why Aunt Judy was stringing out her story to produce the maximum effect. When three women walked up to the front counter and interrupted our conversation I was relieved. Aunt Judy turned to wait on them. "Hello, ladies, what can we get for you?"

Their coffee drink orders — one honey cinnamon latte, one gingerbread latte and one Americano — gave me a short reprieve from what I knew was coming. When they'd paid, picked up their cupcakes and found an empty round table near the front, Aunt Judy turned to me and grabbed my arm.

"Aren't you curious who Evelyn told Maxim to talk to?"

I said nothing because I knew who the expert was, and I wasn't surprised when she answered her own question.

"You! Evelyn told him, 'Go see Bree Somers at the coffee shop. She knows everything about Waconda Springs.' Can you believe it?" For some reason I could.

"Wow. That's something else." My mind raced.

Aunt Judy beamed in triumph and then wrinkled her brow. "I wonder what he wants to know, exactly. How will he use it in a book?"

And how was I going to think and talk at the same time when he came in? I was secretly thrilled he was still in town, which was alarming in and of itself, yet apprehensive about meeting him. To sum it up, I was thoroughly intrigued by this man. Irritated with myself, I turned to the espresso machine and made a mocha latte with a mound of whipped cream in a coffee mug that said, "This Coffee is Making Me Awesome," and drew in long sips as my mind raced.

"You know he writes love stories, right?" Aunt Judy crossed her hands over her heart. "I've read several of his books. I cried every time."

I was certain I'd read his work but couldn't think of a single title. "What's he written?"

Aunt Judy grabbed a cupcake, peeled off the wrapper and took a generous bite. "Oh my God, this is so good!" She filled her mouth with a second bite and continued talking. "Well, there's The Climb. That one was about a mountain climber who wrote a love letter to his ex-wife, telling her he wanted to get back together, before he fell off the side of a mountain and died."

"Sounds cheery. I don't think I've read that one." I sipped my drink and mentally ran through the books I'd read in the past few months.

"Then there's The Day. That one was about how a couple fell in and out of love in one day."

I snapped my fingers. "Oh yeah, and then 20 years later they met and fell in love again and got married."

"Yes. Some of the endings are sad and others are happy. You never know what you're going to get ... it's like a box of chocolates." Aunt Judy stopped to think. She threw away the cupcake wrapper and sipped some coffee. "He's written others, but I can't remember the names. Several of them were turned into movies."

I recalled one of them. "The Street! I was disappointed in the movie because it was nothing like the book."

"Never saw it." Aunt Judy drummed her fingers on the front counter. "He has a new one out that I haven't read. For the life of me I can't think of the title."

"Me either." I didn't really care what the book was called, however, since I was suddenly filled with dread at the thought of Maxim Hall's appearance. My phone rang with an incoming text message. I pulled it out of my back pocket and read it.

"Peggy said she'll come in Monday to bake pies."

Aunt Judy nodded. "That will be perfect before Christmas. Ask her if she'll also make pecan. That's Joe's favorite."

"Will do, but only because you brought me a birthday gift." I tapped a reply into my phone telling Peggy to text me when she planned to arrive on Monday so I could unlock the back door for her.

Aunt Judy vibrated with excitement. "I hope he comes in this morning."

"Who?" I knew full well who she meant.

Aunt Judy's exasperation was clear in her voice. "Bree, would you focus? Maxim Hall, of course. I really hope he comes in while I'm here so I can see him again. What a looker! Now that's a birthday gift a girl can appreciate!"

I rolled my eyes. "You're hopeless." I was desperate to change the subject. "I need to see how Hannah's doing."

"Okay, but when he comes in make sure you introduce him to me."

I was on my way to the cupcake table but stopped dead in my tracks and stared at her. "Since when have you ever been shy about introducing yourself to someone?"

"I just want a proper introduction, that's all." Aunt Judy smiled angelically. "After all, I did bring you a birthday gift."

I agreed just to shut her up. "Okay. I will introduce you to the famous writer. I promise."

"Good girl."

I walked to the table where Hannah was refilling the cupcake towers. "How's it going?"

"Good. No one's tried to sneak an extra … so far." Her laughed echoed off the limestone walls, and I noticed that her young skin was luminous and wrinkle-free. Thick blonde hair was held back in a ponytail and she wore a Bree Brews It cap along with her apron.

"Most people are honest. The ones you have to pay attention to are the little boys and the old boys. Watch them like a hawk." I wasn't kidding.

Hannah laughed again. "Oh, I know. Dave came up and acted like he hadn't already eaten one, but the pink frosting stuck in his beard gave him away."

"That guy is something else." Even as I said it I wasn't mad. I watched the table of retired men, including Dave and Rich, who were drinking coffee and howling at someone's lame joke.

Hannah looked around. "I like the decorations."

"Thanks, honey." Clusters of pink and silver helium-filled balloons and streamers adorned the room. A Happy Birthday banner hung from the front counter. "They clash with the Christmas decorations, but I never claimed to be classy."

Hannah cast me a shy glance. "You're the classiest woman I've ever met."

I was touched. "Thank you. That is so sweet." I gave her a quick squeeze. "Are you just saying that to get a raise?"

"Of course!"

"Good answer!" I patted her on the shoulder.

The bell over the front door rang and Brice walked in carrying a magnificent floral bouquet under a clear plastic cover. I was astonished by the size of the arrangement. "Happy Birthday, Sis!" He kissed me on the cheek before carrying the bouquet to the front counter. "The lady at the flower shop said to keep the cover on until I got them inside because otherwise they'd freeze. Imagine that!" He carefully pulled off the plastic, revealing hot pink roses, white Queen Anne's lace, seeded eucalyptus and curly willow. I breathed in the aroma of flower shop flowers, second only to the smell of outdoor flowers.

"Oh, they're beautiful!" I wrapped him in a bear hug. "Thank you so much."

"They're from all of us … Caitlin and the boys too."

"Did you drive over to Beloit and pick them up this morning?"

He shook his head and shuffled his feet. "No, I got them yesterday when I told you I was going to check cows."

I chuckled. "You're pretty sneaky, B.S."

He pointed at me. "I know, B.S. I learned from the master."

"Insults on my birthday? Don't I get the day off?"

He nudged my shoulder. "You're right. No insults on your birthday." He dropped his head and bowed deeply. "You look stunning today, Bree." When he rose to his full height he was grinning from ear to ear. "How's that?"

"Much better!" I grabbed his hand and led him toward Hannah. "Let's get you a cupcake. Do you want an espresso or a latte?"

He studied the cupcakes and picked out one with extra frosting. "No, just regular coffee for me today."

"Help yourself. I won't charge you since you brought me flowers."

"That's very generous of you." He gave me a thumbs-up on his way to the coffee bar. "Hey. Should I grab some cupcakes for Caitlin and the boys before they're gone?"

"No, I set a few back for when they come in for lunch. Owner's prerogative."

"Good. The boys would be ticked if they didn't get cupcakes." He stopped and turned to me. "By the way, thanks for texting those amazing photos of Caitlin with Nate and Matt. The one of them kissing her cheeks is my lock screen photo now."

"Yeah, I told Caitlin that was the money shot."

"No doubt. And it's the perfect photo because I'm not in it."

I grinned. "Yeah, but you look a lot better today than yesterday … no raccoon eyes. I take it the boys slept in their own beds?"

Brice laughed. "Yes, thank God. I slept like a brick. The moment my head hit the pillow I was out." Brice poured himself a cup of coffee and a group of guys sitting by the window called him over. I heard one man call him B.S. and another said, "Hey, Bullshit, what's new?" I was glad Caitlin wasn't there to hear it; she absolutely detested his nickname.

Two women were ordering at the front counter, so I walked over to the espresso machine to await my marching orders from Aunt Judy. "Two peppermint mocha lattes, for here."

"Alrighty." I set two white ceramic coffee cups on the counter and launched into my espresso-making routine that was so familiar I could make one, literally, in my sleep — or at least when I was trying to sleep.

I was stirring peppermint syrup into the last drink when Aunt Judy, nibbling on her second cupcake, grabbed my arm. "He's here!" I knew who she meant. I inhaled a calming yoga breath and let it out evenly, carried the drinks to the front counter and presented them to the women.

I recited my warning. "That's a lot of sugar, so take it slow and beware of sugar rushes." They giggled and picked up their drinks. "Please help yourself to a free cupcake and don't forget to sign up for our drawing." They murmured their thanks and rushed over to the cupcake table.

I looked toward the front door and there was our well-dressed customer from yesterday, in the flesh, and Mr. Gorgeous now had a name — Maxim Hall. This morning I told myself that I'd blown him up in my mind; surely he wasn't as good looking as I remembered.

I was wrong. He was a beautiful specimen of a man.

I knew I was staring but before I managed to look away he noticed me gawking and walked toward the front counter. To make myself look busy I leaned down to retrieve something imaginary from behind the counter and stood up empty-handed just as he reached me.

"If you're about to grab the bell please know that I'm not going to ask how tall you are." His voice matched his looks — smooth and deep and melodious. I bet he could sing too.

He'd immediately put me at ease, and I grinned. "You don't want a free drink and a confectionary delight?"

Maxim crossed his arms and laughed; his dimples deepened and the lines in the corners of his eyes were pronounced. "It might be worth it, but there are a lot of people in here and I'm not looking for the attention. I'll admit I thoroughly enjoyed the bell-ringing bit, but I felt sorry for the guy until you comped his coffee and muffin."

"I have to do that, or they'll never come back."

He nodded in amusement. "Oh, he'll be back. How do you stop repeat customers from asking your height just to get free drinks and food?"

I explained. "It's a one-time-only sort of thing. I remember who's already asked."

"That's a good way to do it."

There was a pause in the conversation as we stared at each other. He suddenly straightened and extended his hand. "Where are my manners? I'm Maxim Hall." His handshake was firm, and I noticed his hands were callous-free unlike most of the men around here — the life of a writer. The warmth of his hand made its way into mine. "And you're Bree Somers, owner of this fine establishment."

"That I am." I managed a weak smile and was unsure what to say. He held onto my hand and I didn't object. I decided to let him explain his presence.

"It's nice to see you again." His clear blue eyes looked straight into me.

"You too … Maxim." I was suddenly a shy schoolgirl standing in front of her crush, tongue-tied and on the verge of total idiocy. I reminded myself that I'm a grown woman, I support myself and I know how to change a tire. Snap out of it!

He gently pulled his hand away and tucked it into the pocket of his jeans. "I hear you're the local expert on Waconda Springs."

I found my voice. "I consider myself an amateur historian, but I've read everything I could find on the subject. My grandfather lived near the spring and was fascinated by it."

Maxim rested his hands on the counter and leaned forward. "I'm a writer — I write novels — and I'm actually in the area doing research for a new book. I hadn't heard of the spring until I got here, but I'm totally intrigued by it. I found a little info online, but I'd really like to learn more."

I nodded. "I'd be happy to tell you what I know. We're super busy this morning but we could discuss it over coffee later."

Maxim looked pleased. "That would be great."

I smiled shyly, still stuck in schoolgirl mode. He was probably used to it. "We close at 2 and it will take a bit to clean up. Could you come back at 2:30?"

"Perfect. I'll drive around and get a feel for the area before then. Do you mind if we exchange numbers in case someone's plans change?"

I reached for the cell phone in my back pocket. "That's a good idea." We entered each other's numbers into our phones.

"It's really nice of you to help me out." He glanced back and saw several people behind him waiting to order. "I'm sorry to hold up the line. Before I go could you make me a latte? Let's do caramel today. I'll take this one to go."

"Sure." I turned around and ran into Aunt Judy who must have been standing behind me listening to the entire conversation. She gave me The Look and I knew what she wanted. I put my arm around her waist and together we turned toward the front counter where Maxim was pulling a ten-dollar bill out of his wallet.

"Maxim, I'd like you to meet Judy Johnson, my aunt and best employee." I pushed her forward and turned to make the latte.

He offered up a charming smile, revealing straight white teeth and pronounced dimples. "It's a pleasure to meet you, Judy. We weren't formally introduced yesterday."

She giggled and shook his outstretched hand. "It's a pleasure to meet you, Mr. Hall. I've read all of your books. Well, I think I have. Most of them, anyway. At least what I could find in the City Library because I never buy books. Too expensive, you know." She blushed and hurried on. "Your writing is wonderful, really wonderful. The stories are so ... so clever. You never know how they're going to end and I'm always surprised. Sometimes I cry."

Realizing she was babbling, Aunt Judy stopped talking and openly beamed up at the man who was at least a foot taller than she was.

"Well, it's always a pleasure to talk to a reader. I'd love to visit more and get your feedback."

Her jaw dropped and her face turned serious. "It would be an honor, Mr. Hall."

"Call me Maxim."

"Okay … Maxim."

He looked behind him again. "Let me pay and get out of the way. You're busy today."

I glanced over my shoulder. "It's the free cupcakes. Really brings them in."

He laughed. "You've got a great place here."

Aunt Judy silently collected his money and counted back change. I'd never seen her so quiet. She was definitely star struck. By this time I'd finished his latte and handed it to him. "I'll see you at 2:30."

He stuffed the change into his pocket and caught my eye. "See you then." We gazed at each other for a long moment until he broke the spell. "Thanks again. Oh, and Happy Birthday … Bree."

I whispered goodbye, and Maxim smiled, pickup up a cupcake and headed outside.

Five people were lined up, patiently waiting to order, and we managed to focus on the task at hand. Twenty minutes later and caught up, Aunt Judy pulled up a stool and sat down. "I need to take a load off." She swallowed some coffee, peeked up at me and I could tell she was thinking about something. She fluffed her hair and readjusted her glasses. "Did I sound like an idiot when I was talking to Mr. Hall — I mean Maxim?"

My heart went out to her, and I lied. "Of course not." I patted her shoulder and smiled into her trusting face. "He obviously loves to meet his readers. And he seemed genuine when he said he wanted to get some feedback from you."

"I thought so too." She was lost in thought for several minutes and looked up suddenly, a silly grin on her face. "Did you notice he wasn't wearing a wedding ring?"

I didn't admit I'd peeked at his left hand. "Why would I pay attention to something like that?" Disappointment clouded Aunt Judy's face and I felt bad for bursting her bubble. She never gave up hope that I'd date again and eventually marry. I quickly changed the subject. "You could stick around after we're closed and talk to him then."

She shook her head. "No, Joe wants to get stuff together for ice fishing tomorrow and he said something about 'cookies for the guys' which means he promised his fishing buddies my famous chocolate chip cookies which means I'll be baking all afternoon."

I chuckled. "Don't act like you don't love it. Those famous chocolate chip cookies have made you a lot of friends." She laughed and nodded. "So the lake's finally frozen enough for ice fishing, huh?"

"I guess so, around the edges, anyway." She appeared perplexed. "Why anybody would want to sit on the ice and freeze to death while catching barely any fish is beyond me."

"At least you'll have the house to yourself tomorrow." I loved pointing out the obvious.

"So true." Her face lit up. "It will give me a chance to clean the girls' bedrooms. They're coming next Friday for Christmas!"

"That's great." I meant it even though I was less than thrilled with Jane and Joyce, my first cousins who rarely called or visited their mother.

She snapped her fingers. "Oh honey, let me get your birthday gift. It's in the car." She jumped down from the stool and ran to the back door.

I walked to the front and visited with customers about the snow predicted for the weekend, the chances of the Waconda High School basketball teams qualifying for the state tournament, and how the wheat crop was faring in the drought. Brice stood to leave.

I stopped him. "Hey. What time should I meet up with you guys at RJ's?"

"Seven is what I told the others. Will that work for you?"

"Yes. That should give me time for a nap before I party like it's 1999."

He chuckled. "Is that how it's gonna be?"

"Yep, watch out. I'll be dancing on the tables by the end of the night."

"I'll wear my dancing shoes then." Brice turned serious. "Hey, who was that guy you were talking to?"

"You mean the incredibly hot one?"

Brice rolled his eyes. "I mean the one I've never seen before."

"That's Maxim Hall, the writer. Said he's doing research in the area and wants to talk to me about Waconda Springs. Evelyn Foster told him I was an expert."

He crossed his arms and looked amused. "You're an expert, huh?"

"Yep. I'm meeting him here at 2:30."

Brice's eyes lit up with recognition. "Hey, I've heard of him. He's written quite a few books."

I crossed my arms. "Yeah. It's interesting he's out here in the middle of the country. His books are all set on the East Coast."

"Probably looking for something different. Who knows?" Brice turned to go. "See you tonight."

"Thanks again for the flowers. I love them."

He reached over and squeezed my arm. "No prob, Sis. You deserve it. I'd better get to the farm."

He walked out into the cold morning, and I watched until he disappeared around the corner. I grabbed a cupcake on the way to the front counter and met Aunt Judy who was holding a small box wrapped in balloons-and-confetti wrapping paper with a pink curly cue bow on top.

She handed the box to me, and I set down my cupcake. "Go ahead and open it, honey."

"With pleasure!" I tore off the ribbon and wrapping, opened the lid and pulled out a black coffee mug with white lettering. I read the saying out loud. "'Messy Bun and Getting Stuff Done!' I love it."

Aunt Judy practically swaggered. "When I saw the 'Messy Bun' part I knew I had to buy it for you."

"Where did you find it?"

"Where do you think?"

We stared at each other, burst out laughing and yelled in unison. "Stuff n Such!"

"She has the cutest things in that store." I bent down and wrapped Aunt Judy in a long hug. "What would I do without you?"

"Oh, you'd get by." But I could tell she was pleased with the compliment.

I set my new mug on the front counter next to the bouquet of flowers. "My birthday is certainly off to an excellent start."

"That it is, honey. And you get to see Maxim Hall again. Happy Birthday to you." Aunt Judy winked, swung her broad hips and poked me in the ribs.

I nodded. "Yeah, the day just keeps getting better. Will you take a picture of me?"

"Sure."

I pulled my phone out of a back pocket, turned on the camera and handed it to Aunt Judy. She walked around to the front of the counter and snapped a picture of me with my gifts and another of me with the decorations. I posed for selfies with Aunt Judy and Hannah, then took a few candid pictures of the coffee shop with its crazy combination of Christmas and birthday decorations. Dave photo bombed one of my selfies with Hannah.

I posted the pictures on my Bree Brews It Coffee Shop page, answered several birthday texts from friends and one from Mother, slipped the phone back into my pocket and smiled as more customers came in. I walked to the espresso machine and found myself looking forward to meeting with Maxim Hall, novelist, about one of my favorite subjects.

Chapter 7

I heard a knock on the front door and glanced up at the clock: 2:28 pm. Mr. Gorgeous had arrived. My heart jumped and sped up its pace. I inhaled a calming breath, smoothed down my hair and popped a mint in my mouth. I jogged to the front door and Maxim was in the breezeway rubbing his ungloved hands together. He smiled when he saw me, and I turned the lock and hurriedly ushered him inside. "Come in before your fingers freeze off."

He shivered visibly. "I think it's colder now than it was this morning."

"That's probably true. It's from the cold front that's bringing snow tomorrow." In my awkwardness I almost forgot my manners. "May I take your coat?"

He shrugged it off. "Thanks."

I hung the black leather coat on the rack and felt his gaze on my back. My stomach fluttered, and I forced myself to turn and look at him. He was a beautiful man, and the way he carried himself was aristocratic and somewhat otherworldly. His broad shoulders and full chest strained at his blue sweater, and he smelled earthy, woodsy and clean. I noticed a small mole on his neck and a scar above his right eyebrow. His face was a study in thoughtfulness, and his eyes focused intently on mine. I sensed curiosity and hesitancy.

I broke the spell. "Would you like some coffee?"

His eyes lit up. "I would love some."

I walked behind the counter and faced him. "What'll it be?"

Maxim followed, leaned on the counter and studied the menu. He thought for a moment and then grinned broadly. "The peppermint mocha latte sounds intriguing."

I smiled back at him. "Great choice. That's one of our most popular drinks this time of year. Think I'll have one too."

I turned to the espresso machine, hugely relieved by the distraction, and ground coffee beans into the porta filter, tamped them down, slid it into the machine and turned it on. I watched as dark, fragrant liquid was extracted into the two white mugs I'd placed under the spout, and I sensed movement out of the corner of my eye.

Maxim surveyed the room. "This is an amazing building. I read about the limestone in the area. Is this native limestone?"

"Yes, it is. It was actually one of the first buildings in Waconda. The cornerstone says 1894. It was the town's first general store and post office."

"Is that so?" Maxim hooked his thumbs in his pockets and regarded the building.

I poured a syrup made of sugar, peppermint and cocoa into the drinks. "The settlers were isolated and lonely on their claims of land, and the general store was the hub of action. They'd drive for miles to stock up on supplies, catch up on the local news and check for letters from home."

"How long was it the general store?" Maxim walked to a wall and ran his hands over the limestone, studying it closely.

I stirred the syrup into the coffee and glanced at him. "For over forty years. Then it was a millinery where they made hats. It's been a bakery, two restaurants, a lawyer's office, a grocery store and for twelve unfortunate years it was a tavern where there were apparently a lot of fights … and one murder."

Maxim stared at me. "That was unfortunate."

"When I was little it was Rogers Variety Store. I bought the building from their son." I expected him to ask me how long I'd owned the building, but he remained quiet. I poured in some steamed milk to finish the drinks, and then I carried the cups to a small round table and set them down. "Help yourself."

"Thank you." Maxim walked over, picked up one of the cups and sipped the coffee. "Wow! That is amazingly good … very Christmassy." He relished several more drinks of the rich, sweet liquid, and his eyes turned to me. "Tell me about these pictures on the wall. You played volleyball?"

I lifted my cup of coffee and stepped over to the first of two 11 by 14 framed photos of women's volleyball teams. "Yes, I did. This is the 1998 Waconda High School team when I was a senior. We were second at State that year. I'm right there." I pointed to the tallest girl in the back row.

Maxim inspected the picture and glanced at me. "I bet you were good."

I shrugged. "I held my own."

"I'm sure you did. Were you a passer, a hitter or a setter?"

I'm sure my face registered surprise.

He shrugged. "My sister played volleyball and my mom made me go to the games."

"That explains it. I was a passer, a hitter and a blocker."

He leaned toward me. "You obviously played in college so you must have been good. Dazzle me with some statistics. You have my permission to brag. In fact, I insist on it." He drank his coffee and regarded me with amusement.

I hesitated for a moment and forged ahead. "My junior year of high school I set the state record for the most blocks in a single season ... I set the record halfway through the season."

Maxim's eyebrows shot up. "Impressive."

My shyness melted away. "Then during my senior year I broke my junior year record." I chuckled and stared at the picture. "It's not as hard to brag as I thought it would be. Most of the time I was a left-handed hitter, but I was also a switch hitter. I blocked on the offside."

He smiled. "You lost me there."

"I'm just saying that my switch hitting, blocking and height are what caught K-State's attention." I pointed to the second framed picture. "This is the 2002 Kansas State University volleyball team when I was a senior. I wasn't the tallest player, either. I'm second from right in the back row. I got a full ride and played for them all four years of college."

"What was that like?" Maxim seemed genuinely interested.

I drank some coffee and continued. "It was intense. College athletes are worked hard, travel a lot for games and then have full class schedules like the regular students. I rarely went out. I was either playing volleyball or studying."

"What was your major?"

I hesitated. "Music education." My shoulders tensed; I didn't like where this was going.

Maxim's eyes were bright. "So you're a musician. What instrument do you play?"

"Piano." We stared at the pictures and I was surprised, then relieved, when he didn't ask any more questions. I seized the moment to change the subject and pointed to a group of photographs further down the wall. "Over there are some pictures of Waconda Springs when it was a health resort."

"This morning I wondered if that's what they were."

We moved and stopped in front of the black and white photos professionally arranged in rustic frames. I was acutely aware of Maxim's presence yet more relaxed than five minutes ago. I switched into museum curator mode. "The Native Americans viewed the spring as sacred; it was a ceremonial gathering place for generations. In the late 1800s the spring was discovered by the settlers and it wasn't long before one of them capitalized on it." I pointed to the top picture. "There's the spring surrounded by a decorative black wrought iron fence. The buildings you see in these pictures are from when it was a health resort." I pointed to the picture below it. "Here's the first sod house that was built near the spring."

Maxim's eyes focused on the details of the pictures.

I was on a roll. "The first business at the spring was actually a bottling company that distributed the mineral spring water across the country as Waconda Water. In the early 1900s a health resort was built next to the spring. People from all over the country came here to drink the water and bathe in it to restore their health." I gestured to a picture of three women in white uniforms standing behind a bathtub. "The water was piped into bathtubs in private rooms and there was an outdoor pool. In this photo you can see that the main building was huge and quite impressive in its day."

"That is fascinating." Maxim scrutinized the pictures.

"The spring was unique. It was actually a rare phenomenon. A hydrologist hired to study the spring said it was the only one of its kind in the world."

Maxim's eyebrows shot up. "Wow!" He studied one of the photos closer. "So it was a natural spring of water that flowed up from the earth?"

"Yes. It stood 40 feet above the Solomon River Valley — we're standing in the valley — and it was 300 feet wide. Its depth is still subject to debate. Some say it was 15 feet deep and others say it was bottomless. They hired a diver in 1908 and he couldn't find the bottom. Then around 1950 a team of geologists used sonar and said it was 115 feet deep."

"And the water had healing qualities?"

I nodded. "That's what they said." I turned to the tables. "Do you mind if we sit down? My feet are killing me."

"Of course." Maxim set his cup on the table and walked to his coat hanging on the rack. "I need to get out my notebook and write all of this down." He pulled a small blue notebook and pen from the inside pocket of his coat. We sat down across from each other and Maxim jotted down notes in handwriting that would rival a doctor's.

He paused and glanced at me. His blue eyes were intense and focused. "I drove around the lake today and stopped at a historical marker that tells the Legend of Waconda and the Great Spirit Spring." I propped my feet on a chair, sipped my drink and listened. "It said that Waconda was a beautiful princess who fell in love with a warrior from another tribe and when they weren't allowed to marry there was a war between the tribes. The warrior was struck by an arrow and fell into the spring. In her grief Waconda jumped in after him and the natives believed her spirit lived on in the spring." Maxim paused for a moment. "What I understood is that the lake is named after the spring which is named after the Legend of Waconda."

I set down my coffee. "You're right. It all started with the Native American princess, Waconda."

"The story really fascinates me. I'm one-eighth Native American — Cheyenne, actually. I haven't done much research on my ancestry, but I enjoy the year-round tan."

I laughed and sat back in my chair. "Yes, that's a major advantage. Some believe Waconda's tribe was Cheyenne."

This was a revelation to Maxim. "Really?"

"That's what I've read. There's no way to prove it, of course. The stories were handed down verbally from generation to generation." I tapped the table with a fingernail. "There's definitely a chance she was Cheyenne … they lived and hunted on the Great Plains, along with the Sioux and other tribes."

Maxim shook his head. "This story just keeps getting better."

I crossed my arms and leaned back. "The legend you read on the sign is actually just one version of the story; it's the most common. My favorite is the one my father told me when I was a little girl. In this version Waconda's father, Chief Mansotan of the Cheyenne…" I nodded and emphasized the word Cheyenne. "…allowed Waconda to choose her own mate even though many young chiefs and warriors offered him gifts for her hand in marriage. She fell in love with a warrior named Chillotan but before they were married the Sioux from the north invaded their hunting grounds and all of the warriors from the village went to join the fight." I stared into the corner, lost in the story. "Waconda told Chillotan that she would visit the spring every day to pray for his safe return, and she did. When Waconda heard that Chillotan had been killed in the fight she threw herself into the spring, never to be seen again."

I paused and watched Maxim scribble in his notepad. After a few minutes I continued. "The Native Americans believed Waconda's spirit resided in the spring. The mineral water was valued for its medicinal qualities. The natives made pilgrimages to worship the Great Spirit, they drank and bathed in its waters, and made offerings of trinkets, beads and weapons."

He looked up from his notes, wonder filling his face. "Is the legend true?"

I gazed into his indigo eyes. "We'll never know. But it's a beautiful story, don't you think?"

Maxim stared down at his notepad. "Love is a powerful force."

I fiddled with the pendant hanging at my throat and felt a weight push down on my heart. We sat in silence for several minutes, but it was comfortable and peaceful without a trace of awkwardness.

He spoke first. "So this spring we're talking about ... Waconda Spring ... it's covered up by the lake?"

"Yes." I couldn't hide my sadness. "The dam was finished in 1968, and when they closed the gates the Solomon River flooded and formed Waconda Lake. The spring was covered up forever."

Maxim frowned. "Why did they build the dam?"

"Flood control for eastern Kansas, which I agree was necessary. I just wish they hadn't built the dam here and destroyed the spring."

"That is a shame." Maxim noticed my change in mood and set down his pen.

I gazed into space. "My grandfather was born on a farm where the lake is. He grew up there, married my grandmother, settled there with his family and farmed the land. When the dam project was proposed he was one of the people who fought it. They lost, obviously. The government bought out all of the landowners and forced them to move." I sighed deeply. "My father was 20 when they had to pack up and leave; by then he was farming with my grandfather. They bought a farm south of town; that's where I grew up. Some of the homes and buildings were moved before the dam was completed but the rest were torn down. My father said the Waconda Health Resort buildings were destroyed and thrown in the spring. Can you believe that?"

Maxim's face was filled with sympathy. "It does seem callous."

I caught myself brooding and snapped out of it. "I'm sorry. It doesn't take much to get me up on my soapbox when it comes to Waconda Springs."

He shook his head. "Please don't apologize. I admire your passion. I see why Evelyn sent me to you." He bent over his notebook and scribbled a few more illegible lines. Finished, he closed the book and set down his pen.

I switched gears. "The book you're researching … what's it about?"

He sat up straight and his cheeks turned a light shade of pink, a clear indication I'd caught him off guard.

I rushed to apologize. "I'm sorry. It's really none of my business."

He recovered rapidly. "No, it's okay." Maxim rubbed his forehead, ran fingers through his thick black hair and forced a lop-sided grin. "You've been more than gracious in helping me out. You have the right to ask." He scratched his chin and stared off into the distance for a moment. When he turned to look at me he was once again composed. "I guess I became flustered because I'm not sure yet, and that obviously bothers me. That's kind of how it works when you're writing a book. An idea either comes to you or you go searching for it. Right now I'm doing the latter. Does that make sense?"

I nodded and smiled warmly. "Of course it does. Thanks for being honest with me."

A curious look, along with a little apprehension, crossed his face. "Have you read any of my books? Please don't say yes if the answer is no."

I leaned my elbows on the table and folded my hands. "Well, the answer is yes. I've read The Day and The Street. They were both excellent."

He exhaled and leaned his elbows on the table, closing the space between us. "Excellent, huh?" His look was teasing, and he held up a hand. "Do you pinky swear that you're telling the truth and nothing but the truth?"

I raised my hand next to his and grinned. "Yes, I pinky swear it's the truth and nothing but the truth." We linked our little fingers and burst out laughing. His hand was warm and soft. I gazed into his eyes and felt my pulse quicken. Our laughter faded and we studied each other with open interest. Those incredible dimples and full lips were just inches away; I felt the urge to trace the contours of his face with my fingertips.

Awareness of the intimate situation snapped me back to reality. I pulled my hand away, jumped up and grabbed the empty cups. "Would you like more coffee?"

"No, thank you."

I carried the cups to the coffee bar and set them in the plastic tub. When I finally turned around, Maxim's head was down, and I couldn't read his expression. I searched for something to say. "I forgot to tell you that there's a replica of the spring at Waconda State Park."

Maxim glanced up with interest. "I'd love to see it."

"You probably drove right by it today and didn't notice. We need a bigger sign out there. I keep telling them that and no one will listen to me."

He stood and rested his hands on the back of the chair. "Now that I've seen a picture of the spring I'm sure I drove past the replica; it isn't close to the road."

"No, it's a bit of a trek but definitely worth it." Awkward silence filled the room. I wished I knew what to say. I suddenly had an idea. "I'd be happy to show it to you tomorrow."

His face lit up. "That would be great. But isn't it supposed to snow tomorrow?"

I rested my hands on my hips. "A little snow doesn't slow us down here in Kansas."

He scratched his chin. "I guess I forgot to tell you that I'm from New York City. It gets cold there but we're kind of wimpy about the snow."

I glanced at his feet. "Did you bring boots?"

"Will suede work?"

"Absolutely not." I thought for a moment. "I'll find you some boots. You just show up. And we can take my pickup. It has four-wheel drive."

His amusement was palpable. "What time?"

"How about 2:30 again? We'll leave from here."

"I'll be here at 2:30." Maxim pulled on his coat, buttoned it up to his chin and slipped the notebook and pen into a pocket.

I stopped him as he reached for the door handle. "Hey. Where are you staying?"

"Lakeside Bed and Breakfast."

I chuckled. "What do you think of Lucy?"

He grinned. "I think I love her. She makes the best biscuits and gravy I've ever eaten."

"That's the truth. She's a pretty special lady. Lost her husband last year to cancer but she plows ahead and never complains. She's a tough old gal. The B and B is also made of native limestone."

"Lucy told me all about it." He emphasized 'all' and looked amused. "Well, I'll see you tomorrow. Thanks again, Bree." He turned to leave but paused and reached toward his back pocket. "Let me pay you for the coffee."

I shook my head. "Nope, it was on the house."

He hesitated then smiled, and I could feel the warmth emanating from his body to mine. "That's very kind of you. Thanks for everything … the conversation and the coffee. I really enjoyed both."

I blushed and looked down. "You're welcome … Maxim."

He left and I walked to the front window to catch another glimpse of him as he hopped into a shiny black SUV, backed up and sped off.

I breathed a sigh of relief and wondered what I'd gotten myself into.

Chapter 8

My high-heeled boots clicked a steady beat on the sidewalk as I hurried through the chilly air of the town square. I walked past the evergreen tree glowing with Christmas lights and between two rows of brightly-lit plastic candy canes cleverly named Candy Cane Lane. I tucked gloved hands deep into the pockets of my long black coat and whistled the Happy Birthday song to the rhythm of my steps, a ploy to warm myself that didn't work.

When I arrived at the front door of RJ's Bar I grabbed the handle, pulled hard and stepped into the blessed warmth. As my eyes adjusted to the dim lighting I headed to our favorite corner table where Caitlin, adorable in a white cashmere sweater, matching skinny jeans and grey ankle boots, jumped up and waved. "Get over here, birthday girl."

The moment I was within reach Caitlin wrapped me in a hug, squeezed tightly, and even though it was a challenge to breathe, I squeezed back. Brice loved to joke about the sheer strength packed into Caitlin's petite body, and he was right. "Happy birthday, Bree." She let go, stepped back and beamed up at me, her entire body buzzing with excitement. She turned and pointed to the large round table where a wildly-colored balloon bouquet sat in the center surrounded by wrapped presents and two bottles of my favorite white wine. "Ta Da!" She bounced and clapped her hands.

I laughed as I removed my coat, tucked the gloves in a pocket and hung it on the back of a chair. I inspected the charming table and patted Caitlin's back. "You shouldn't have ... but I'm glad you did." I kissed her cheek and picked up a bottle of wine just as Brice appeared with wine glasses. "Perfect timing for once. I need a drink."

He grinned. "Let me do the honors." Brice reached for the wine bottle, peeled off the wrapper and twisted the cork until we heard a soft pop. He poured three glasses, handed one to Caitlin, one to me and then raised his in the air. "A toast to my sister on her 37th birthday." Caitlin and I raised our glasses next to his, and I could tell by the smirk on his face that Brice was about to dazzle us with his wit. "May your B.S. stand for Bree Somers and not bullshit. Here's to many more years of happiness, laughter, coffee, wine ... and me as your favorite brother. To Bree!" I giggled, Caitlin groaned, and we clinked our glasses together in a toast.

"Thanks, B.S. Poetry. Pure poetry." I tilted my head back and chugged half the glass of white wine.

Caitlin raised her eyebrows. "Oh, yes, Brice is the Poet Laureate of Waconda." She sipped at her wine while I drained the rest of my glass.

"Lordy, Bree, you might want to slow down a bit." Brice poured more wine into my glass.

"Like this?" I stuck out my pinky finger and daintily sipped the sweet liquid. I giggled and high-fived Caitlin while Brice shook his head.

He regarded me with an amused expression. "You must have gotten a nap. You're absolutely peppy for someone who's been up since 5."

I offered a thumbs-up sign. "Yep. I actually slept for about an hour. I'm ready to go."

I turned when I heard the front door open, and Robert, Michelle and Tracey hurried in and rushed over to our table. Tracey, a petite redhead in a cinnamon-colored sweater dress, embraced me and a surge of floral fragrance swirled around us. With her crimson manicured nails she placed a perfectly-wrapped present with gold ribbon in my hands. "Sorry if we're late. Happy Birthday, honey. Hope you like it."

"Thanks, Tracey." I set the present next to the others on the table. "I'm sure I will."

"You look great tonight, Bree."

"Well, I did wear my nicest pair of jeans and brand new boots." I kicked up a leg to show off my knee-high black boots.

Tracey whistled. "Very nice. And I love it when you wear your hair down." She smiled and rearranged the navy and teal scarf around my neck. "Is this new?"

"You know it is since I bought it at your store."

She laughed. "Thanks for the free advertising." She turned to Brice. "Where's the wine?"

He chuckled and poured her a glass which she sipped while chatting with Caitlin.

Robert and Michelle walked over holding glasses of wine, and Michelle hugged me tightly. "Happy Birthday."

Her husband shook my hand. "The same from me." He was clearly uncomfortable and cleared his throat. "You know I'm not much of a hugger."

I patted his hand. "That's okay, Robert. Michelle hugs enough for both of you."

He snapped his fingers and looked pleased. "You're right." He tapped his wife on her shoulder. "Did you hear that, Michelle? You hug enough for both of us so that gets me out of hugging for the rest of my life." He held out his arms. "I'm free."

Michelle snorted. "Whatever. I was going to hug you later, but I guess since you're never hugging anyone again we'll just cancel it." Robert seemed at a loss for words and scratched his head.

She hooked her arm through mine. "Did you have a good day? We didn't make it to the shop for your birthday cupcakes."

"No problem and yes, it's been a great day. We actually had two dozen cupcakes left over which surprised me. We usually run out by late morning."

Michelle sipped her wine. "I'm sure they were yummy as always."

I nodded. "Of course. I ate three."

"Well it doesn't show. I wish I was tall and could eat whatever I wanted."

I smiled. "That's all I've eaten today, so I'm starving."

She rummaged around in her purse and pulled out a small wrapped box. "Here's a little something for you."

I squeezed her arm. "Thank you. That's very kind." I placed Michelle's gift beside the others in the middle of the table. "I'll open it later."

Michelle apologized. "It's not much, really. Just a token of our friendship."

I put my arm around her waist and pulled her close. Her navy wool jacket looked sharp over a fitted white T-shirt and boot-cut jeans. Michelle always wore true-to-God cowgirl boots. "You know I never want any gifts."

She frowned and cast a sideways glance at Tracey. "I know, but Tracey always shows up with something fabulous from her store and makes the rest of us look bad."

"It's not a competition, Michelle. Your presence is my present."

She shrieked with laughter. "Did you really just say that?"

"Too much?"

"Way too much." We doubled over in laughter.

Brice caught my eye and took charge as he loved to do. "Why don't we all sit down?" I snagged the chair next to Caitlin, Tracey sat down by me, Michelle settled in by Tracey and the two men — Robert and Brice — grabbed the two remaining spots. Brice rested his hand on Caitlin's shoulder. "Honey, would you give a toast for Bree? I'm thinking that mine was a little tacky."

Tracey was insulted. "You did a toast without us? How dare you!"

Caitlin reached out and patted her hand. "Don't worry. You didn't miss much."

Brice tried to look offended but couldn't hide his amusement.

Caitlin raised her glass and regarded me. "I want to wish you a happy birthday on the anniversary of your 37th year on earth. We are truly blessed that God sent you to us, and I'm lucky to call you my best friend. May the coming year be filled with health, happiness and love. To Bree."

Tears pooled in the corners of my eyes, and the group answered "To Bree" in unison as we clinked our glasses in a toast. I pulled a tissue out of my pocket and dabbed at my eyes. "That was beautiful, Caitlin. Thank you."

"Was it better than my toast?" Brice wrapped his arm around Caitlin's shoulders and kissed her forehead.

I held up two fingers an inch apart. "Maybe just a bit … but it's the thought that counts."

Caitlin turned to Brice. "At least I didn't call her B.S. like you did. That is the most God-awful nickname I've ever heard." She wrinkled her nose. "Did your parents even stop to consider your initials when they named you?" She poked a finger in his shoulder. "Why do you think I didn't want to use the names you had picked out for Nate and Matt when they were born?"

Michelle leaned forward, her eyes bright with interest. "What did he want to name them?"

Caitlin squinted and looked like she'd sucked on a lemon. "Brad and Brent. Can you imagine? Might as well have called them the B.S. Boys."

Michelle snorted noisily and caught the attention of two gray-haired, wrinkled men nursing drinks at the bar. She lowered her voice. "Thank God you stopped him, Caitlin. Brad Somers and Brent Somers. They'd be teased mercilessly in junior high, I can tell you that."

Caitlin dropped her fist on the table. "That's what I told him … and you would know. How you can stand teaching thirteen-year-olds is beyond me, but I'm glad someone is willing to do it."

"They're not that bad, really." Michelle poured more wine into her glass. "It just takes love, patience and plenty of wine on Friday nights. Thank God it's Friday!" Michelle raised her glass in the air, and we burst out laughing.

Tracey snapped her fingers and grabbed my arm. "I forgot to tell you guys … I heard there's a famous writer in town and he's staying at Lucy's B and B."

Caitlin leaned forward, her face a study of intense curiosity. She was a big-time reader. "Who is it?"

Tracey sat back, a smug look on her face, and folded her fingers together. "Well, I'm not much of a reader but even I've heard of his books."

Michelle drummed her fingers on the table. "You're going to drag this out for all it's worth, aren't you?"

"Yes, I am." Tracey grinned in delight.

Caitlin was having none of it. "Come on, Tracey. Just tell us who it is."

Tracey twirled a ringlet of hair around her finger. "I'm not one to spread rumors."

Michelle shrieked in laughter and the old guys at the bar stared at her again. "Yes, you are!"

Brice and Robert were in a heated debate about possible Super Bowl contenders, but Brice overheard Tracey's announcement and caught my eye. As Robert droned on about his New England Patriots, Brice conveyed with a simple shake of his head that he wouldn't mention my meeting with Maxim Hall. I nodded briefly and kept my mouth shut.

Tracey, satisfied that she held our full attention, finally relented. "I heard from a reliable source that it's Maxim Hall."

Caitlin's mouth fell open. "Oh my God. He's my favorite writer."

Michelle leaned forward. "I've read all of his books, except for the most recent one. I think it came out this fall."

"It did." Caitlin stared off into the corner. "I haven't read it, either, but it's called The Chair. I usually cry at the end of his books."

Tracey shrugged and inspected her fingernails. "You know I don't like to read so unless the books were made into movies I won't know them."

Michelle touched Tracey's shoulder. "Remember when we all went to see that movie called The Day?"

Tracey jumped. "That's his movie?"

"Well, book turned into movie, but yes."

Tracey clapped her hands. "I loved that one."

Caitlin pointed at Tracey and sat up straighter. "The book was even better. You should read it." Tracey stuck out her tongue.

Michelle kept her focus on Tracey. "Is he in town right now?"

"That's what I heard from a reliable source."

"What's he doing here?"

"Researching a new book, apparently." Tracey sipped at the wine, a satisfied expression on her face.

Michelle turned her attention to me. "Bree, have you read any of Maxim Hall's books?"

I avoided eye contact and counted the balloons in the bouquet. "A couple of them, I think."

"I'm a huge fan of his work. Did you enjoy them?"

I rubbed my elbow. "Sure. His books are pretty good." Brice gazed at me, and it was clear he enjoyed my discomfort immensely. He twirled the wine in his glass and snickered.

Michelle shook her head. "Pretty good? They're better than that. As an English teacher I'd rate his work a nine out of ten." She crossed her arms. "And you know how hard it is to get a ten out of me. He's able to convey a simple yet profound story line with colorful images and engaging dialogue. He's a wordsmith."

Caitlin gazed at Michelle. "Wow, that's an amazing way to describe his books. You're right. He's a gifted writer."

Finished with his speech about Tom Brady's expertise as a football quarterback, Robert joined in. "My secretary mentioned the writer you're talking about, Maxim Hall. She's a big-time reader and was excited to hear that he's in town. But how famous can he be? I've never heard of him."

Michelle frowned. "How would you know who the hot writers are? Do you secretly read novels at the insurance office? Because in the twelve years we've been married I have never once seen you read a book." She jabbed her finger in his chest. "Name one book you've read."

"Okay." He thought for a few seconds and suddenly snapped his fingers. "In Cold Blood. Truman Capote."

Michelle rolled her eyes. "I mean a book that wasn't assigned in Junior English class."

Robert crossed his arms and didn't say anything.

Michelle raised her chin and smiled in triumph. "That's what I thought."

In desperate need to change the subject I caught Tracey's attention. "Have you been busy at the store with customers buying Christmas gifts?"

Tracey set her wine glass on the table and leaned forward, obviously delighted to talk about her favorite subject. "Yes. This morning I ran the numbers and we're already ahead of last year's December sales figures. I think my Christmas ad campaign is working." Tracey raised her voice and imitated a radio announcer: "Amazon may deliver to your door, but do they support the Waconda High School Lakers? No! Shop at Stuff n Such, proud financial supporter of the Waconda Lakers." She beamed in triumph. "And the free wrapping with any gift purchase is really bringing in the men."

Robert uncrossed his arms. "Hey, you got my attention. I heard your ad when I was driving to work and stopped by that very day. I can't wrap a gift to save my life."

Tracey's face lit up. "My hunch was right on that one. Poor guys. Most of them don't have a clue what to buy when they come in the store but luckily I know most of the women around here and I help them pick out something special."

Michelle grabbed Robert's hand, her eyes huge. "You were in Stuff n Such?"

Robert pretended to be insulted. "Yes, I was in Stuff n Such. I bought you a Christmas gift and it's beautifully wrapped and everything. You're going to love it."

Tracey beamed and patted Michelle's leg. "Yes, you will, honey."

Michelle squeezed Robert's hand. "It has to be better than last year's four-slot toaster."

"Oh, it's much better." Tracey smiled. "Trust me."

Robert placed his hand on his heart in mock insult. "What's wrong with our four-slot toaster? We use it every morning. It was a romantic gift; very hot. Sometimes it's so hot the toast burns my fingers." He smiled at his attempt at humor.

Michelle patted his hand. "Yes, nothing screams romance like four pieces of toast at a time."

Robert pointed at Michelle. "At least our three children aren't fighting over two pieces of toast anymore. You're welcome."

Caitlin called to Tracey. "Has Brice been in the store to pick out something special for Yours Truly?"

Brice raised his hand like a traffic cop and stopped Tracey before she could speak. "Don't say a word, Tracey. Whether I have or have not been in Stuff n Such to buy a Christmas gift for my wife is no one's business but my own."

Tracey nodded. "Don't worry, Brice. What happens in Stuff n Such stays in Stuff n Such." Caitlin shrugged and poured more wine into her glass.

A shadow fell across our table, and I looked up to see RJ standing between Brice and Caitlin, his hulking body-builder form straining at the black T-shirt that was at least one size too small. He grinned, set a stack of menus on the table and turned on the charm. "Wow, look at you guys. You clean up pretty good."

Brice slapped the table. "Clean jeans and everything tonight, RJ. Only the best for my sister on her birthday."

RJ looked straight into my eyes and smiled, revealing ultra-white teeth with a small gap in the center. "I agree. Happy Birthday, Bree."

"Thank you, RJ." I sank down in my chair.

He winked and crossed his massive arms. "You look gorgeous this evening. I hope you've had a pleasant day."

The man's chutzpah never failed to surprise me. "I have, thank you." The table descended into silence.

RJ eyeballed me for a few seconds, his short blond hair spiked with gel and a light coating of stubble covering his face. With his eyes still pinned on me he addressed the group. "Tonight I'm not only the owner and bartender, but I'm also your waiter."

"Is Sandy sick?" Tracey always got straight to the point.

"No, just out of town for the weekend, and my high school waitresses are all at the basketball game." He shook his head. "Thank goodness my cook showed."

Robert piped up. "Do you think you can handle us?"

"I'll try, Robbie." Robert frowned at the nickname, but RJ didn't notice. "How are we doing on the wine?"

Brice checked the levels in the bottles. "Better bring out another, RJ, and we could use some water. And how about an extra-large order of loaded nachos? Is that good with everyone?" We all nodded in agreement.

RJ clasped his hands. "Sure thing. Why don't you guys look at the menus while I put in your appetizer order and grab some water. Be right back."

He disappeared into the kitchen behind the bar, and I glanced around the room. In addition to the old bachelors at the bar, a young man and woman were huddled together in serious conversation by the front window, and two middle-aged couples convulsed in laughter in the corner booth. Most of Waconda had driven thirty minutes north to Mankato to watch the Waconda High School Lakers play basketball against the Rock Hills Grizzlies.

I felt a finger jab in my side. "Bree." Tracey's words were in a hushed tone, her face just inches from mine. "Has RJ asked you out lately?"

I groaned. Not this again. The woman was tenacious. I picked up a menu and pretended to read it even though I knew exactly what I was ordering. "Not since November. You know he's too young for me."

"Well, he's not too young for me." Tracey eyed the bar where RJ was mixing two whiskey sours for the old guys who were almost permanent fixtures in the place. She sat up straight and fluffed her hair. "I sure wish he'd ask me out. Unlike you, I'd say yes."

I exhaled slowly. "You know I'm not interested in dating. Every time he asks me out I explain this to him, he listens patiently, acts like he understands and then a few weeks later he asks me out again. Either he's as stubborn as hell or not very bright."

"Oh, he's bright alright and extremely good looking." Tracey almost drooled. "His hair is so thick and gorgeous; it's healthier than mine, for Lord's sake. And don't you love that stubble? So manly." She leaned in closer. "I heard he has a snake tattoo that starts on his chest, wraps around his arm and goes down his back. Some lucky gals saw him at the lake last summer and told me all about it." She scrutinized RJ as he leaned on the counter, talking with the ancient drinkers. "And did you notice his butt in those jeans?"

In exasperation my voice rose. "Tracey, I do not make a habit of looking at RJ's butt." I felt eyes on me and noticed that my friends had stopped studying their menus and were staring at me.

Brice didn't even try to hide his amusement. "Anything we need to know about, Sis?" The others chuckled.

I shrugged and plowed ahead. "Tracey thinks RJ's butt looks good in the jeans he's wearing tonight." I dared to glance sideways at Tracey and the woman was actually blushing. I snickered; victory was mine.

Robert chimed in. "If it makes you feel any better, Tracey, I also noticed how good RJ's butt looks tonight." We froze in place, eyed each other for a few moments and suddenly shrieked with laughter. Tracey glared at us and tried to remain stoic, but her attempt was futile; she was soon laughing as hard as we were.

RJ chose that moment to appear at our table with a pitcher of water and a stack of drinking glasses. "Sounds like I missed a good joke."

Silence settled over the table and Tracey was the one to break it. "We were just talking about a prank from our high school days. You're too young to get it." She pinched my leg and I suppressed a giggle.

RJ's smile didn't leave his face as he set down the water pitcher and glasses. "Yeah, I heard you guys were big troublemakers back then." He peeked at me and pointed to the kitchen. "I need to bring the meals out to table five and then I'll come back and get your orders."

Brice tipped back in his chair. "No hurry, RJ. We're got a babysitter and I'm staying 'til you kick us out." Caitlin leaned over and kissed Brice on the lips.

When RJ was gone Robert slapped Brice on the arm and wrinkled his brow. "Troublemakers? Us? We were never in trouble." Brice appeared equally baffled.

Caitlin poured water into the glasses and passed them around. "Keep up the innocent act, boys, but we know better. Right, ladies?" Michelle, Tracey and I nodded. "Who snuck a goat into Principal Heide's office when he was in the bathroom?" She looked at Robert and Brice who feigned innocence. "Who picked up Karen McKay's tiny car and balanced it on the half wall at the Stop n Shop?" She pointed her finger at Robert and Brice who were staring at the ceiling and twiddling their thumbs. "Who talked Daryl Sullivan into log rolling down the side of the dam, and when he broke his leg…."

Robert interrupted. "Okay, we get it. We were troublemakers. Will you stop?" He rubbed his forehead in agitation. "And please don't go telling those stories to our kids." He glanced at Michelle. "That's the last thing we need at our house of horrors." Michelle chuckled and rubbed his back.

Brice crossed his arms. "Yeah, Caitlin, I give. What's with the memory skills? Are you part elephant?"

Caitlin slapped Brice on the back, a cheesy grin plastered across her face.

RJ carried a tray of food out of the kitchen and served four steak dinners to the corner booth. He walked to the bar, set down the tray, grabbed a new bottle of wine and set it in the middle of our table. "You guys ready to order?"

Brice pointed at me. "The birthday girl goes first." I smiled warmly at my brother who, in spite of his orneriness and teasing, was a pretty thoughtful guy.

RJ strode to my side of the table and stood so close I could smell his pungent aftershave. "What can we get for you, Bree?"

"I'll have the ribeye, medium rare, a baked potato with all the fixin's and instead of the side salad bring me a cup of whatever soup you're serving tonight."

"Broccoli cheddar."

I nodded. "I love broccoli cheddar soup."

Caitlin piped up. "I don't know. Broccoli is a vegetable and you usually avoid those."

"But it's a vegetable disguised by cheese. That's the best kind."

Caitlin crossed her arms and shook her head.

RJ peeked at me over the order book. "Broccoli cheddar soup it is." His pointed stare unnerved me, and I was relieved when he worked his way around the table and wrote down everyone else's orders. RJ glanced at me one more time before disappearing into the kitchen. I sighed when he was gone, and Tracey cursed softly under her breath.

We refilled our wine glasses and discussed everyone's plans for the upcoming Christmas holiday. Michelle was in master storyteller mode, describing the nightmare of driving their three children in a chaotic minivan on a 12-hour road trip to Michigan to visit her grandparents. My chair was facing the door, and in the midst of the laughter I glanced up and saw him walk in.

At the sight of Maxim Hall my muscles tensed, and my forehead grew hot. I was suddenly hyper aware of my body and the chills running up and down its length. I inhaled deeply and watched him stroll to the bar, remove his coat and sit down, oblivious to my presence. When he leaned his elbows on the oak countertop I noticed the outline of his wide shoulders and trim back through his blue sweater. I exhaled slowly and placed two fingers on the opposite wrist: my heart was racing. I folded my hands in my lap and breathed evenly as I stared at Maxim's back. He talked to RJ in what appeared to be a pleasant exchange. RJ served Maxim a beer and I watched the muscles in his back move under the thin sweater as he lifted the mug to his lips.

I was so caught up in the moment that I didn't notice Caitlin talking to me until she waved her hand in front of my face. "Earth to Bree. Come in, Bree."

I snapped out of my daze and zeroed in on Caitlin. "What is it?"

"You were a million miles away, honey. What were you thinking about?"

I dug up an excuse. "I must be tired. It's been a long day."

Caitlin stroked my back. "Yeah, when you get up at such an ungodly hour, every day is a long day ... but I'm not letting you sneak out early tonight, lady.

You're mine until midnight, anyway. That's when the babysitter needs to go home." She tossed her blonde hair and giggled.

RJ set an enormous platter of loaded nachos and a stack of plates on the table. "You guys need anything else?" We glanced around at each other and shook our heads no.

"It looks amazing, RJ." Brice handed out the plates and we dug into the nachos. RJ retreated behind the bar.

I stuffed a nacho chip covered with melted cheese, bacon, tomatoes and jalapeños into my mouth and was reveling in the heavenly combination of flavors when I sensed a presence approaching our table. I chewed hastily and swallowed at the very moment Maxim Hall walked up, rested his hands on his hips and focused his attention on me. His eyes were shadowed in the dimly-lit bar, but I sensed interest and curiosity.

"Hello, Bree." The way he said it reminded me of butter melting on rolls hot out of the oven. My heart resumed its frenzied pace.

My friends, their mouths filled with nachos and wine, looked up in puzzlement and curiosity. Maxim apologized and kept his eyes on mine. "I don't want to interrupt but I noticed you sitting over here and thought I'd say hello. It looks like you're having a birthday party."

I managed to find my voice as Brice, Caitlin, Tracey, Michelle and Robert glanced at Maxim, then me, then Maxim again, as if watching a tennis match. "It was nice of you to come over. Let me introduce my friends." I cleared my throat and swallowed hard.

Questions hung in the air as I rose to my feet, inhaled deeply and plowed ahead. I pointed at Brice who wore a devilish grin on his face. "That's my brother, Brice Somers." He jumped up and shook Maxim's hand then sat back down. I gestured to Caitlin. "This is Brice's wife, Caitlin." She looked up at Maxim and smiled sweetly. I placed my hand on Tracey's shoulder. "This is my friend, Tracey Miller." Tracey gawked at Maxim with her mouth hanging open. "And these are my friends, Robert and Michelle Dobson." Robert and Michelle said hello.

I screwed up my courage and blurted it out. "Everyone … this is Maxim Hall."

Time seemed to stand still at our table in RJ's Bar in Waconda, Kansas. Brice crossed his arms and studied his wife who openly stared at the famous writer, star struck by his appearance. Tracey's gaze remained on Maxim's clean-cut face; she twirled a red ringlet and crossed her legs. Robert and Michelle sat in stunned silence; the outspoken English teacher was suddenly at a loss for words.

Maxim crossed his arms and studied my friends; I could almost see the wheels turning in his head, recording and filing away every look, every nuance, every single moment for the perfect line in a future novel.

I broke the spell. "Maxim is in town researching a new book."

Maxim's clear blue eyes met mine. "Bree was kind enough to meet with me at her coffee shop this afternoon to tell me about Waconda Springs. She is a proven expert on the subject."

My friends roused from their stupors and regarded me with unabashed surprise. They eyed me, then Maxim, then me again, the mental tennis match continuing. Robert remembered his manners. He stood and extended a hand. "It's nice to meet you, Mr. Hall. Welcome to Waconda."

Maxim firmly shook his hand. "Thank you ... Robert, right?"

"Yes. And this is my wife, Michelle." Robert leaned over and helped Michelle to her feet.

She offered her hand and Maxim squeezed it gently. "It's a pleasure to meet you, Michelle."

When his wife didn't say anything, Robert filled the silence. "Michelle is the English teacher at the middle school in town."

Maxim's eyebrows raised and his eyes sparkled with interest. "How wonderful. A fellow word nerd."

Michelle forced a smile and spoke softly. "It's an honor to meet you, Mr. Hall. I've read all of your books ... except the newest one, anyway."

"Well, I hope you won't hold that against me. They're not exactly literary masterpieces."

Michelle gripped his hand tightly. "You shouldn't say that. Your writing is beautiful. It's a gift to the world."

"That's kind of you to say but I wouldn't go that far."

She leaned toward him. "I hate to pry but I have to ask: The book you're researching ... what's it about?"

Maxim rubbed his chin. "Well, I'm not sure yet. I was out of ideas, so I decided to drive across the United States and see if something grabbed my attention. When I got here I read about the Legend of Waconda Springs and was immediately intrigued. I asked around for the local expert and was directed to Bree." He caught my eye and winked.

Michelle fidgeted and spoke quickly. "The writing process is fascinating. I've been discussing it with my students."

"It may be fascinating but it can also be frustrating."

Michelle nodded in agreement. "They always whine when I make them write an outline for a story."

Maxim laughed. "I would too."

Tracey stepped in front of Michelle and linked her arm through Maxim's. "Hello, Mr. Hall. As Bree said, I'm Tracey Miller. What she failed to mention is that I'm the owner of Stuff n Such, a gift shop just across the square. You should stop by while you're in town and I'll help you pick out something for your wife. I bet she'd love a special souvenir from Kansas." Could the woman be more obvious?

Maxim blushed and dropped his head. "That's kind of you. I'll have to see if my schedule allows it."

"We're open from 9 to 6, Tuesday through Saturday." She drew her body closer to his side and regarded him boldly. "I'm always there." If a siren had been nearby it would have gone off.

I grabbed Caitlin's arm, pulled her to a standing position and dragged her next to Maxim who was clearly uncomfortable with Tracey's advances but nevertheless visited with her pleasantly. I tapped him on the shoulder. He was just inches away and smelled of lemon soap and shaving cream. "Maxim, my sister-in-law, Caitlin, is one of your biggest fans."

He turned his eyes to Caitlin, and she beamed up at him from her petite stance. "Mr. Hall…"

He corrected her. "Please call me Maxim."

"Maxim … I hope you'll forgive me for being so forward, but I want you to know that your books have affected me profoundly. The Day filled me with gratitude for the blessings in my life. I don't take my days for granted anymore."

Maxim smiled warmly, leaned down and gently placed his hands on Caitlin's shoulders. "That's the best compliment I've ever received. It means the world to me. Thank you." He looked over his shoulder at Brice. "Your husband is a lucky man." Caitlin blushed.

He dropped his hands and regarded the group. "My apologies. I've completely disrupted your dinner. Please sit down and continue your meal. I'll get out of your hair."

I reached for his arm as he turned to go. "Would you like to join us?"

He shook his head. "I wouldn't want to intrude. I know it's a special night."

Tracey glided between us and flashed a mischievous grin. "I can assure you it would be no intrusion." She reached for an empty chair at the next table and slid it by hers, patting the seat. "You sit right here. I don't bite … at least not very hard. I want to hear all about these books you've written." She giggled, sat down and crossed her slim legs seductively, beckoning him to follow.

Maxim sent me a questioning glance; I smiled and nodded my approval. "We really would love to have you join us." He hesitated for a moment and finally sat down. I settled in next to him.

Our group returned to their chairs and Brice grinned at Maxim. "Well, it looks like you have no choice but to stay. Would you like some wine? Or I could get you something else." He glanced at the bar where Maxim had been sitting.

Maxim shook his head. "No, I'll take some wine, thank you. I had a beer at the bar, but I can tell I'm going to need to keep drinking to survive this group." He managed a weak smile and shrugged his shoulders.

Tracey laughed and leaned toward Maxim, resting her hand on his thigh. "Don't worry, we won't be too hard on you." She grabbed a plate and handed it to him. "Have some loaded nachos … they're delicious."

Brice filled a wine glass and handed it to Maxim. "Here you go. There's plenty, so drink up."

Maxim thanked him and sipped at the drink, glancing sideways at Tracey as she boldly examined the length of him. He peeked at me and my heart went out to him. Tracey was clearly on a mission; she seemed to have forgotten all about RJ and his snake tattoo. I was keenly aware of Maxim's presence just inches from mine, and I gulped what was left of my wine.

Maxim scooped a generous serving of nachos onto his plate and had just slid a bite into his mouth when Tracey pounced. "So I saw your movie, The Day, and it was absolutely incredible! What a love story!" She gestured to the table. "Us girls saw it together, and I can honestly say it was the best movie I've ever seen!" She leaned on the table and studied his face as he chewed. "It must have been so exciting to be on the movie set while it was filming! I'm sure you know the stars, Claire Hampton and Trey Logan. What are they like?"

Maxim picked up a napkin and wiped his mouth, keenly aware that the entire table was watching him. "I can't say that I know them well, but they're nice people … great actors. Claire is a sweetie. Very nice." Tracey's eyebrows shot up in suspicion. Maxim hurried ahead. "Actually, I got to know her husband the best during the shooting because he was on the set with her. Quite a guy."

Tracey moved even closer to Maxim, if that was possible. Michelle sat back and crossed her arms, clearly disgusted, and the guys watched Tracey with amusement. Caitlin still seemed starstruck and studied Maxim closely, her mouth hanging slightly open. I knew Maxim needed rescued but was unsure what to do.

Tracey continued. "So … Trey Logan. Is he as hot in person as he is on the screen?"

Maxim coughed in surprise and reached for his wine glass. He gulped what was left and moved slightly away from Tracey. "I really couldn't tell you since I prefer women."

Tracey's laugh was devilish. "That's good to hear." She twirled a ringlet of hair with one finger while her other hand continued to rest on his thigh. "Is he as hot as you?"

Brice chuckled, clearly amused. "Down, girl." Tracey ignored him.

Robert shook his head and mumbled. "We really need to find you a man." Tracey pointedly ignored him.

Maxim's cheeks turned red and I'd suddenly had enough. I cleared my throat as my brain searched for a way to change the topic. I stumbled ahead with the only thing that came to mind. "Maxim and I had a wonderful discussion about Waconda Springs this afternoon." Maxim turned to me, a grateful smile lighting his beautiful face. I looked at Michelle. "You know a lot about the spring. Do you have anything you'd like to share?"

Maxim leaned on the table eagerly, and I saw him gently move Tracey's hand to her lap as he watched Michelle's face.

Michelle sat forward and smiled, clearly pleased with the change in topic. "I've always been fascinated with the spring and the Native Americans who would travel for miles to visit it. They worshipped the spirit of Waconda like some of us worship God." Her eyes lit up and her hands were animated as she talked. "They truly believed that Waconda resided in the waters. They'd throw beads, trinkets, buffalo robes, whatever they had into the spring as offerings to her spirit, asking her to bring favorable weather and good hunting."

Maxim nodded in agreement and zeroed in on Michelle. "Bree said Waconda may have been Cheyenne, which interests me because there's some Cheyenne in my family tree."

Michelle's eyes widened. "Looking at you, I can see it. How fascinating! That must make you even more interested in the Legend of Waconda."

"It really does! The older I get the more intrigued I am with my family genealogy, especially the Cheyenne branch."

Tracey rested her shoulder against Maxim's and placed her hand on his back. "I can see it too. I've always found Native American men to be quite handsome."

Caitlin glared at Tracey, then turned to Maxim with a sweet smile. "Maybe your next book could be about a man who goes looking for his Cheyenne genealogy and stumbles across the Legend of Waconda." She suddenly stopped and stared at Maxim in total seriousness. "Maybe he finds out he's related to Princess Waconda!"

Maxim laughed with obvious delight and clapped his hands. "What a marvelous idea! Will you be my writing assistant?"

Caitlin blushed lightly. "It's just an idea. You know what works best in a novel, obviously."

"Well, you can bet I'll be writing down your idea and considering it seriously." His kindness toward Caitlin melted my heart.

Brice put his arm around his wife and pulled her close. "Yep, she's not only gorgeous but damn smart!"

Caitlin appeared embarrassed and pleased at the same time. I could tell she was searching for something to say when RJ walked out of the kitchen carrying three plates of food. He walked over and set an enormous steak dinner and cup of soup in front of me, and my mouth salivated at the sight of it. He leaned close to my ear. "Enjoy." His voice was smooth and seductive. I resisted the urge to gag. RJ set plates of food in front of Caitlin and Brice. "I'll be back with the rest of your orders."

I turned to Maxim. "Did you get any food? We'd hate to eat in front of you."

"I've got a grilled chicken salad coming, so please go ahead and eat while it's hot." He studied my plate and then regarded me with amusement. "Can you really eat all of that food?"

I waved my hand in the air. "Watch and learn, Mr. Hall. I'm a champion eater. Just ask anyone."

He sat back, crossed his arms and grinned. "With pleasure. This will be fun."

Tracey frowned in annoyance at Maxim's interest in me and I secretly patted myself on the back. I cut into the steak, popped a bite into my mouth and proceeded to show Maxim how a real Midwestern girl eats.

Chapter 9

The air felt like the inside of an icebox as we gathered on the sidewalk in front of RJ's Bar at a quarter past midnight, my birthday party breaking up. Caitlin offered a quick hug and hurried after Brice to their white minivan, yelling over her shoulder. "Happy Birthday! I love you, doughnut girl!"

I laughed and yelled back. "You too, half pint. Thanks for the party!" She jumped in the passenger seat, and Brice waved as he drove off.

Tracey sidled over and leaned into Maxim. "Don't forget to stop by Stuff n Such tomorrow." She pointed across the square to her store with its giant sign over the front door. "It's right over there. You can't miss it. We're open from 9 to 6. I can help you pick out something for the special woman in your life." She grinned up at him. "Good night." She winked and skipped to her grey Honda Accord, backed up and sped away.

Robert held out his hand to Maxim. "It was a pleasure meeting you."

Maxim gripped Robert's gloved hand with his bare one. "You too Robert. Good luck with the insurance business."

He nodded. "And good luck with your next novel."

Michelle kept her hands in her coat pockets but smiled warmly. "It was really great visiting with you, Mr. Hall."

"Likewise, Michelle. Keep those English students in line. You may have the next Great American Novelist in one of your classes."

She threw her head back and laughed. "Not so far! They're abysmal writers. It's really quite awful."

Robert waved. "We'd better get going. My mother is watching the kids, and it's way past her bedtime." They hurried off into the night, their house just two blocks away.

I was suddenly aware that I was alone with Maxim, and the thought both thrilled and terrified me. I was a little tipsy, and there was no telling what would come out of my mouth.

Maxim turned to me. "Well, Miss Somers, can I drive you home?"

"No, I'll walk. It's not very far."

His eyebrows furrowed. "Where do you live?"

I pointed to the second story of my coffeehouse, across the street from the square. "Up there."

He followed my direction and recognition crossed his face. "So you live above your coffeehouse. That's handy."

I agreed. "Yes, it is. I have the easiest commute in the world."

"No kidding." A smile played at the corners of his mouth. "Do you mind if I walk you home?"

I studied his face to see if he was joking. His eyes bored straight into mine, and my heart skipped a beat. "Sure. That would be nice."

Without asking he grabbed my hand and led me into the street. My other hand held a plate of leftover chocolate birthday cake covered with plastic wrap, and I was determined not to drop it.

Maxim pointed ahead. "Let's walk through the square since it's lit up like a Christmas village. Okay with you?"

"That's my favorite way home. Wait 'til you see Candy Cane Lane."

Just as we started to cross the street two boys raced by on their bicycles, mere inches from us. I stumbled backward and lost my balance, but Maxim caught me. I somehow managed to hold onto the cake. When I was steady he yelled after the receding bicyclists. "Watch where you're going, you juvenile delinquents! And get home! Do your parents know where you are?"

I broke into a spasm of laughter. "Are you 100 or what? You sound like an old man ... juvenile delinquents?"

He chuckled. "You're right. I needed a cane to shake at them."

I bent over and caught my breath. "That would have been perfect."

He grabbed my hand again. "Come on. Let's get out of the street before we really do get run over."

We walked through Candy Cane Lane and casually made our way to the center of the park where the miniature Statue of Liberty, wrapped in clear twinkle lights, watched over the town. I was suddenly dizzy from the wine. "Do you mind if we sit down for a bit?"

Concern was etched on Maxim's face. "Are you okay? Do you feel like passing out? Throwing up, maybe?"

I waved away his concern. "No, just a little light-headed is all. Too much celebrating." I smiled weakly and plopped down on a bench, bright Christmas lights draped overhead like a psychedelic spider web. Maxim sat next to me, and I noticed he was still holding my gloved hand. I set the cake plate down on the bench.

His shoulder brushed mine, and I leaned into it, grateful for the support. His head tilted toward me, and I caught the scents of lemony aftershave and pine forest that must have been his high-dollar cologne. I closed my eyes, inhaled deeply, and the combination of Maxim and the frigid outdoors sent my head soaring. His toned leg pressed against mine, and I didn't move away.

We sat in silence for a few moments and then he shook his head and grinned. "You and your friends can certainly put away the wine. Did you have fun?"

I rubbed my forehead and moaned. "God, yes — the kind of fun that'll need 800 milligrams of ibuprofen tomorrow morning."

He laughed. "May take more than that." He turned and looked at me. "I suggest you take some pain reliever tonight before you go to bed. Get a jump start on that hangover. Couldn't hurt."

I nodded in agreement. "Good idea, doc."

He shrugged. "Just trying to help. That'll be eighty dollars for the house call."

"So worth it! Can I pay you in coffee?"

Maxim chuckled and squeezed my hand. "Absolutely!"

He leaned back and sighed in contentment, seemingly mesmerized by the lights and the cool, crisp air. "I've always loved towns with a square. We used to visit my grandmother in South Dakota, and her little town had a square with a playground in it like this one. We spent hours swinging and sliding. I was really good at the monkey bars." His nostalgia was palpable.

"Where did you grow up?"

He looked down. "Kansas City."

"Really." I hesitated before continuing. "And you live in New York City?"

"Yes."

"How did you end up there?"

He glanced at me sideways. "I wanted to be closer to my book publisher." I was about to ask how long he'd lived in New York City when he continued talking. "This square in this exact moment would be the perfect scene in a novel. Probably a romance … except I'd add lots of snow and a tragic ending."

I turned and gazed at him. "Why tragic?"

He shrugged his shoulders. "I've come to learn that most endings are. Not to sound melodramatic, but reality is a bitch. A beautiful and idyllic setting like this could lead to only one type of ending … they wouldn't live happily ever after. I save the happy endings for dark settings."

I turned to him, and even though my brain was fuzzy, his meaning was clear. "So what you're saying is that if the setting is ugly you give your characters a happy ending, and if the setting is beautiful you give them a tragic ending?"

He smiled and looked down, suddenly bashful. "Don't tell anyone my writing secret."

I was incredulous. "Oh my God!" We sat in silence for at least a minute, each lost in our own thoughts. "So if I went back and read all of your books I'd clearly see this pattern?"

"Yep. You got me. I'm surprised none of the writing critics have caught on yet."

I grinned and looked up at the lights twinkling overhead, moving cautiously in the soft breeze. "Not everyone has a tragic ending. Some people live happy lives and die happy, surrounded by loved ones. You do know that, right?" I thought of my own tragic life, but I knew there was still the possibility of happiness finding me, however elusive it seemed to be.

"True, but there are a lot of tragic endings out there. That's why some of my books end well and others … not so well. I like to reflect reality in my writing. Not every romance is a happy ending. Life is complicated."

I nodded. "Don't I know it."

His voice was barely above a whisper. "Me too."

The air suddenly seemed much colder, and not because of the temperature. I pulled my hand from his, picked up the birthday cake and gingerly rose to my feet. "I need to be getting home now. The coffee drinkers will be here bright and early. I've got to get to bed."

Maxim stood and shoved his hands in his coat pockets. "I'll walk you to the door."

I shook my head. "That's not necessary. I'm just over there. If you like you can watch me until I'm inside."

He peeked at me shyly, and in the glow of the Christmas lights his face was softly illuminated and so damn handsome that my breath caught in my throat. "I had fun tonight. Thanks for inviting me to join your birthday party."

I shrugged. "It was nothing. Thanks for staying."

We stared at each other for a moment until I turned and headed for the coffeeshop.

He called after me. "Bree!"

I looked over my shoulder. "Yeah?"

"See you tomorrow. 2:30 sharp."

Warmth spread through my body at the thought of spending more time with him. "See you tomorrow."

I watched him smiling amidst the twinkling lights, and then I hurried to the front door of my coffee shop, unlocked it and slipped inside. I spied from the darkness as he stared my way for a minute, walked to his black Lexus and drove away.

Chapter 10

I fell onto the plush red couch in my apartment and exhaled the breath I'd been holding all day. It was past midnight. I turned on the television and found an episode of Seinfeld, hit the mute button and pulled a cozy fleece blanket over my blue and white snowflake-print pajamas. I settled my head on a throw pillow and stared at the TV screen. The images blurred as the effects of the wine unearthed memories and emotions I'd spent years burying.

I turned my head and focused on one of the framed pictures sitting on the end table. I picked it up and stared at the image of the ribbon-cutting ceremony on the opening day of my coffeehouse. In the photo I'm standing on the sidewalk in front of the building holding a giant pair of scissors near a giant red ribbon that's held by Dad on one side and Brice on the other. Mother stands next to Dad, Aunt Judy and Uncle Joe are positioned beside Brice, and the town's mayor beams at the camera with both hands in the thumbs-up position. It's 105 degrees and our faces glisten with sweat. I'm grinning straight at the camera. It was the beginning of my new life. Plan B.

I turned over the picture frame and slid the lock clasps open, removed the back of the frame and set it on the couch. Tears formed as I lifted a faded picture and birthday card from behind the ribbon-cutting photo. I clutched the treasures to my heart and closed my eyes, breathing evenly and gathering the courage to visit the past. Slowly, very slowly, I opened my eyes and gazed at the photo of an attractive red-haired man smiling that gorgeous smile, the one that made me weak in the knees and willing to do anything for love. My heart was heavy with sorrow. The shot captured him at the height of laughter, his bright green eyes full of life, his smile captivating. God, I missed him.

I propped the photo against my bent leg where I could see it and picked up the homemade birthday card. A white piece of paper was folded in half with a drawing on the front of two hands holding a heart. In the heart was written the name Danny, and underneath it said: My Heart Belongs to You. I opened the card and read the note that brought both great joy and deep pain:

Dear Bree,

Happy 27th Birthday to the woman who stole my heart and wouldn't let go. Tonight I asked you to marry me and you said yes, otherwise you wouldn't be reading this card because if you'd said no I would have thrown it away and driven off a cliff.

I hope you love the ring I picked out. The blue sapphire surrounded by diamonds looks like a flower and I chose it because I know how much you love flowers. Since honesty is important in a healthy marriage I need to tell you the truth: I didn't plan on buying the diamond earrings as a birthday gift, but the lady at the jewelry store sold them to me for half price because I was buying the ring at full price. I knew you would appreciate the deal, and you get to enjoy authentic diamond earrings. I know they're the real thing because I used them to cut a circle in a window like I saw in an old movie.

All joking aside, I can't believe I get to spend my life with you. I'll do everything in my power to keep you smiling. You are the most beautiful woman I've ever seen — you knock me out with your looks, your kindness and your intelligence. And those legs — my God! Why you picked me is a mystery, but I'll never question it. I love you so much. Let's set the world on fire!

All my love,

Danny

I gently held the photo and card as tears flowed down my cheeks and neck, soaking into the collar of my pajamas. I don't know how long I cried but I allowed the tears to stop in their own time. When my eyes finally dried up I laid the precious mementoes back in the picture frame, replaced the back, slid the clasps closed and set it on the end table where I stared at the ribbon-cutting ceremony until it blurred into nothingness.

The frame represented my life. The picture on display featured a happy and smiling Bree, a woman who forged a new life after the old one shattered into a million pieces. But what the world didn't know — what the world couldn't see — was that my heart was still living in the past, a past that had me in its grip and wouldn't let go. I was stuck and I knew it. My heart was frozen in time ten years earlier, trapped under layers of ice, and yet I didn't fight to free myself because I didn't really want to be free. I was wallowing in sorrow — and I knew it — but I was content, somehow, to wallow.

What would it take to finally let go?

I had no idea.

Lara Ketter
ANOTHER CHRISTMAS WITHOUT YOU

106

SATURDAY, DECEMBER 16, 2017

Chapter 11

I heard a knock on the front door and pressed the home button on my phone to check the time: 2:25 pm. The man was certainly punctual. My heart jumped and hammered in my chest. I inhaled deeply, pushed away from my cluttered desk and walked to the front where Maxim stared at the door as if willing it to open. The collar of his black leather coat was turned up and he held it closed in front. The poor guy looked chilled to the bone. I unlocked the door and he hurried inside.

"My God, it's cold out there!" He stomped the snow off his suede boots and shivered visibly.

I smiled. "We're living the dream."

He gestured to the window. "There must be two feet of snow out there … and it's still coming down." He sounded incredulous, astonished even.

I sighed and gazed at the white flakes floating to the ground. "I know. Isn't it beautiful?"

He removed his coat, draped it over a chair and when I glanced his way I was suddenly distracted as his muscles moved with supple ease under a light grey sweater. I knew I was staring, but I couldn't help myself; he hadn't shaved, and the light coating of stubble was ruggedly masculine and overwhelmingly attractive. His jet black hair, damp from the wet snow, hung in waves and curled around his ears.

He rubbed his hands together. "It's more beautiful from in here than out there."

The man didn't know it, but he was seriously messing with my head, stirring up feelings I'd thought were lost in an ocean of grief. Whenever he was near me my body pulsed in awareness, acutely tuned in to the fact that I was a woman and he was a man. It was disarming and confusing. I moved a few steps away, scolding myself for dredging up my teenage hormones. I shifted my attention and regarded the snow. "I bet the kids in town are thrilled."

He smiled and sat down. "Oh yeah, they're out in full force … sledding, sliding across the icy streets, throwing snowballs at each other and building snowmen. I didn't think anything could tear kids away from their screens, but I was wrong."

I laughed. "I'm happy for them. Would you like some coffee for our big tour?"

Maxim propped an ankle on his knee and leaned back. "I've only had one cup today so yes, I could go for more caffeine."

I walked to the espresso machine. "I'm making an Americano for myself with foam and stevia."

"That sounds great. Make it two."

I pushed the porta filter under the coffee grinder and watched as the dark grounds piled up. I tamped the coffee and slid the filter into the espresso machine, placed a go-cup under the dispenser and turned on the machine. As the espresso poured into the cup I peeked across my shoulder; Maxim stared out the window in concentration, his brows furrowed into deep grooves. Butterflies had been dancing in my stomach all morning as the anticipation of seeing him built, but somehow, right now at the espresso machine, I was surprisingly calm.

I repeated the process for the second drink and added hot water to within an inch of the top of the cups. I foamed milk and poured it, added several drops of stevia, stirred to combine and pushed on the lids. I carried the drinks to the front of the store and set them on the table next to Maxim. My arrival snapped him out of his reverie.

I settled into a chair and sipped at my drink. "Mesmerizing, isn't it?"

He looked at me curiously. "What?"

I pointed outside. "The snow. When it's coming down like this, so gently, it's hypnotic. I could sit here all afternoon and watch it."

Maxim lifted the cup to his full lips. "You're right." He smiled at me over the rim. "I didn't even realize the snow had me in its hypnotic grip, but you caught me zoning out."

"I don't think people spend enough time zoning out; it's actually one of my hobbies."

Maxim laughed. "Is it, now? Novel writers consider 'zoning out' part of the job. If we can't daydream we're out of luck."

"I bet that's true." We fell into silence, drank our coffee and regarded each other across the table. He was an easy man to be with, and I sat back and crossed my legs, totally relaxed in his presence. His blue eyes bored into mine, and I didn't look away as my heart picked up its pace. Why was I so drawn to this man? True, he was no longer a stranger, but I knew practically nothing about him. I found that his good looks weren't as disarming as I came to know him better.

Maxim uncrossed his legs and leaned his elbows on the table. "How was business this morning with the snow? Did it keep any customers away?"

"Yes, it did, but I'm not complaining. After polishing off all that wine last night I'm feeling it today. I had to drag myself down here and opened fifteen minutes late. Thank God Rich and Dave don't come in on Saturdays ... they would never let me live it down."

He chuckled and shook his head. "That was a lot of fun last night. Thanks again for including me. I had a great time getting to know your friends and family. The food was good, too, especially Caitlin's homemade birthday cake."

I sat up and stared at him. "Listen, I want to apologize for Tracey. She means well but she's an in-your-face type of person. She wants a man and isn't afraid to show it."

"No worries. I mean yes, it was a bit uncomfortable, but she really didn't bother me that much. Don't take this the wrong way, but I'm used to the attention. It's part of the book-selling game."

I sat back and crossed my arms. "I bet you get more attention from women than from men." He didn't disagree. When he lifted the coffee cup with his left hand I noticed again the absence of a wedding ring, but that didn't necessarily mean he wasn't married. Curious about his status, my boldness amazed me. "How does your wife feel about women throwing themselves at your feet?"

Maxim blinked in surprise; his shoulders hunched, and he looked down at the table.

When he remained silent I hurried to recover. "I can't believe I asked that. I apologize."

He directed his attention outside at the falling snow and his empty look spoke volumes. He suddenly exhaled and spoke quietly. "It's okay. She actually died four years ago."

I stared at his pained expression. "Oh, I'm so sorry. I wish I hadn't said anything."

He turned his eyes to the coffee cup and fiddled with the lid. "It's okay. We can't live in bubbles, can we?"

I reached for the pendant at my throat and ran a finger over the blue sapphire. Silence filled the room.

"Strange as it sounds, she died of pneumonia."

I couldn't hide my astonishment. "People still die of pneumonia?"

He pinched his lips. "Yes, they do. Our sons were 16 and 14 at the time. It was hardest on them."

I covered my mouth and stumbled forward. "What are their names?"

Maxim sat up and a smile tugged at his lips. "William and Henry. William prefers to be called Will. They're in college now. Will is at Yale and Henry's at Wake Forrest. Henry's a freshman. He moved down there in August, and I'm out of sorts with the apartment to myself."

"Is that why you decided to drive across the country?"

He rose abruptly and walked to the front window where he gazed at the town square. He hooked his thumbs in his jeans pockets. "Partly."

I didn't know how to respond so I sat stiffly in my chair and prayed for inspiration.

Maxim rocked on his heels. "I'm actually in the middle of a book tour but I needed a break, so I rescheduled most of my December appearances."

I absorbed this information and neither of us said anything for several minutes until Maxim turned around and abruptly changed the subject. "So what's the population of Waconda?"

Filled with relief at the shift in conversation I walked to the window and stood next to him. "One thousand, three hundred and five in the most recent census, but I suspect a few pets were snuck in."

Maxim burst out laughing. "Thirteen hundred including pets. I love it." He grinned and glanced my way. "You have a great sense of humor."

I shrugged. "More like skepticism in the form of humor."

"It suits you well." He directed his gaze across the street. "Tell me about the businesses in town."

I stretched to my full height and he was still several inches taller. "You're in luck, because you're standing next to the president of the Waconda Chamber of Commerce."

Maxim's eyebrows raised and he studied me with approval. "So ... you're one of the bigwigs around here, huh?"

I crossed my arms. "I'm on the city council as well." His look of surprise thrilled me. "Somebody's got to do it. Keeps me out of trouble, and I know everything that goes on in this town."

"Well, then, Ms. Chamber of Commerce, how is business in small-town America?"

I deflated a bit. "The retail trade isn't what you would call thriving. Between shopping in bigger towns and ordering off the internet, it's a wonder people shop local anymore."

Maxim frowned. "I'm sorry to hear that."

"But we're doing okay. Tracey's ad for Stuff n Such is clever. She points out that Amazon doesn't support the Waconda High School Lakers — and she does. Her business sales have actually increased in the past six months. Plus she sells amazing things in her store."

"Like what?" Maxim had directed his gaze across the square to the limestone building with a mammoth Stuff n Such sign hanging over the front door.

"She describes it as a general store, and it's packed — and I do mean packed — with a wild mix of home decor, clothing, jewelry, greeting cards, seasonal decorations, toys, board games, candy and even some lake supplies and hardware items. I've forgotten a few things, I'm sure."

"No kidding." His tone conveyed interest.

"The square is practically empty on Saturday afternoons, but there are at least six cars in front of her store today. She pulls customers from all over. Christmas is her biggest sales season, of course." I nudged his shoulder. "Would you like to go over and see her? We know she'd be thrilled if you walked through the door."

Maxim shook his head. "I'll pass, thanks, but she's got moxie. I admire her drive and determination, but it will take a special man to handle a whirlwind like her. I'm not that man."

"She's always on the prowl. She wants a husband in the worst way. She drives me nuts sometimes, but she's been a good friend — and she definitely has a mind for business. She's helped me with several big decisions regarding the coffeehouse."

Maxim turned and eyed me with approval. "I love seeing women business owners. We need more women in positions of power. If you gals ran the world we'd be in much better shape."

I lifted my chin. "You were certainly raised right."

He smiled and shook his head. "What other businesses do you have in town?"

"Why don't I just work my way around the square, okay?" He nodded in agreement. "In the building next to Tracey's store, the space is shared between the City Office, Waconda Library and Senior Center. Aunt Judy was the City Clerk for over three decades before she retired a few years ago. On the corner is Farmers and Ranchers Bank; it's actually locally-owned which is pretty rare these days. On the corner across from the bank is Dare Your Hair, then there's RJ's Bar where I drank a gallon of wine last night, Lakeside Liquor, and the rest of the block is taken up by the Waconda Cable Company."

Maxim grinned. "It's ironic that RJ's Bar and Lakeside Liquor are next to each other."

"Yeah, we call it the boozers' side of the street."

He clapped his hands and chuckled.

I continued the tour of Waconda's business district. "On my side of the street we have the post office, an antique store that advertises 'flexible' hours which means it's closed most of the time, and the insurance agent and attorney share offices in the building on the corner. You met Robert last night. He owns the insurance business."

"Yes, he seems like an insurance man."

I couldn't suppress my laughter. "I totally agree. Finally, across from the playground we have the city swimming pool, which was built just three years ago with grant money, our weekly newspaper, The Waconda Observer, then the American Legion building where they play bingo and eat pie on Wednesday nights, and on the corner is Waconda Foods, our only grocery store."

"I was in the grocery store looking for snacks. They have an impressive selection for a small store."

"Yes, they do. We're lucky they're still open." At Maxim's curious glance I explained. "There just aren't as many people around as there used to be, and most of our high school graduates move to cities where the jobs are. Without enough customers, sales dwindle, and a lot of small-town grocery stores just can't make it ... it's pretty sad. People drive to Waconda from other towns just to buy a gallon of milk. I get all of my food and supplies through Waconda Foods, and they give me discounts on a lot of stuff. I'm friends with the owners, so that helps."

Maxim unhooked his thumbs from his pockets, turned from the window and looked pleased. "I can see why you live here. It's the idyllic small town. A lot of novels have been set in such a place. I didn't see a police station, though."

I nodded. "That's because crime is almost non-existent. The County Sheriff's Department sends a patrol car through once a day, more for our peace of mind than to catch criminals. A couple of months ago old man Hawkins forgot to put his car in Park in his driveway and it rolled backwards into the street and hit a car driving by. No one was hurt but the Sheriff encouraged his family to take away his keys. That's about as dangerous as it gets around here; it's a sleepy little town."

"Well, there's something to be said for that. The sound of sirens is a regular backdrop in New York City. My apartment's on the twentieth floor but we can still hear it. I use one of those noise machines when I sleep to block it out."

We stared out the window in silence until a semi-truck and trailer drove by, its wheels sloshing through the wet snow. Maxim snapped his fingers. "I forgot to ask ... what are all of the big trucks hauling?"

Amused by his ignorance, I suppressed a smile. "I forgot I'm dealing with a city boy. The big trucks are called semi-trucks because they haul semi-trailers. Did you notice the three huge cement grain bins on the south edge of town?"

Maxim nodded. "Yes. I drove by there. The sign said Waconda Grain Company."

"The bins hold hundreds of thousands of bushels of wheat, soybeans and milo, depending on the time of year." He was clearly amazed, and I explained. "During harvest time farmers haul their grain into town and are paid by the bushel depending on the market price the day they sell it. Then in the winter months Waconda Grain hires truckers to haul the grain to bigger markets. This time of year it's crazy with semi-trucks coming and going all day. Some of the residents complain about it, but since I make money selling drinks and food to the truckers, I keep my mouth shut."

He laughed. "If it's good for business, why complain?"

"Exactly." I looked up at the clock. "Wow! It's almost 3. We'd better get to the Waconda Springs replica before the snow's too deep to walk in." I walked to the front door and locked it. "My ride is in back. Are you ready to go?"

Maxim picked up our drinks. "Don't forget the coffee."

He handed me my cup and I popped off the lid and peered inside. "I could use a refill. How about you?"

"Yeah, top mine off, if you don't mind." He gave me his cup.

"No problem." I stepped over to the espresso machine.

He followed and leaned against the counter. "Can I pay for my coffee? I feel like a freeloader."

I dismissed his concern. "I wouldn't think of taking your money." I set his cup under the dispenser and turned on the machine. "Don't tell anyone but I make a lot of money on these specialty coffee drinks. They're not expensive to make." He inched closer and his scent swirled around me, a combination of citrus and pine. It was intoxicating.

"Your secret is safe with me. And thanks, by the way, for the coffee … and everything." I felt a gentle touch on my shoulder and turned to see Maxim's hand resting there, a beautiful smile on his face. I looked into his vibrant blue eyes and knew it would be easy to fall for this incredible man. Conflicting emotions churned in my heart; it felt as if it could explode at any moment.

Abruptly, he dropped his hand and looked at the floor, pink coloring his cheeks. He glanced around the room as if searching for something. His voice was soft. "Could you tell me where the restroom is?"

I released the breath I'd been holding, grinned and pointed to the back of the building. "On your right there are separate men's and women's bathrooms. Take your pick depending on your gender preference today."

He chuckled. "There's that great sense of humor again."

"I'm here all day."

He smiled and disappeared into the men's room.

Chapter 12

I pulled into a parking spot at Waconda State Park and pointed to my left. "There's the replica of Waconda Springs … at least what we can see under all the snow."

Maxim hunched down and peered out my window. "I thought it would be level with the ground."

"No, but there's a reason for that. I'm on the committee that maintains it…"

Maxim interrupted. "Of course you are."

I ignored him and continued. "…so I know a bit about it. The replica was built when the lake was put in, and they decided it would be more realistic if it was constructed similar to the original one which laid at the top of a rise 40 feet above the Solomon River Valley. This one isn't 40 feet high, but do you see that slope to the right?" His gaze moved to where I was pointing. "They designed a gradual rise to make it easier for people to walk up to the spring. There's a great view of the lake from up there. Want to give it a try?"

Maxim gestured to his feet. "Since Brice was nice enough to lend me his boots — socks too — I'm game for anything."

I opened the center console and pulled out a blue and white-striped stocking cap. "Put this on … you'll be glad you did."

Maxim slipped on the stocking hat and grinned. "If my friends could see me now."

I grinned. "Oh, I'll be taking a picture when we get up there. Maxim Hall, famous novelist, in muck boots and a woman's stocking hat. You're looking mighty fine, sir."

"The lengths I go to for research."

I retrieved a pair of men's work gloves from under the seat. "Brice sent these for you."

He shook his head. "No, thanks. I'm fine without them."

I stared at him in amazement. "You don't want to wear gloves? Why not?"

His answer was simple. "I don't like them."

"But your hands will get cold."

"I have pockets … I'll be fine."

His logic made no sense, but if the man didn't want to wear gloves, I couldn't force him. I patted his shoulder. "Let's go."

We stepped out of the pickup amid huge, wet snowflakes that stuck to everything. My boots sank into the deep snow and disappeared above my ankles. Our hats and shoulders were soon covered with snow, and I pulled my red scarf tighter around my neck. The land before us was a blanket of white, and it reminded me of a picture you'd see on a postcard. A limestone fence was gathering several inches of snow on its posts, and I spotted movement in a small shrub next to the trail — most likely birds nestling together for warmth. We were, like the song, walking in a winter wonderland.

We hiked to the base of the spring and I was soon breathless from the exertion of tramping through the thick snow in heavy boots. We reached the bottom and stared at each other.

Maxim spoke first. "Are we crazy?"

I chuckled. "Yes, we are definitely crazy."

We started up the rise and, about halfway up, paused to rest for a moment. When Maxim reached for my hand I didn't stop him. "Pull me the rest of the way. Writers don't get much exercise, and I live on takeout food." He grinned and looked pleased with himself; it hit me that I was likely heading for trouble with this man.

Although I doubted he actually needed my help making it to the top, I forged ahead and pulled him behind me. When we finally arrived at the Waconda Springs replica I leaned forward against the black wrought-iron fence that surrounded the spring and, looking out over the lake, caught my breath. Maxim leaned on the fence, his coat sleeve brushing mine, and surveyed the white expanse with me.

Lake Waconda stretched out before us, its center translucent and sparkling, its edges covered in thick snow. The lake was a sheet of glass reflecting the gray sky, and the branches of the trees surrounding it were weighed down with the heavy, white stuff.

I marveled at the stillness around me, the serenity of snowflakes gently falling to the ground; in Kansas, snow usually arrives with a blizzard and driving winds that force everyone inside. Today was a beautiful gift, and I was filled with awe.

I turned to Maxim. "Let's get a picture before I forget. Give me your phone." He didn't move or even acknowledge I'd spoken. "Come on, Maxim." He was frozen in place and not because of the cold. "I brought you out here. It's the least you can do." He waited a few seconds, sighed and finally pulled his phone out of a coat pocket, opened the camera and handed it to me.

He frowned. "I'm not sure why I agreed to this."

"Because you're a nice guy." I backed up a few feet and faced Maxim. "And your fans will love it."

"I am not posting this picture."

"Move a little to your left. Okay, now stop. Right there. Hold on a minute." I was surprised to see he was actually pouting.

"Is this really necessary?"

"Yes, you'll be glad to have a picture of the historic day when you hiked to the replica of Waconda Springs. Now smile ... that's an order!"

He shook his head and forced a smile. I quickly snapped the picture before he grabbed his phone back.

He held up a hand. "Okay, now that the torture's over let's get one of us together."

"What? No way. I look stupid in this hat."

"You're complaining about that hat? I'm pretty sure the one I'm wearing looks goofier than yours." I didn't move. "Come on. It's the least you can do. Please?"

"I hate it when people use my words against me." I trudged over to Maxim's side, handed him the phone and turned around. I was surprised when he pulled me close with one arm, and I had to admit it was not an unpleasant feeling to be crushed against a strong, solid man. Maxim held the phone in front of us, raising it until he was satisfied with the shot. The angle he settled on showed our faces in the bottom of the frame with the Waconda Springs replica and lake behind us. He snapped the picture and let go of my waist.

"Thank you."

I wiped a layer of snow off his shoulders. "You know, you have my permission to post that picture in spite of my silly hat ... it would be instant fame for me and if you mention my coffeehouse I'll give you a free cappuccino."

"I'll consider it." He shoved his phone in a back pocket.

I decided to change the subject and pointed to the lake. "See how the snow is melting in the middle of the lake where it's not frozen yet? In the shallower areas, where the water is frozen, the snow is piling up. They say there's 100 miles of shoreline on Lake Waconda. Do you believe that? But it's the third largest lake in Kansas, so that's probably true."

Maxim looked slowly from left to right. "One hundred miles, huh? That seems crazy. But I can't see the other end of the lake so who am I to argue?"

"It goes on and on." I lifted my face to the sky, catching snowflakes on my eyelashes, and breathed in the smell of earth and pine and the crisp outdoors. Birds called to each other in the barren trees near the lake, and the wet snow piled up on the branches and stuck to the fence posts in decorative patterns. "Isn't it gorgeous?"

Maxim stared at the lake. "It really is. I could write pages about what I'm seeing right now."

I studied his striking profile. "What would you write about Waconda?"

He grinned. "Nothing like putting me on the spot, but I'll see what I can do." He was lost in thought for a moment. "The charming town of Waconda, Kansas, clings to the eastern edge of Lake Waconda like a child clings to its mother." He smiled down at me. "How's that?"

"Not bad." We stared at the lake in companionable silence. "I wonder if Uncle Joe is still ice fishing."

"Is that Judy's husband?"

"Yep. He's addicted to fishing. As long as the fish are biting he'll fish anytime, anywhere. Aunt Judy said he was going out today with his buddies."

"Sounds peaceful."

"It must be. I don't care to fish, but whatever floats your boat."

Maxim laughed. "That's a good way of putting it, especially at the lake."

I looked down at my gloves resting on the fence. "This is an exact copy of the fence that was erected around the spring when it was Waconda Health Resort." I indicated the area inside the fence. "And this is the replica of Waconda Springs. It's perfectly round, like the original spring. During the warm months it's filled with water. It was designed to drain so it could be emptied before winter."

"I'd love to see it full of water, but this is nice too."

I gazed at snow piling up inside the fence. "You'll have to come back this summer. It's more impressive then." I was shocked I'd verbalized my thoughts, and I stumbled over my words. "For your book, I mean … if you use this in a book." I stared at my gloves.

After a brief silence Maxim cleared his throat. "Where was the spring before the lake covered it up?"

I pointed to the center of the lake. "Out there in the middle. I've actually considered hiring a crew to dive down there during the summer and see if there's anything that can be salvaged. I haven't mentioned it to anyone around here because they already think I'm crazy."

Maxim furrowed his brow. "Doesn't sound unreasonable to me. Divers explore sunken ships and search for lost civilizations all the time. People spend millions of dollars and often recover nothing, but some are luckier." He stared into the distance. "I remember reading about a crew that found a sunken ship full of gold off the coast of North Carolina. I can picture a crew searching Lake Waconda for relics from Waconda Health Resort."

I wiped the snow off my shoulders and shook my head. "If I set out exploring the lake they'd fit me with a strait jacket and lock me up for sure."

Maxim grinned. "I'd like to see that."

I pointed to the left side of the lake. "There's the dam, just in case you missed it."

"How tall is that thing?"

"It's 115 feet high and almost three miles long. Most of Waconda sits at the base of the dam on the east side. Only a few of the homes are high enough to actually see the lake. The Richie Riches live up there."

Maxim rubbed his chin. "The who?"

"Didn't you ever watch Richie Rich when you were a kid?" His expression was blank. "The boy with millions of dollars and every gadget and gizmo you could ever want?" Maxim's face still registered nothing. "He lived in a mansion?"

"Did he carry around a green bag of money and run it through the washing machine and dryer?"

I raised my fist in the snowy air. "Yes! Do you see the beautiful homes overlooking the lake?"

Maxim turned his attention to the large, ornate houses in the distance on our left. "Yes. Very impressive."

"The people who can afford to build mansions overlooking the lake … I call them the Richie Riches of Waconda."

Maxim laughed. "I get it now. You should do standup comedy."

"You're not the first one to suggest it." I stared at the dam and clapped my gloved hands together. "In the summer we have The Dam Run. D-A-M. Clever, huh?"

Maxim chuckled. "I love the play on words."

I nodded. "I call it the Damn Dam Run. I'm one of the organizers…"

Maxim interrupted. "What a surprise."

I ignored him and continued. "…and we split the runners into age groups and hand out prizes." I crossed my arms over my heavy coat. "I've won my age division every year I've run."

Maxim scrutinized me and grinned. "You are something else." He hesitated and continued. "I hate to dampen the mood but what year did you say the dam was built?"

"The groundbreaking was held on October 1, 1964. The newspaper article said 6,000 attended. My father was there. He was just 17. It was a sad day for the family. My grandfather was there too. Dad said his mom stayed home and cried."

"The emotions are understandable. They lost their farm because of the lake. It was a tragedy."

I bit my lip. "I try not to be bitter because I understand the need for flood control. But yes, it was a tragedy for our family. By the time the dam was completed my father and his parents had moved to our farm south of town."

"Do your parents still live there?"

I stared across the lake at nothing in particular. "Mother does. Dad died in 2012."

"I'm sorry." Maxim covered my gloved hand with his bare one, a tender gesture that touched me deeply. He stepped over to a bench, wiped the snow off and urged me to sit down beside him.

I joined him and became slightly dizzy as I focused on the hundreds of snowflakes swirling in the still air. I closed my eyes and exhaled. "Dad was born to farm — Brice is just like him — and he loved working the land, planting seeds, watching them grow and harvesting his crop. It was fall harvest and Dad was driving his combine to the field to cut soybeans." I opened my eyes, inhaled and let the air out slowly. "He was crossing an old bridge with the combine when the bridge collapsed. The combine pitched forward and Dad was thrown against the front window. The coroner said he died instantly … which was some comfort and still is."

Maxim squeezed my hand. "I sense that you were very close to your father."

"I was." A tear slid down my cheek and Maxim wiped it away. "He was a strong yet gentle man, if that makes any sense."

"It does make sense. I know exactly what you mean. I've met men like that … they're the best of both worlds."

I glanced up and stared at the scar above his right eyebrow. "That's exactly what he was." I shivered and hugged myself. We sat in companionable silence for several minutes as snowflakes floated around us.

Maxim rose and pulled me to my feet. "I've seen enough. Let's get out of here before you freeze to death." He grasped my hand and led me down the slope and through at least a foot of snow. "I hope to God our coffee is still warm."

As we neared the pickup, an ancient Ford Bronco pulled into a parking space and screeched to a stop followed by a newer Jeep Cherokee. The doors of both vehicles flew open and a group of lively teenagers donned in heavy winter gear spilled out and raced across the road to a clearing near the lake. Laughter and screeches filled the crisp air as boys and girls tumbled onto each other, threw snowballs and fell backward to create snow angels.

I leaned against my pickup and watched them frolic, reveling in the display of unbridled joy. Maxim joined me, crossed his arms and smiled in amusement.

His voice took on a wistful tone. "I remember being young and carefree like that." He laughed as a full-on snowball fight ensued with boys versus girls. "Life hasn't kicked them in the ass yet, and it shows."

I grinned and punched him in the arm. "God, you're cynical. I suggest you don't take a job writing for a greeting card company." I watched the teenagers and sighed deeply. "I just love seeing them out here acting like kids." A few had separated from the pack and were forming what looked to be the base of a snowman. The others continued hurling snowballs at each other and whooping with laughter. "No phones, no screens, just friends and fun. That's how it's supposed to be."

I reached back in time twenty years and remembered how it felt to be that unencumbered, that innocent, that free. It hadn't been so long ago, really, and yet it seemed a lifetime. I drifted away, recalling days when happiness was just assumed, when I thought everything would always be magical and easy and fun.

Maxim nudged my shoulder. "What are you thinking about? You're a million miles away."

I snapped back to reality and turned to him. "Just remembering the last time I played in the snow. They're so completely happy."

His look was serious, and he inspected my face; his eyes were an intense blue and I found myself paralyzed in his gaze. We didn't move a muscle, and the snow fell around us in a canopy of white. We stayed like that for a long time, and the world seemed to fade away.

His voice was gruff. "God, you're beautiful." My heart leapt and my eyes grew huge at his statement, yet I was secretly pleased. He noticed my quick intake of air and furrowed his brows. "I'm sorry. I didn't mean to be so forward."

I dropped my head and studied the snow. My cheeks flushed an even deeper pink than they'd been from the frosty air. "It's alright." I screwed up my courage. "You're not so bad yourself."

His laughter surprised me, and I glanced at his face. "I'll take that as a compliment. Come on. Let's get out of the cold."

He let go of my hands, opened the driver's door like a true gentleman, and when I was inside he slammed the door shut. He hurried around to the passenger side and jumped in the pickup. I was visibly shaken from our encounter, but I pulled myself together and started the pickup. When the engine rattled to life I breathed a sigh of relief. "I was afraid it wouldn't start." I removed my gloves and hat, revved the engine and waited for the vehicle to warm up. I lifted the coffee cup out of its holder and sipped at what I thought would be icy liquid. "Hey, it's still warm!"

"Thank God." Maxim turned the heat to high, grabbed his coffee and swallowed the rest of it. He set the cup back in its holder and held his rosy hands in front of the vents. "Maybe your pickup will take pity on us and actually produce some hot air."

"Don't count on it. She has a mind of her own."

I rubbed my hands together and willed my heart to slow to its regular pace. We sat in silence until Maxim looked over at me and covered my hand with his. "Bree, what I said outside … I want you to know that I don't expect anything from you." He rubbed his forehead and exhaled slowly. "It's just that a woman as beautiful as you deserves to hear it — that she's beautiful, I mean." He searched for the right words. "I just hope I didn't make you uncomfortable. I feel like we're becoming friends and that means the world to me."

I peeked up at his face. "Thank you for explaining. I'll admit it was unexpected, but you're right … a woman loves to hear that. You're a kind man."

He squeezed my hand and let go. "Can I take you out for supper to thank you for the tour?"

All at once I realized how tired I was. "Not tonight but thank you. I'm exhausted and, I'll admit, a little hung over. No surprise there." His eyes crinkled as he grinned. "I just want to go home and do nothing."

He stared out the window. "I completely understand."

"How long are you staying in town?" I was more curious than I wanted to be.

"A few more days at least."

"Just so you know, my coffee shop is closed on Sunday and Monday, but give me a call if you have any more questions."

"Thank you. I will." His eyes conveyed warmth. "And I really enjoyed today."

"So did I." I was surprised at how much I meant it.

I exhaled and shifted the pickup into reverse. I'd spent the afternoon with a man … talking, laughing, revealing myself. Maybe there was hope for me yet. I smiled in spite of myself as I backed out of the parking space and turned toward Waconda.

Chapter 13

I padded to the kitchen in my new fuzzy snowflake-patterned socks, one of my birthday gifts from Tracey, and picked up the plate of leftover birthday cake Caitlin sent home after my party. I pulled open the utensil drawer, grabbed a fork and shuffled to the living room where I sat on the couch and pulled away the plastic wrap to reveal a dark chocolate cake with whipped chocolate frosting half an inch thick. I sank my fork into the cake and devoured the biggest bite I could handle. I exhaled and settled into the cushions as the chocolate melted in my mouth and dreams of heaven flashed before my eyes. If I'd died right then I would've left this world one satisfied lady. I propped my feet on the coffee table and relished several huge bites of cake until my chocolate craving was satisfied.

I pulled the plastic wrap over the remaining cake, set the plate on the coffee table and stared at my laptop computer sitting just inches away on the couch. Before I lost my nerve I grabbed it, opened the internet browser and typed "Maxim Hall Novelist" into the search bar of a new window. I chewed on a fingernail and scanned the page of results. The first listing was Maxim Hall's official website, so I clicked on the link.

When the page loaded I was overwhelmed by the sight of Maxim's elegant face stretched the full length of the screen. In the black and white image Maxim gazed past the camera, his face pensive as he searched the world for stories. The only color on the screen was in his eyes, and the vivid blue was striking against the monochromatic scheme of the site.

I stared at his face for a long time and then pulled my gaze away from his eyes and studied the features I hadn't been able to examine in real life. The light wrinkles under his eyes and the laugh lines in the corners only added to the beauty of his face. The scar above his right eye hadn't been Photoshopped away, and I wondered what caused it. His jaw and chin were covered in light stubble but didn't hide the dimples that showed even though his smile was slight. His nose was somewhat crooked in the center, which I liked; perfection was overrated. I traced the contours of his cheekbones with my eyes and traveled up and down his face several times, drinking in every nuance. Maybe it was the chocolate coma, maybe it was the hangover, maybe it was the years of fatigue and sadness taking over. Maybe it was just the man himself. What was I going to do?

I looked for the Links bar, clicked on the About Me page and read his biography: "Maxim Hall is an award-winning novelist with nine books to his name, seven of which reached the New York Times' Bestseller list. Maxim has achieved worldwide acclaim for his emotional stories of love, loss, forgiveness and redemption. Four of his books have been adapted to film, with the fifth in production. His novels have been translated into five languages. Maxim's latest novel, The Chair, was released this fall and hit #1 on the New York Times' Bestseller List in its first week. He is currently touring the country to promote The Chair. Maxim lives in New York City with his sons, William and Henry." The writing was simple and classy, not unlike the man himself.

I clicked on the Books link and stared at nine impressive book covers lined up with release dates printed underneath. I scanned the title of each cover and assessed that I'd read all but three of Maxim's books — two of the old ones and his most recent. I clicked on the cover picture for The Chair and read the description: "In his latest novel, writer Maxim Hall takes us to the day the world fell apart for Rebecca King, the day a careless accident snuffed out two innocent lives and landed her in a wheelchair." I gasped and inhaled sharply, emotions rushing to the surface, but I forced myself to continue reading. "As Rebecca enters a new life without the use of her legs, she buries the feelings of guilt and works to move on, but an unexpected letter threatens to send her over the edge. With life spiraling out of control, Rebecca must decide whether to accept forgiveness or lose herself in the depths of anguish and despair."

My heart beat wildly, sweat dotted my forehead and the laptop started sliding out of my lap. I grabbed it before it hit the floor when, without warning, a sensation of dizziness overwhelmed me. I rested my head on the couch cushion and stared at Rosie the Riveter hanging on the far wall, a framed World War II poster I found at an auction after I moved into my apartment. I'd always related to Rosie's attitude of, "We can do it."

I focused on Rosie's face and breathed evenly, willing my heart to return to its normal pace, which it did after several minutes of meditation. When my nerves had calmed and I was certain the panic attack had passed, I lowered my gaze to the computer screen, clicked on the Home page button and stared at Maxim's picture for a long time. What was it about this man that cut to the core of my soul? Yes, he was a gifted writer, but it was more than that; Maxim was able to tap into the emotions produced by trauma and create real characters his readers could relate to. He was terrifyingly introspective and accurate in the human experience, and he wasn't afraid to delve into the darkness left behind by tragedy. I shuddered and rubbed my temples, continuing my close scrutiny of Maxim's image.

In the far right-hand corner of the Home page I noticed a link titled Tour Dates and clicked on it. What loaded was a calendar filled with the cities Maxim was visiting to promote The Chair. On the December calendar his scheduled appearances from December 11 to 31 had been crossed through and marked Rescheduled, but an autograph session at a bookstore in Denver, Colorado, on Monday, December 18, wasn't crossed off. December 18 was this coming Monday. I wondered if he still planned to attend. Would he drive there? Fly? Take a train? I was far more interested in this man's life than I wanted to be, but I couldn't seem to help myself. Was I flirting with obsession, heading toward the stalker stage with Maxim? I reminded myself that I was simply reading his website, that's all. It was totally innocent. If he didn't want me to know about his life, he shouldn't have put it out there.

I jumped as my cell phone rang, and when I saw it was Caitlin I tapped the Accept button and picked up the phone. "Hi, Caitlin."

"Hey, Bree." Caitlin's tone was flat, and her voice was muted.

"You don't sound very good, honey."

Caitlin groaned and sighed heavily. "One too many bottles of wine, I guess. Did you see me putting that stuff away? Why didn't someone stop me?"

I laughed and sank into the couch. "Because you were having fun … and we were having fun watching you."

"Oh Lord, I was afraid of that. Did I do anything stupid? Brice won't tell me a thing; every time he looks at me he's wearing that shit-eating grin of his." I pictured her twirling a strand of hair, something she did when she was irritated.

"Your rendition of Baby One More Time from the bar was a big hit."

"You're making that up." Her voice moved away from the phone and she yelled into the distance. "Brice, did I get on the bar and sing Britney Spears last night?" Brice's laughter reached my ears and Caitlin returned to the phone. "He's just laughing and won't tell me. You guys totally suck. Why do I put up with you?"

"Because you love us, Catey."

"Don't go using your cutesy little nickname and expect me to roll over like a puppy."

"Okay, you didn't sing Britney Spears from the bar."

She released a loud sigh of relief.

I continued. "You were actually standing on the table. And dancing. Removal of vital clothing may have been involved."

She mumbled something under her breath. "I give up. You are totally useless and a little mean."

Knowing how much appearances meant to Caitlin and the fact that a large group of Waconda's finest had joined us at RJ's Bar after returning to town from the high school basketball games, I decided to put her out of her misery. "Don't worry, you didn't do anything stupid last night. Honest. You were a true lady all evening and hosted one hell of a birthday party."

I sensed a smile on her end of the conversation. "You're welcome. Even though you're a total pain in the butt most of the time, I do love you."

"Love you too. And I really did have a great time. Don't feel bad … I'm still hung over. That wine was smooth and tasty!"

She agreed. "Oh, I know. It just proves that since the boys were born I don't get out enough. And then when I do get a night off I think I'm still 21 and drink a bottle of wine by myself."

I giggled. "That's motherhood, kiddo. And you love every minute of it."

"I know. But when I was 21 I could have slept in 'til noon. The boys were jumping on our bed at 6:30. I'm exhausted."

I sympathized. "Right? I was 15 minutes late opening the coffee shop."

She laughed. "It's a good thing Rich and Dave don't come in on Saturdays."

"That's what I was telling Maxim today. If Rich and Dave had been forced to wait out in the cold 15 minutes for their coffee I would have never heard the end of it."

Caitlin's voice was teasing. "So … Maxim Hall, the brilliant and drop-dead gorgeous novelist. That's actually what — or who — I was calling about."

"Really? What about him?" I studied my fingernails that were always chewed short.

Caitlin didn't hide her exasperation. "What about him? Last night we're all shocked to find out you already know him, and today you spent the afternoon giving him a tour of Waconda. Or did you cancel because of the snow?"

"No, I didn't cancel."

"Okay, so give me the scoop. Brice is playing with the boys in the living room and I'm alone in the bedroom, so we won't be interrupted. Go ahead."

As my best friend, Caitlin was used to hearing all the details of my life. She commiserated with me during the low times and celebrated with me during the high times. I could trust her with anything, but for some reason I was reluctant to share my feelings about Maxim. I decided to stick with the facts.

"Well, I drove him out to the lake, and we hiked to the Waconda Springs replica. By the way, tell Brice thanks for loaning him the boots. Maxim's suede boots wouldn't have held up in all of this snow."

"I'll tell him. What happened when you were up there?"

I traced the edge of the cushion with one finger and stared at the ceiling. "It was pretty straightforward. I showed him the replica and told him about the lake and the dam. It was cold, of course, so we didn't stay long." I left out the parts that Caitlin would have loved to hear, like Maxim telling me that I'm beautiful, but she didn't press for more information.

She sounded disappointed. "Oh. I guess I thought you'd spend more time with him."

I cringed as I lied to my best friend. "No, it was pretty quick. He just wanted to get a little info and I was tuckered out. When we were done I drove him back to the coffee shop, he thanked me and then left."

There was a brief pause in our conversation. "When is he leaving town?"

I looked down and picked at a loose thread in the sofa. "In a few days is all he said. I told him the coffee shop is closed on Sunday and Monday, and to call if he needed any more information on Waconda Springs. I didn't ask what day he's leaving town, and he didn't tell me."

"I see." I could sense Caitlin's mind racing. She sighed. "Well, it was amazing to meet an author I've actually read. His books are life-changing."

"Yeah, he's a good writer."

"And he seems like a good man. Is that the vibe you get when you're around him?"

I thought about her question. "I don't know him very well, but he's been kind and considerate to me."

"That's a relief. Sometimes you meet famous people and they're the opposite of what you expected. It's so disappointing. The way he writes makes it seem like he'd be a real person, you know, not some phony out to make a buck."

I nodded. "He does seem like a real person."

We sat in silence for several minutes until Caitlin spoke. "What were you doing when I called?"

I quickly shut the laptop and set it on the couch. "Just eating more of my birthday cake."

Caitlin laughed. "I'm glad to hear that. We ate the rest of ours for dessert tonight."

"The cake I ate was both supper and dessert."

I pictured Caitlin shaking her head in disappointment. "You should consider putting some vegetables and fruit into your system. If you ate a salad I think your organs would literally applaud."

"No, they'd go into shock and shut down completely. They're more comfortable with coffee and sugar. It's worked for me this long."

"Well, you may be getting away with it now, but very soon, my friend, your body will rebel against all of the junk you put into it. I'm just saying that a piece of fruit every now and then wouldn't kill you."

I crossed my feet and inspected my new socks. "But why risk it?"

She moaned. "You, Bree Somers, are one stubborn woman. What am I going to do with you?"

"If it makes you feel any better I plan to go for a run before church in the morning. My organs will love it. Are you happy now?"

"Yes, that does make me happy. And we're planning on you at our house after church for Sunday dinner. I'm trying out a new crockpot recipe. The boys can't wait to see you."

I smiled. "I can't wait to see them, either. I told them we'd play in the snow after dinner."

She chuckled. "Oh yes, they mentioned that. But first they want you to play Legos with them."

"Are we adding to their town?"

"Yep. They want you to help them build a church, since it will be Sunday."

"Well, aren't they clever boys. Our Lego Waconda just keeps getting better."

Caitlin yawned loudly. "Listen, I'll let you go. Try to get some sleep." She paused. "Well, as good as you can sleep, anyway."

"Will do."

"And Bree?"

"Yes?"

"There will be a vegetable served with the meal tomorrow and I expect you to eat it."

I imitated a little girl's voice. "Yes, Mommy. I pwomise."

Caitlin was still laughing when I tapped the End Call button.

I set my phone on the coffee table and picked up my Kindle. I turned it on, tapped Books, then Store and typed in The Chair. When Maxim's novel popped up I stared at the cover artwork, an empty wheelchair sitting on a beach in front of a gorgeous sunset. The image blurred and my mind wandered. I really wanted to read the book, but I was filled with trepidation and nerves. I knew that if I allowed fear to stop me I would never get better. After several minutes of contemplation I gathered up my courage, tapped the button that said Buy for $9.99 and watched the little bar fill with green as the book downloaded onto my Kindle.

When the Download Complete sign appeared I tapped on Read Now and there it was, Chapter 1 of Maxim Hall's latest novel. My heart picked up its pace as I sank back into the couch cushions and began to read.

SUNDAY, DECEMBER 17, 2017

Chapter 14

"Here you go, Aunt Bree." Nate's hands were heaped with red Lego pieces, and he dumped them in a pile on the cream carpet next to my knee.

"Good job, Nate." I patted his back, picked up several of the pieces and pushed them, one by one, onto the slanted roof of the white Lego building.

Matt knelt beside me and helped assemble the red roof. "Will our church have a bell in the tower?"

"I don't know. Is there such a thing as a Lego church bell?"

Matt's forehead scrunched in concentration and he shrugged dramatically. "I dunno."

Nate, who preferred to search for pieces and leave the assembling to his brother, resumed digging through the giant tub of Lego pieces. "If there's a church bell, I'll find it."

I laughed. "If you can't find a bell we can just make one with Legos."

Matt's eyebrows drew together. "How do you make a Lego bell?"

My right hip had fallen asleep, so I shifted the weight to my left hip. "First we need to know what color a church bell is ... do you know?"

Before Matt could answer Nate turned from the tub of Legos. "Brown."

"No, it's not." Matt cast an exasperated look at his brother. "It's gold."

Nate shook his head. "Church bells are brown."

Matt stopped building Legos and put his hands on his hips. "They're gold."

Nate jumped up and faced his brother. "Brown."

Matt sprung up and poked a finger in Nate's ribs. "Gold."

"Brown!"

"Gold!"

I held up my hands in the time-out sign used by referees. "Calm downs, guys. You're both wrong. Church bells are actually bronze."

The twins scrutinized me, their faces twisted in confusion. Nate spoke first. "What's bronze?"

I smiled. "It's a shiny brown." Nate pointed at Matt and stuck out his tongue.

Matt mirrored the gesture back to his twin. "Whatever." I suppressed a smile as Matt dropped down beside me and finished the red roof of the church.

"You boys need to watch the Olympics in February. They give bronze medals to the third-place finishers."

Matt peered up at me. "What's Olympics?"

"It's when the best athletes in the world compete in sports like ice skating, skiing and snowboarding."

Nate stared at me. "Are the medals like what we got in baseball last summer? I wore mine around my neck. Is that what those people do?"

"Yes. If you win first place you get a gold medal, second place gets silver, and third gets bronze."

Nate scratched his head. "But I don't think they make bronze Legos."

"It's okay, kiddo. Brown or gold will be fine."

Nate jumped up in excitement. "I know. We could make the bell brown and gold."

Matt grinned at his brother but remained quiet.

I gave Nate instructions. "Okay, Master Lego Finder, what we need are the smallest brown and gold Legos you can find."

Nate saluted formally. "Yes, Ma'am."

I turned to Matt. "Master Lego Builder, it's time to assemble the bell tower."

Matt saluted like his brother and giggled. "Yes, Ma'am."

"Do we have enough white pieces?"

Matt studied the pile of white Legos that Nate had found in the tub. "Yes."

"Okay, let's get to building."

Matt and I pushed white Legos onto the bell tower of the church, taking turns at each level. When the steeple was about two inches tall I told him that it was time to build the belfry.

Matt tried out the word. "Belfry?"

"Yep. That's where the bell hangs."

Recognition lit his face. "Hey Nate, did you hear that? The belfry is where the bell lives."

Nate sat beside the huge tub of Legos, his brows furrowed in concentration as he pushed brown and gold Legos together. After several minutes he broke out in a triumphant grin. "I made the bell!" He jumped up, ran to me and threw his arms around my neck. He smelled like crayons and strawberry shampoo. "Aunt Bree, I made the bell!"

He handed it to me, and I studied it closely. "This is the best Lego bell in the history of Lego bells." He beamed in triumph and Matt smiled. "Since you made it why don't you place it on top of the tower, and we'll build the belfry around it."

Nate bent down near the Lego church and carefully pushed the brown and gold bell onto the tower. When he was done he planted his hands on his hips and grinned broadly. "We almost done?"

"Yes, we are. Okay, Matt, let's finish this church." I used the smallest pieces to build the belfry and we pushed more red pieces on top of the bell tower to form its roof.

Matt stretched out his arms. "Ta-da."

I chuckled. "That is one good-looking church."

Nate ran out of the playroom, yelling as he went. "Mom! Dad! Come see our church!" Nate returned with Caitlin and Brice following closely behind.

When Caitlin saw our creation she broke out in a broad smile. "Oh boys, that's a beautiful church." She knelt down to examine it from every angle. "Wow. You made double front doors and even put windows on the sides."

Nate rolled his eyes. "Of course we put in windows, Mom. The people couldn't see out if we didn't have windows."

Matt piped up. "And it would be really dark in there since Lego towns don't have 'lectricity."

Caitlin nodded in agreement. "You're right."

Brice squatted down beside his wife. "You guys really outdid yourself. And finally, the people of Lego Waconda will have a church to attend." He smiled at his twins.

Matt slung an arm around my neck. "Would you put the church in our town?"

I placed a hand on my heart and gasped. "I would be honored. Where does it go?"

Nate and Matt ran to their Lego town in the corner of the playroom and pointed to an empty spot near the wall. I rose slowly from my awkward position on the floor and stretched out the tightness from my early-morning run. I reached down and lifted the Lego church and walked to the corner where I placed it between the bank and the hair salon.

I knelt down between my nephews. "Give me high fives, boys." I high-fived Nate with one hand and Matt with the other. "Now give me big hugs." They threw their arms around my neck and we were a jumble of big and small body parts linked together. I kissed them each on the cheek.

Caitlin raised her voice. "Dessert is ready if anyone wants it."

Nate and Matt untangled themselves from me and raised their fists in the air. "Dessert!" They raced from the room. Caitlin followed the boys to the kitchen, and when Brice and I arrived we joined them at the round oak table tucked into a bay window that filled the room with natural early-afternoon light.

I was always up for sweets. "What are we having?"

Matt was happy to fill me in. "Cheesecake!"

Nate looked at me and grinned. "Cherry cheesecake!"

Caitlin used a spatula to dish up generous servings onto dessert places, added forks and passed them out. "Dig in."

The twins grabbed their forks and set out to see who could finish first. Brice frowned. "Slow down, guys. Enjoy the taste of each bite."

Caitlin smiled as she lifted a dainty bite of cheesecake to her mouth. "Good luck with that suggestion, honey."

I'd eaten just three bites of my dessert when the boys declared they were done and asked to be excused from the table. Caitlin pointed to the other side of the kitchen. "Put your dishes in the sink and then you can go play." Nate and Matt hopped down from the chairs, ran to the sink where they deposited their empty plates with a loud clank and then ran from the room.

I took another bite of dessert, closed my eyes and savored the sensation as the cheesecake melted together with the cherry topping. When I opened my eyes Caitlin was gazing at me in amusement. "You know I'm only letting you have dessert because you ate your vegetable at lunch."

"Yes, and thank you, mommy." I fed myself another bite of cheesecake. "I actually thought the green beans were quite good."

"Probably because I cooked them with bacon."

I smirked. "That didn't hurt, either."

Caitlin ate another small bite and set her fork on the table, a clear indication that she was done eating and that Brice would finish her dessert. She sat forward with her elbows on the table and folded her fingers. "Hey, I meant to tell you after church that the piano music this morning was really beautiful. I teared up."

I grinned. "Thank you, but I know for a fact that you cry over pictures of baby squirrels."

She swatted my hand. "Only if they're super cute. What's the name of the song you played right before church started? It was a beautiful arrangement. I know I've heard it, but without the lyrics I was lost."

"'How Beautiful'."

Caitlin snapped her fingers. "Yes! 'How Beautiful.' The lyrics are amazing. I wish you would have sung along."

"I know, but my throat's a little sore. I'll wait a few weeks and do it again with the lyrics."

"I'll hold you to it."

Brice pushed his empty plate to the middle of the table and grabbed Caitlin's. He had just lifted a forkful of cheesecake to his mouth when his cell phone rang. He set the fork back on the plate and pulled the phone out of his back pocket. His eyebrows shot up. "It's Mother." He glanced at Caitlin.

She gestured to the phone. "Please answer it. I've been thinking about Trudy and would like to know exactly where she is." I tossed the fork on the table and crossed my arms, my appetite suddenly vanished.

Brice answered. "Hello, Mother." He sat back in the chair and crossed his ankles. "Yes, we're all together for Sunday dinner." Another pause. "Yes, Bree is here too." Brice's eyebrows furrowed as he focused on Mother's words. He listened for what seemed like two full minutes before he spoke. "Wow, that's amazing news. Congratulations." He pointed to his wedding ring and grinned. Caitlin clapped her hands and smiled. I couldn't suppress the groan that passed my lips.

Brice scratched his forehead and leaned forward. "I'll tell them the news." More silence followed as he nodded and grinned. "Tell Hank congrats. Okay. See you soon." He ended the call and set the phone on the table. "Wow. Mother's engaged."

Caitlin propped her elbows on the table, clasped her hands together and rested her chin on top. "Did she tell you how he popped the question?"

Brice grabbed Caitlin's dessert and devoured a huge bite. "During dinner last night a cake was delivered to Mother, and when it arrived there were lit sparklers sticking out the top of it and the cake read, 'Will You Marry Me?'" Brice glanced at Caitlin and avoided eye contact with me. "She said that when the cake was set down in front of her, Hank dropped to one knee holding a wedding ring with a diamond the size of a golf ball. I guess it's huge."

"That's pretty sweet." Caitlin stared at Brice. "Anything else?"

Brice ate the last bite of her dessert and dropped the fork on the table. "Yeah. She said she would have called right after Hank proposed but they went back to their room and fed cake to each other … among other things."

I moaned out loud and held up both hands. "Too much information."

He grinned. "It's the middle of the night there and she hasn't been to sleep yet."

I couldn't hide the sarcasm from my voice, and I suppose I didn't want to. "My God, who are you? Her therapist? If she told you any more, please keep it to yourself." I dropped my head into my hands and bent forward in the position people use when they hyperventilate.

"Nope, that's it."

Caitlin tucked a stray blonde hair behind her ear. "Did she tell you where they are?"

"No. Somewhere near Alaska, I presume."

Caitlin sighed. "I know that. I was just curious where the ship stopped last."

"Honestly, I don't think Mother cares where she is. She got the ring she wanted and now she can relax."

We sat at the table in silence for several minutes, lost in our own thoughts. Caitlin spoke first. "Bree, are you okay?"

I didn't bother to look up. The hyperventilation pose was working for me. "I'm trying to be Zen about this, Caitlin. It's like Brice said: hopefully she'll move to Hank's mansion in Beloit and leave me the hell alone."

Brice's exasperation was obvious. "That's not exactly what I said."

I lifted my head and glared at Brice. "What's the difference? As long as she's not in Waconda I truly don't care what the hell she does."

I dropped my head back down and noticed two small feet near my chair. I turned and found Matt gawking at me, his eyes bugging out in his small face. "You shouldn't say hell, Aunt Bree. It's a bad place and really hot. My Sunday school teacher said that no one wants to go there."

Caitlin hid her smile with one hand and tousled Matt's brown wavy hair with the other.

I softened and placed an arm around Matt. "You're right, honey. I'm sorry I said that bad word. Do you think I should go stand in the corner?"

Lara Ketter

ANOTHER CHRISTMAS WITHOUT YOU

He considered my question and finally shook his head no. "I'll let it go this time, but if I hear you say it again you'll have to stand in the corner. Okay?"

"I can respect that. Thank you."

Brice's face turned red and his body shook as he held in laughter. Caitlin continued to cover her mouth.

Matt didn't move so Caitlin finally pulled him to her. "Do you need something, honey?"

"Yep. I'm thirsty." He looked at his mom with a crooked grin. "Can I have a juice box?"

Caitlin smiled and tapped his nose. "Yes. I'm sure your brother will want one too."

Matt walked to the refrigerator and pulled out two juice boxes. "Thanks, Mom." He ran out of the room.

When he was gone Brice erupted in laughter. "I guess he told you. Someone needs to watch your smart mouth. I'll tell you this — if anyone can do it, it's Matt."

"I know. He should consider a career in law enforcement." I rubbed my temples as the beginning of a headache made its appearance. "Maybe if I'd had a better mother I wouldn't be such a wise-ass."

Caitlin leaned back and locked her fingers behind her head. "There goes that mouth of yours again. Do I need to put you in the corner, young lady?"

"Very funny." I turned my attention to Brice. "But you know I'm right. Mother wasn't much of a mother. If it weren't for Dad I'd be in a loony bin somewhere."

Caitlin dropped her arms and regarded me with tenderness. Brice scooted his chair closer to mine until our knees were touching. "Bree, you've got to let it go. So she sucked at being a mom. Don't you think I know that?"

I slapped his knee. "But don't you remember how she acted after you and Dad brought me home from Olathe? She had no clue how to handle my emotions. She'd tiptoe into my room, leave a glass of water and some food, then tiptoe back out. So she fed me. Big deal. She never talked to me or asked how I was doing." I fiddled with the pendant at my throat. "I heard later that she'd been telling people in town I was 'just fine' and made up things I was doing on the farm. She even told one lady I'd taken up macramé. I was mourning and sleeping, not tying knots in a rope. What's up with that?"

Brice leaned even closer. "She obviously didn't know how to handle it."

143

"You think? Dad's the one who saved me. I would have wasted away in that room if it had been up to her to help me."

He touched my hand. "She is who she is. You have to learn how to accept it."

I hung my head and stayed quiet.

He continued. "Listen, I get where you're coming from. I think she hugged me one time, maybe two, when we were growing up, but after Nate and Matt were born she just showered them with hugs and kisses every time she saw them; I was blown away. And now, when they go out to the farm, she bakes cookies and plays games with them."

I looked up and peered into Brice's brown eyes where I saw a mixture of happiness, sadness and bewilderment.

He reached for my hand. "I'm going to tell you a secret that only Caitlin knows. Well, and Mother, although she'll never admit it happened." He had my full attention. "A few months ago Caitlin brought the boys out to the farm while I was working in the shop. Mother baked chocolate chip cookies, let them eat as many as they wanted, and then played hide-and-seek. After she hugged and kissed them goodbye I followed her into the kitchen. Guess what I asked her."

My attention was riveted to the story.

Brice stared into my eyes and continued. "I asked her, 'Where the hell were you when Bree and I were little?'"

I gasped and covered my mouth with both hands. "Oh my God. What did she say?"

"Nothing. She stomped off and didn't speak to me for a week."

I laughed. "Lucky you."

"Ol' Ice-T had thawed out, and it took the cutest twin boys ever born to do it."

"They have that effect on people."

Brice squeezed my hand. "Here's the deal. That day I decided to let it go. All of it. I forgave her. She was a terrible mother but instead of being bitter about it I thank God every day we had Dad. He was amazing, wasn't he?" Brice seemed lost in his memories. "I wish I'd asked him why she's the way she is, but I thought I had plenty of time to talk about that stuff." His focus returned to me. "The thing is, we'll never know why she was a lousy mom. What I know now is that she's a loving grandmother, and I'm thankful for that. Do you think you can let it go? Can you try to forgive her?"

I wiped a tear from the corner of my eye. "But she hasn't asked forgiveness."

"You know that forgiveness is about you and not about her."

"What, are you a preacher now?" Brice sat back and crossed his arms. "I'm sorry. I know you're right. It's just hard to forgive someone who won't even admit they did anything wrong."

He rubbed his chin. "If you won't do it for yourself, do it for Nate and Matt. She's good to them, and they really love her. As their Godmother you want what's best for them, right?"

His comment caught me off guard. I looked at him and grimaced. "Ouch. Using the old guilt trip on me, huh?"

"Whatever it takes."

Caitlin, who'd remained silent during the conversation, leaned on the table and reached for my hands. "This is none of my business, but I'm thinking of you. The anger and resentment are eating you up inside. And without fruits and vegetables in there, your organs are already stressed out." I smiled in spite of myself. "If you could forgive Trudy I think you'd feel a lot better."

I nodded and squeezed her hands. "I know you're right, and I value your opinion. I'll see what I can do."

Caitlin let go of my hands and rose to her feet. "Well, that's enough of the heavy stuff. Let's go see what the boys are doing and lighten things up around here. We should all go out and play in the snow!" She hurried from the room.

Brice and I stood at the same time and he grabbed me in a bear hug that lasted longer than usual. His voice was soft. "I just want what's best for you. Caitlin's right. Forgiveness is powerful." When he pulled away there were tears in his eyes.

I choked up with emotion. "I'll try. I really will."

"That's my girl." He put his arm around my shoulder and led me to the playroom where Nate and Matt had set up their collection of dinosaurs in the middle of Lego Waconda. When we walked in they looked up and smiled the sweetest smiles you'll ever see, and my heart melted.

Brice leaned in close. "Do it for them. It will be worth it. I guarantee."

Chapter 15

I was half asleep on the couch, curled up under an old quilt with a rerun of Friends playing on TV, when my cell phone rang. After the third ring I grabbed it off the coffee table and my heart jumped when I saw the name on the screen: 4:10 pm and Maxim Hall was calling. I tossed off the quilt, sat up straight and hit the Accept button.

"Hello." My voice was scratchy and quiet.

His voice sounded smooth and rich like double cream chocolate frosting. "Hello." A slight pause. "It's Maxim … Hall."

I cleared my throat. "Hello, Maxim."

"I woke you, didn't I?"

"No." I rubbed my eyes with my free hand and ran fingers through my tangled hair.

He chuckled. "You're a terrible liar."

I sighed. "You caught me. I was taking a nap. Kind of."

"What do you mean you were 'kind of' taking a nap?"

I crossed my legs on the couch and relaxed into the cushion. "The deal is I'm a terrible sleeper. I nap during the day because I can't sleep at night. But I can't even nap like a normal person. It's like I'm sleeping but I'm still aware of what's going on around me."

"That sounds terrible." I sensed sympathy and was touched.

"It's no picnic. I would give anything for a solid night of sleep."

"So when I called, you were asleep, but only kind of."

"Yes. The TV is on and I could hear it the whole time I was asleep, or half asleep, or whatever you call it."

"I'm sorry to hear that." He seemed sincere. "I wish there was something I could do to help."

I laughed. "That's nice of you but I've been to several doctors, taken medicine, tried one of those CPAP machines, which I hated, and even saw a hypnotist. Nothing helps. It's just my lot in life, I guess."

Maxim understood. "Every rose has its thorn."

"Yes, that's how I look at it." Another pause. "What are you up to today?"

"That's why I called you. I've been compiling my notes on Waconda Springs and I'm really interested in the water bottling company and the health resort that were built next to it. Do you mind if I ask you some questions?"

I picked up the remote and turned off the TV. "Sure. What do you want to know?"

I heard him rifling through papers. "The whole thing continues to fascinate me. The bottled water from the spring — was that business started before or after the health resort was there?"

I picked up the quilt and draped it across my legs. "Before. The U.S. government started parceling out land in the late 1800s, and the settlers were fascinated with the spring. A man named Pfeifer made the first claim on the property and built a sod house near the spring. A mineral company bought the spring to harvest the salt, but the business failed. A few years later a guy named Burnham bought the spring and established a bottling works on the site; the mineral water was bottled and sold as Waconda Water."

He must have been writing down the information because he didn't speak right away. "Okay. So after the health resort was going did they continue to sell the bottled water?"

I picked at a loose thread in the corner of the quilt. "Yes. Burnham kept selling the bottled water while he convinced an easterner named McWilliams to invest financially in the future health resort. It was ten years before the first building was finished, an impressive hotel and resort. They hired G.W. Cooper to run it and continued distributing Waconda Water to all parts of the country."

"That must have been something."

"I can only imagine." I laid my head back on the cushion and stared at the ceiling. "In 1906 Dr. G.P. Abrahams purchased the property from McWilliams, and the business stayed in his family until the lake covered it in 1968."

"Yeah, I read that on the local website, which needs some serious editing, by the way. It's so badly done that I wouldn't trust the information unless I verified it with a valid source. You're my valid source, by the way."

I chuckled. "I'll do what I can. Evelyn Foster, the City Clerk — you've met her — is in charge of the website, and her spelling and grammar are atrocious. No one has the guts to say anything because we're all afraid of her. We'd love to turn it over to a professional. I suggested my friend, Michelle ... you met her at my birthday dinner. She's an English teacher and has experience with website design. She'd be perfect for the job."

"Has anyone asked her to do it?"

I laughed. "Asked? I begged her is more like it, but she, too, fears the wrath of Evelyn."

Maxim roared with laughter. "Well, I can't rag on Evelyn because she sent me to you. I'll forever be grateful to her."

I blushed and stayed quiet.

"Okay, I'm going to read you what I wrote down and please tell me if I'm right." I heard papers moving around. "Dr. Carl Bingesser married Dr. Abrahams' daughter, Anna, and they moved to Waconda Springs and helped run the resort until Dr. Abrahams died in 1924. At that point Carl and Anna took over in the daily operation. Their son, Dr. Carlos Bingesser, and his wife, Marjorie, ran the health resort in later years..."

I interrupted. "And dreamed of passing it onto their children, who would be the fourth generation at Waconda Springs."

"Yes, but that didn't happen."

I sighed. "Nope. Dr. Carlos fought the dam project, but of course he lost. Generations of work and all his adversaries could say was that Waconda Springs was a 'mud hole.'" I couldn't hide the melancholy in my voice. "I mean, even if the buildings were run down, it was worth saving and could have been restored. Think of the history of the place. I can't believe sane people did such a thing. I wonder if it would happen today."

Maxim agreed. "It does seem crazy, but the fear of another huge flood is what drove the builders of the dam. And you have to remember, some people don't care about nature or history. It's all about the needs of man. More often than not, that takes precedence."

I stayed quiet and traced a star on the quilt.

I heard Maxim tapping a pencil or pen on a table. "How do you remember all of those facts and dates?"

"I've always been able to remember information like that. I think I have a photographic memory, but I've never been tested. It came in handy at school, especially during college when I was so busy I barely had time to study. If I read or heard it once, I'd remember."

"Wow. I wish I could do that. I have to write everything down, especially dates, or they just float away into the great abyss. Do you have time to answer another question about the spring?"

An idea was forming in my head, an idea that both scared and thrilled me at the same time. I was surprised at myself and questioned my motives. Before I had the chance to chicken out I screwed up my courage and jumped into the deep end of the pool.

"I had a thought."

"I'm all ears."

I pictured his well-proportioned ears and smiled. "Well, my grandfather, my dad's dad, put together a scrapbook of historical items from Waconda Springs ... pictures, newspaper clippings about the dam project, lots of interesting stuff. I have it here in my apartment." I paused, breathed deeply and forged ahead into the realm of no return. "Would you like to come over and look at it? As a bonus, I'm planning to burn up some frozen pizza, and you're welcome to join me." I closed my eyes and dropped my head, once again the shy schoolgirl, which irritated me to no end.

After a short pause, Maxim spoke. "I would love to come over. Thank you. What time?"

I continued to surprise myself. "How about now?" I held my breath.

"Sure. I'll gather my notes and bring them along. Is the entrance at the back of your building?"

I exhaled and started folding the quilt in anticipation of his arrival. "Yes. You were in the alley behind the store yesterday ... you'll see my pickup parked there. Look for the red door — Bree Brews It is painted on it. Come up the metal steps to the second red door."

"I'll be there in a few minutes."

I thought of something. "And Maxim? Be careful on the steps. With all of this snow it will be slick." My voice turned playful. "I wouldn't want to be responsible for injuring America's Writer."

He laughed. "Thanks for the warning. See you in a bit."

I tapped the End Call button and sat perfectly still. Maxim Hall, famous novelist, nice guy and super hottie, was coming to my home because I'd invited him. Me — Bree Somers — had asked a man to come over to see me. Well, I'd actually asked him to come over and see a scrapbook. A scrapbook that was in my home, and if he wanted to see it he'd have to see me. And this man would be here in five, maybe ten, minutes.

As if hit by lightning I jumped up and finished folding the quilt, threw it in the basket of blankets and plumped the pillows on the red couch. I picked up two dirty glasses and a cereal bowl from the coffee table, rushed to the kitchen and set them in the sink. I opened a cabinet, grabbed the dust rag and ran to the living room where I wiped down the end tables, coffee table, and hurriedly dusted the TV and the stand it was sitting on. With no time to spare, I shoved the dust rag under the couch.

I jogged into the bathroom and inspected myself in the mirror. My hair was a mess and I attacked it with a brush. When it was free of knots I parted it on the side, smoothed it flat and tucked it behind my ears. I pulled out my bag of makeup and reapplied mascara, blush and lip gloss. I wiped down the sink with the dirty hand towel, tossed it in the hamper and hung a clean towel on the rack.

In the closet I changed out of my faded black yoga pants into dark skinny jeans. I pulled off my K-State sweatshirt with the frayed hem and slipped into the grey knit sweater Tracey gave me for my birthday. The softness of the V-neck sweater caught my attention for a moment, and I remembered to pull off the price tag. I heard a knock on the door and slipped my feet into a pair of black flats.

I stepped out of the closet and stopped short at the sight of Maxim through the window of the only door in my apartment. His face was in profile, and I could see his breath in the frigid air as he stood on the landing. I realized he was looking away from the door because he was much too polite to snoop in the window of someone's home; I'd left the blind up. After a calming yoga breath I marched to the door and opened it quickly. Maxim's head turned my way and a broad smile filled his face.

I ushered him inside. "Sorry to keep you waiting. You must be frozen."

When Maxim stepped into the apartment I was overwhelmed by his presence. The man filled the space without knowing it. "It's nice and toasty in here." My apartment wasn't the only thing that was nice and toasty. I felt the heat rush to my forehead even though cold air cascaded off his black coat. He stepped inside and I hurriedly shut the door.

Maxim's eyes were pinned on my face. "Hello."

My stomach did a backflip and I clasped my hands behind my back. "Hello." We stared at each other for several long seconds. His bright blue eyes were alert and missed nothing, an excellent trait for a writer but disarming for me. He needed a shave, like in his website picture, but it was a pleasing look on him. His ebony hair was slicked back, and he smelled like the forest after a rain shower. I was extremely attracted to this man, and it scared me a little. Okay, it scared me a lot. I was walking the high wire without a net.

I broke the trance. "Let me take your coat." He set down a shiny black leather briefcase, pulled off his coat and handed it to me. I hung it on the rack near the door and looked at the briefcase by his feet. "That must be your research."

He reached down and picked it up. "Yes. Where should I put it?"

"I'll take it for you." He handed me the briefcase and I set it on the kitchen counter.

Maxim stepped onto the rug by the back door and wiped his shoes. "Should I take these off?"

"Not unless you want to. I wear my shoes in here all the time. Hardwood floors can handle anything." He seemed unsure of what to do next. "Take a seat wherever you like." He walked to the living area, sat down in one of the cream-colored chairs that flanked the couch and studied his new surroundings. I remembered my manners. "Would you like a beer?"

He glanced up in surprise. "Yes, I'd love a beer."

I stepped to the refrigerator and peeked inside. "I have bottled wheat and canned light."

"I'll take a wheat beer."

I grabbed one of each and used an opener to remove the lid from the bottle. I walked over to Maxim, handed him the wheat beer, sat down on the couch and popped open my can of Coors Light. He drained a third of the bottle and sighed in contentment. "That tastes wonderful. It's been one of those days."

I swallowed some beer and set the can on a coaster. "How so?"

He frowned. "Conference call with my publisher. They're furious I cancelled the rest of December's book tour, especially right before Christmas." He lifted the bottle to his lips and downed another drink.

"You're not in charge of your schedule?"

My innocent question sent him into a fit of laughter. "Contrary to popular belief, writers are not the captains of our own ships. Publishers run the show."

"That's news to me."

He set the bottle of beer on a coaster, crossed his ankle over a knee and locked fingers behind his head. "In all fairness, the publisher is the one taking the risk.

They invest money in producing a book that may or may not sell. I signed a contract that stated I would make a certain number of public appearances before Christmas to promote the new book, and I've backed out on that. They're not happy." He ran fingers through his thick hair. "My agent, Laurie Lane — and yes, that's her real name — is smoothing it over for me but I've put her in a tough spot. I'm sending her a cashmere sweater and a hefty bonus check for Christmas." He grinned and picked up his beer.

I slipped out of my shoes and rested my feet on the coffee table. "I never even considered the stress of promoting a book."

Maxim took a long drink of the wheat beer and examined the label. "Sure, it's stressful, but with people starving in the world I'll never whine about it. I told Laurie that the folks at my publishing house need to get over themselves. To them, this stuff is the difference between life and death. It's crazy." He smiled and looked around. "Enough of that boring stuff. Let's change the subject. I love your studio apartment. I can't get over that limestone."

I studied the walls and nodded. "Can you believe that when we remodeled this place there was paneling on the walls? Downstairs too. The first thing we did was tear out all of the paneling and then we hired a crew to clean the limestone, inside and out. I decided not to fix the flaws in the limestone, and we left all of the nails and screws exactly where they were. I think it adds character to the place. If these limestone walls could talk … man, they could tell some fascinating stories."

"Was it open like this when you remodeled, or did you have to remove some walls?"

I laughed. "No, it was open, but the 1970s decor was atrocious. We completely gutted the kitchen and bathroom and started over. The kitchen had orange Brady Bunch countertops and the bathroom was entirely pink — pink tub, pink toilet, pink sink and pink tile."

"Wow. That sounds awful. Who is 'we'?"

"I hired a construction crew to do the work, but I was referring to my father. We put our heads together and came up with a plan for the building."

Maxim's expression was tender. "That's wonderful."

"Yes, it was."

"Who did you buy the building from?"

I grinned. "Do you want the short version or the long one?"

He grinned back at me. "I'm a writer. Of course I want the long version." He picked up his beer and emptied the bottle.

"Okay, but you may be sorry you asked." I pointed to his drink. "Before I bore you for who knows how long, would you like another beer?"

He set down the bottle and nodded. "Please. It's been years since I drank wheat beer, and I forgot how much I like it."

I jumped up and walked to the kitchen where I retrieved another bottle of wheat beer and popped off the lid. I returned to the sitting area and handed it to him.

"Thank you." As Maxim reached for the bottle our fingers touched and I felt a yearning deep in my gut that surprised me. His tender smile tugged at my heart and stirred up feelings I was hesitant to acknowledge. I dropped onto the sofa and crossed my legs. Maxim inhaled a long draw of beer. "Go ahead. I'm like a little kid … I love stories."

"Don't say I didn't warn you. Okay, here goes. When I was a girl, Rogers Variety Store was downstairs, and Harvey and Verna Rogers ran the place and lived up here. It was my favorite hangout because they had the best selection of candy and gum in town, and along one wall they had rows of toys, games, dolls and puzzles."

Maxim drank more beer. "Sounds like a kid's paradise."

I watched his lips on the bottle and noticed that the small mole on his neck moved slightly when he swallowed. I looked away and chewed on a fingernail. "It was. The Rogers seemed at least 100 years old back then, and the town kids were terrified of them. Harvey was deaf and grumpy, and Verna was stern with eyes in the back of her head. She may have smiled once, but that's just a rumor. I never saw it happen."

Maxim convulsed in laughter. "I can remember women like that from my childhood."

I leaned my head on the cushion and stared at the wall. "Even though the kids were deadly afraid of Harvey and Verna, they had the best candy in town, so it was hard to stay away. In fact, it was considered an act of bravery for a kid to come in here alone, so that rarely happened. When the craving for candy hit they'd come in groups, dollar bills and quarters shoved in their pockets, and while they were looking at the candy Verna would hover and watch them like a hawk, ensuring there was no funny business or shoplifting. The children would grab what they wanted, pay quickly and race out of the store to the park, slowing down only when they reached the Statue of Liberty. You saw it on Friday night, right?" I lifted my head and peered at Maxim, recalling how gorgeous he looked among the bright, twinkling lights.

"The miniature Statue of Liberty in the park?" He laughed. "How could I miss such a grand symbol of freedom?"

I crossed my arms. "I'll have you know that we're very proud of our little Statue of Liberty. It's been in the park since 1976 — the bicentennial year if you missed history class that day — and they even had a special ceremony to unveil it."

Maxim was unfazed by my lecture and chuckled in amusement.

I rolled my eyes. "Anyway, the kids would meet there and eat the candy they bought, right under the torch of freedom."

Maxim beamed. "God, what a great story. I can just see the kids tearing out of the store to the park, pennies and nickels falling to the sidewalk as they ran. Did Harvey and Verna have gray hair and wrinkles? Please tell me they did."

I nodded. "Oh, yes. Like I said, Harvey and Verna seemed ancient to me, although they were probably in their 60s. Verna had the biggest selection of quilting fabric and accessories in the area, and this attracted lots of business. Harvey was a fix-it man — back then he could fix anything — and people brought in broken toasters and television sets. He sat quietly at a large work bench in the back of the store, surrounded by tools and projects. He never charged enough for his work and then complained about it."

"I had an uncle like that who fixed things." Maxim stared off into the past. "He didn't charge enough, either, and then complained that people were taking advantage of him."

I uncrossed my arms. "The weird thing is, I wasn't afraid of them. Just the opposite, in fact. The other kids thought I was super brave because I would walk in here alone, buy a candy bar or gum, and then browse the rows of colorful fabric that was stacked up on large tables in the middle of the store. Maybe it was because I wasn't afraid of her, but Verna liked me." I quieted at the memory, and a smile tugged at the corners of my mouth.

Maxim set his beer on the coffee table and gazed at me. He remained silent as I continued. "Verna kept a large pot of coffee going all day and had two small round tables with four chairs each that were for customers only. After the purchases had been made, she and her customers would drink coffee, discuss quilting patterns and gossip. Because she liked me, Verna let me sit with the women and join in their conversations. She'd give me a can of Coke 'on the house' and I'd drink it while listening to the chatter." I chuckled at the memory. "It was amusing to watch her chase off the lazy coffee drinkers — all men — who didn't buy anything. To my young mind this place was heaven."

Maxim folded his hands in his lap and regarded me with kindness. "It sounds like it."

I sipped at the beer and set the can on the coffee table. "The smell of coffee combined with the smell of the old building was mesmerizing. If I close my eyes I can smell it now." I paused for a few seconds, my eyes half closed. "We lived in the country and Dad often brought me to town when he ran errands. He knew I'd be safe at Rogers Variety Store, and so I was here a lot." I frowned. "Mother thought it was odd for me to hang out with Verna, so Dad and I never mentioned my visits to the store."

Maxim leaned back and laced his fingers behind his head. "I wonder if that's why you turned it into a coffeehouse. The smell of coffee brought you so much comfort, and this was a happy place for you as a child. Smell is a powerful component of memory. A certain smell can instantly transport me back to a childhood event."

I stared at the scar above his right eyebrow. "I think it was. I really do. Coffee was synonymous with this building. It seemed the right fit. And when I came home after …"

I stopped short, shocked that I'd almost gone there, and instinctively reached for the pendant hanging at my throat. Maxim remained quiet and his gaze never left my face. I wondered if I was imagining the tears I saw in his eyes. Even though he was a curious man, he didn't ask me to continue, and I was grateful. He seemed to have a sixth sense for such things. I cleared my throat and shook my head, as if those actions would loosen the memories threatening to surface.

I reached for my beer, drained a generous swallow and then held it in both hands. "Anyway, when I moved home I was looking for something to do with my life, and Dad suggested we buy this building and restore it. It had been vacant for about ten years after Harvey and Verna's health deteriorated and they moved to an assisted-living facility near their son, Stan. They tried to sell it, but no one was interested. Stan was grateful to finally have a buyer, and when I told him about all the time I'd spent here as a child, he sold it to us for a song."

Maxim was silent, his expression unreadable.

"Stan had sold all of the stock and most of the fixtures out of the building, so I was surprised that the two round tables and chairs were still here."

Maxim leaned forward. "You mean the round tables by the front window? Those are the ones you sat at when you were a little girl?"

I grinned. "Yes. You can imagine how thrilled I was. The other tables down there I found at auctions and second-hand stores, and I spent a lot of time sanding and re-staining them. But I left Verna's tables and chairs exactly as they were, except for some wood cleaner and polish. They're the most valuable things in my shop."

Maxim smiled and leaned back in the chair. "Well, I think it's fitting you turned the building into a coffeehouse. I think Verna would be pleased. I'm not sure about Harvey, since he was so grumpy. Did he drink coffee too?"

I nodded. "Oh, yes. They both drank coffee all day." I laughed and set the beer on the table. "I honor their memories by doing the same."

Maxim's eyebrows shot up. "You drink coffee all day?"

I tucked my feet under my legs. "Yep."

"Wow. I can't handle that much caffeine. I'd never sleep." He snapped his fingers. "That's probably why you don't sleep at night."

I shook my head. "I may have exaggerated when I said, 'all day.' I drink as much as I can handle until we close at 2, then I'm done. Well, except for the past two afternoons with you." I looked at him and blushed at the memory of his compliment in the snow. I hurried on. "My doctor said to stop drinking caffeine at 2 pm because of my sleeping problem, and I'm a good girl and follow her instructions … most of the time, anyway. It hasn't helped, but I see where she's coming from."

We sat in silence, lost in our own thoughts, until Maxim spoke. "I started drinking coffee in college. We pulled a lot of all-nighters studying. When did you start?"

"When I was a little girl I would beg Mother for a sip of her coffee, but she said it would stunt my growth." I smiled at the memory. "When she wasn't looking I'd sneak sips, and when she was out of the kitchen I'd drink what was left in the bottom of the pot, grounds and all."

Maxim screwed up his face in disgust. "That nasty stuff? You were desperate." He grabbed his beer and swigged it, as if to wash down some imaginary coffee grounds stuck in his throat.

"Yes, I was. On the morning I turned thirteen I walked into the kitchen my usual groggy, grumpy self, and Dad handed me a cup of coffee in my very own Birthday Bear mug — remember the Care Bears? I was shocked. Dad grinned from ear to ear as I greedily slurped the Nectar of the Gods, as he called it. Mother frowned the entire time but kept her mouth shut. Dad said, 'I don't think it will stunt your growth now that you're a teenager.' I was already five-foot-ten and still growing. I've drunk a pot of coffee every day since."

Maxim grinned. "You're addicted to coffee."

I laughed. "You're right. I guess it's not the worst addiction in the world."

"No, it's not."

I was searching for something to say when my cell phone dinged with an incoming message. "Excuse me a minute." I grabbed the phone off the coffee table and saw I had a text from Peggy. I tapped the message and read it. "I'm sorry about the interruption but I need to answer this. It's the woman who bakes pies for my shop." I grinned. "We call her The Pie Lady. She uses my kitchen and wants to know if it's available in the morning."

Maxim furrowed his brows. "Why wouldn't it be? You're closed tomorrow, right?"

"Yes, but several bakers use my kitchen because it's so big and the fact that it's already been cleared by The Health Department. In Kansas, if you make food in your home you can only sell it at farmers markets or directly to consumers."

Maxim nodded. "I didn't know that. By all means, please answer The Pie Lady's text. Sounds like serious business."

I pointed an index finger at him. "You have no idea, Mr. Hall. My customers take their pie very seriously. Peggy is a celebrity around here."

"Sounds like I need to try it. While you do that, may I use your bathroom?"

"Sure." I gestured behind him. "It's the first door on your right. The second door is my closet, and right now it looks like a tornado went through it, so please stay out of there."

Maxim stood and smiled. "You're tempting me to take a peek." At my look of disapproval he held up both hands. "On second thought I'll stay out of there. Be right back." He disappeared into the bathroom, and I heard the door lock.

I opened the text from Peggy and typed a reply: "Yes, the kitchen is open in the morning. Text me when you leave your house and I'll unlock the back door for you." I hit send.

Several seconds later she answered: "I was thinking around 8. See you then."

I sent her the thumbs-up emoji, turned off my phone and set it down. I jumped up and walked to the bookcase where I bent down and picked up a thick, brown notebook with frayed edges and papers sticking out the top and side. Its weight was substantial, and I hurriedly carried it to the kitchen table and set it down with a thunk.

Maxim stepped out of the bathroom and eyed my closet door. "Are you sure you don't want me to take a look?" He grinned broadly and I was blown away by his brilliant blue eyes, dimples and straight, white teeth. I wondered if he knew his effect on me.

I shook my head and smiled in spite of myself. "You do have an ornery side, don't you?"

"That's not the first time I've heard that." His gaze dropped from my face to the book my hand was resting on. "Is that your grandfather's scrapbook?"

I nodded and he walked over and stopped right next to me beside the table. He smelled earthy and woodsy and clean — thrillingly like a man — and his aura grabbed my senses and sent my head spinning. I reached for the back of a chair to steady myself and was transported back in time to another tall, strong man who always smelled wonderfully masculine. It would have been so easy to turn and lean into Maxim's chest; I imagined his body against mine, his fingers in my hair, his breath on my forehead. I could almost feel his lips on my cheeks, my chin … my lips. God, it had been so long since I wanted a man to touch me, and I was shocked that I wanted to touch him. I shook my head to clear it and hurriedly stepped to the opposite side of the table where I sat down, folded my hands in my lap and stared at the scrapbook.

If Maxim sensed my jumbled feelings he didn't let on. He sat down in the chair next to the scrapbook and lifted the cover. "This is a huge book. Everything in here is about Waconda Springs and the lake?" His tone was incredulous.

"Yes. Grandpa Somers was born in 1924 and was 40 years old when they broke ground for the dam. The farm he grew up on was only a mile from Waconda Springs. He lived through all of it and kept everything … pictures and souvenirs from the spring, newspaper articles about the dam, pictures of when the dam was built … it goes on and on."

"He was a man of foresight."

"Yes, he was."

As Maxim turned the pages with extreme care, almost reverence, he studied each one in meticulous detail. "The main building at the health resort was enormous for the time and place it was built. Looks like it was three stories tall with dozens of guest rooms."

I relaxed and sat back in my chair. "Yes. And there were family cottages as well. The reason people came to the Waconda Health Resort or whatever it was called at the time — they kept changing the name — was because the mineral water was thought to be medicinal. A lot of sick people came here hoping the water would heal them."

Maxim glanced up. "Did it?"

I nodded. "There are numerous accounts of people being cured by the water."

Maxim lifted a small, aged brochure from the scrapbook and carefully opened it. "This is when it was the Nature Cure Sanitarium." He turned several pages and stopped. "Here's a picture of G.F. Abrams. It says he's the founder."

I smiled. "Close enough. He didn't actually start it, but he's the one who expanded and improved upon the original plan."

Maxim looked at the next page. "Here's a picture of Dr. Carl Bingesser. It says he's the superintendent, and here's his wife, Anna. She was a naturopath. I guess I thought that was a modern term."

"No, they did lots of cutting-edge treatments here."

Maxim nodded. "The brochure says hydrotherapy, massage, neuropathy, chiropractic, electrotherapy and dietetics."

"Carl and Anna's son, Dr. Carlos Bingesser, said the water 'will clean your works until your works work.'"

Maxim chuckled. "Marketing at its best. I love it." He returned the brochure to the scrapbook, flipped to the next page and stared at me in awe. "Are these what I think they are?" He ran a finger down the page and stopped. "These are labels for the bottles of Waconda Water, am I right?"

I smiled at his excitement. "You're right. Aren't they beautiful? The profile of the Native American Chief is so regal."

Maxim read the label. "Greatest of natural waters. Waconda Water. From Great Spirit Spring, Waconda, Kansas. Nature's best remedy for sick headache, indigestion, constipation and biliousness." He directed a curious look at me. "What's biliousness?"

"Too much bile from the liver or gallbladder."

He frowned. "Sorry I asked."

I leaned on the table and studied him with interest. "Don't forget that curiosity killed the cat."

"Well, right now I am one curious cat." Maxim continued turning the pages of the scrapbook, stopping to study what caught his attention. "Here's a photo from the ground-breaking of the dam. It says 6,000 attended on October 1, 1964. Your grandfather dated and labeled everything in here."

I sat up straighter. "Like I said, he was a true historian. He knew that it was important to keep a detailed record. In the back of the book are a bunch of photos he took ... the dam being built, houses and buildings being moved to different locations and others knocked down before the lake covered everything."

Maxim gazed up at me. "This is a treasure. Thank you for inviting me over to see it." He looked at his briefcase on the counter. "I should take some notes."

"Don't worry about that right now. I'd like you to take it with you and spend some time studying it. Return it to me when you're done."

He stared at me as if I'd grown a second nose. "I couldn't do that."

"Why not?"

He stumbled over his words. "It wouldn't feel right. I mean, what if it gets damaged while I have it?"

I crossed my arms. "How could you possibly damage it?"

"I could drop it in the snow. Or Lucy's B and B could burn down." He snapped his fingers. "Or I could forget to return it and take it with me to New York."

I sighed. "You have quite the imagination. Just take it with you, okay? That way you can spend some time looking through it and then just drop it by the shop when you're done."

He remained quiet for a few minutes as he turned the pages of the old scrapbook. Finally he shrugged and sat back in his chair. "Okay, you win. But if something happens to this family treasure while it's in my possession, it's on you. I can tell it's a waste of time to argue." He crossed his arms and glanced at me. "Do you always get your way?"

I rose and walked to the refrigerator. "Not as often as I wish. Are you hungry yet?"

"Now that you mention it, I'm starving. I haven't eaten since Lucy's ham and cheese omelet for breakfast."

I opened the freezer, pulled out a boxed pizza and set it on the counter. "What time was that?"

"Around 9, I think."

"You haven't eaten since 9 this morning?"

He rubbed his chin. "I'm one of those people who forgets to eat. Like I said, I was on a conference call for several hours today."

I set the oven to 425 degrees, turned to face him and leaned against the counter. "I never forget to eat. I can't imagine."

Maxim scanned the length of me, running his eyes over my body from head to toe. "Well, I'll tell you one thing. It looks damn good on you."

My face instantly turned hot, and if the counter hadn't been holding me up I might have fallen over. I blushed and stared at the floor.

Maxim rubbed his forehead. "I've made you uncomfortable again. And in your own home. I'm sorry."

I kept my gaze on the floor, studying the pattern in the wood. "I'm not very good with compliments. I never know what to say, especially with men."

"Well, I'm not very good at keeping my mouth shut."

I lifted my face and looked at him. His eyes were closed, and he was massaging the space between his eyebrows and shaking his head. "It's okay. I should have just thanked you. It was nice of you to say."

His eyes opened but he focused on the scrapbook in front of him. "You're a beautiful woman. It's hard not to mention it."

I smiled. "Thank you."

He looked at me then, and when he saw my expression he relaxed visibly. He sat forward, turned another page of the scrapbook and became absorbed in a picture of the dam construction, this one showing bulldozers pushing dirt up a steep incline.

I glanced at the oven temperature … 250 degrees. I turned around and pulled a pizza pan from a drawer, and then I opened the box of beef and bacon pizza, removed the plastic wrapping and placed the pizza in the center of the round pan. I sat down at the table and interrupted his study of a newspaper clipping. "By the way, I started your newest book last night."

I was not prepared for the look on Maxim's face, a combination of shock, confusion and panic. He didn't move a muscle and his mouth was a straight line. I didn't know what to make of his reaction, so I sat in silence as my mind ran over what I'd said. The simple act of reading a book seemed innocuous. What was going on here?

Maxim dropped his gaze to the scrapbook. "What chapter are you on?"

I couldn't remember. "I'm not sure. I think I read three, maybe four chapters before I fell asleep on the couch." I studied his expression, but it was flat and unreadable.

He still didn't look at me. "What do you think of it so far?"

I stumbled over my words. "It's good. I mean, I really can't give you a review yet because I just started reading, but it certainly grabbed my attention. It's beautifully descriptive, as all of your books are." I didn't tell him that the story line was hitting close to home but that I was determined to push past my insecurities and anxiety. I waited for more questions, but he was quiet, stoic even. I stumbled on like a drunk leaving a bar at 2 in the morning. "I'm looking forward to reading more tonight." The silence extended and multiplied.

When the buzzer rang, indicating the oven was at 425 degrees, I jumped up, relieved at the interruption. I slid the pizza into the oven, shut the door and set the timer for fifteen minutes.

I opened the refrigerator and pulled out a bagged salad and a bottle of ranch dressing. I found a glass bowl in a cabinet, pulled open the plastic bag and dumped in the salad. I turned and set the bowl and dressing in the middle of the table. Maxim was reading a newspaper clipping and didn't look up when I spoke. "Please don't tell Caitlin I served you salad. I'd never hear the end of it."

Maxim didn't react right away. When he finally glanced up he looked like all of the energy had been sucked from his body. He forced a smile, and I wondered why the conversation had deteriorated when I mentioned his book. "Is Caitlin the salad police?"

I sat down. "Pretty much. I'm not a healthy eater and she's always lecturing me about eating 'greens and fruits.' To Caitlin, all of the world's problems would be solved if we ate enough 'greens and fruits.'"

In spite of his somber mood, Maxim laughed. "Rest assured I won't say a word." He peeked at me and then dropped his gaze, once more, to the scrapbook which I could tell he wasn't really looking at anymore. "She seems like a sweet person. Caitlin."

"Oh, she is. Brice got lucky with that one. He was a confirmed bachelor, and then she moved back to town."

"One look and he was a goner?"

I grinned and tucked a stray hair behind my ear. "Pretty much. Caitlin grew up in Waconda but she's six years younger than Brice, so he never paid any attention to her. She went to college on a track scholarship — she was a state champion in pole vault — and when she moved home to work at the bank she was gorgeous. Lots of guys wanted to date her. I really think it was love at first sight, at least for him." I laughed. "She didn't make it easy. He had to work to win her over, but he finally did. They're a good match."

I watched Maxim perk up as I told the story. With his natural curiosity it was easy to see why he was an exceptional storyteller. "Were you and Caitlin best friends growing up?"

"No, I knew her, but we didn't hang out. After she and Brice got married we became close." I leaned forward. "She's a wonderful listener and a kind person. I'm lucky to have her as a friend. She really does care about me eating healthier; I guess she's rubbing off on me. Why else would I buy a bag of salad?"

Maxim sat back and crossed his arms. "Consider yourself lucky to have someone care enough to nag." He shook his head and chuckled. "That's what my mom always said when she was nagging me, anyway."

"I know you're right. She sounds like a smart woman." I jumped up and pulled two dinner plates out of a cabinet, and then I opened a drawer and grabbed forks and the basket of napkins. I set the items on the table and turned on the oven light. "Let's see if I've burned up the pizza yet." I bent over and peeked through the oven's window. "No, it looks good. There's still plenty of time to ruin it." I pulled two clear drinking glasses out of a cabinet. I glanced at Maxim over my shoulder. "Seltzer or plain water?"

"Seltzer sounds good."

I filled the glasses with ice, retrieved two cans of seltzer water from the refrigerator, opened them with a hiss and poured the bubbly water into the glasses.

I handed one to maxim. He reached for it but didn't look at me. "Thank you."

I sat down, drank some seltzer and set the glass on the table. Although the mood was lighter, silence settled between us, and I loathed the awkwardness. Maxim stared at the scrapbook, but I could tell he was in his own world. I was baffled by the emotional turn in our conversation and struggled to come up with something to say. I suddenly remembered his website.

"So I found your 'official' website last night." Maxim glanced up and his gaze was intense; I couldn't read his expression. Was it surprise again or dismay at my audacity? I fumbled around and continued. "It's great … I mean, I really like the black and white theme. It's striking." He didn't say anything but continued to stare into my eyes. "So I was reading your scheduled appearances this month and

I noticed they were canceled for the rest of December, like you said, but a book signing in Denver, Colorado, tomorrow night is still listed." He rubbed his forehead and looked down. "I know it's none of my business, but I was just wondering if you're going to that one."

After several seconds he raised his head and smiled weakly. Everything I said seemed to be causing him angst, and I was helpless to explain it. "Yes, I'm going to Denver tomorrow." My heart sank at the news. "That was the main argument with my publisher this morning. I wanted to cancel but he put the screws to me concerning my next book." He drummed his fingers on the table. "If I don't show up at the book signing in Denver tomorrow they're going to terminate my contract."

I gasped. "Did they really say that?"

"Believe it or not, they did." He ran his hands through his hair. "I've been with them for over ten years and they're ready to dump me if I don't obey like a little lap dog. Do you know how much money I've made them? It really pisses me off."

I was at a loss for words. No wonder he was moody; I would be too.

He locked fingers behind his head. "Laurie found a flight from Hays to Denver that leaves at 2:20 tomorrow afternoon. She said the flight takes less than an hour. Hays is west of here, right?"

"Yes, it's about an hour and a half drive. It's on Interstate 70." I chewed a fingernail.

Maxim's irritation was palpable; his cheeks were red, and the muscles of his jaw were clenched. "They made it clear I have no choice in the matter. 'Show up or you're out' were the exact words. I'll fly back Tuesday and pick up my stuff at Lucy's before I drive home for Christmas."

So he was coming back to Waconda. My shoulders relaxed and I shook my head. The relief I felt surprised me, and I wondered if he could sense my growing feelings for him. I was powerless to control the emotions that swirled inside of me when it came to Maxim Hall.

The buzzer went off, and I jumped up and opened the oven. "Good news! I didn't burn it this time." Using hot pads, I lifted the pizza pan and set it on the stove. I turned off the oven and left the door open a crack to warm the room.

Maxim closed the scrapbook and slid it to one side of the table. His face was returning to its regular color and he grinned broadly. "Congratulations on not burning the pizza." He paused. "And thanks again for inviting me over. I'm sorry I'm such a mess tonight. There's a lot going on in my brain."

I cut the pizza into six slices, served us each one and sat down at the table. "You really don't need to apologize. You're under a lot of pressure."

"And obviously about ready to explode." He focused his attention on me. "But tonight helps. You have no idea. Supper with a smart and beautiful woman. I'm feeling better already." Suddenly aware of the compliment that had slipped out, he peeked at me shyly.

I sat up straight. "Smart and beautiful? Why, thank you, Mr. Hall." I reached for the bowl of salad and scooped a small amount onto my plate. I handed it to Maxim.

"I'm proud of you for accepting the compliment so graciously." He loaded his plate with salad, and after I doused mine with ranch dressing, I handed the bottle to him.

He poured dressing on his salad and set the bottle on the table. "Is this a formal dinner or can I eat the pizza with my hands?"

"This is definitely not a formal dinner." I picked up my slice of pizza and bit into it. Maxim did the same. It was hot but manageable.

After three generous bites I nibbled at the salad. "The flight from Hays to Denver is amazingly easy. I've been on it several times."

Maxim stared at me, his mouth full of pizza. He swallowed and tilted his head. "You've flown from Hays to Denver?"

I pretended to be insulted. "I do have a life outside of Waconda."

"I didn't know the Chamber of Commerce President had time to travel. I guess I shouldn't be surprised."

I grudgingly stabbed the salad with my fork. "I love the mountains. In fact, I'm quite the snow skier." He stopped chewing and regarded me in what seemed like admiration. "But when I take that flight to Denver it's for the shopping. The first weekend of December Caitlin and I take a girls weekend and fly to Denver for some power shopping. We've also gone a couple of times in the summer."

Maxim grinned. "A shopping weekend for the girls. I actually know Denver quite well. Where do you shop?"

"Our favorite spot in the 16th Street Mall."

"That's an amazing area, and there are loads of excellent restaurants. Where do you stay?" Maxim popped the last bite of pizza into his mouth.

I shrugged. "Wherever we can get the cheapest room. As long as it's clean and the bedding has been washed, we'll take it. We don't spend much time in the room anyway." Seeing his plate was empty I rose and turned to the stove. "Would you like more pizza?"

"Please."

I picked up the spatula. "How about two slices?"

"That would be great. I'm really hungry."

I slid two slices onto his plate and one onto mine. I sat back down. "Where do you stay when you're in Denver?"

"My publisher always puts me up in The Brown Palace." He took a huge bite of pizza and chewed quietly.

I was stunned. "You mean that fancy hotel and spa on 17th Street?" He nodded and continued chewing. "I've heard it has the most amazing atrium, but I've never been there. Caitlin and I love looking at all of the Christmas decorations in the city. Denver at Christmastime is magical."

Maxim smiled in agreement. "It really is." He finished his second slice of pizza and dove into the third.

I sipped my seltzer and sat back in the chair. "On our trip earlier this month Caitlin saw a purse she absolutely loved in a store at the 16th Street Mall. It was an Americana design — red, white and blue. She's a sucker for anything patriotic. She spent 20 minutes debating whether it was worth $85 and finally decided it was too expensive. That's Caitlin." I smiled at her frugality. "After we left the store my plan was to sneak back and buy it for her as a Christmas gift, but she wouldn't let me out of her sight, so I finally gave up. I looked for one like it online but apparently it's handmade and one-of-a-kind." I shook my head. "I called the store, but they don't do mail orders. The owner is pretty snooty. Apparently it's beneath them to package an item and mail it to a customer. Caitlin would have loved that purse." I frowned and bit into my pizza.

Maxim ignored his unfinished pizza, sat back in the chair and furrowed his brows in concentration. I continued chewing as he rubbed his chin and regarded me with scrutiny. After a minute he leaned forward, looked me straight in the eye and proposed an idea that was so preposterous it mentally blew me out of my seat. "Why don't you come to Denver with me tomorrow?"

My fork stopped in midair and ranch dressing dripped off the lettuce and onto the plate. My mouth dropped open and my brain was rocked in shock and awe. Bewilderment swept through my body. Did I hear right? Surely not. I think

Maxim Hall just invited me to Denver, but that couldn't be. Confusion racked my brain. Why would Maxim Hall want me at his book signing? Did I need a hearing aid?

He rushed to explain as I set down my fork and fiddled with the pendant on my necklace. "Honestly, I would love the company. You have no idea how boring these book tours are. You travel alone to a city, sign some books, and then travel to another city, still alone." He ran his fingers through his hair, standing it up on end. "And listen, it would be totally platonic. I'm a gentleman. In fact, I'll have you talk to my agent, Laurie. She can vouch for my character." He stopped talking and watched me, but I didn't know what to say.

He continued at a fast pace. "I'll pay for everything … flight, hotel room, food. You'd have your own room and I would stay away from it, cross my heart." He actually lifted his index finger and crossed his heart. I smiled and looked down at my hands. "And we can stop by that store and see if they still have the purse Caitlin wanted." When I remained quiet he sat back and folded his hands behind his head. "You think I'm crazy, don't you?"

I was at a loss for words. I picked at a cuticle and avoided his gaze.

He lowered his hands and leaned forward. "You've been so kind to me, and I'd just like to return the favor."

I laughed and glanced up. "So I drive you to the Waconda Springs replica in my old Ford pickup, and to return the favor you fly me to Denver and pay for me to stay in one of the fanciest hotels in the city?" He grinned and rubbed his forehead. "Yes, I think you're crazy."

After a minute he sat back and rested his hands on the table. "Okay, you got me there, but I still think you should come with me." His face was animated as he continued. "Think about it. Denver at Christmastime. You know how beautiful it is. The Brown Palace Hotel. Did you know that at Christmas they decorate the chandelier with thousands of twinkle lights? You'd be blown away by their Christmas decorations. And you said you've always wanted to see the atrium. It really is spectacular. And let's not forget the purse for Caitlin. She'd love you forever if you bought it for her. As a bonus, The Bookworm, where I'm signing my book, is world-famous … it's in historic LoDo."

My head was spinning with the arguments he was throwing my way. "You're really going for the hard sell here, aren't you?"

Maxim folded his hands and stared into my eyes. "Are you hesitating because you have a boyfriend?"

I shook my head. "No, that's not it. I'm just wondering what the people around here would say about me traipsing off with a man I just met … that's so unlike me."

"You already told me they think you're certifiable. Besides, it would give them something to talk about. I get the feeling that gossip grows pretty stale in Waconda."

I laughed. He had a point. "But what would my family think? Brice would totally freak out. I mean, I don't even know you very well."

Maxim crossed his arms. "Okay, so we're still getting to know each other, but like I said, this would be an innocent trip between new friends. We'd leave late morning tomorrow and be back in the afternoon on Tuesday. You said you're closed on Mondays, so you'd just miss Tuesday. Could you swing it?"

It felt insane to even consider the idea of flying with him to Denver, but I ran through the options. "I'd have to call Aunt Judy and see what she thinks. She can't run the place by herself, but one of my summer workers, Hannah, is home from college for Christmas break and she may be able to work for me. She was the one handing out cupcakes on Friday. She's always looking to make a few extra bucks, and she's filled in for me before. That's the only way I could go; Aunt Judy refuses to touch the espresso machine. I don't know. Can I just take off like that, and right before Christmas?"

Maxim steepled his fingers. "I get the feeling that you don't take much time for yourself. Just think of my invitation as an early Christmas gift from a writer to one of his readers. And if you're worrying about the money, I can afford it. I love to splurge on special people."

I ran my fingers through my hair and sighed. "What are you doing to me? Now I'm actually considering your crazy idea."

Maxim laughed. "I knew I'd wear you down. Listen, I'm going to call my agent, Laurie, and have her talk to you. She'll vouch for the fact that I'm a good guy and a total gentleman. She's been my agent for five years so she should know me by now."

I didn't argue as he pulled out his phone and dialed Laurie. My brain had quickly moved from shock to disbelief to acceptance. I was already picturing us rushing through Denver International Airport. He was a persuasive man.

I watched him hold the phone to his ear, brows furrowed in concentration as he listened to Laurie's phone ring. He sat up when she answered. "Yeah, it's me." There was a short pause as he listened. "No, everything's fine. Don't worry, I'm still going to Denver tomorrow." He rolled his eyes and twirled a finger in the air as Laurie talked. His impatience amused me. "No, you're right. I will be a good little boy at the book signing. Listen, I'm sitting here with Bree Somers, the woman who owns the coffeeshop in Waconda. She's been helping me with research … I told you about her." He winked at me and I blushed. He'd been talking to his agent about me? I didn't know what to think. "I've invited her to fly to Denver with me tomorrow for my book signing, and I'm trying to convince her that I'm a good guy and that she will be totally safe traveling with me. Would you talk to her, please, and vouch for my character?" He listened and grinned. "Okay. Thanks. Here she is."

Maxim reached across the table and handed me his phone. Suddenly nervous, I accepted it with shaking hands and held it to my ear. "This is Bree."

"Hi, Bree. This is Laurie Lane, Maxim's book agent." Her voice was light and bubbly. I pictured a brunette with perfect hair and a thick day planner.

"Hi, Laurie. Um, this is a bit awkward for me."

"I can imagine. But listen, Maxim is an amazing man. I've known him for five years and he really is a stand-up guy. He always treats me with respect and goes out of his way to show his appreciation for my work. You would be totally safe traveling with him, and I think you'd have a really good time." She paused and lowered her voice. "Don't tell Maxim I told you this, but the guy's lonely. I know he's a well-known writer and all, but in my line of work I've learned that it's often the famous people who are the loneliest. I worry about him. With his boys both in college now, I think he's a little lost. And listen … if he asked you, he really wants you to go. He doesn't make a habit of inviting women along on his book tours."

I'd wondered about that and was relieved at the news. Maxim was sitting at full attention and staring a hole through me, so I decided to have a little fun at his expense. "So you're saying he's a ladies' man and I should stay as far away from him as I can? Thanks for warning me, Laurie. You're a good woman."

The look on Maxim's face was priceless, a mixture of surprise and fear with a touch of skepticism. He couldn't tell whether or not I was joking. He sat back, closed his eyes and rubbed his forehead with both hands.

Laurie chuckled. "Good for you, sister. I'm so glad you just did that to him. He's a great guy, like I said, but he can be a real pain in the ass sometimes, especially when it comes to negotiating his contract." She laughed and then returned to the business at hand. "Anyway, if you decide to go, I'll book your flight and hotel room. I know the flight still had some seats left. The hotel will be a little more challenging since it's right before Christmas, but I have a few tricks up my sleeve and should be able to get you a room. The manager owes me a favor."

I chewed on a fingernail. "Okay. Let me think about it. I appreciate you talking to me. I'm going to give you back to Maxim."

I handed the phone to Maxim; he grabbed it and held it to his ear. "So I'm a ladies' man, huh? Thanks a lot." He listened to Laurie for a few moments and suddenly understanding crossed his features. He pointed an accusing finger at me. "So did you actually give her a good sell?" He ran his fingernail along a groove in the table as she talked. "Thank God. I told Bree that she should be a stand-up comic. She has quite the sense of humor." He sat in silence and then looked at me. "I can't really tell on this end. She's chewing her fingernail and frowning. It's never good when a woman does that." He smiled at me and twirled his finger in the air again. "Okay. The moment she gives me the go-ahead I'll call you back so you can make the arrangements. Thanks again."

He tapped the End Call button on his phone and put it in his back pocket. I rose and walked to the couch where I sank into the cushions and propped my feet on the coffee table. "What have you done to me, Maxim?" I laid my head back and closed my eyes.

He walked over and sat in the chair closest to me. He folded his hands behind his head and remained quiet.

My mind played like a tennis match, back and forth, back and forth.

It would be insane to take off on a trip with a man I'd met just two days ago. But wouldn't it be equally insane to turn down the chance to fly to Denver with a bestselling writer? As the old axiom goes, "You only live once."

Brice would no doubt question my common sense. He'd probably blame my recklessness on Mother's engagement. But Caitlin would encourage me to take a chance and live a little, I knew she would. She constantly prodded me to date, and wouldn't this be the ultimate first date?

The people of Waconda, my own customers, would gossip about me. Would I lose their respect if I threw caution to the wind? On the other hand I didn't really care what they thought or said. In fact, the gossip would sustain them for weeks. I'd be doing them a favor, actually. Level-headed Bree Somers takes off with world-famous author, Maxim Hall, to an undisclosed location for a romantic rendezvous. Or to Denver for a book signing. They're similar.

I wondered how Dad, if he were alive, would react if I jetted off with Maxim. I waited for inspiration from beyond, but nothing came to me, no great oracle guiding the way.

Danny didn't speak to me, either. It was crazy to listen for words of direction from my dead fiancé, and yet I somehow expected him to tell me whether or not a trip to Denver with Maxim would upset him. If he was truly in heaven as we were taught in Sunday School, I figured he was engaged in more enlightening pursuits than my day-to-day life. Maxim defined our relationship as a friendship, and I would simply need to make sure it stayed that way.

One thing I knew for sure … life is short. The tragedies I'd been dealt proved that when happiness came along you needed to grab it and hold on for dear life. And when a kind person offered you a generous gift it was best to accept and say thank you. I was tired of living safely, of coloring within the lines, of crossing my t's and dotting my i's.

I peeked at Maxim. His head was lowered, his eyes were closed. His long lashes touched his cheeks, and I wondered what he was thinking. Was he truly lonely as Laurie guessed? My heart fluttered. Here was an amazingly gorgeous and kind man, admittedly a little moody, sitting next to me in my living room, and he'd invited me to Denver as a friend. To sum it up, I'd be crazy not to go. It was only Denver, for Lord's sake. It's not like I'd be flying to Paris with him.

I cleared my throat and Maxim opened his eyes, the question hanging between us as we gazed at each other. I smiled. He smiled. "Let me call Aunt Judy."

"Yes!" Maxim sat forward and pumped his fist. He jumped up and moved to the couch, sat next to me and reached for my hands which he squeezed gently, stroking my fingers. His tender look melted my heart, and I felt the heat travel up my fingers, into my arms and radiate through my body. I desperately wanted to pull his fingers to my lips and kiss them, but I restrained myself. He would be so easy to love, and the thought surprised me.

"Thank you. You won't regret this. Denver, here we come!"

Chapter 16

I dreaded this phone call most of all, but I had to make it. I tapped the number on my phone, settled back into the cushions of the couch and pulled the quilt across my knees. Caitlin answered on the third ring.

"Hey, Bree. Whatcha doin'?"

"Not much. What's up there?"

"Oh, just got the boys to bed. Three days of school this week, the music program, then Christmas break. With all of the excitement it's hard to get them calmed down."

I nodded. "I remember the feeling."

"Hey, just a friendly reminder about the boys' school program on Wednesday. Are you still planning to come?"

I traced a star on the quilt. "Of course. I wouldn't miss it. 7 pm?"

"Yes. They won't tell me a thing about their parts. Apparently it's a big secret."

"I can't wait." Silence settled between us and Caitlin yawned. I pulled the quilt across my chest and tucked it under my arms. "I need to tell you something, but I want you to promise to stay very calm and don't yell for Brice right away like you usually do. Are you alone?"

"Yes, I'm in the kitchen. Brice is watching TV."

I hesitated for a moment, finding the right words. "Well, I invited Maxim Hall over tonight to look at Grandpa's scrapbook about Waconda Springs, and we had a great time. We talked and he ate supper with me. It was nice. He's ... well, he's quite a man. Anyway, he sort of ... he kind of ... well, he asked me to fly to Denver with him tomorrow for a book signing." I closed my eyes and prayed she'd understand.

Silence settled on the other end of the phone. Caitlin's voice was soft. "What did you tell him?"

I picked at a small hole in the quilt. "Well, at first I was like, hell no, of course not. What kind of crazy person would do something like that? But then I started to imagine how much fun it would be, and he had me talk to his agent, Laurie, and she said he's a really great guy and a true gentleman. And then I thought about how you only live once, you know, and would I regret it if I said no."

I knew I was rambling, but I couldn't stop. "And then I thought about the people in town and wondered what they would think, but then I decided they can say what they want, this is my life and it's about time I lived it. And then I thought about Brice, and I knew he'd freak out, and I'm still kind of worried he's going to totally freak out. Well ... anyway ... I finally said yes." Caitlin was quiet and then I heard muffled sobs. "Catey? Are you okay, honey?"

"I don't know what to say." Her tears worried me. She sniffled and I heard her blow her nose. "I'm so happy for you. This is what I've wanted for a long time now."

I was surprised. "Really? You don't think I'm totally loco for flying to Denver with a man I met two days ago?"

"You know I already think you're crazy, right? I'm just thrilled you're finally taking a chance with a man. I'm so happy I could explode." She actually cheered and I was afraid Brice would hear her. "I only met him one time, but I can tell he's a good man. And I mean, you talked to his agent, and she's a woman; if he was a total pig she would know about it by now, right? I say go for it. Life's too short." She sniffled again and blew her nose with gusto.

I stared at Rosie the Riveter hanging above my TV. "Oh, I don't know. I'm still not sure if it's the right thing to do. He really does seem like a good man, but I don't know if I'm ready for this. Am I ready? He's been nothing but a total gentleman, and he even said the trip is platonic and we're going as friends, but I'm sure that if I made a move he would reciprocate. I'm scared of what might happen. Is that what I want?" I paused and a sob caught in my throat. "What would Danny think?"

Caitlin's voice gained strength. "I'll tell you what Danny would think. Danny O'Neill would tell you that it's been ten years, that you've suffered long enough, and that it's time for you to focus on yourself. He would tell you to go. I know he would."

I cried openly. "I'm sure you're right, but it still feels like a betrayal. I don't even know if anything will happen with Maxim, or even if that's what he wants.

We've become friends and it feels really good to have a man as a friend again. I've missed that."

"Of course you have, honey. You need to quit thinking so much and go with your heart." She paused and I could hear her goofy smile. "I'll want all of the details, of course."

I laughed through my tears. "Of course you will. There may not be any to give."

"I have a feeling you'll have some tidbits to share. I mean, you're going to a book signing, right? That will be exciting. There are women who would kill to be in your spot."

She had a point. "Yeah, I bet there are. I'll probably see some of them tomorrow night."

"So you said you're leaving tomorrow. When do you come back?"

"Tuesday."

"That's a quick trip."

I nodded. "We're taking the 2:20 flight from Hays to Denver, his book signing is tomorrow night, and then we'll be back here late Tuesday afternoon. I think he's going to leave town on Wednesday. His boys will be home for Christmas, and I can tell he's anxious to see them."

"How old are they?"

I paused to consider. "I can't remember exactly, but they're both in college."

"Okay. And who's manning the espresso machine on Tuesday? I know Judy won't go near that thing."

I grinned and crossed my ankles. "Hannah said she could work on Tuesday. You should have heard Aunt Judy when I told her that Maxim Hall was taking me to Denver." I laughed. "She actually screamed. She was so thrilled she may have peed her pants. She told me to have fun and not to worry about the coffee shop; she'd man the ship. She literally said that."

Caitlin giggled. "Good ol' Aunt Judy."

"I know. She's a gem." My smile faded and I turned serious. "It's really Brice I'm worried about. He won't like this at all."

Caitlin agreed. "No, I don't think he will."

I sighed and traced another star on the quilt. "What do you suggest?"

There was silence on the line as Caitlin considered my question. "Listen. Why don't I tell him about it tonight and then you won't have to deal with his reaction. He'll have time to cool down before he talks to you."

I was touched. "Really? Oh, that would be wonderful. Do you think he'll try to talk me out of it?"

"I don't know but let me handle him. You know I'm good at that."

"You're the best, Catey. If he's calm and wants to visit about it, tell him to call me. I'd rather talk to him tonight than in the morning. I've got Peggy coming to make pies right away tomorrow, and I'll need to do some laundry and pack."

"Okay, honey. I'll go talk to him right now."

A tear slid down my cheek. "What did I do to deserve you?"

"I feel the same."

Brice called ten minutes later. His voice was subdued. "Hey, B.S."

I smiled. "Hey, B.S."

"I hear you're going on a trip."

"Yep."

"With that writer fella'."

"Yep."

"To the Mile High City."

"Yep."

"Do you have anything to say besides 'yep'?"

I laughed. "Nope."

Brice chuckled. "Listen, I know you were afraid to tell me about your trip to a distant city with a man you met on Friday, but you've got me all wrong. You're a 37-year-old woman who runs her own business and kicks ass on the City Council. I trust your judgment, and it sounds like the trip is legit. I just want you to be happy, and if this will make you happy … well, then you need to go for it. It's about time you put yourself out there." There was a long pause. "I know Danny would agree."

Tears slid down my cheeks, and a sense of relief washed over me. "Thanks, B.S." I grabbed a tissue and dabbed at my face. "I still think it sounds crazy, and I can't imagine what people will say, but I'm actually excited about tagging along on Maxim's book signing. He said the bookstore we're going to is world-famous.

And his agent got me my own room in the hotel where we're staying, so you don't have to worry about any funny business."

"Actually, I think you could use a little funny business in your life."

I was utterly shocked. "Wow. How long have you felt this way?"

"For several years now. I think a roll in the hay would do you a world of good."

I never knew what would come out of my brother's mouth. "You're probably right, but one step at a time, big brother. I know you're confused and bewildered by my self-imposed celibacy but that's because you're a man. We all know which body part makes men's decisions … at least when it comes to women."

Brice laughed. "I use my brain once in a while."

"Sure you do." My tone was patronizing. "Anyway, this is an innocent trip between new friends, and I've decided I would be a fool not to take Maxim up on his generosity."

"I agree. When a rich man wants to spend money on you, I say let him. He seems like an okay guy. I mean, he's a writer. How bad could he be?"

I grabbed a throw pillow and hugged it. "He said it gets boring traveling from city to city on his book tour. His wife died four years ago, and his sons are both in college. He seems absolutely thrilled that I'm going along."

"Well, use your good judgment, and you'll be fine. When are you leaving?"

"He said he'd pick me up at 11:30 in the morning. I have a lot to do before then."

"I'll let you go so you can try to get some sleep. Would you do me one small favor and text me when you get to Denver? It would make me feel better knowing you've arrived safely."

I rested my chin on the pillow. "Will do."

"Okay. Well, get some sleep. Love you."

"Love you too. And Brice? Thanks for trusting me. It means a lot."

"No prob. Night."

"Good night."

I tapped the End Call button and smiled. I didn't need Brice's approval to fly to Denver with Maxim Hall, but the trip would be much sweeter now that he'd given it.

MONDAY, DECEMBER 18, 2017

Chapter 17

Interstate 70 to Hays is a vast expanse of pastures and fields dotted with farms and the occasional town clinging to life along the major highway that runs horizontally across the state of Kansas. Wind farms, with their hulking white turbines slicing through the air like butter knives, break up the monotony of the long, sparse drive, and passers-through complain that there's nothing to see.

I saw beauty in the landscape as we raced west along Interstate 70 toward Hays Regional Airport in Maxim's black Lexus RX. The plains were a blanket of snow that rose and fell with the terrain, and the sun was so blindingly bright reflecting off the snow that sunglasses weren't just a fashion statement, they were a necessity.

I spoke of the towns we passed; they were as familiar to me as the coffee drinks I created, and nostalgia rose to the surface as I thought about my ties to each community. "There's Wilson." I pointed south to a small town a mile off the interstate that was no bigger than Waconda. "We played sports against the Wilson Dragons. They had this one volleyball player, Beth Sims, who was my height. She'd taunt me from the other side of the net, and I swear her only goal in life was to block my shots." I shook my head at the memory. "She did it a few times and then she'd jump and holler like she'd won the Olympics. God, I hated her."

Maxim glanced sideways, keeping one eye on the road as he drove. "I can't imagine you hating anyone."

I crossed my arms. "Well, I hated Beth Sims, and she felt the same. I got the last laugh, though, when she was recruited by a junior college and fizzled out after the first year." I stared out the window at the passing scenery. "I sound like a bitter old lady."

Maxim watched the road and checked the speedometer. "Sports bring out the competitors in all of us. It's not always pretty."

I turned to face him. "That's true. When Wilson came to Waconda to play football, it was a huge rivalry. The stands were packed, and tempers flared. During my senior year one of the Waconda dads got a technical foul for screaming at the referee even though the call was bogus. The players were usually good sports, but the parents were a mess."

Maxim nodded. "That's how it was when my boys played sports." He signaled to pass a slow-moving Taurus and pulled into the left lane. "Were you a cheerleader?"

I threw up my hands. "You think I was a cheerleader?"

"No, I asked if you were a cheerleader, I didn't assume. Big difference."

"Okay, fair enough. No, I was not a cheerleader." I grinned and stared at his profile. "I was too tall for the uniform."

Maxim looked skeptical. "Are you messing with me?"

As we passed the Taurus I turned to look at the driver, a white-haired, older man with thick glasses who gripped the steering wheel with both hands and peered closely at the road. "Yes, I'm messing with you, because it's so much fun. I just didn't want to be a cheerleader."

"Why not?"

I thought about it for a moment. "I've never been naturally perky, and none of the cheerleaders were taller than five foot seven. I would have looked like a freak."

"Yeah, you probably would have." Maxim grinned and pulled his Lexus in front of the Taurus.

I punched his arm. "You think you're so funny." He just shrugged and kept his eyes on the road.

My cell phone dinged with an incoming text message. I pulled it out of my pocket and saw that it was from Caitlin. I tapped the message and read it: "Hey. Been thinking of you. Have fun in Denver with the hunk. Wish I was you today. Except for the height thing. That would totally suck. Otherwise I'd give my right arm to go to a book signing with Maxim Hall. Oh well, I still have Brice. Call me tonight with the details. Love you."

I giggled, drawing Maxim's attention for a few moments before he returned his eyes to the road. "Anything you'd like to share?"

"No, just a text from Caitlin. They're always funny."

I texted a response: "The hunk is even hunkier today. Not sure how he does it. I will definitely call you later. Love you." I sent the message and waited for her reply which was the thumbs-up emoji. I returned the phone to my pocket.

I reached behind the plush black leather seat and grabbed a small white bakery bag. "Want a chocolate chip cookie?" I opened the bag and reached inside.

"Am I breathing? Of course I want a chocolate chip cookie." I handed Maxim a cookie and he bit off half of it. As he chewed, contentment spread across his face. "Wow, that's amazing. Did you make these?"

I pulled another cookie from the bag and bit into it. "No, I can't bake to save my life."

Maxim was incredulous. "But you sell all of those delicious baked goods in your store."

I pointed my finger in the air. "That's because I hire all of it done. A bakery delivers the doughnuts, muffins and bagels every morning, and you already know about The Pie Lady."

"Yeah, I'm planning on a piece of pie when we get back to Waconda." I pictured Maxim eating pie at one of the small, round tables next to the front window in my coffee shop. And who would be sitting next to him eating pie? Me, of course. It was a cozy scene.

I continued my explanation. "Well, another Waconda woman — Aubrey Krug — bakes the cookies. Let's see … she makes chocolate chip, obviously, oatmeal raisin, white chocolate cranberry, mint chocolate chip, whatever I ask for, really."

"The white chocolate cranberry sounds intriguing."

"You'll have to try one … God, they're fantastic. Anyway, Aubrey has five children, all 10 and under, and she uses my kitchen to bake cookies — and also to escape her wild house. She bakes in the evenings, and when she's finished she always comes up to my apartment for a glass of wine. She never seems too eager to go home."

I relished another bite of cookie: the rich chocolate chips melted into the sugary dough, and I closed my eyes in satisfaction.

Maxim popped the last half of cookie into his mouth. "Do you have another one in that magical bag of yours?" I nodded and handed him a second cookie. I finished mine and set the bag behind my seat.

The miles passed in silence as we sped closer to Hays, but it was a companionable silence without the trace of awkwardness that often plagues new friendships. It was obvious from the interior of his vehicle that Maxim was a city boy — not a trace of dust marred the pristine black interior. You can't get away with that in the country. I shifted in my seat and studied Maxim's profile; his sunglasses reflected the maroon SUV we were following. "You haven't said much about your family."

Maxim kept his eyes on the road. "What do you want to know?"

"Well, you said your sons are in college. Tell me about them."

Maxim's face lit up. "They're great kids. Will is at Yale University — that's in New Haven, Connecticut — studying business. He has the foolish idea of becoming a lawyer like his old man."

I'm sure my face registered surprise. "You're a lawyer?"

He laughed. "Recovering. I gave it up to become a writer."

"I see." As I peeled away the layers of Maxim Hall, he continued to astonish me. "Tell me more about your boys."

Maxim signaled and pulled into the left lane to pass the SUV. "Will's on the debate team. Man, that kid can argue. It's a gift, really. I could see him becoming a courtroom lawyer. I hope he doesn't wind up defending sleaze balls. That would break my heart."

I agreed. "Yeah, that would put a real damper on Thanksgiving dinner. You'd ask him what he was up to, and he'd say, 'Oh, just trying to get a serial killer off on a technicality.'"

Maxim slapped his hand on the steering wheel. "Exactly! I guess time will tell. He plays the guitar, loves to snow ski and hinted that there might be a special girl in his life. He's being pretty close-lipped about it right now." He stared at the road in thought.

I prompted him. "And Henry?"

Maxim smiled and turned to me. "You remembered his name."

I tapped my head. "I have a photographic memory. Remember?"

"No, I forgot. I didn't write it down." We stared at each other and burst into laughter. Maxim signaled and pulled into the right lane ahead of the maroon SUV. "Henry is at Wake Forrest University in Winston-Salem, North Carolina."

"That's a mouthful."

"Oh, I know. I usually end up saying Winstom instead of Winston."

I inspected my ugly fingernails and suddenly wished I'd thought to paint them for my special outing. "What's he studying?"

"He's undecided right now, just getting a feel for the school since he's a freshman. I worry about him because he's never been very focused, kind of roams about aimlessly. He'll be interested in something for a month or so and then moves on to the next thing. I have no idea what he'll do."

I pushed back a cuticle. "Maybe become a writer like his dad?"

Maxim shook his head. "He has no writing talent, whatsoever. He struggled through his writing assignments at school. It was painful. I had to restrain myself from re-writing all of his work. It was pretty bad."

I studied Maxim, his expensive Aviators focused on the road. "He'll find his way eventually."

"I hope so."

We rode in silence for several miles. I stared out the window. The turbine of an old rusted windmill struggled to turn. A barn with faded red paint leaned precariously to the left. A huge new green combine sat beside a dilapidated farmhouse, a foot of snow clinging to both.

I turned my attention back to Maxim. "You don't say much about your wife."

His shoulders instantly stiffened, and I noticed that he gripped the black leather steering wheel tighter. His jaw clenched and unclenched, but he remained quiet.

Even though it was awkward I forged ahead, surprised at myself. "It must still be very painful … her death." I stared out the windshield at the back of a semi-trailer, its logo emblazoned in red and blue lettering: We Transport USA.

Maxim finally spoke. "She was a beautiful woman and I loved her very much, but you're right … it's painful to talk about. Don't take it personally … I don't talk about her to anyone." Maxim's tone softened. "Her death was hard on all of us, especially the boys. They're both in counseling at school to help deal with it, and I worry about them. I have a hard time talking about it." He peeked at me. "But you're kind to ask."

I turned and gazed out the passenger window. "No, I completely understand. Believe me, I do. I apologize for being so nosy." I ran my fingers over the stones in my pendant necklace.

Maxim reached over and squeezed my arm. "No, it's okay. It's natural to be curious." He returned his hand to the steering wheel. "She was an amazing mother. She loved Will and Henry so much. She started her own interior design business from the ground up, she volunteered at the boys' school, she was a great cook, she was a great person. She had a lot of talents. It's just painful to think about her, you know?"

I nodded. "I know."

We were both lost in our thoughts, and the miles passed in silence. I was the one to break the spell. "Do you mind if I turn on the radio?"

Maxim sighed in relief and smiled broadly. "That's a great idea. I have satellite radio … just none of that country crap, okay?"

I exaggerated a gasp and planted my hands on my hips. "What do you mean, country crap?"

Maxim glanced at me. "Country music. I don't like it. All the twang and my girlfriend left me and big trucks and kegs of beer. I can't stand it."

I pointed a finger at him. "So you mean to tell me you're driving in the middle of the country and I'm not supposed to play country music?"

He nodded his head vigorously. "Yes, that's what I'm saying. I prefer '80s rock."

"Is that a request from Maxim or an order from the writer, Maxim Hall?"

He rubbed his chin. "A request?"

I laughed and turned on the radio. "I was just messing with you. I don't like country music, either. I'll punch in 80s on 8 for Mr. '80s, even though I'm a girl of the '90s."

Maxim shook his head. "You're quite the piece of work."

I smiled in delight. "Thank you, Sir!"

Chapter 18

Maxim pulled into a parking space in front of the Hays Regional Airport, a modest brick structure on the edge of Hays, population 21,000. He put the vehicle in park, pulled the keys and pushed the button that automatically opened the tailgate. He stared at the building and frowned. "That's got to be the smallest airport I've ever seen."

I laughed. "Yeah, but the parking is too legit to quit."

Maxim stopped and turned to me. "You did not just say that."

I grinned. "You know I did." I pointed to the building. "Look how close we are to the front door. I bet that never happens in New York City."

He glanced back at the building. "At least in New York City we have real airports. This looks like an oversized garage."

In spite of the sunny day the air was wickedly cold and stung my eyes, so we quickly retrieved our carry-on bags from the back of the car — his black, mine royal blue with a pink bow on the handle — and rolled them through the automatic double sliding doors and into the airport's lobby. The center of the space was lined with chairs and couches typical of waiting rooms across the country — uncomfortable, firm as a board and dark in color to hide the stains. A recessed skylight showered the room with early-afternoon sunlight. Just off the lobby, to our right, was Airport Security, and a room to our left held the lone ticket counter; it was empty. Straight ahead, in a smaller room lined with windows on two sides, was the boarding gate. People milled about, some waiting on passengers currently departing the jet from Denver, others eager to board the same jet back to Denver.

Maxim stared, disbelieving, at the inside of the airport, and I noted the look on his face, a cross between a sulk and a pout. I nudged his arm. "Follow me, city slicker." I led us to the self-service check-in kiosk in front of the ticket counter and, surprise, there was no line. I entered the flight number, tapped the pertinent information into the computer, confirmed that I had no bags to check and finally printed my boarding pass. I turned to Maxim, my voice teasing. "Do you know how to use one of these?"

He held up his phone to show me his boarding pass already pulled up on the screen.

The smile left my face. "Well, I guess you showed me."

He shrugged. "I have the United app. I fly a lot."

"Makes sense." I checked the time on my phone. "It's 1:45 and the flight leaves at 2:20. They should be boarding any time now, and I'd like to use the restroom before we get on the plane. Will you watch my bag?"

"No problem." We rolled our luggage to the seating area and set them together. I headed to the ladies room, and when I returned five minutes later Maxim went to the men's room. I sat on my suitcase and watched two elderly ladies walk by, their heads together in deep conversation. They strolled through the double sliding doors and out of sight. A few seats over a middle-aged couple sat together and held hands but didn't talk.

An announcement came over the loudspeaker. "Flight number 35 to Denver International Airport will board in ten minutes. Please form a line and proceed through the security checkpoint. That's flight number 35 to Denver International Airport, departing at 2:20 pm."

Maxim walked out of the bathroom during the announcement; his sulk/pout had turned into a grimace, and he looked bewildered. We grabbed our bags and rolled them to the short line just feet from where we'd been sitting. In less than a minute we reached the front of the security line, and a plump young woman with bright red hair and black nail polish compared my boarding pass to my driver's license. "Have a night flight." Her voice was monotone, and she didn't bother to look up. It appeared she might actually die from boredom.

Maxim handed the woman his driver's license and held out his phone with the boarding pass on the screen; she looked at the license, looked up at him, looked at the license a second time and then looked up at him again. Her eyes grew wide in recognition; surprise, then delight, filled her round face. "I love your books." Her hand went to her throat and she smiled. "Have a night flight, Mr. Hall."

Maxim leaned down and turned on the charm. "Thanks … what's your name?"

Her black-rimmed eyes were huge. "Olivia."

Maxim smiled, revealing his straight white teeth and dimples. "Thanks, Olivia. I take it you've read one or more of my books?"

Olivia puffed out her ample chest and stretched to her full petite height. "I've read all of them."

"Wow." Maxim stared at her in deep respect. "Well, thank you for that. We'd better get going, but I just want you to know that I love your hair."

Olivia blushed two shades of pink, batted her thick, black eyelashes and touched her artificially red locks. "Thank you, Mr. Hall."

As we moved to the security checkpoint I turned to him. "Do you ever get tired of that?"

The frown was back on his face. "Nope."

I bent down to pull off my boots, but a security officer stopped me. "No need to remove your shoes, Ma'am. Just place your bags on the conveyer and walk through the metal detector." Maxim insisted on lifting our bags onto the conveyor belt, and I laid my purse flat behind them. When I walked through the metal detector it remained silent, but not so for Maxim. He was asked to back up, remove his belt and walk through it again. Once past the metal detector he rolled his eyes, put on his belt and retrieved his pocket change from a bowl. He mumbled something under his breath about "incompetent airport security" and "Mickey Mouse airport," and I covered my mouth to keep from laughing.

We picked up our bags and walked no more than twenty feet to the boarding gate, the only one at the airport. I noticed that the sign said Boarding Gate 1. We found two empty seats and sat down.

Maxim stared through the huge windows at the 50-seat Bombardier jet. "Thank God. With this miniature setup I was afraid the plane would look like something the Wright brothers built."

I slapped his arm. "Don't you think you're acting just a bit pretentious? The city boy is leaking out of you."

He grimaced and hung his head. "You're right. I'm being an ass, and I know it."

I leaned into his shoulder. "Yes, you are. Just remember that this is a regional airport." I emphasized the word regional. "It's small, but they get the job done. Those of us who live out here in the middle of nowhere are mighty thankful for this 'regional' airport and the flight to Denver … so get over yourself!"

He peeked at me through his long eyelashes. "You're good for me. Sometimes I need a kick in the butt."

I patted his back. "Well stand up, then. I'm wearing my cowgirl boots."

He laughed with abandon, drawing attention from the other passengers. "You would love to kick me in the butt, wouldn't you?"

"You know it." We stared at each other and I squeezed his arm. "I'm glad to see you're in a better mood."

He shook his head. "I've been a grump since we got here. I'm sorry. Do you forgive me?"

My heart melted. "Of course I do. I have my grumpy days too."

"Now that's something I'd love to see." He pulled his phone out of his coat pocket, pushed the home button and glanced at the screen. "I'm in seat 3D. What about you?"

I pulled the paper boarding pass out of my purse and checked my seat assignment. "12A."

"I'll ask the flight attendant if I can switch seats and sit by you. Laurie said the flight is about half full so it shouldn't be a problem."

Warmth spread through my body. "Sounds good." I glanced at his handsome face and marveled that this man had come into my life and wanted to switch seats to be near me. I almost pinched myself.

The plump redhead with the black fingernails walked past us to the boarding gate desk and picked up the microphone. "Flight number 35 is now boarding at Gate 1." She looked right at Maxim and batted her eyelashes. "All passengers heading to Denver on Flight 35, please form a line and have your boarding pass ready." She stepped to the outside door and propped it open, then returned to stand by the desk where she electronically scanned each passenger's boarding pass before allowing them to walk to the airplane.

We rose and stepped to the end of the line. Maxim leaned in close to my ear. "Do you think Olivia will be flying the plane too?" I laughed and reveled in his close proximity.

When I reached the front of the line Olivia scanned my boarding pass and avoided eye contact. "Have a night flight." I walked to the door and stopped to wait on Maxim. When he showed his young fan his boarding pass she glanced up at him. "Are you flying to Denver on business?"

He gave her another one of his dazzling smiles. "Yes. I have a book signing tonight."

She beamed up at him. "Well, enjoy your flight. Keep writing."

"I will. And please keep reading."

"No problem there." She smiled broadly and scanned the next passenger's boarding pass.

We walked outside toward the jet that was parked about fifty feet away. My hair blew with abandon in the frigid Kansas wind, and we stepped up the long ramp that led us to the cabin of the small jet airplane.

Maxim's seat was near the front of the plane, and he heaved his bag into the overhead bin. "Do you need any help with your bag?"

I shook my head. "Nope. I'm a strong country girl."

Maxim studied me, his eyes playful and bright. "I noticed." He sat down to make room for the passengers behind us.

I walked back to my seat two rows in front of the bathroom and effortlessly lifted my bag into an overhead bin. I removed my coat, folded it in half and laid it on my suitcase, then I sat down by the window and fastened the seatbelt. Outside my window, two male airport employees were loading a handful of suitcases into the belly of the airplane, and I was surprised that Olivia wasn't with them, heaving baggage to and fro.

I pulled my Kindle from my purse, unwrapped a piece of chewing gum to keep my ears popping during the ascent, and stowed my purse under the seat in front of me. As I turned on my Kindle, chewed the fresh minty gum and tapped open Maxim's book, I prayed the seat beside me would remain empty. I settled in and started reading Chapter 5, soon caught up in the story of Rebecca King: The Chair was a heartbreaking tale that both disturbed and intrigued me, and Maxim was a master at drawing out the emotions and feelings of each character until they seemed real enough to touch. I half listened to the safety demonstration and barely noticed the lone flight attendant shutting the overhead bins and securing the door.

I was floating in Maxim's fictitious world of struggle, outrage and grief when a final announcement interrupted my trance: "We ask that all passengers remain in their assigned seats until we've reached cruising altitude, and once the captain has turned off the seatbelt sign you may move about the cabin. Our flying time will be approximately 55 minutes. Thank you for choosing United."

The airplane pulled away from the boarding gate and the engines roared to life. When the plane was ready for takeoff I shut my Kindle and focused my attention outside the window. I loved flying, and takeoff was by far the best part. We were soon speeding down the runway, and as the plane lifted off the ground my pulse quickened, and I felt the sheer power of the engines thrusting us into the air and the thrill of being propelled to a new destination. I marveled, as I did every time I was in an airplane, at the invention of flight. I watched the houses and cars grow smaller and smaller, and the cloudless, sunny day offered a spectacular view of the snow-covered fields and pastures. The plane lifted higher and higher, and when I couldn't make out any more distinguishable landmarks I opened my Kindle and resumed reading Maxim's book.

I was halfway through Chapter 5 when I heard a ding and saw the seatbelt sign turn off. The flight attendant's voice came over the speaker. "Ladies and gentlemen, the captain has turned off the seatbelt sign. You may now move about the cabin. Several have asked to change seats, and you may do so at this time. Be advised that FAA regulations require that you keep your seatbelts fastened when you're in your seats. I'll be coming through the cabin with complimentary beverages. You'll find a drink menu in the seat in front of you that specifies which drinks are complimentary and which require payment. We accept all major credit cards."

Just as the flight attendant finished her speech, Maxim dropped into the aisle seat beside me and smiled. "Hey."

I shut the Kindle and focused on him. "Hi there."

He glanced down at my Kindle. "Whatcha been doing?"

"Reading your book."

He slumped in the seat and massaged his forehead. "Oh." He fidgeted with a button on his shirt. "Maybe I'll go back to my seat."

I rolled my eyes and sighed. "If it makes you that uncomfortable, I won't read it in front of you." I reached for my purse and slipped the Kindle inside.

We sat in silence, each staring straight ahead. The plane hummed reassuringly, and muted talk and laughter reached my ears. The tension between us was so thick I could have cut it with a knife; I didn't like it one bit. As I grew to know him I was learning that Mr. Maxim Hall could be a bit of a drama queen. I wondered if all writers were so temperamental.

Maxim finally spoke. "I'm sorry. I guess I'm a little sensitive about my writing. I've never been able to watch someone read one of my books."

I crossed my arms. "You know thousands of people read them, right?"

He cringed. "Yes, but I'm not there when they read them, like physically in the room. It just throws me when I know someone is reading one of my books as I'm sitting next to them. I've heard other writers say the same thing."

I shook my head. "What do you think will happen … they won't like it and they'll insult you, throw the book at you … what?"

He rubbed his forehead. "No, I don't know what I'm thinking. I realize it's not rational. It's just how I am." He glanced at my purse on the floor. "What chapter are you on."

"Well, I was in the middle of Chapter 5 when this rude guy sat down and basically told me to stop reading."

Maxim grinned and stared at the floor. "You got me there. Once again, I apologize … but thanks for not reading in front of me." He reached for my hand, gazed at me and smiled. "You have permission, however, to read my book anytime I'm not around. How about that?"

I thrilled at his touch. He squeezed my hand and rubbed his thumb across my fingers. His hands were smooth and warm like a caramel macchiato; I responded and squeezed back. As if on cue we turned our heads to face each other, and I was suddenly shy as his blue eyes bored into mine. We were just inches apart, and I could smell his minty breath. He glanced at my mouth and licked his lips — my stomach fluttered, and heat radiated from my heart to places that had been cold and numb for a long time. A slow smile spread across his face, and I couldn't help but smile too. It was the happiest I'd been in a long, long time.

Our flight attendant broke the spell. "Would you like something to drink?" I ordered a can of seltzer and Maxim did the same. When she left I noticed with delight that Maxim was still holding my hand. I laid my head back on the seat and sighed in satisfaction.

The flight attendant returned with our drinks, and I reluctantly released Maxim's hand to accept the small package of roasted almonds she handed to me. We lowered the tray tables, sipped our drinks and munched on the almonds. Maxim turned to me. "Do you have any of those amazing cookies left?"

"Yes, I do." I set my drink and package of almonds on his tray, returned my table to its upright and locked position, and pulled the white bakery bag out of my purse. I lowered the tray again and removed three chocolate chip cookies from the bag. I handed two to Maxim and kept one for myself. "That's the last of them." I picked up my seltzer and sipped at it.

Maxim bit into a cookie and sighed. "Bless you. That McDonald's lunch at Russell isn't sticking with me, and these almonds aren't very filling."

I nibbled at my cookie and savored the view outside the window. "I've got to say, this is the life: jetting off to a book signing, eating a chocolate chip cookie and sipping on a seltzer. How do you ever get tired of this?"

He finished the first cookie and bit into the second. "Try doing it alone for years. It's not as glamorous as it seems." He turned his full attention on me and smiled warmly. "It's much better to travel with someone, especially someone as wonderful as you."

I blushed but remembered my manners. "Thank you. I enjoy traveling with you, too, even though you can be a total grump at times." I poked his arm.

He laughed. "You're not only wonderful, you're honest ... brutally honest, but that's good for me."

I finished my cookie and popped an almond in my mouth. "Tell me about the bookstore we're going to."

"Oh, you're gonna love this place." Maxim turned to me, his face radiating excitement. "It's called The Bookworm, and it's an iconic bookstore in the middle of Denver. A woman named Willow Jones opened it in 1972. She's a total hippie and her bookstore has huge, overstuffed chairs, a coffee bar and free hugs from the employees. Books are crammed into every corner and crevice they can find. They're known for author events — it's a huge hangout for published writers — and Laurie said Willow is preparing for several hundred people to show up tonight. I'll read an excerpt from my book and then sign copies."

My curiosity and interest grew at the image that formed in my mind as Maxim described the bookstore. "Will Willow be there?" I laughed at how funny that sentence sounded.

Maxim reached for my hand again and rubbed his thumb across my fingers. "Yes, Willow will be there. She's become a friend of mine, and she's a huge promoter of my books." He stared past me out the window. "If Willow likes you, everyone likes you. She's kind of a big deal. She has four chain bookstores in Denver and twelve in other big cities, but the original Bookworm is where all of the authors want their book signings. When Willow invites you to the main store, you've arrived."

"Impressive. I look forward to meeting her."

Maxim squeezed my hand and intensified his gaze. "Just a warning: I'll introduce you to Willow as my friend, but she'll probably think you're my girlfriend. The woman has no filter, and I have no idea what she might say to you. Just be prepared for anything."

I picked up my seltzer. "Thanks for the warning. I'll brace myself for Willow."

"Don't get me wrong; she's a wonderful old gal. I love her dearly even though she lectures me about eating meat — she's a vegan — and she hounds me about finding a woman. 'You need love, Maxim. We all need love.' Just expect to be hugged a lot and, because you're with me, treated like a queen."

I grinned and enjoyed the warmth of his hand over mine. "I've never been treated like a queen. I wonder if I'll like it."

Maxim's face was pensive, and he stared straight into my soul. "If anyone deserves to be treated like a queen, it's you." I could have sworn I saw tears in his eyes, but he looked away before I could tell.

Chapter 19

Denver International is a behemoth of an airport with four terminals accessible via an underground train called the Airport People Mover Train. This always struck me as amusing somehow. The airport itself sits in the middle of nowhere 25 miles northeast of downtown Denver. It's one of the largest airports in the country, and the architect who designed the iconic white sculpted roof on the main terminal was striving to evoke the snow-capped Rocky Mountains, the covered wagons of the pioneers, and Native American teepees.

Our plane landed at United's Gate 95, the eastern most gate of Terminal B. Pulling our bags behind us, we walked and walked, stopped for a bathroom break, then walked some more until we saw the sign pointing us to the train. We rode the escalator down and waited a few minutes until the Airport People Mover Train, bound for the Main Terminal, pulled up. It was standing room only, and Maxim and I squeezed in together near the door. His aftershave was intoxicating, and I stared at his full, red lips and the smoothly-shaven skin on his chin. The train started moving, and in less than five minutes it arrived at the Main Terminal; we stepped out and rode the escalator up to the main level.

Maxim pointed to the exit and pulled out his phone. "I'll get an Uber driver. It shouldn't take long."

I shook my head and grabbed his arm. "No, it's a lot more fun to take the train. It goes right to Union Station and we can take an Uber to the hotel from there."

Maxim stopped walking and seemed unsure what to do. "I've never taken the train into Denver."

I pushed him because I was certain the writer in him would relish the experience. "It's fairly new, but Caitlin and I love the ride." I nudged his arm in encouragement. "This way we can say we took a plane, a train and an automobile."

Maxim laughed and shrugged his shoulders. "Why not? You only live once, right?"

I linked my arm through his. "Truer words were never spoken."

We followed the signs to the Transit Center and rode another escalator down five flights to the platform where we purchased tickets at a kiosk to ride the University of Colorado A Line to Union Station in downtown Denver. Tickets in hand, we sat on a bench and waited for the next train. From experience I knew the trains were spaced 15 minutes apart. Cold air swirled around us, and I gathered my scarf tightly around my neck and leaned into Maxim; he leaned back, and I closed my eyes in contentment. A few minutes later the train arrived.

We pulled our suitcases into the train car and located two empty seats. It was a tight squeeze with our bags parked in front of us, and my right leg touched Maxim's left one. Needless to say, I didn't mind. The train moved smoothly forward, and Maxim pulled his phone out of a pocket. "Guess I'd better turn this thing back on." He held the button on his phone until the apple logo appeared and then he pressed the home button. He scrolled down the screen and frowned. "Two missed calls from Laurie, ten texts from people I don't want to text back, and twenty emails from people who want me to make appearances."

"Are all of those new since we left Hays?"

His frown deepened. "Yep."

"But I've hardly ever seen you on your phone."

"That's because I hate it. I usually leave it in my hotel room on purpose." He stared at the screen with distaste. "I'd better call Laurie back. She and my boys are about the only reason I carry this damn thing around."

He tapped his phone screen twice and held it to his ear. It didn't take long for Laurie to pick up. "Hey. We're in Denver." He turned to look at me while he listened to Laurie. "Yep, right on schedule. We're on a train now, headed to Union Station." He paused for a few seconds. "Yes, I'm on a train. Bree suggested it. She said it's the way to travel." A grin lit up his face. "Yes, I agree, she is good for me." He eyed me and smiled. "We'll get a ride to the hotel from Union Station." He smiled and twirled his finger in the air. His eyebrows raised in surprise. "Wow, that's amazing. Guess I'd better brush my teeth, then." He laughed and listened for a minute. "Okay, Laurie. Thanks again. You're the best. I'll call you in the morning." He tapped the End Call button and slipped the phone into his coat pocket.

"What was that about brushing your teeth?"

He grinned and I marveled again at his straight, white teeth. I suddenly wondered if they were real because they were almost too straight.

"Laurie said Willow is expecting a record crowd tonight, and when I'm going to be meeting that many people the joke is that I'd better remember to brush my teeth. I guess Willow, the most laid-back hippie I've ever met, is actually stressed out about what she'll do with all the people."

"Is her bookstore big enough for a huge crowd?"

Maxim rested his hands on his suitcase. "Not originally, no. When she opened The Bookworm it was a tiny bookstore, and that's one of the reasons people loved it. She was determined not to move, and when the large building next door came up for sale she was smart enough to purchase it. She made the entire first floor a meeting room; it can seat about 200. You can access it from inside her bookstore or just walk in there off the street. It was a good move."

I nodded in agreement. "I'm really excited about meeting Willow … and seeing you in action."

Maxim reached for my hand and was suddenly shy. He peeked at me through his long eyelashes. "I'm glad you decided to come along. I can't begin to tell you how nice it is to have a beautiful, fun woman with me. Any man would be lucky to have you as a companion."

I stared down at our hands, the fingers entwined effortlessly like we'd been together forever. "That means a lot." I glanced up and we grinned at each other like silly 13-year-olds.

The train turned south, and my attention was drawn out the window west toward the city of Denver spread out at the base of the Rocky Mountains, the jagged peaks bathed in snow and stretching for miles in each direction. "Summer or winter, the mountains are beautiful. I bet there's some amazing skiing going on up there."

Maxim stared at the spectacular view. "Do you wish you were up there now, skiing down one of those mountains?"

I turned and gazed into his profoundly blue eyes. "There's nowhere I'd rather be than here with you." I was shocked at the words that fell out of my mouth before I'd had time to think. I sounded like a cheesy line from a Hallmark movie. I hadn't lied — it was certainly how I felt — but I was surprised I'd verbalized my feelings. My cheeks turned red and I sat in silence.

Maxim's face registered shock, and then he grinned from ear to ear. "I feel the same way."

I relaxed and surveyed the mountains; I'd done enough talking for the time being.

The train made six quick stops and arrived at Union Station, in the heart of downtown Denver, 37 minutes after leaving the airport. When the train doors opened we rolled our luggage onto the platform and walked through double doors into Union Station's great hall, a white three-story chamber with a domed ceiling, arched windows and a magnificent chandelier hanging in its center. I'd walked through this impressive room many times with Caitlin, but it was different with Maxim.

When we reached the center of the room we paused, and Maxim looked up and turned in a complete 360-degree circle, taking his time to mentally photograph the remarkable place. I watched in fascination as the gifted writer proved why he was a master storyteller: his brain was taking in every nuance of the room and recording it in vivid detail. Busy people with places to go scurried around us, but I barely noticed.

He put his hands on his hips and smiled. "When I come to Denver I always take a cab, Uber or Lyft to my hotel, but man, this is the way to go. What a gorgeous building. I've never been here."

That intrigued me. "Really?"

He nodded. "Really. I'll need to come back when I have some time to look around. Right now we'd better get going. We need to check into our rooms, change clothes, eat supper and get to the book signing a little early. I'd like to arrive by 6:30 at the latest. The signing starts at 7:00."

I saluted Maxim. "I'm ready to go."

Maxim used his Uber app to schedule a driver, then returned the phone to his pocket. "He's five minutes away." Maxim glanced at the front doors. "You stay here where it's warm. I'm going to walk outside and look at the building. When he gets here I'll come back for you and the bags."

I didn't argue. I had no desire to stand out in the cold any longer than necessary. Maxim walked outside, and I watched him step to the curb, turn and stare up at the building. The man's powers of observation were the key to his writing, and it was fascinating to witness him at work. Everywhere he went Maxim observed his surroundings, soaking up details like a sponge. His writing was so vivid, so real, and it was because of his attention to detail that he was able to draw the reader into his compelling stories. I was suddenly eager to resume reading The Chair, but I knew there wouldn't be much of a chance on this busy trip.

A black four-door car pulled up to the curb. Maxim leaned down to talk to the driver, pointed toward the building and then rushed inside. "Kevin has arrived." We pulled our suitcases out to the car where Maxim heaved them in the trunk before we ducked into the back seat. I shivered, rubbed my gloved hands on my thighs and we huddled together for warmth as Kevin raced us the fourteen blocks to our hotel. Apparently Kevin was not only lead-footed, but hot-blooded as well because his car felt like a meat locker. Maxim slipped his arm around me and pulled me close. "This guy will not be getting five stars today or a very big tip." With Maxim's arm around me and his warm breath in my ear, I suddenly didn't mind the cold.

It didn't take long to arrive at The Brown Palace Hotel & Spa at the corner of 17th Street and Tremont Place. I stared at the luxury hotel, a spectacular red brick triangular-shaped building with green awnings and rows and rows of windows in its eight floors. Maxim leaned toward my ear. "This is where I always stay when I come to Denver. It was built in 1892 and it's the second-longest operating hotel in Denver. The Beatles used to stay here. Wait 'til you see the inside."

Kevin screeched to a stop at the main entrance and jumped out to retrieve our bags from the trunk. By the time we stepped out of the car the bags were waiting for us. Maxim turned to our driver. "Thanks, Kevin."

Kevin waved and rushed to the driver's door. "Have a nice stay in Denver." He hopped in his chilly car and sped off.

We pulled our bags up three steps, walked through an arched doorway with cherubic figures carved into the stone, passed through an enclosed entryway, and when Maxim opened the door and led me into the 8-story atrium of the iconic hotel … the view astonished me. I gasped and my eyes were immediately drawn to the atrium's enormous crystal chandelier that was covered with what must have been thousands of clear twinkle lights, plus greenery, red glass balls and red bows. Eight floors up, late-afternoon sunlight streamed through the stained-glass ceiling. Each floor of the hotel was open to the atrium, lined with decorative metal panel railings.

The magnificent open room of the atrium was filled with ornate tables and chairs, and guests were sipping wine and eating hors d'oeuvres. A grand piano sat off to one side on a small stage, and a professional pianist filled the room with

"Winter Wonderland," his fingers flying up and down the keyboard as he effortlessly played the challenging rendition.

Enormous archways with marble columns surrounded the room and were lined with clear twinkle lights. A mammoth Christmas tree stood ceremoniously in the center of the room and it was also covered with clear lights, red glass balls and red ribbons. I sensed a theme and noted that a professional decorator was certainly in charge of such grandeur.

I felt Maxim's hand at my waist. "It's a thrill to see the hotel through your eyes. I must admit I've gotten used to it but watching you I'm reminded that it is a magnificent place."

There was so much to look at, and my eyes absorbed every detail in the grand room. "I've just never seen anything like this. It's stunning."

Maxim glanced up at the chandelier and regarded it for a moment. "Yes, it is." He allowed me a few more minutes of gawking and finally reached for my hand. "Let's get checked in." Maxim led me to the front desk; I was still slack-jawed but tried to rein in my enthusiasm for his benefit.

At the registration desk a middle-aged man with gray hair lit up when he saw Maxim. "Ah, Mr. Hall. How wonderful to see you again."

Maxim turned on the charm. "Mr. Nimoy. It's good to see you too."

"We have your rooms ready. This must be your guest." Mr. Nimoy acknowledged me and bowed slightly.

"Yes, this is Bree Somers. Bree, this is Mr. Nimoy, the Assistant Manager here."

Mr. Nimoy nodded and smiled. "It's my pleasure to serve you, Miss Somers. If you need anything during your stay don't hesitate to dial zero on your room phone and we'll take care of it immediately."

I smiled back at him. "Thank you. I'm still a bit stunned … the hotel is breathtaking."

"It certainly is! Why else would I have worked here for 23 years?" He turned his attention to the computer screen. "Miss Somers, we have you booked in Room 312. That's on the third floor, in one of our classic queen rooms." He slipped a keycard into a paper sleeve, wrote 312 on the cover and handed it to me. "And Mr. Hall, you're in the Eisenhower Suite on the eighth floor." He handed Maxim a keycard sleeve and grinned. "I believe you know where that is."

"You know that I do."

Mr. Nimoy leveled a dazzling smile on us. "Enjoy your stay, and welcome to The Brown Palace Hotel and Spa."

"Thank you."

I turned around and almost knocked over a small girl who appeared to be about the same age as Nate and Matt. The look of distress on her face brought me to my knees, and I squeezed her shoulders and asked where her parents were. She remained quiet but held up her hands and moved her fingers in various positions as her eyes implored me to understand.

"It's sign language." Maxim knelt down and smiled tenderly at the child. When he held up his hands and joined in a signed conversation with her, my mouth fell open. Was there nothing this man couldn't do? The little girl, now fully engaged in her familiar language, smiled joyously. When their conversation was finished Maxim rose and turned to Mr. Nimoy. "This girl's name is Susan Fisher. She and her parents are staying here, and she lost her mother in the gift shop…"

At that moment a woman swooped in and picked up Susan, relief crossing her features. The girl threw her arms around her mother and then leaned back, signed for a few moments and pointed at Maxim. The mother beamed at him in genuine gratitude. "My daughter said you helped her when she was lost."

Maxim shuffled his feet. "That's right."

The mother grabbed his hand and shook it vigorously. "I'm Susan's mother, Margo. Thank you so much. I was frantic with worry."

Maxim pointed to the child. "Well, Susan was a very smart girl to come to the front desk when she was lost. She just happened to be lucky to run into someone who knows sign language."

Margo laughed. "Very lucky. Well, thanks again … we need to be going." Still holding Susan, she rushed off toward the staircase.

Maxim placed his hand at the small of my back and led me away from the registration desk. We pulled our suitcases to the double elevators, pushed the Up button and waited.

"How do you know sign language?"

His expression was casual, as if it was no big deal. "I had a friend who couldn't speak." He didn't seem interested in talking about it, so I decided not to press for the details.

Maxim pulled the phone out of his pocket and pressed the home button. "With the time change it's 4:15 right now. I'd like to leave for the book signing by 6:10."

He turned to me. "They have some great restaurants here in the hotel. Why don't we meet in the atrium by the Christmas tree at 5:30. That's pretty early for a big meal — I don't like to eat a lot before my appearances — but we could have an appetizer or two before we leave and then eat supper after the book signing. Does that sound okay to you?"

I leaned in. "That sounds great. I'm along for the ride, so whatever works for you works for me."

Maxim shook his head. "You're every man's dream — beautiful and low maintenance."

"I hate it when men compare me to their vehicles."

Maxim dropped his head and laughed. "That was pretty bad on my part. Sorry."

I reached out and squeezed his arm. "Well, since you whisked me away on a glamorous trip to Denver, I'll forgive you this time."

He bowed deeply. "Thank you, Ma'am. That's mighty generous of you."

The elevator arrived and interrupted our playful exchange. We rode it to the third floor, and Maxim insisted on helping me find my room. As we followed the discrete signs pointing us to Rooms 300-320, I turned to Maxim. "I suppose you're unfamiliar with the commoners' area down here on the third floor."

He was unfazed. "Actually, the first time I stayed here I was on the second floor. But you're right — I've moved up in the world. Just so you know, Laurie tried to get you into one of the suites, but they're booked solid through New Year's Eve."

That was unexpected. "She really tried to get me a suite?"

Maxim nodded. "I told her to."

We'd reached Room 312. I pulled the keycard out of its sleeve. "I'm certainly glad she didn't succeed. I'm really not a suite kind of gal."

Maxim shrugged. "I guess I've gotten used to it."

I slid the keycard into the door and pulled it out when the green light came on. "I can't imagine what your suite must look like."

"You'll have to come up later. It's really worth seeing."

I'd opened the door a couple of inches, but his comment stopped me in my tracks. I glanced at his face, but it registered nothing. I stayed quiet, pushed the door open and rolled my suitcase behind me into Room 312.

Maxim stayed in the hallway. "I'll see you by the Christmas tree at 5:30."

I offered a small wave. "Okay. See you in a while." He turned on his heel and headed back to the elevators.

I pulled my suitcase into the narrow hallway of the room, closed the door and locked it. The bathroom was to my right and I peeked inside — white marble countertop, white tile, white toilet, white tub with shower, white shower curtain, white was the word in here. I stepped through the hallway and into the small but attractive room dominated by a queen-size bed with white plush bedding. The accent wall behind the bed was charcoal grey, and a tan upholstered panel headboard with diamond tufting stretched to just a few feet from the high ceiling. I rolled my suitcase into a corner and inspected the tan carpeting with its swirls of white, red and dark blue. I stepped to the window and looked out: the mountains were on the other side of the building, but the city of Denver was beautiful in the fading light of late afternoon.

I stepped over to the bed, sank down on its edge, pulled off my brown ankle boots and laid back into the softness of the comforter. Staring at the ceiling fan, I assessed my current situation: this small-town girl was in a famous hotel in a big city with the eminent author, Maxim Hall, who held my hand, proclaimed my beauty and sent my heart racing. I'd come close to kissing him, and I'd need to rein in these feelings because it would be easy to fall under his spell and do something I hadn't done in a long time ... a very long time, indeed. Lordy.

My eyes fluttered closed, and I succumbed to a cat nap before my big evening with a man who was, quite literally, sweeping me off my feet.

.

Chapter 20

I bit into a wedge of the prime rib quesadilla I'd ordered at the Ship Tavern Restaurant. As the melted cheese, beef, guacamole and salsa settled onto my tongue, I closed my eyes and savored every moment of its exquisite taste. I'd considered ordering the truffled French fries, but after Maxim described the truffle as a type of fungus, I'd changed my mind.

"You certainly enjoy your food." Maxim watched me closely, the corners of his eyes crinkled in amusement.

I pushed my plate toward him. "You've got to try this. Put some guacamole and salsa on top first. It's amazing." I watched as he did what he was told, and after he'd taken a bite, a look of pleasure filled his face.

"You're right. It's very good." He wiped his mouth with the cloth napkin.

"How are the crab cakes?"

He pointed to his plate. "Please try one. They're excellent, as usual."

I speared one of the appetizer-sized crab cakes with my fork and took a small bite. "You're right. I'm not usually a huge fan of fish, but if you add enough breading and fry it — I'm in." I ate the rest of the crab cake and returned to my quesadilla.

Maxim sipped his water and checked the time on his phone. "We have about twenty minutes before we need to leave." He picked up his fork and cut into another crab cake.

I wiped my fingers on the white cloth napkin, settled back in my chair and inspected Maxim. He'd showered and his charcoal hair was still slightly damp and combed back neatly from his forehead. His tan skin glowed with health in spite of the harsh winter weather, his aftershave was glorious — he smelled of pine and woods and earth — and he wore dark gray pants, brown dress shoes and a navy V-neck sweater over a white button-down shirt. He was basically every woman's dream sitting across from me nibbling on a crab cake.

I wondered if he knew his effect on the female population. The women we'd come across — whether it was the busty blonde hostess who showed us to our table tonight or the red-haired airport employee earlier today — had responded immediately to his very presence. Dozens of female heads had turned when we'd hurried through the airport. Was he totally oblivious to the ladies who stared and whispered, did he choose to ignore them, or was he so used to the attention that he didn't even notice anymore?

He caught me staring and leveled his clear blue eyes on mine. "In case you were wondering, I have a stylist. If it were up to me I'd be wearing one of those plaid jackets with patches on the elbows."

I laughed. "Well, she does a great job. I assume it's a she?" He nodded. "Anyway, I like the outfit … it looks like you're trying, but not too hard."

Maxim glanced down. "I wasn't sure about the brown shoes with the dark pants, but Heather assured me it's the 'in' thing. I always thought you wore black shoes with black pants and brown shoes with brown pants, but I guess that's not the case anymore."

I gave him the thumbs-up sign. "No, the gray and brown really do look good together. I'd noticed women wearing brown boots with black leggings and asked Tracey about it — she's my fashion consultant. She said it's all the rage."

Maxim rested his chin on one hand and openly admired the length of me. I wore white skinny jeans with black high-heeled boots and a slate gray cowl-neck sweater. I'd twisted my long hair into a casual chignon at the nape of my neck and wore silver leaf leather earrings. "You look totally stylish. Really, you're stunning. And I love your hair like that. Very classy."

I blushed and glanced at my fingernails. They were chipped from washing dishes, but there wasn't anything I could do about it now. "Thank you. That's kind of you to say."

He frowned. "I'm not just saying it. I'm proud to be seen with you. Surely you've noticed the men who stare at you everywhere we go."

I looked around the room. "They do?"

He smiled and crossed his arms. "You really don't notice?"

"I guess not. I'm usually in my own little world."

He leaned forward. "Well, they're looking."

I sat up and studied the room. When my gaze reached the bar I noticed two men in dress suits sitting together drinking and watching me. As our eyes met they raised their wine glasses as one and smiled pleasantly. I managed to smile back, just to be polite, and turned my attention to the last wedge of quesadilla. I picked it up and devoured a huge bite.

Maxim's expression was smug. "I told you they were looking. Consider it a compliment."

I chewed and stared at the table. "I'll try."

We finished our food and sat in silence for several minutes. I was curious about something. "Do you get nervous before your speaking engagements?"

Maxim sat back and crossed an ankle over his knee. "I usually have a few butterflies right before I'm introduced, but nothing like when I was a new author. Back then I almost threw up before I had to speak in front of a crowd; I was a nervous wreck. I guess time and experience have mellowed me out. There's so much I can't control — the crowd, the weather, the moods of the people. Nowadays I just show up and go with the flow."

I grabbed my purse and dug out my lip gloss. "How do you think it will go tonight?" I opened the tube and slid on a new layer of Perfectly Pink.

Maxim watched my lips as I applied the gloss, then he linked his fingers behind his head and leaned back. "Willow's events are the biggest — the best, really — of anywhere in the country, at least of the bookstore signings. Some events I dread, but I always look forward to hers. You're going to love the store." He reached for his phone and checked the time. "Why don't we head over there now?"

Maxim motioned for the waitress and graced her with one of his beautiful smiles. "We need to get going. Would you charge this to my room? Maxim Hall, the Eisenhower Suite. Add a twenty percent gratuity for yourself." The waitress thanked him, gathered the dishes and hurried to the kitchen.

We stood and slipped into our coats. I wrapped a scarf snugly around my neck as Maxim tapped his phone and ordered an Uber driver. "Jasmine will be here in seven minutes." He reached for my hand and led me to the atrium where we waited on our driver. The pianist was playing "Silver Bells." As I stared at the stunning chandelier, Maxim linked his fingers with mine, and I thrilled at his touch. I could get used to this.

When our driver was one minute away, according to Maxim, I reluctantly pulled my hand away from his and slipped on my black leather gloves. He didn't seem to own any gloves. We stepped outside in the early-evening darkness just as a bright blue four-door car pulled up. Maxim spoke to the driver and confirmed it was our ride. We slipped into the back seat, and I was pleased with the warmth that surrounded me. Our driver, Jasmine, was pleasant but quiet, and we rode in relative silence for twenty minutes to The Bookworm.

I was curious about something else. I leaned into Maxim's shoulder and pointed to his bare hands. "Do you not own a pair of gloves?"

"I hate gloves."

"Don't your hands get cold?"

"Yes."

"Then why don't you buy some gloves?"

"Because I hate gloves."

"But if you'd put on gloves your hands wouldn't get cold."

"Ah, logic. Don't confuse me with logic."

Jasmine pulled to a stop in front of a narrow white-washed brick building tucked between two larger buildings in Denver's trendy LoDo district. The building sported a bright red door and navy awnings over the two front sash windows. A wooden sign hanging above the door read:

> The Bookworm
> New and Used Books
> Weekly Author Events
> Denver, Colorado

The building was cute and quaint — exactly what you'd dream of in a famous bookstore — and my excitement reached a crescendo. I opened the door, stepped out of the car and when I saw the crowd of people huddled around The Bookworm's front door, and the line extending down the block, I was filled with awe. Maxim stepped out of the car and a hush fell over the crowd. My first impression was one of quiet respect — that's what I felt — and Maxim stopped and addressed the group. "With this many of you out on such a chilly night you must be waiting on a well-known writer … Nicholas Sparks?" The group laughed. "Thank you all for coming tonight. I'm sure Willow will let you in soon." He raised his hands in the air. "In fact, I'll insist on it." Several people clapped; the women closest to us beamed in pleasure, and many clutched Maxim's new book to their chests.

Maxim pulled out his phone and turned to me. "I should have thought to do this sooner. You're throwing me off my routine." He grinned, tapped out a text message and sent it. "I'm letting Willow know we're here so she'll let us in."

Within a minute I heard the dead bolt turn, the door opened, and Maxim ushered me inside.

The smell of food hit me first — several delicious aromas swirled in the air — and then I caught a whiff of coffee and suddenly craved a rich cup of joe. I marveled at the sight of more books than I'd ever seen in one place: there were shelves filled with books, chairs filled with books, tables filled with books, refurbished dressers filled with books and even a baby crib filled with children's books. How in the world did the staff keep track of all these books?

The inside of the store was as bright and cheery as the outside. The walls were a creamy white with hand-painted butterflies and flowers scattered about, and the overstuffed chairs and couches were an eclectic mix of colors.

The woman hugging Maxim was so tiny she didn't even reach up to his chin, and with her floral chiffon kimono, red eyeglasses and silver hair pulled into a loose bun, I guessed she was Willow Jones. I was correct. Willow released Maxim and turned her fierce green eyes on me.

"My God, Maxim, she's a tall one. Where in the world did you find her?" She smiled, reached around my waist and pulled me into one of the tightest hugs I'd ever received. I hugged her back, although not with as much force, and when she let go she peered up and studied me closely. "What a beauty. I'm Willow Jones, and I own this joint. And you're Bree Somers. Welcome." She turned to Maxim. "Good job, my dear. She looks like a keeper."

I didn't have a chance to respond before Willow hurriedly led us to the back of the long bookstore and ushered us into a room with two small couches and a desk piled with paperwork. She glanced up at Maxim. "Okay, hon, you know the drill. You stay here until I come and get you." She turned to me and then back to Maxim. "It's like talking to two giraffes. You guys need anything to eat or drink?"

I found my voice. "No, thank you, we just ate. I want to say how nice it is to meet you, and your bookstore is lovely. I look forward to seeing the rest of it."

Willow folded her hands together in a prayer pose. "Well, isn't that nice of you, dear. I'll show you around personally after Maxim's little talk." She clapped her hands together. "I'd better get going. Now that you're here I'll unlock the door and let the peasants in." She giggled, turned to leave and then looked over her shoulder. "Don't tell anyone I just said that." And she was gone.

I leaned against Maxim. "Well isn't she a tiny ball of fire!"

Maxim shook his head. "I wish I knew where she got her energy. She's always like that."

We removed our coats and hung them on the rack in the corner. I sat on the green couch that was probably new in the 1970s, and Maxim remained standing.

I looked at the stack of papers threatening to topple off the desk. "Is this Willow's office?"

Maxim stuck his hands in his pockets and rocked back and forth on his heels. "Yes, but she's rarely in it. The woman hates to sit … she's in perpetual motion. An employee comes in here once a week and sifts through the paperwork." He opened the door and peeked into the narrow hallway. "I'm going to sneak out for a bathroom break. Are you okay?"

I nodded yes and he left. I sat back on the couch, crossed my legs and tapped out a text message to Caitlin: "Sitting in The Bookworm, waiting for Maxim's book signing. Wish you were here."

Caitlin's response was immediate: "Me too. I am beyond jealous. You're out hobnobbing with a celebrity and I'm filling the washing machine with stinky underwear. Send me some pics. And call me later. I'm dying for details."

I texted back: "Will do. You would not believe how many people are waiting outside. I couldn't see the end of the line."

Caitlin: "OMG! I bet it's mostly women."

Me: "Looked like it when we got here but I'll be able to tell more when everyone's inside. The bookstore owner is a trip. Her name is Willow."

Caitlin: "Get a pic of her too, please."

Me: "OK. I'd better go. This thing will be starting soon."

Caitlin: "Have fun. Call me later."

I sent Caitlin the thumbs-up emoji, put my phone on silent and slipped it into a back pocket of my jeans.

Maxim returned to the room and shut the door. "The place is almost full. They're bringing more chairs up from the basement, but a few people may have to stand."

We waited in silence, and I watched as Maxim's nervous energy consumed him: he paced back and forth in the tiny space for a few minutes; he adjusted the collar on his shirt and asked if it looked okay; he literally twiddled his thumbs; he blew air out of his mouth and stretched his jaw; he swung his arms and rolled his shoulders; and he opened the door three times to peek outside. "I guess I do get a little nervous before these things."

I laughed. "That's what I was just thinking."

He stopped and regarded me. "I think it's because you're here. I usually don't get this worked up before a speaking engagement."

I uncrossed my legs and sat forward on the couch. "You're nervous to speak in front of me? Little old Bree Somers who peddles coffee for a living in a Podunk town in the middle of Kansas?"

Maxim pointed at me. "Yes you. You have a strange effect on me." He put his hands in his pockets and looked down at his shoes. "Maybe I'll say something stupid and you'll figure out that I'm just your typical guy and not some popular writer."

"Oh, I already know you're a typical guy. I've seen you eat pizza. It's not a pretty sight."

He laughed and was about to respond when Willow opened the door and rushed in. "Well, we have the peasants corralled and calmed. My God, there's a lot of them here tonight. I think it's a record crowd; I told Stevie to count."

She led us from her office, through the bookstore and into the adjoining building where at least two hundred people — mostly women as Caitlin had guessed — sat on folding chairs and leaned against the walls facing a small stage at the far end of an enormous room. One chair sat empty in the front row with a RESERVED sign on it; Willow pointed. "We saved that one for you."

I thanked her and sat down, but I grabbed Maxim's arm before he was out of reach. "Good luck."

"Thanks ... I'll need it."

Willow grabbed Maxim's hand and pulled him onto the stage; he sat down in the lone chair and Willow walked to the wooden podium. She stepped onto a stool that must have been placed there just for her, tapped the microphone to see if it was working, smiled warmly and addressed the crowd.

"Welcome to The Bookworm. My name is Willow Jones, and I opened this bookstore in 1972 with the dream of someday hosting author events like the one you're attending this evening. My dream was not only realized but grew far beyond anything I could have ever imagined. At our weekly author events we bring in some of the most-recognized names in the book industry along with up-and-coming authors who are ready to take the literature world by storm.

"Tonight we have with us one of our regulars, an award-winning novelist with nine books to his credit. Seven of those books have reached the New York Times Bestseller List, and four have been made into films ... with the fifth in production." Willow glanced at Maxim and pointed a finger. "I can't wait to see it. It better be as good as the book." The audience laughed, and Willow returned her attention to them.

"Tonight's author released his latest novel this fall and, in my opinion, it's one of the most poignant books I've ever read. I cried at the end, and Willow Jones doesn't cry easily." The audience nodded in unison. "The Chair hit number one on the Bestseller List in its first week, and I'm thrilled that Mr. Maxim Hall is with us tonight. Maxim will speak for a bit, read an excerpt from his book and then he'll sign copies. It's a pleasure to introduce my friend and novelist, Maxim Hall."

As Maxim rose to his full height, the crowd jumped to its feet and applauded wildly; I heard a few whistles and cat calls among the clapping. I stood and joined them, astounded at the noise that filled the room and bounced off the exposed brick walls. Maxim hugged Willow, bent down and lightly kissed her on the cheek, stepped to the podium where he pushed aside the stool, and then he slowly and assuredly surveyed the room. After a solid minute the applause tapered off and the book lovers returned to their seats.

I sat down and stared at Maxim who was more attractive than ever under the single spotlight illuminating his elegant face. He was such a beautiful man, and not just on the outside. Since first meeting him three days ago — had it really been just three days? — I'd peeled back several layers to reveal a kind and thoughtful man with a keen intelligence. He was also fun to be around, even though a pompous ass occasionally showed up in his place. He was quick to rebound, though, and self-aware.

I turned to inspect the sea of faces eager to hear whatever he had to say. Maxim, I realized with sudden clarity, was a God in his realm, a master standing before his subjects, a king in his court. He wasn't just a famous writer, he was a hero in the land of books, and the people — because of his writing — felt they knew him intimately. If he'd told them to sit on the floor, they would have done it. If he'd led them outside, they would have followed. If he'd asked for a kidney, someone in the room, I'm almost certain, would have donated hers, no questions asked. I wondered if he knew the power he wielded, and how he could have manipulated it for personal gain. As far as I knew, he'd never done it — Maxim Hall, writer, simply asked his fans to buy a $15 book and see a $10 movie. It wasn't highway robbery.

Maxim surveyed the room, and his smile was sincere. "Thank you all for coming. It means so much that you would venture out on such a chilly winter night." His voice was smooth and rich like chicken gravy poured over mashed potatoes. "I'm glad that Willow finally let you in." Maxim turned and smiled at Willow who was now seated in the lone chair on the stage. Even as she rolled her eyes and threw her arms in the air, she couldn't resist smiling back at him.

Maxim returned his attention to the crowd and turned serious. "Benjamin Franklin said, 'Either write something worth reading or do something worth writing.'" He paused and a chorus of heads nodded in agreement. "I've devoted my life to the former, and it seems to be working out okay." The group laughed as one.

"In my latest book Rebecca King did something worth writing about. Rebecca may be fictional, but her story is real. It's a story of pushing forward when you want to give up, of choosing life when you want to die, of taking the next step when you want to turn and run." The woman beside me clutched the book to her heart as tears streamed down her face. "If you haven't read the book yet, Rebecca King's character will show you what real bravery is." The woman cried openly; she reached into her purse for a tissue and blew her nose.

Maxim glanced at Willow. "I'd like to express my gratitude to Willow Jones for inviting me here tonight. Back when e-books became popular in the early 2000s, and bookstores across the country started closing, Willow announced that e-books were a fad and said that she wasn't going anywhere." The crowd laughed in unison.

"According to Willow, real books were here to stay, and she was in it for the long haul. 'Besides,' she said, 'authors can't sign e-books.' I'm thrilled that Willow was right; we must all support our local bookstores and the heroes who run them." Maxim paused, and thunderous applause filled the room. "Thank you, Willow, for keeping the dream alive for writers like me." Willow blew a kiss to Maxim.

He turned back to the crowd. "My books are known as the 'THE' books — THE Climb, THE Day, THE Wall, THE Street and so on." Heads bobbed in agreement, and almost everyone smiled knowingly. "My newest 'THE' book, The Chair, was the most difficult one I've written." Out of the corner of my eye I saw more nodding, and several 'Amens' erupted from the audience. Maxim glanced at me and I noticed a light sheen of sweat on his forehead.

"Rebecca King is a woman who has been thrown into a situation that most of us can't imagine — life in a wheelchair without the use of her legs. When Rebecca is told that she'll never walk again, life as she knows it is forever transformed into Before and After the accident. Most of us have experienced what Rebecca feels in this book. We've lived the Befores and Afters — Before Mom died versus After Mom died, Before the cancer diagnosis versus After the cancer diagnosis, Before the hurricane versus After the hurricane, Before the stupid decision versus After the stupid decision.

"At this book's center is Rebecca's struggle as she comes to grips with Before versus After, and yet she knows the fault is hers, that she's to blame for her life as it has become. One of the most difficult components to write was Rebecca's internal dialogue as she worked through physical therapy and began to understand the damage she'd done to the lives of people she didn't even know, people she hurt when she wasn't thinking."

Maxim looked at me then, a deep frown etching his elegant face. "Many of us have done things we regret, things that hurt other people, things that we would take back in a heartbeat if we could." He observed the crowd and braced his hands on the podium. "But life's not like that. We can't go back in time and change the past, our stupid mistakes, our blunders, our gaffes, our complete lacks of judgment." He paused and looked down. "Our selfishness."

He rubbed his forehead and wiped the damp hand on his pants leg. He looked up at his readers. "Rebecca is pulled in so many directions; it's a miracle she survived. It's a miracle she thrived." He smiled then. "But she did." Maxim stared into the corner for several seconds, lost in his thoughts.

He reached down and pulled a copy of The Chair from the podium and turned to a spot marked with a yellow sticky note. He held up the book for everyone to see. "The cover of The Chair shows an empty wheelchair sitting in the sand on a beach. Before the accident Rebecca lived along the ocean and loved to surf; it was her religion. Every day she'd wake at dawn and surf before work, an exhilarating routine that nourished both her body and her soul. After the accident Rebecca would sit in her wheelchair and look at the ocean she'd never surf again — at least not the way an independent, able-bodied woman could. She'd lost not only the use of her legs but the spiritual connection she'd forged with God when she defied gravity and sliced through the water on a surfboard. She'd found God out in that water and couldn't feel him anywhere else. In this scene Rebecca sits along the beach staring at the ocean the same day a letter arrived that rocked her to the core."

Maxim held the book and read:

I used to love the ocean — the strength of the waves was both thrilling and terrifying — and I'd push my surfboard past the swells and wait for the perfect wave to carry me back to shore. I'd do it over and over again, the saltwater knotting my hair, the wind caressing my skin, until the sun rose high in the sky and I'd head for home, happy and satisfied and filled with the wonders of God and creation.

Now I hate the ocean, and God's nowhere to be found. The waves taunt me — Remember us, Rebecca? — and by the time they reach the wheelchair I'm forever stuck in, they're nothing more than bubbles that swirl around the tires and dissipate in the sand. The ocean laughs at me. Look who won in the end, Rebecca. You thought you could conquer us, but you were a fool. We win, we win.

If I had the strength I'd fling myself into the ocean and let the waves take me for one last ride. I'd enjoy the darkness, the blackness, the nothingness. They would swallow me whole, eat me for lunch, nibble on me for an afternoon snack.

But I'm not strong enough to hurl myself out of this wheelchair and into the ocean — it's a ridiculous thought, anyway — and I'd probably do it wrong like everything else in my life.

Why did he send the letter? What was he thinking? He doesn't even know me, and he wants to forgive me? He must be a fool, an idiot stuck in grief who thinks the only way to feel better is to forgive. He wants to meet me in person but that is never going to happen. Never. I don't know if I should write him back or just ignore the letter, pretend I didn't receive it. Maybe I should have my attorney contact him and tell him to leave me alone. I don't know what to do. I'm not worthy of forgiveness. I should rot in hell for what I've done. Maybe rotting in a wheelchair is better than death.

I need to get away from the ocean ... the saltwater eats away at the raw pain that is my life, and the wound in my soul festers and scabs over, then breaks open to repeat the process. I don't know why I stay here. I should sell the house, move to Kansas ... Oklahoma maybe. Somewhere inland — far, far away from any body of water that reminds me of what I've lost, of what was and what could have been.

I'll move to a land where no one has read the news reports, where no one knows what a terrible person I am, how I destroyed lives because I was selfish, thoughtless, stupid. I'll live alone in a bungalow in a tiny Midwestern town, and when I'm old I'll tell the grandchildren I don't have about my life Before and After — I'll tell them to slow down and think and live consciously.

Then they'll never have to destroy a life and wonder ... what if. What if.

Women were sniffling into tissues and gently blowing their noses. I heard sighs as people released the breaths they'd been holding. A tear slid down my cheek and I wiped it away. I hadn't read the section Maxim shared tonight, and I was moved by what I'd heard. Emotions churned within me, but I pressed them down and regained my composure. Maxim stepped back from the podium and stared at the far wall; his face was poised and serene. As one, the crowd rose to its feet and clapped in reverence for the author they loved.

Willow jumped up, bear hugged Maxim and rushed to the microphone. "Maxim, from the bottom of my heart, thank you for your presence here tonight, your beautiful soul in the universe … and for standing as a champion for the literature lovers of the world."

She held out her arms toward the audience, the sleeves of her kimono hanging loosely. "We're now going to move into the book signing portion of the evening." As if on cue, two of Willow's employees — I supposed one of them was Stevie — carried a rectangular table into the room, set it in front of the stage, slid two chairs behind it and piled one side with dozens of copies of The Chair.

Willow continued. "You received a number as you came in tonight. When you hear your number please stand and Stevie …" She pointed to a man standing next to the table with dread locks and a clipboard. "… Stevie here will lead you to the front where Mr. Hall will autograph your book and pose for a picture. Once you have reached the table, Saffron will guide you through the process." Willow gestured to the tall stacks of books. "If you would like to purchase a book for Maxim to sign, they are available at the front table, as you can see. If you are purchasing a book tonight, once your book has been signed you will be handed a green card; please take this card to the cashier and pay for your book before you leave. Thanks again for coming."

Willow turned to Maxim and hugged him again. He squeezed her shoulders and stepped off the stage where he spoke with a young woman I assumed was Saffron, and then he sat down at the table, smiled at me and shrugged his shoulders; Saffron sat next to him. Two more employees appeared — one held a stack of green cards and planted herself by the piles of books, and the other hovered off to one side near the table. The low murmur in the room grew louder as Maxim's fans patiently waited their turn to meet him.

Stevie, clipboard in hand, asked "Number One" to come forward. "Let the book signing begin!" His voice was surprisingly powerful. The woman sitting next to me jumped up, and I moved out of the way as Stevie ushered her to the front table. Her bottle-blonde hair was teased and hair-sprayed at least three inches high; she was prepared for hurricane-force winds in the middle of Colorado. Her long, red manicured fingernails held a paperback copy of The Chair, and I could see that the corners of the book were tattered; she'd obviously read it more than once. Saffron reached for the book, opened it to the title page and set it in front of Maxim. He peeked up at the woman and smiled. "Who should I sign this to?"

The lady vibrated with excitement. "Tonya. Make it out to Tonya. That's T-O-N-Y-A."

Maxim opened a black Sharpie and wrote, in his scrawling, doctor-like handwriting: "To Tonya, Keep Reading, Maxim Hall."

He closed the cover and handed her the book. "There you go, Tonya. Would you like a picture?"

Her face lit up. "Yes!"

The employee who'd been hovering near the table rushed over. The name tag on her shirt said AFTON. "I'll take the picture, Ma'am. Just step behind the table and stand beside Mr. Hall." Tonya tapped the camera app on her phone, handed it to Afton and dashed around the table where she leaned down next to Maxim. His mere presence seemed almost too much for Tonya. Her eyes blinked rapidly, and I was afraid she might faint.

Afton held up the phone. "Smile." Tonya and Maxim grinned at the phone and Afton snapped two pictures.

As Tonya trotted off with her book and inspected the pictures on her phone, the process was repeated over and over again. I was impressed by the well-oiled machine that was the Author Book Signing. Willow appeared at my shoulder and led me into her bookstore. "How about I show you around and then we'll get some food. Do you like coffee?"

I laughed. "I own a coffeehouse."

Her green eyes were filled with wonder. "You do? How marvelous!" She grabbed my hand and pulled me through the crowds of people to the coffee bar at the opposite end of the store. It was crazy busy with two long lines and four occupied baristas. She turned and peered up at me through her red glasses. "What would you like?"

I scanned the menu. "Honestly? Coffee with cream and sugar sounds perfect."

"Coming right up." Willow stepped behind the counter and filled a large yellow ceramic mug with black coffee. She returned and handed it to me. "Doctor it up however you wish." She pointed to the row of sugars and creamers lined up near the counter. I retrieved two sugar packets — raw turbinado sugar, of course — and two individual-sized creamers, emptied the contents into my coffee cup and stirred it with a swizzle stick. As I lifted the cup to my mouth I noticed a smiley face painted on the side and couldn't suppress a giggle. I sipped the hot drink and sighed as the dark roast tickled my senses and slid down my throat.

Willow beckoned for me to follow. "Let's get you something to eat." She led me to a long table filled with colorful food, most of which I didn't recognize. Willow clapped her hands and grinned in delight. "So we have quinoa spinach bites, string pea guacamole, three-color hummus, cherry tomato bites, cashew cheese spread, stuffed mushrooms, black bean dip, spring rolls, plantain chips and lots of other delicious vegan goodies." She turned to me. "Do you like vegetables?"

If Caitlin had been there she would have dropped to the floor and laughed her ass off. I had no choice, really, but to lie. "Of course. It looks wonderful."

She clapped her hands again and picked up a plate, loaded it with a little bit of everything and then topped it off with what looked like a brownie. Could it be? If so it was most likely a vegan brownie, but did I care? No, I decided, I did not. Willow ran on one speed — fast — and I chased after her as she sped off toward the front of the store and found a huge, overstuffed blue chair in the corner that had just been vacated.

Willow nodded in satisfaction. "Well, that's good timing." She set the plate of food on the small table next to the chair and ordered me to sit. I didn't argue. In fact, I could tell it would be futile to argue with this woman.

I sat down in the chair, sinking into the cushions. "Thank you. I appreciate your hospitality. You've been very kind."

Willow settled her hands on her hips. "Well, any friend of Maxim's is a friend of mine. When he said he was bringing a lady along, I was thrilled … absolutely thrilled. I've known him since before he was famous. I just think the world of him, and I want him to be happy. He really deserves it, you know, after what happened with his wife. It was so awful for him, taking care of her for so long. She was a sweetheart, but it was still terribly stressful." I heard someone call Willow's name. The tone was urgent, but she seemed unconcerned. "I'd be happy to give you that tour I promised, but you've pretty much seen the entire store." She laughed. "We're small but mighty here at The Bookworm."

I crossed my legs and leaned back, curious about the details of Maxim's wife, but it wouldn't be right to ask Willow. Maxim would tell me when he was ready. "I'll eat my food and then mosey around until Maxim is done."

She peeked over her shoulder at the meeting room. "Well, that will take a couple of hours. The place is packed. There's an upstairs you haven't seen that's filled with used books; the staircase is at the back of the store. Help yourself." She stretched to her full height. "And there's more food up there as well."

"Thanks. I'll check it out." I picked up what I guessed was a plantain chip and bit into it timidly. I almost gagged but managed to smile as I choked it down.

Willow's name was called again, and this time the tone was frantic. "Well, I'd better go … sounds like the place is on fire." She hurried away.

I set down my cup of coffee and picked up the plate of vegan food which I eyed suspiciously. I was overwhelmed by all of the vegetables. Caitlin would scream if she saw my plate. I decided to take a picture to show her. I pulled out my phone and snapped two pictures, one with the brownie and one without. I ate the brownie first — it wasn't half bad — and then I nibbled at a spring roll that was filled with thinly-sliced carrots, celery, peppers and other vegetables I couldn't identify. I picked up a whole-wheat cracker and dipped it in the hummus. It wasn't terrible, but I opted out of a second bite. I popped a stuffed mushroom in my mouth — icky — and forced it down, and then I swallowed a cherry tomato bite — yuck again. I was glad we ate at the hotel or I would have been near starving.

I was proud of myself for trying everything on the plate — and would report as much to Mommy Caitlin — but in the end the only thing I actually liked was the brownie. I picked up the plate and located a trash can where I tossed the entire works upside down so no one would see how much food I wasted. I returned to the chair in the corner and picked up my coffee cup that was still half full. I walked around the bookstore and discretely snapped photos for Caitlin, including one of Willow working behind the front counter, and then I stepped to the door of the meeting room and captured several images of Maxim signing books. He was absorbed in the process and didn't notice me.

I decided to inspect Willow's little bookstore, and I took pictures of the nooks, crannies and unusual spots filled with books. When I reached the back of the building I saw the staircase and made my way up to the second floor. It, likewise, was crammed with books and overstuffed chairs. I zigzagged around the throngs of people and came across a long table filled with exact replicas of the food downstairs. I snagged two of the largest vegan brownies on the platter and nibbled at them as I inspected the titles of the used books.

I waited until the narrow stairs were clear of people and stepped back down to the main level. My smiley face coffee cup was empty, so I carried it to the coffee bar and set it on the counter, then I turned and scanned the room and noticed a wall filled with photos. Upon closer examination I saw that the frames were filled with photos of Willow posing with famous writers. "Willow's Wall of Fame" was painted in block letters in the center of the collage. I recognized authors whose books I'd read, and I found a photo of a younger Maxim bending down to give Willow a kiss on her cheek.

I walked into the meeting room and surveyed the crowd — over half of the seats were now empty. I pulled out my phone and checked the time: 9:04 pm. We'd be here awhile. I settled off to the side and watched Maxim sign books and pose for pictures. He must have sensed my presence because he glanced over, and when he saw me standing there he grinned broadly, tapped an imaginary watch on his wrist and shrugged his shoulders as if to apologize for how long this was taking. I was unconcerned and shook my head to let him know that I had all the time in the world.

And it was true. Where did I have to be?

It was time for another cup of coffee.

Chapter 21

We stumbled into the atrium at The Brown Palace Hotel and sank onto one of the couches facing the Christmas tree. It was 11:04 pm and there were few people about. The piano was even vacant. My stomach growled in protest; the vegan brownies hadn't stuck with me.

Maxim read my thoughts. "Man, I'm hungry. Willow offered to send me a plate of her vegan food, I guess they call it, but I'd rather starve to death."

I laughed. "Yeah, she filled a plate for me, and I ended up throwing most of it away. Damn good brownies, though."

He slouched down on the couch and rubbed his temples. "Did you get high off the brownies?"

I stared at the piano, tempted to play it. "What do you mean?"

"You know, Rocky Mountain High? Willow is known to partake in marijuana, especially after a stressful day at work. She told me once that she makes a mean pot brownie."

I smiled at the image of Willow smoking a joint. "Well, I ate three brownies and I think I'd know if I was high. They were vegan, though. No doubt about it."

"All the talk of brownies is making me even more hungry." Maxim pulled out his phone. "It's past 11. The restaurants here stop serving food at 11."

I rested into the couch cushion. "Should we go out?"

"If it's all the same to you, I'd rather not. I'm beat. You may not believe it but signing your name and smiling for three hours is exhausting work."

"No, I believe you. After the first hour I would have bolted."

Maxim sat up and turned to me. "Listen, they have 24-hour room service here. Why don't you come to my suite and we can order some food?" Before I could protest he rushed to explain. "I promise I'll be a perfect gentleman. You sit wherever you like, and I'll sit on a different piece of furniture, cross my heart. I won't come anywhere near you. What do you think?"

I paused to consider and decided to continue the day's theme which was, You Only Live Once. "That sounds nice, actually, but on one condition."

Maxim eyed me closely. "Name it."

I sighed. "I could really use a drink … of the alcoholic variety."

He laughed. "So could I." He jumped up and held out his hand. "Let's show you the Eisenhower Suite. You're not going to believe it."

We rode the elevator to the eighth floor, and my stomach clenched at the thought of being alone with Maxim. He used his keycard to open the door to the Eisenhower Suite and then stepped aside, allowing me to enter first. When I walked into the foyer that featured black and white checkerboard tile, I gasped at the sight. The large opening directly in front of me led to an elegant living room, and when I looked through the spacious doorway to my left I was shocked to see a dining room with a formal table that seated eight. To my right was a half bath which meant there was a full bathroom elsewhere in the suite.

Maxim placed his hand at the small of my back and led me straight ahead through the doorway and into a long living room that looked utterly presidential with navy and gold carpet, swagged draperies in cream and navy with gold tassels, a maroon- and blue-striped couch, maroon chairs with scalloped wooden backs, and cherry end tables. I walked to the fireplace with its white mantel and examined two photos of President Dwight Eisenhower — one of him golfing and the other with Winston Churchill. I noted the presidential-looking desk in the corner.

I turned to Maxim. "This suite is as big as my apartment."

He shook his head. "But not as cozy."

I surveyed the room and scrutinized the furniture. "You're right. This furniture doesn't look very comfortable, but it's an impressive room nonetheless."

Maxim pointed to a doorway on the far wall of the living room. "The master bedroom is in there. I'm going to change into something more comfortable."

I raised an eyebrow. "Doesn't the woman usually do that?"

"I'm not going to change into a negligee … well, not unless you want me to." He paused and I remained quiet. "No, I'm going to change because there's way too much starch in this dress shirt and it itches like crazy."

"Okay, I'll let you change." I waved my hand. "Be off with you now."

He laughed and disappeared into the bedroom. I strolled into the dining room and inspected the beautiful presidential china on display in the corner cabinets. A few minutes later Maxim found me. "That feels much better." He'd changed into a cream V-neck sweater and jeans and motioned me into the living room. "Why don't we order some food?"

I sank into in a navy blue lounge chair and Maxim handed me a room service menu. Flipping through the pages, I was surprised at the lengthy selection.

He sat on the couch and scanned a second menu. "I suggest we each order a different item from the entree menu, and then we can share. What do you think?"

I told him that sounded like a great idea. I spent several minutes perusing the options. "I think I'll have the Slow-Roasted Prime Rib. Make sure they send up some horseradish."

Maxim nodded. "And I'm going to have the Filet Mignon. How do you like your prime rib?"

"Medium rare."

He grinned. "That's exactly how I like my steak cooked. I'm going to order a bottle of wine. Anything specific you like?"

I shrugged. "If it's wine I'll drink it. You decide."

Maxim jumped up and walked to the desk where he picked up the phone and punched zero. While he was placing our order, I removed my boots and walked to the master bedroom off the living area. It was a sea of maroon: the carpet was solid maroon and the bedding, draperies, chairs and wallpaper were white- and maroon-patterned. The four-poster bed was so high off the ground that two steps led up to it. A full bathroom with tile and granite was just off the bedroom.

I didn't hear Maxim sneak up behind me, and I jumped when he spoke. "I always sleep well in here. Must be all of the maroon. Is there enough for your liking?" I detected a teasing tone in his voice.

I was suddenly flustered; his body was just inches from mine, and I could feel his breath in my hair. "I think it would look better in the dark." I immediately flinched at the unintended double entendre.

Maxim laughed, and I knew that if I turned around I'd be so close I'd feel the heat radiating off his body. I imagined him against me, his hands in my hair, his lips on my neck. It was a tempting thought, giving myself to this man. We were already in the bedroom, and I imagined the bed was as comfortable as it looked. But was that truly what I wanted? My mind raced and I felt for the pendant at my throat. After what seemed like an eternity but was only a few seconds, I stepped forward and walked around him to the living room where I sat down in one of the matching chairs facing the window. My hands were trembling.

Maxim was either oblivious to what had just happened, or he chose to ignore it out of politeness. He walked into the living room and sat on the couch across from me. "The food will be here in about 30 minutes. I told them to go ahead and send up the wine."

I crossed my legs and sat back. "Wonderful. I could really use a drink."

That was the understatement of the day.

It was after midnight when we finished eating. Maxim refilled my wine glass.

"Thank you." I swirled the liquid, inspected the color and sipped it slowly. "This Cabernet is amazing."

Maxim drank some wine and set his glass on the coffee table. "I agree, but I can't take credit. When I placed our order I asked what wine they suggested … this was it."

I tipped back my head for a long drink, and then I held the wine glass in both hands. "Do you always treat yourself like this after a long evening of signing books?"

Maxim sat back on the couch and rested his head on the cushion. "Sometimes … it just depends on the mood I'm in. Tonight I convinced a beautiful woman to come to my room, so I'm living it up." He smiled and traced the pattern on the couch.

I sat forward and studied the room, pretending to look for someone. "Where'd she go? Did you run her off already?" I giggled, sat back and sipped some more wine.

Maxim grinned and reached for his glass. "No, this one stayed … although I'm not sure why."

I crossed my legs. "This one stayed because she's having a great time with a wonderful man who has a lot of money and isn't afraid to spend it."

Maxim raised his glass in the air. "To the woman who stayed."

I lifted my glass. "To the man who paid for the wine."

We smiled at each other and drained our glasses. Maxim pointed to the bottle. "More?"

I nodded yes even though I was a bit light-headed. "Absolutely. It goes along with my motto for this trip."

Maxim walked over and filled my glass with wine, then steadied his gaze on me. "Which is?"

"You only live once!" I picked up my wine glass and raised it in the air.

He smiled and returned to the couch where he filled his glass half full. "Sounds like an excellent motto." He rested his elbows on his knees and regarded me with interest. His blue eyes boldly ran the length of me, and I felt butterflies stir in my stomach as he inspected my mouth, my chin, my neck. He steepled his fingers and rested them on his rosy lips. "I can't tell you how amazing it was to have you there with me tonight. I usually feel so alone at these things, but just knowing you were there — even if I couldn't always see you — filled me with a happiness I haven't felt in a long time."

I spent a few moments thinking about his statement. "I know what you mean. I've been happy today and that's not always the case with me."

He smiled, but there was a sadness to it. "Today has been very special. I'm not afraid to tell you that I really don't want it to end."

My stomach flipped and I matched his intense gaze instead of looking away. His eyes were so clear, so captivating, so mesmerizing. "I don't want it to end, either."

I was utterly drawn to everything about this man: his incredible looks, his kindness, his intelligence, his thoughtfulness. He was the most gorgeous man I'd ever seen, and I knew that if I let him, he would take me to the king-sized bed in the Eisenhower Suite and make love to me until dawn. The attraction was there — I knew it was mutual — and it would be so easy to give in to what my body was begging for. I wanted him.

My own brother said a "roll in the hay" would do me good.

Maxim's eyes never left my face. He watched me drain the rest of my wine, set the glass on the end table, stand up … and when I walked to the couch and sat next to him, surprise registered on his face but was soon replaced with desire. It was clear that he wanted me as much as I wanted him.

I gently placed my hands on his shoulders and stared into his blue eyes. He sat completely still, and I knew it was up to me to make the next move. I leaned in, brushed my lips against his and felt him shudder. He was hesitant at first, but as I kissed him he tilted his head to the side and kissed me back with an intensity that sent tingles to my toes; our mouths melted together, and the sensations that passed through my body awakened a part of me that had been dormant for what seemed like eons.

Maxim suddenly pulled away and stared into my eyes. "Are you sure this is what you want?"

I nodded my head. "Yes." With that one word the dam that had been holding Maxim back shattered into a million pieces. His hands caressed my back as he kissed my lips and then moved down to my neck where he ran his teeth along the skin and nibbled my jawline. He moved to my ear and tickled it with his tongue. His hands found my breasts and he moaned in pleasure. "God, I want you."

I caressed the muscles of his back, and when he lowered his head to my neck I inhaled the scent of him and was overtaken with desire. I ran my fingers through his thick, black hair and pulled back so that I could study his face in detail, trace the contours of his jaw and touch his full, red lips. He kissed my finger and held my gaze as he slowly lowered me onto my back. His breath was erratic, and his eyes were black with desire. I wanted to feel the weight of him, the hardness of him, but when I pulled his body on top of mine, it happened.

Danny flashed before my eyes.

Maxim moaned in pleasure, buried his head in my neck and gently bit the skin under my ear. I could feel him responding to my touch, growing harder as his excitement rose. I reached down to feel him — God, it had been so long — but when my fingers reached the button on his pants it happened again.

Danny flashed before my eyes.

I sat up abruptly, my brain fuzzy from desire, four glasses of wine and Danny appearing from the deep recesses of my mind. I leaned forward and dropped my head into my hands. Maxim sat up and pulled me close. "What is it? Did I do something wrong?"

I didn't know what to say. How do you explain to your new boyfriend that your dead boyfriend suddenly appeared just as you were about to make love to him?

Maxim bent down to kiss my lips, but I pulled away and shook my head. "I can't do this. I'm sorry. I really didn't mean to lead you on. I thought I was ready, but I guess I'm not." I rubbed my right temple as a headache threatened to appear.

Maxim reached for my other hand and stroked it. "I understand."

We looked at each other, and I read sadness in his eyes. I touched his cheek and leaned in for a gentle kiss. When our lips parted I pulled back and rested my forehead against his. "You're a good man. Just give me a little time, okay?"

He nodded but remained quiet. Unsteadily I rose, retrieved my coat, purse and boots, and held them tightly in my arms. Maxim walked me to the door, and when we reached it I turned to face him. "I'll see you in the morning for breakfast?"

He crossed his arms. "Sure."

"Thanks again for everything today. I really enjoyed it."

He stared at his feet. "I'm glad. You deserve the best."

"Well, good night, then." I opened the door and stepped into the hallway.

I barely heard Maxim mumble goodnight as I padded toward the elevator in my socks.

Chapter 22

I laid on the bed in Room 312, fully dressed, and stared at the ceiling. Five floors above me a gorgeous man in the Eisenhower Suite was wondering why I'd left him.

Danny, what are you doing to me? Was that really you or did my guilty conscience conjure your image to get me out of that room, away from that man?

Since I didn't believe in ghosts I supposed it was the latter. It was guilt. I felt guilty for wanting another man even though Danny had been dead for ten years. Well, almost ten years — in three days it would be exactly ten years since he died. A tear streamed down my face and I wiped it on the comforter.

For the first five years after Danny died I was heartbroken and never looked at another man with any kind of romantic interest. I kept my head down and stayed busy in order to survive. For the past five years my celibacy had been a decision — I would not dishonor Danny's memory by cheating on him. The thought of replacing him made me sick to my stomach, and it wasn't an issue because I hadn't met anyone who interested me in that way. Until three days ago, that is.

My brain was in torment. I could take the elevator to the eighth floor and offer myself to Maxim, but I knew what would happen when he led me to his four-poster bed — Danny would show up again. That's what happens with unresolved issues — they keep resurfacing until they're dealt with.

The day I met Danny O'Neill I was tacking cardboard snowmen to a bulletin board in the music room at Prairie View Elementary School in Olathe, Kansas, a suburb of Kansas City. It was January 2, 2004, and I'd been hired to replace the music teacher who resigned after she fell in love over Thanksgiving and eloped over Christmas. The principal at Prairie View Elementary was in a bind and I was in need of a job. It was my first gig as a newly-minted music teacher.

School would be back in session in just three days, and I was frenzied as I put my mark on the classroom and drew up lesson plans. I was pleased with the snowmen I'd designed: they each held a music note and its value, and I'd hung a blue background that contrasted nicely with the white snowmen and their colorful hats and scarves. The bulletin board was titled, "Music Is Snow Much Fun!"

I was focused on taping up the snowflakes I'd cut out of coffee filters when I heard a male voice behind me. "Miss Somers?" I spun around and was face-to-face with the biggest Irish cliché I'd ever seen.

The man held out his hand. "I'm sorry I startled you." I extended my hand and he gripped it in a firm handshake. "I'm Mr. O'Neill, the Assistant Principal here. Danny's my first name. I just wanted to welcome you to Prairie View Elementary School. We're excited you've joined our teaching staff."

Then he smiled, and I was totally blown away; his grin stretched from ear to ear and lit up the entire room. When I say Danny O'Neill was the biggest Irish cliché I'd ever seen, I wasn't exaggerating. The man looked like he'd stepped straight out of Dublin, Ireland. He was 6'5" with a mop of red hair, fair skin and a light dusting of freckles across his nose and cheeks. His eyes were so green it looked like he was wearing colored contact lenses. (He wasn't.) There was a hint of mischief in his smile and a gleam in his eye. He was a striking man with broad shoulders and a trim waist. I guessed he was in his early 30s. The sheer size of him was imposing but my first impression was that he was a gentle giant. I would soon learn that life was fun for Danny O'Neill, and he wanted everyone around him to also have fun.

"It's nice to meet you, Mr. O'Neill."

He gazed into my eyes, and his expression was kind. "Do you have time for a friendly chat? I'd like to get to know you before school starts."

"Of course." I gestured toward my desk. "Why don't we sit down." I walked to my chair and he retrieved a folding chair from the corner. He laughed as he unfolded it and sat down. "I've learned not to sit in the student chairs. I've broken several, and the principal said that the next one I destroy will come out of my paycheck. If you hadn't noticed, I'm not a small man."

I'd noticed. "I guess we still learn the hard way."

"Unfortunately, we do." He crossed an ankle over his knee and settled back in the chair. "So I've looked through your file and read your resume. I see you're a graduate of Kansas State University. That's a great school."

"Yes. I really enjoyed it there." I straightened a file on the desk.

"And you were a star on their volleyball team."

I blushed, picked up a stray paper clip from my desk and bent it between my fingers. "Well, I wouldn't say I was a star, but I did have my moments."

Mr. O'Neill crossed his arms and noted my unease. "I admire your modesty. After reading your resume I was curious, so I Googled you. In the world of college volleyball, you were definitely a star."

I pulled out the small part of the paperclip and bent it backward. I avoided his gaze. "I'm not sure what to say."

He paused and watched me fidget. "I can see I've made you uncomfortable, so I'll shut up about your college volleyball days. I just want you to know that we're thrilled to have someone of your caliber here. We pride ourselves on giving new teachers their first jobs. I've found that teachers fresh out of school are full of great ideas and lots of enthusiasm. You have the support of the staff, the principal, the school board..." He pointed to himself. "...and me."

I dropped the paperclip, looked up and smiled. "Thank you. That means a lot to me. I love children and music, so teaching seemed the perfect fit for me."

He uncrossed his legs and leaned forward. "I'm glad to hear it. I hope you'll like it here. We currently have an enrollment of 302 students, and there are 35 elementary schools in the Olathe School District." He paused and looked out the window. "Do you have a place to live? I hope you're not in a hotel until you find an apartment."

I put his mind at ease. "No. The music teacher who resigned..."

"Miss Hamel. Well, I guess that's not her name anymore since she got married. Unless she kept her maiden name ... some women do. Anyway, you were saying..."

"Well, Miss Hamel left town with her new husband and skipped out on her apartment lease. I was asking the school secretary for suggestions about where to live and she said I should talk to Miss Hamel's roommate, Trina. We met for coffee and got along surprisingly well so I moved in with her. It worked out for both of us."

Danny nodded. "I'm happy to hear that. Do you have any questions that I can answer?"

I thought for a moment but drew a blank. "Not right now. I'm sure I will later."

He jumped up. "Well, my door is always open, Miss Somers. Stop by any time. Do you know where my office is?" I told him that I did, and then I followed him to the door. "It's great to have you on board. I'll be seeing you around." He shook my hand and turned to leave but stopped to admire the cardboard snowmen. "I've got to tell you ... I love this bulletin board. And I agree. Music is snow much fun!" He grinned and was gone.

My first semester of teaching flew by, and I'm sure I learned more than my students. Teaching was everything I dreamed it would be, and the children were lively and engaging. Every moment of my downtime was devoted to preparing lesson plans, and I knew I was going above and beyond what was required of me. I heard that was common with new teachers. The veteran teachers laughed and shook their heads at the new teachers, but they'd also been guilty of over-zealousness in their first years of teaching.

I saw Danny in the hallways engaging with the students, and he was always smiling. His personality was like a magnet, drawing children to his side. I soon learned he was the master of silly jokes and bad puns, and the kids ate it up. If he'd been the pied piper, they would have followed him anywhere.

I heard the other teachers talking about Mr. O'Neill's anti-bullying policy. He counseled children who were being bullied, but he believed the bully needed support as well. He had a sixth sense for the children who needed a little extra attention, and it was common for him to show up at students' homes with food, warm coats, whatever they needed. I once spotted him slipping a bag of packaged food into a student's backpack on Friday afternoon.

I also heard he had a serious girlfriend who was a pediatrician in Kansas City. When Danny saw me at school he was kind and courteous. "If there's anything you need, don't hesitate to ask."

The school year ended, and I spent most of the summer in Waconda helping out on the farm. In my spare time I created games, projects and worksheets to engage my students and teach them the fundamentals of music. I returned to Olathe in August filled with excitement and a pile of new teaching ideas.

Danny O'Neill was back as well, and our relationship remained professional but friendly. His caring attitude and sense of humor livened up the school. He ran the faculty meetings, and they were never boring. He roamed the hallways during breaks searching out the students who needed words of encouragement. He ate lunch in the cafeteria, sat with a different group of students each day and wouldn't allow any student to eat alone.

I loved teaching music at Prairie View Elementary School, and with each passing month I gained confidence in my ability to teach effectively.

I fell into a comfortable pattern: I lived with Trina in Olathe during the school year and spent my summer breaks on the farm. Summer was a source of rejuvenation for me. I drove a truck during wheat harvest, water skied with friends at the lake on the weekends and sat on the front porch in the evenings drinking beer with Brice and Dad. After the Fourth of July holiday I turned my thoughts to the coming school year and threw myself into creating new material that would excite my students.

When I returned to Prairie View Elementary School in August of 2006 it was soon clear that Mr. Danny O'Neill's interest in me had turned from friendly to something more. He'd drop into my classroom unexpectedly, "just to say hello," and he'd linger for no apparent reason. When he saw me in the hallways he'd fast track it over to see how I was doing. He tossed compliments my way almost daily. "That's a beautiful dress." "Your hair looks especially nice today." Strangest of all, he sometimes called me by my first name. "Bree, that's an amazing necklace. The color brings out your eyes."

An attraction between us was brewing, and I looked forward to our interactions. I asked around and learned he'd broken up with his girlfriend in April after he caught her cheating on him. Ouch. I wondered when, and if, he would make his move.

One day in October of 2006 I returned to my classroom from a bathroom break, and Mr. O'Neill was in my room studying the musical staff on a bulletin board. He heard me walk in and turned around. "You know, I never learned to read music. I regret it."

I walked over to him and clasped my fingers behind my back in a classic teacher pose. "That's a shame."

"If I'd had a teacher like you there's no doubt I would have been in a rock band. Lead guitar, of course." He grinned and sat down in a red kid-sized chair; it strained under his weight.

I laughed. "You know that if you break the chair, you'll have to pay for it."

"Yeah, but I don't care right now." He pulled over a blue kid-sized chair and patted the seat. "Would you sit down?"

I did what he asked and waited for him to speak. Normally confident, he seemed unsure what to do. He leaned back, crossed his arms and regarded me seriously. I noted the beads of sweat on his forehead. His right knee bobbed up and down.

"You've put me in a bit of a bind, Miss Bree Somers."

I couldn't imagine what he meant. "How's that?" My mind raced. Had a parent complained about my teaching style? Was I in trouble with the school board? Did I talk excessively at faculty meetings?

He noted my panic and shook his head. "I don't mean as a teacher. You're doing a fantastic job." I breathed a sigh of relief, and he patted the left side of his chest. "I mean in here. I'm afraid I'm falling for you." He waited a moment and then continued. "No, that's not right. I've already fallen for you."

I blushed and chewed on a fingernail. I knew exactly what he meant because I'd also felt the chemistry between us.

He leaned forward and propped his elbows on his knees. The tiny chair groaned under his weight. "It doesn't feel right to talk about this at school, but I was wondering if you'd go to dinner with me Friday evening. I need to tell you how I feel about you, otherwise my head's going to explode." He sat back and locked his fingers behind his troubled head.

His honesty was refreshing. The man obviously did not believe in playing dating games. I hated them too.

I smiled and folded my hands. "I'd love to go to dinner with you."

His smile lit up the room. "Really? Wow." He sat and stared at me for a minute. "That's great. Okay. What now? I didn't expect you to say yes."

I chuckled. "You didn't have a plan for yes?"

He ran his fingers through his thick, red hair. "I guess I'd talked myself into believing you'd say no so I could handle the disappointment better." We sat in silence and stared at each other. I smiled and then he smiled. Finally he spoke. "Okay, here it is. Why don't I pick you up at 6:30 on Friday and then we'll decide where to eat? Let's dress casual, like nice casual, okay?" He slapped his hands on his thighs and sat up straight. "Wonderful. Okay. It's a date."

We stood up at the same time, and I walked him to the door. He turned and our bodies were just inches apart. His beautiful green eyes gazed down into mine. "I'm really looking forward to spending the evening with you … Bree."

"So am I … Danny." His eyes brightened when I said his first name. He turned and walked down the hallway whistling "Oh Happy Day," off key but with gusto.

Our date that Friday evening was instant chemistry, and by midnight we were making out in his car in front of my apartment building. After that it seemed natural to spend most of our time together, and within a few months I knew I was in love. Danny was sweet and tender … he showered me with attention and random acts of thoughtfulness. I never knew what would show up on my desk at school … it might be flowers, M&Ms (my favorite), jewelry or a handmade card with a sweet note in his sloppy handwriting.

I was extremely attracted to him, and I knew he felt the same, but when we were alone I sensed he was holding back. We kissed, of course, but when I'd start to unbutton his shirt or take it to the next level he'd invent an excuse: he was tired, or he had to wake up early the next morning.

Finally, he explained: when he was in his early 20s he drank every weekend, did drugs and slept around. One of his various "girlfriends" became pregnant, but during the first trimester she lost the baby in a miscarriage. It rocked Danny to his core, and he determined to shape up his life. He deeply regretted his recklessness. On his 25th birthday he took a vow of chastity: he would wait until he was married to have sex. He stopped doing drugs and focused on his future.

I loved his honesty, respected his decision and so when we spent time at his apartment we stayed away from the bedroom and limited our interactions to kissing and snuggling. As you can guess, it wasn't always easy, but in the end our mutual attraction was strong — but our will was stronger.

The day of my 27th birthday — Saturday, December 15, 2007 — Danny arranged a day filled with my favorite things. In the afternoon we shopped at The Plaza and ice skated at Crown Center, and in the evening we ate at the 1950s-style diner, Shake, Rattle & Roll. Their cheeseburgers and fries were the best in Kansas City.

I was sipping on a chocolate shake when Danny pulled a jewelry box out of his pocket and pushed it across the Formica table. "Happy Birthday."

I batted my eyes. "Why Mr. O'Neill, you shouldn't have." I opened the box and screamed when I saw the diamond stud earrings. "Forget I said that." I lunged across the table and kissed him, and then I pulled out the cheap hoop earrings I was wearing and replaced them with my new diamond earrings. I dug in my purse for the compact mirror and admired myself from several angles.

Danny's smile stretched from ear to ear as he watched my face. "Just so you know, they're real."

"So are you." I leaned across the table and kissed him again. "I love you."

He pulled my fingers to his lips. "And I love you."

Danny drove us to Union Station, one of Kansas City's most iconic buildings. We held hands as we walked into the Grand Hall, and I marveled at the magnificent architecture. I'd been staring at the 95-foot ceiling, a piece of artwork unto itself, and when I looked down Danny was kneeling on the marble floor holding yet another jewelry box. My breath caught in my throat.

I knew what he was about to ask me, but when I glanced at his face I was suddenly concerned. Danny didn't look well. Beads of perspiration dotted his forehead, his skin was pasty white, and his lips were the color of blood. It appeared he would topple to the floor at any moment, and when he spoke his voice was shaky. "Bree Somers, I love you, and I want to spend my life with you. Will you marry me?" He managed to open the jewelry box, and I was blown away by the most beautiful ring I'd ever seen, a blue sapphire mounted in the center of five diamonds in the shape of a flower.

I knelt beside Danny and wrapped my arms around his shoulders. "Yes, I will marry you, Danny O'Neill."

He managed a weak smile. "Thank goodness or it would have been a really embarrassing story to tell them at the ER." I helped him stand and we sat down on a nearby bench where he pulled the ring out of its box and pushed it on my finger. The color slowly returned to his face and he smiled brightly. "I guess we'll have quite a story for the grandkids, huh, about the day Grandpa almost fainted when he asked Grandma to marry him."

"Yes, we will." I held him close and laid my head on his shoulder.

Could life get any better, I wondered, as we drove to Danny's apartment. Once inside we tossed our coats on the couch and, without saying a word, we walked into his bedroom, tore off each other's clothes and spent the night making love. I couldn't get close enough to him, and I knew he felt the same as we kissed and explored each other's bodies. When I opened my eyes on Sunday morning we were a tangle of arms and legs, and even with our bad breath and wild hair I felt like the luckiest girl in the world.

Danny offered a goofy grin. "That was fun."

I laughed out loud. "That's an understatement, Mr. O'Neill."

He linked his fingers with mine. "Whatever you say, Mrs. O'Neill."

I couldn't believe I'd get to spend the rest of my life with this man, and I looked forward to thousands of nights together. We'd broken Danny's vow of chastity, but it didn't seem to matter anymore; we were deeply devoted to each other and engaged to be married. I knew he was the only man for me. How fortuitous we didn't wait. There would be no wedding night for us.

Five days later the dream came crashing down. Literally.

The last day Danny O'Neill walked this earth was Friday, December 21, 2007. He roamed the halls of Prairie View Elementary School, as usual, delighting the children with his presence, and when he saw me he winked, and I blushed at the memory of rolling around in his bed the weekend before.

It was the last day of school before Christmas break, and the teachers had organized "holiday" games in the gymnasium. I was in charge of the caroling, and I led groups of children through the hallways singing Christmas — excuse me — "holiday" carols.

I'd been stressed for weeks planning and rehearsing the winter musical program, "Let It Snow." It went off with only a few hitches two nights before, and I was eager for Christmas break.

After school Danny dropped by my room to pick me up. He shut the door and rushed over to hug me. "Guess what I want to do tonight?"

I linked my arms around his neck. "Go bowling?"

He laughed and rubbed my back. "No, I was thinking about a fun activity we can do at my place."

I kissed his cheek. "Monopoly?"

He smiled and nuzzled my neck. "You're getting warmer."

I frowned. "I can't imagine what you mean."

He pulled me as close as possible. "Why don't we drive to my apartment now and I'll show you what I mean."

I kissed him on the lips. "It's a deal."

I pulled on my coat, grabbed my purse and bag, and we left the school. Danny drove us through the busy streets of Olathe and regaled me with a hilarious story about one of our students; we roared with laughter. Talk turned to Christmas break and our plans for visiting each other's families. It was the happiest I'd ever been. Love is a drug, and I was totally high.

We'd been hitting mostly green lights, and Danny even commented on it. "Must be my lucky day." At the next green light I looked over at Danny; he was smiling his beautiful smile that took my breath away. I remember thinking how much I loved this kind and gentle giant, and in the next instant I saw the car that would destroy our lives veering directly toward us. I didn't even have time to scream before the grey SUV slammed into Danny's door. My air bag deployed. Glass shattered at the impact, and the sound of metal on metal and screeching tires was deafening. My head and right arm hit the passenger door as the car spun around to face the direction from which we'd come. The crash seemed to last forever and yet it was over in seconds.

When the car stopped I was dazed and confused, yet coherent enough to lean toward Danny and see if he was okay. He wasn't. His body was slumped forward, and his head was resting on the steering wheel where the air bag hadn't deployed. Blood was everywhere. I remember screaming but I couldn't hear a thing. I lifted Danny's head off the steering wheel, and when I saw his face I knew in an instant there was no longer life in my 6'5" guy. Even as I held his face and called his name, my heart told me he was gone. I couldn't feel him anymore.

In that moment my world ended.

It didn't matter that strangers stopped to help. He was gone.

It didn't matter that the paramedics showed up in three minutes. He was gone.

It didn't matter that I'd suffered a concussion and my right arm was severely broken in three places. He was gone.

It didn't matter. Nothing mattered.

I was in disbelief. Grief and sadness would come later, but in that moment I was numb. Dead inside. Paramedics lifted me from the car and laid me on a stretcher. I watched Danny's lifeless body as they wheeled me to an ambulance, lifted me inside and shut the doors. From that moment on my memories are hazy at best, but I do remember a doctor explaining the injuries to my arm and that she wanted to operate immediately. I must have signed a release for the surgery; I don't recall. I didn't care what happened to my arm.

My roommate, Trina, showed up at the hospital; months later, when I was piecing together that day, I wondered how they knew to call her. We lost touch so I never found out. Trina called my father and sat with me until I was wheeled off to surgery. One rod and six pins were needed to put my right arm and elbow back together. Dad and Brice drove the four-hour trip from Waconda to Olathe in just three hours. I was under heavy sedation and slept until Sunday when the doctor lowered the dosage of medication. I woke up at 10:32 am.

At first I was confused by my surroundings. It appeared I was a patient in a hospital room, but why? My right arm was heavy, and I couldn't lift it. When I looked down I saw a white cast running from my shoulder to my wrist. I glanced up and saw Dad and Brice standing at the foot of the bed; their faces were ashen, and they didn't say a word. I stared at Dad's face; a lone tear ran down his cheek.

And then it hit me. Danny was dead.

The full force of this reality landed like an elephant on my chest. My heart … my heart felt like it would explode into a thousand tiny pieces. I cried softly at first, and soon sobs shook my body. Wordlessly Dad and Brice flanked the bed and comforted me. Dad spoke soothing words in a comforting tone and ran his fingers through my hair. Brice held my hands and cried openly. I bawled for what seemed like hours, and in the midst of it I threw up until there was nothing left in my stomach, much like my heart.

When I was able to speak I asked what day it was. Sunday. Had I missed Danny's funeral? Dad said no, it was in the morning, on December 24. I insisted that I would be going, and he nodded his head. The doctor was reluctant to discharge me so soon after the surgery, but she finally agreed if I promised to use a wheelchair at the funeral. I didn't fight it. I was actually relieved; I was neither physically nor mentally prepared to walk into Danny's funeral on my own.

The next morning, on Christmas Eve, a nurse helped me shower and wash my hair. Trina brought black pants, a gray sweater and black boots to the hospital and helped me dress. The sweater's sleeve wouldn't fit over the arm cast, so the nurse cut it along the seam and we discretely taped it to the cast. They draped my heavy winter coat over my shoulders, settled me into the wheelchair and discharged me from the hospital. We drove in silence to St. Elizabeth Catholic Church in the Kansas City neighborhood where Danny grew up. When his family saw me they rushed to the back of the church and surrounded my wheelchair.

Danny's mother, Catherine, sobbed and clung to me; she practically sat with me in the wheelchair. "Oh, you poor girl. We love you so much."

One of Danny's brothers, Bobby, bent down and kissed me on the forehead. "We're so glad you're going to be okay." Tears streamed down his face.

Danny's casket was covered in a white cloth and rolled down the main aisle at the beginning of the Funeral Mass; his huge Irish family streamed in behind him. Catherine pushed my wheelchair to the front pew, sat next to me and held my hand during the entire service. I was the last link to her little boy, and she needed me.

I remember bits and pieces of the service. It was long; Catholic funeral masses always are. There was much sprinkling of holy water and countless prayers. Dozens of plants and flower arrangements flanked the casket and altar. A giant photo of Danny sat on an easel; he was smiling and joyous. He'd always been the life of the party. I chewed on a fingernail and stared at Jesus hanging on the cross behind the altar.

At my insistence Dad drove us to the cemetery. Brice lifted the wheelchair out of the trunk, set it up and pushed it over. I was able to stand, take a few steps and then I practically fell into the chair from exhaustion. My arm hurt like a bitch, and I just wanted the day to be over. Once Danny was buried properly I would leave town and never return.

When the short graveside service was over I heard Danny's father, brothers and uncles talking about the woman who caused the accident. Danny's father was justifiably angry, and his voice was filled with venom. "She'll be charged with vehicular homicide, but I plan to file my own lawsuit. I've already talked to a lawyer. That woman will not get away with killing my son." I asked Dad to take me back to the car.

I rode home to Waconda in Dad's car, and Brice followed in mine. I slept most of the way. Once settled into my childhood room I swallowed anything the doctor would prescribe because the drugs made me drowsy. I craved sleep, because in sleep Danny was still alive and life was still wonderful. Mother tiptoed in with food, but I didn't want it.

A few days later Dad and Brice drove back to Olathe, packed up my belongings, wrote Trina a check for the remainder of the lease and came home. On the first of January I turned in my resignation to Prairie View Elementary School. I wondered how the children would ever get along without Danny. How would I get along without Danny?

I fell apart. For months I laid in my double bed under the pink chenille bedspread of my childhood. I lost 20 pounds that I didn't have to lose. I couldn't cry. I was numb, dead. There was nothing left inside of me. Friends stopped by but I sent them away. Family members stopped by, but I sent them away too.

What did I do day after day after day? On Mondays, Wednesdays and Fridays Dad or Brice drove me to physical therapy where I was indifferent as the therapist forced me to exercise my right arm. She prescribed home exercises that I didn't do. I slept for hours at a time. When I was awake I stared at the walls. I stared at the ceiling. I counted the pink roses in the wallpaper. I daydreamed of a future I would never have with a man who was dead.

Details of the accident trickled in under the door. Jacqueline "Jackie" Green, a 33-year-old mother, was searching for her ringing cell phone when she ran a red light, crashed into the car and killed Danny. Distracted driving is what they called it. There wasn't a drop of alcohol or any drugs in her system; she was sober as a judge.

Three months after the accident Brice walked into my bedroom carrying the Kansas City Star newspaper. "There's a story in here about Jackie Green's sentencing. Do you want to read it? If not I could read it to you."

I shook my head. "No, give it here." I sat up in bed and held out my hands. He turned to page 5, folded back the newspaper and gave it to me. I expected to see a picture of Danny staring at me from the page, but the simple story was void of photos. Danny deserved more. I chocked back a sob.

DEFENDANT SENTENCED TO $2,500
FOR VEHICULAR HOMICIDE
Published March 25, 2008

<u>By Karen Jennings</u> *The Kansas City Star*

An Olathe woman was sentenced to the maximum fine of $2,500 for vehicular homicide with no jail time to be served.

Jacqueline "Jackie" Green was sentenced Tuesday in Johnson County District Court after pleading guilty to one count of vehicular homicide, which is a misdemeanor.

The charge stemmed from the December 21, 2007, crash that resulted in the death of Daniel "Danny" O'Neill, also of Olathe.

Assistant County Attorney Derek Mathers laid out the facts of the case: on December 21, 2007, Jacqueline Green was driving her '07 Mercedes-Benz SLK northbound on Pine Street when she ran a red light at the intersection of Pine Street and Washington Avenue, which resulted in a fatal collision with Daniel O'Neill, who was driving an '01 Buick Regal westbound on Washington Avenue. A front-seat passenger, Breanne Somers, was injured in the accident. Distracted driving was blamed for the accident.

Mathers said both parties were ready for a plea agreement.

Two family members of the victim spoke during the hearing.

Catherine O'Neill, Daniel O'Neill's mother, said that no sentence would bring back her son. "She has her life sentence," said Catherine O'Neill of Jacqueline Green. "She has to live with what she's done, and I hope she takes the time to think about how she killed my baby and devastated our family."

Bobby O'Neill, Daniel O'Neill's older brother, also spoke. "Our family believes in forgiveness," he said, "and we forgive Jacqueline Green for what she has done. But we will never forget. Every day we miss Danny. We always will. The world lost a great man on that terrible day."

Jacqueline Green was not present for the sentencing, but her family issued this statement: "The family of Jacqueline Green deeply regrets her role in the accident that caused the death of Daniel O'Neill. She is truly sorry that she caused the accident that ended the life of such an upstanding man. She hopes that at some point Danny's family can forgive her. She has endured months of physical therapy with the dream of returning home to spend the rest of her life with her family."

During the hearing Judge Martha Wolesky said she'd taken into consideration the fact that Mrs. Green was still recovering in a rehabilitation facility in Nebraska, and that she would be a paraplegic for the rest of her life.

"In light of this life sentence I am considering her condition 'time served' and fining her the maximum of $2,500."

I read the story twice and handed the newspaper to Brice. "Thanks for showing it to me. Once everyone has read it, get it out of here. I never want to see it again."

"Sure, I understand." Brice left the room, and for the first time since coming home I cried. It felt good.

We rarely talked about the accident among our family, and we never spoke of Jackie Green. There wasn't anything to say.

My roommate, Trina, forwarded a letter addressed to me from a law firm in Kansas City that had arrived at our apartment in Olathe. Dad brought it to my room along with a lunch of chicken and noodles that I barely touched. Inside the envelope was a cashier's check for $100,000. A letter on the law office's stationery was included with the check.

April 1, 2008

Ms. Breanne Somers:

On behalf of Jacqueline Green, find enclosed a cashier's check in the amount of $100,000 to be used in whatever way you see fit. Although I have advised against it for the obvious legal reasons, Ms. Green insists that I convey to you her deepest apologies for the accident that killed your fiancé, Daniel O'Neill. While the money in no way makes up for the loss of such a fine young man, Ms. Green is concerned about your medical bills and the cost of physical therapy to rehabilitate your arm. If the money is not needed for medical bills, Ms. Green is hoping you'll be able to use it to advance your future needs.

Larry Bogart
Attorney at Law
Bogart & Bogart, LLC

Mr. Bogart didn't need to worry. I had no intention of suing Jacqueline Green now or in the future. Brice said the O'Neills filed a civil suit against her for distracted driving, but I didn't follow the case, and I only heard from Danny's parents in December when they sent a Christmas card and a poinsettia. I wondered if they'd sue the car company since Danny's airbag hadn't deployed.

I stared at the zeroes on the check. Blood money. I thought of Danny and wondered what he would suggest — should I tear the check to pieces, pay medical bills that my health insurance didn't cover or save it for a memorial to Danny? I thought about it for the rest of the day, and as darkness settled into my room I made a decision; I folded the check into thirds and slipped it under the mattress.

It took time but I eventually left that bedroom, at Dad's insistence, and used the $100,000 to buy the old Rogers building and remodel it to its former glory. I felt Danny would have been pleased with my decision, but of course I didn't really know.

It was good to live again, but I was empty inside. My body was moving on, but my heart was buried with Danny in that grave in Kansas City.

That's grief. It's such a personal thing. Some people wrestle it to the ground and others are frozen in its grasp. It was clear that I was of the frozen variety. Ten years is a long time and yet grief was still leading me around, calling the shots. Guilt had also made an appearance, disguised as Danny, and had driven me from the arms of a man I cared about. I'd hurt him deeply, and he'd done nothing to deserve it.

How would I get past the grief? How would I overcome the guilt?

And most important of all, could I?

Lara Ketter
ANOTHER CHRISTMAS WITHOUT YOU

TUESDAY, DECEMBER 19, 2017

Lara Ketter
ANOTHER CHRISTMAS WITHOUT YOU

248

Chapter 23

I was savoring my second cappuccino when Maxim finally showed up for breakfast at Ellyngton's, a somber look on his face. He leaned down and spoke with the petite hostess who smiled and pointed to me sitting by a window at the far end of the restaurant. When Maxim spotted me he averted his eyes, thanked her and shuffled to the table like a child who'd been called to the principal's office. I pressed the home button on my phone: 9:06 am. When I texted him we'd agreed to meet at 8:45.

Maxim forced a smile, pulled out a chair and sat across from me. "Morning. Sorry I'm late."

I set my cup of cappuccino on the table. "Good morning." I waited for him to explain his tardiness, but he didn't bother. Maxim cast a nervous glance my way and remained quiet.

Our waiter, who'd introduced himself earlier as Phillip, appeared and offered Maxim a menu but he waved it away. "Bring me a double espresso, please."

The waiter nodded. "Would you like anything to eat, sir?"

Maxim shook his head. "Not yet. Maybe a little later."

Phillip turned to me. "Are you ready to order, ma'am?"

"No, I'll wait a bit too."

Phillip nodded again. "Very well." He looked at Maxim. "Your espresso will be right out." He hurried off.

Maxim unfolded the white cloth napkin and spread it on his lap. "How did you sleep?"

I picked up my cappuccino. "About like usual, but I'm sure neither of us slept well last night. I finally gave up at 5 and spent an hour on the hotel's treadmill."

Maxim glanced up, then, and I noted the dark circles under his eyes and the pallor to his skin. His hair was a mess and he wore the same clothes as last night.

He leaned forward and rested his arms on the table. "I'm so sorry. I've been up all night kicking myself for what happened."

I stared at him in amazement. "You feel bad? I'm the one who should apologize for leading you on and then bolting like a frightened child."

Maxim hung his head. "No, this one's on me. You were very clear that you didn't want to come to my suite in the first place, but I twisted your arm until you didn't have a choice."

I glanced around to make sure no one was listening and lowered my voice. "Of course I had a choice. And you were the perfect gentleman you promised to be. I'm the one who came onto you and then left without an explanation. I'm sorry."

Phillip arrived with Maxim's espresso. He set it on the table and turned to me. "Is there anything else you'd like?"

I smiled and turned my attention to our waiter. "Yes, I think I'll have a chocolate croissant and an orange juice."

Phillip nodded. "Excellent choice, ma'am. The chocolate croissant is one of our specialties." He turned to Maxim. "And you, sir? Would you like anything else?"

Maxim glanced up at the waiter. "A bagel and cream cheese would be good."

"I'll have those out in a few minutes." Phillip nodded politely and rushed off.

Maxim slurped at his espresso, sat back and regarded me. "I've made a total mess of things." He ran his fingers through his disheveled hair. "I promised that this would be an innocent, friendly trip, and that's truly what I thought it would be. But honestly, by the time you came to my suite last night I wanted something to happen." He stared straight at me. "And I'm not going to lie — I'm glad it did."

I averted my eyes and stared at the linen tablecloth. I didn't know how to respond.

Maxim cleared his throat and continued. "I know we met only a few days ago, but you've gotten under my skin … I'm falling for you."

I was amazed by his candor, and I glanced up and gazed into his beautiful blue eyes. Suddenly shy, my voice was quiet. "I'm falling for you too."

Maxim smiled, but there was a sadness to it. I wished I knew what he was thinking.

I leaned forward and rested my arms on the table. "I want to explain what happened last night, why I left so suddenly."

"You don't need to explain anything to me. A woman has the right to change her mind."

I shook my head. "But that's not what happened. I mean yes, I changed my mind, but not because of you."

He steepled his fingers and fixed his gaze onto mine.

Suddenly nervous, I drank some cappuccino and sat back in the chair. "I was in love with a man — ten years ago. We were engaged, actually." I stared past Maxim and lost myself in the design of the wallpaper. "His name was Danny O'Neill and he was the most wonderful man I'd ever met. We were crazy about each other." I returned my gaze to Maxim. His eyes hadn't left my face. "I was working as a music teacher in Olathe and he was the assistant principal at the school. Danny was the sweetest, kindest man." I swallowed and felt for the pendant hanging at my throat. Maxim watched my every move.

"Anyway, it was Christmastime and we were really happy, you know? Danny was driving us to his apartment, we were joking and laughing." I looked down at my hands. "The light was green … I mean, he didn't even do anything wrong … and this car — SUV, actually — just came out of nowhere and crashed into us." I looked at Maxim and saw tears running down his face. I was touched that this man cared so deeply. A sob escaped my throat, and I bit my lip. "He died instantly."

Phillip chose that moment to appear with our food. His smile was bright as he set the chocolate croissant and orange juice in front of me, and the bagel and cream cheese in front of Maxim. "Will there be anything else?" He glanced back and forth between us and noted the tears and our somber faces. He lowered his gaze and fidgeted. "I'll leave you to your breakfast." I managed to thank the waiter before he raced off.

Maxim wiped the tears from his face and slouched back in the chair. He clenched and unclenched his jaw. "I'm so sorry. I really am." His words rose from a place deep within his soul; I knew they were sincere. He stared past me, lost in thought.

I pulled a tissue from my purse and dabbed at my wet face. "Well, you of all people know how I feel since you lost someone you loved." Several minutes passed in silence as we sat completely still. Conversation, laughter and the clanking of dishes snaked around us. Finally, I continued. "The reason I'm telling you about this is because it's related to last night. When we were kissing, an image of Danny flashed in my mind." Maxim looked at me, then, concern etched into his face. I chewed on a fingernail. "It freaked me out."

Maxim sat forward and reached for both of my hands, which he held gently on the table. "I'm sure it did."

"I mean, I know it wasn't really him. It was obviously my own guilty conscience telling me to stop kissing you." My voice trembled and I stumbled ahead. "It's been ten years since Danny died. It may sound crazy to you, but I haven't been with another man since then. Not even a kiss. Well, until last night."

Maxim frowned and stared at me. "There's nothing crazy about that. I haven't been with anyone since my wife died, either."

My eyes bored into his. "But it's been ten years. That's a long time. I know I need to move on, but I just can't get myself to do it."

Maxim squeezed both of my hands and stroked my fingers with his thumbs. His voice was low and soothing. "That's because you loved him so much. There's no rule book that tells us when we have to stop grieving or how long we have to wait to love again. You're a person who feels things deeply. You have a big heart. I've known that since the first day I saw you."

"Really?"

He smiled. "Really. You're a woman who only gives herself to a man who's worthy of her. And when you do, you love him with all your heart. We need more people like you in this world."

"That's sweet of you to say."

"I'm not just saying it … I mean it." He stared down at our hands for a few moments, and when he looked up there were tears in the corners of his eyes. "Thank you for telling me about Danny. The fact that you trusted me with something so personal … well, it means a lot to me." His smile was excruciatingly sweet. "You're a special woman, and you deserve to be loved."

My heart swelled in gratitude, and I thanked heaven for sending such an amazing man into my life. "You're a special person too." I hesitated and then grinned. "And one hell of a kisser, I might add."

Maxim laughed and pulled my hands to his lips. He lightly kissed my fingers and peeked at me through his long eyelashes. "You're one hell of a kisser too." His voice turned teasing. "Maybe we could try it again sometime soon."

I stared at his full red lips on my fingers, and my breath caught in my throat. "Maybe we could."

We regarded each other with interest for a few moments until he released my hands and sat back in his chair. He looked down at his shirt. "I'll shower and put on clean clothes before we kiss again, of course."

An image of Maxim in the shower popped into my head. "You do that." I didn't tell him that he could shower and skip the clothes before our next kiss, and I wondered how he would react if he knew what I was thinking. I forced my mind to change the subject.

I suddenly realized I was starving and studied my chocolate croissant with its flaky layers and dark chocolate drizzle. "This looks scrumptious." I picked up the puffy confection, bit into it and as the chocolate filling oozed into the flaky, buttery crust, I closed my eyes in delight; it was one of the most decadent pastries I'd ever eaten. "Oh my God! This confectionary delight is so amazing."

Maxim looked amused. "I've had one of those here, and I totally agree with your assessment." He sat up, pulled the cover off the cream cheese and spread a thick layer onto his bagel. He bit into it and sipped at his espresso. "So I was thinking we should head out pretty soon and see if that purse you wanted to get Caitlin is still in the store. Then we'll grab our suitcases and take the train back to the airport."

"That sounds great." I dove into the rest of my chocolate croissant and drank orange juice and cappuccino between bites. Maxim ate his bagel and watched with interest as I oohed and aahed over the chocolate croissant. "These would really sell in my store!"

I sighed in contentment. I suddenly felt light as a feather and somehow less burdened than before our intimate conversation. Maxim was good for me. I peeked at his beautiful, exhausted face. We'd moved to a new level in our relationship, and I was anxious to see where this was going.

Lara Ketter
ANOTHER CHRISTMAS WITHOUT YOU

.

Chapter 24

"You kissed him? Oh my God! Give me all of the details." In her excitement at my dramatic confession, Caitlin, sitting cross-legged on my couch, jumped up and sloshed white wine out of her glass onto the hardwood floor. I ran into the bathroom where I grabbed a hand towel off the rack. I walked back to the living room and threw it at her.

"Yes, I kissed Maxim Hall. On the lips. In the Eisenhower Suite. In Denver, Colorado." I sank into one of the plush chairs that flanked the couch and rested my feet on the coffee table.

Caitlin was stunned into momentary silence. In one hand she held the half-full glass of wine, and in the other hand the towel. I picked up my glass and sipped wine while she processed my startling piece of news. Her eyes were huge, and after a minute she finally spoke. "Oh my God! This is incredible! I need the details."

I pointed to the floor. "Only after you clean up the wine you spilled, young lady."

"Of course." Caitlin set her glass on the coffee table and bent down to clean up the mess. When she was done she tossed the towel over my head where it landed in the vicinity of the bathroom door. She picked up the bottle of wine, filled her glass to the rim, sank into the cushions of the couch and drained a third of her drink. "Okay, go ahead. Did I mention I want the details? Talk slowly and don't skip a thing."

I swirled the wine in my glass and stared past her at the wall. "What can I say? It was amazing." The silence stretched between us as I traveled back in time to last night with Maxim, his mouth on my neck, my fingers in his hair, our hands exploring each other. I grinned like the Cheshire Cat and sipped at my drink.

"That's it?" Caitlin leaned forward and set her wine glass on the coffee table. "Come on. You can do better than that." She pointed her finger at me, a deep frown on her face. "As your best friend I think I deserve more than, 'It was amazing.' I mean, was he a good kisser? Was there tongue involved? Did he feel you up?" She stopped and stared at me, willing me to talk, but I stayed quiet. "Did you feel him up? Come on, give me something."

I relaxed into the chair. "Okay, you're right. You deserve some details." I held up one finger. "As to your first question — yes, he's a good kisser. He's quite skilled, actually." I held up a second finger. "Yes, there was tongue involved." Caitlin's face broke out into a huge smile. I produced a third finger. "Yes, he felt me up." Caitlin's eyes were huge, and she slapped her knee. Finally, I added my fourth finger to the group. "And yes, I felt him up … kind of. Above the waist, anyway."

Caitlin's hands flew to her mouth. "Oh my God. This was more than a kiss." She bounced up and down on the couch. "You made out with Maxim Hall." Caitlin was practically vibrating with excitement. She dropped her hands and leaned toward me. "He is so gorgeous. How did he feel? I bet there's a lot of muscle under those clothes. Does he have a six pack?"

I rested my head into the cushion and stared at the ceiling. "He felt … like a man. I'd almost forgotten what it's like to be with a man. That physical contact, you know? It's been so long …." My voice trailed off, and I looked at Caitlin whose face had transformed from curiosity into concern.

She scooted to the end of the couch and reached for my hand. "This is the first man you've been with since Danny." Her voice was soft and tender. "How did it go?"

Tears welled in my eyes. "Not so good."

Caitlin reached for the wine glass I was holding and set it on the table. She tugged on my arm. "Come sit by me." I did as she asked, and when I was next to her on the couch she put her arms around me and hugged me tightly. She laid her head on my shoulder and rubbed my back. "Tell me about it, honey."

Her love and concern were a balm to my soul, and the tears flowed freely as she held me. We stayed that way for several minutes until I pulled back and stared into her teary eyes. "When I was kissing Maxim … I saw Danny."

Caitlin's brows furrowed. "What do you mean you saw Danny?"

"He just flashed before my eyes."

"Oh, wow." Caitlin's mouth dropped open, but she quickly regained her composure. "What did you do?"

I shrugged. "The first time it happened I tried to ignore it, but then a little while later I saw Danny again."

Caitlin released me from her grip. "Did you tell Maxim?"

"No, I just made an excuse and left his room. I didn't even put my shoes back on. I just grabbed my stuff, told him goodbye and left."

Caitlin reached for my hands. "What did he say … before you left?"

I shook my head and looked down. "He didn't say anything. He was very quiet and just let me go." I returned my gaze to Caitlin's face. "You must think I'm losing my mind having visions of Danny, but don't worry — I know it wasn't actually Danny making an appearance from the Great Beyond, warning me to stay away from Maxim."

Caitlin nodded. "I know you're not crazy. Any therapist would say you were feeling guilty for kissing Maxim, and that's why you saw Danny." She smiled tenderly and squeezed my hands. "Even though it's been ten years, and we both know that Danny would want you to be happy, you feel like you're cheating on him if you're with another man."

A tear ran down my cheek. "Exactly. My mind knows I'm not cheating on Danny, but my heart feels differently. Does that make sense?"

Caitlin wiped the tear from my face. "Of course it does. You loved him and thought you'd spend your life with him. That's hard to get over … especially the way he died and with you right there beside him when it happened. I can't imagine."

I sank back into the cushions of the couch. "This morning at breakfast I apologized for what happened." I smiled at the memory. "He's a very considerate man."

Caitlin leaned against the cushions and watched my face. "I'm glad to hear it."

"I told him about Danny this morning and he was very understanding." I rested my hand on Caitlin's knee. "He lost his wife a few years ago."

"I didn't know that."

"Yeah, it was pneumonia."

This was obviously a revelation. "People still die of pneumonia?"

I patted her knee. "Yes. I was really surprised." Silence settled between us and I stared at Rosie the Riveter hanging over my television.

"So, everything's okay between you two … you and Maxim?"

I propped my feet on the coffee table. "Yes, it is." I turned to her and smiled. "You should have seen his face when I told him about Danny and the car accident. He actually cried; he was so tender and caring. It touched me deeply." I folded my fingers under my chin. "I have strong feelings for him. When I said I hadn't been with anyone since Danny's death, he said he hadn't been with anyone since his wife died, either."

Caitlin crossed her arms. "Wow. You two really did have quite the talk."

"Yeah, we did. And even though I just met him, I feel close to him." I grabbed her knee. "He told me that he's falling for me."

Caitlin uncrossed her arms and reached for my hand. "Oh my God! You made out with Maxim Hall and he's falling for you? What a lucky woman!"

I lowered my gaze and blushed lightly. "One more thing … when we got home from Denver a few hours ago we kissed before I got out of his car. It was amazing." I laughed. "There's that word again, but it pretty much sums up kissing Maxim Hall."

Caitlin clapped her hands together and reached for our glasses of wine. "Well, this calls for a toast." I accepted my glass of wine and we raised them together in the air. Caitlin grinned and stared into my eyes. "To Bree Somers, who took one giant step forward and kissed a real, live man … on the lips. To Bree." We clinked our wine glasses together and sealed the toast with a drink.

I lifted my glass into the air a second time. "I'd also like to propose a toast. To Caitlin Somers, who is the best friend a gal could have. To Caitlin." We laughed and clinked our wine glasses together again and drained them.

Caitlin smiled and squeezed my arm. "I'm proud of you. I mean, look at what happened when you relaxed with Maxim. I know it won't be easy, but you need to see where this thing goes. Quit thinking so much and follow your heart. You never know where it might lead you."

I nudged her arm. "You sound like a greeting card." I set down my glass and wrapped her in a quick hug. "But I think you're right. Maxim said he's falling for me, and the truth is, I'm falling for him too."

Caitlin grinned and refilled our wine glasses. "Good for you, honey. If you're going to fall for a man, I can't think of a better one than Maxim Hall." She suddenly turned serious and placed her hand on mine. "Danny would be happy for you."

I nodded and smiled through my tears. "I know."

After Caitlin left at midnight I changed into my snowflake pajamas, plopped down on the couch and opened my Kindle. I tapped the cover picture of Maxim's book, The Chair, stretched out my legs and started reading where I'd left off in Chapter 5 when Maxim sat beside me on the airplane and basically asked me not to read the book in front of him. He was a fascinating mixture of confidence and shyness. But, I reasoned, I'd never met a writer — maybe they were all high-strung about their work.

In Chapter 5 the main character, Rebecca King, was enduring intense physical therapy after the accident that put her in a wheelchair and snuffed out two innocent lives. Rebecca was responsible for the accident, and her mind was in turmoil at the damage she'd caused in a moment of carelessness. She was plagued by nightmares of the couple who died, and she questioned her very existence. Maxim skillfully pulled me into the mind of Rebecca as she navigated her extreme emotions and, at one point, even contemplated suicide.

Without warning my thoughts turned to Jackie Green, the woman who ran a red light and killed Danny. I'd never considered the accident from Jackie's point of view, but surely she felt some of the same emotions as Rebecca. For the first time ever, I wondered how difficult Jackie's life had been since the accident. Did she think of Danny and wish she'd slowed down, not been in such a rush, paid attention to the road? Did she consider ending her life to quiet her racing thoughts?

What did I know about Jackie Green? Aside from the fact that she'd been found guilty of vehicular homicide, I actually knew very little. My photographic memory recalled the news article I'd read ten years ago when she was sentenced: As a result of the accident Jackie Green was a paraplegic and would be one for life, she drove a high-end SUV and she lived in Olathe with her family. The check I'd received for $100,000 offered a hint about her financial situation. Or maybe her family had money. My knowledge of Jackie Green was rudimentary, at best.

I shut the Kindle and stared at the ceiling. Where was Jackie Green now? Was she married? Did she have children? Was she still living in Olathe? Was she able to work? Was she an outgoing, bubbly person before the accident or was she a quiet loner? Did she have a career?

When I pictured Jackie Green I always saw her as a monster, but in truth she was a woman who made an enormous and costly mistake. An ironic thought occurred to me — before the accident, would I have liked her?

My thoughts surprised me. It had taken ten years, but for the first time ever I actually pictured Jackie Green as a human being.

WEDNESDAY, DECEMBER 20, 2017

Lara Ketter
ANOTHER CHRISTMAS WITHOUT YOU

Chapter 25

I carried two fried chicken dinners to a round table near the window and set them down. "Here we are … dark meat for you, Darrel, and white for Ruth." I slid the plates in front of my customers.

Darrel rubbed his hands together and grinned at the chicken thighs, mashed potatoes, gravy, creamed corn and whole wheat roll like they were long-lost friends, picked up a plump thigh and bit into the juicy meat. Ruth glanced up at me through her wire-rimmed glasses. "Thanks, Bree. It looks delicious … Darrel is always happy when Wednesday rolls around." As Darrel chewed, an enormous smile spread across his wrinkled face.

I patted his shoulder and smiled. "I'll let Marv know he has a fan."

Ruth spread a napkin in her lap. "Please do. He and Sally have their fried chicken recipe down to a science."

"I agree. Speaking of which, I'd better see how they're getting along. Enjoy your lunch." I turned and headed back to the kitchen, but Aunt Judy stopped me at the front counter.

"Hey, Rex just ordered his panini." I glanced over my shoulder and spotted the retired mailman sitting at his usual table in the corner.

I returned my attention to Aunt Judy. "That man never fails to amaze me. It's Fried Chicken Wednesday and he still wants a panini." I muttered under my breath as I turned on the panini press and gathered bread, olive oil, ham and cheese. I glanced at her. "The customer's always right … right?" I spread olive oil on two pieces of bread and checked the heat on the press.

Aunt Judy rested her hands on her ample hips. "That's what we keep telling ourselves, honey, but in some cases I totally disagree. Maybe you should just march over there with a chicken dinner and force him to eat it." She was decked out in black Christmas lights leggings and an oversized green sweater with a Christmas tree that sported actual flashing lights.

"I have a feeling that would go over like a pregnant pole vaulter." I layered ham and cheese on the bread, slipped the sandwich onto the griddle and lowered the lid. "If Rex wants a panini, Rex gets a panini." While the sandwich grilled I grabbed a plate, a bag of potato chips and a chocolate chip cookie. I drummed my fingers on the counter and stared at the light on the machine.

Aunt Judy sidled up to me and grabbed my arm. "You're practically glowing today."

I leaned against the counter and scrutinized her smug face. "What do you mean?" I knew exactly what she meant.

She nudged me in the ribs and winked dramatically. "You look happy, honey." She was absolutely beaming.

I returned my gaze to the light on the panini press. "I guess I am happy." A small smile tugged at the corners of my mouth.

"Well, from what you told me about your little trip with Mr. Tall, Dark and Handsome, you should be." She winked again and turned to wait on three customers who'd just walked to the front counter.

Happiness was a new sensation for me; for years I'd been sleep walking through life, but now I felt awake and the world was vibrant and filled with light. I watched the steam escape from the sides of the panini press and thought about Maxim. He'd texted earlier this morning that he was planning to stop by for lunch. My heart skipped a beat in anticipation of seeing him again.

When the light on the machine turned off I lifted the lid and slid the perfectly-browned panini onto the plate next to the potato chips and cookie. I carried the meal to the front table where Rex was reading a romance novel. I slid the plate in front of him, and he peeked up at me and smile. "Thanks, Miss Bree."

"Sure, Mr. Rex." I crossed my arms and rocked back and forth on my heels. I didn't normally question my customers, but I was intrigued with Rex's panini addiction. "I was wondering … have you ever thought about trying Marv and Sally's fried chicken?"

Without hesitation, Rex shook his head. "Nope. Never been a big fan of chicken." He frowned and looked up at me over his black reading glasses. "That's about all we ate growing up. Mom raised chickens and sold the eggs. You know, I think we ate chicken almost every night." He pointed to the panini and grinned. "Mom never made these." He picked up the sandwich and sunk his teeth into it.

"That makes sense, Rex. Glad I asked." I patted his shoulder. "I'll make you a panini whenever you want one."

"You're the best." He turned back to the sandwich and resumed reading his book.

The bell over the door rang and Maxim walked in. At the sight of him my breath caught in my throat and my heart raced. His eyes scanned the room, and when he spotted me he smiled and headed my way. I noticed that my grandfather's Waconda Springs scrapbook was tucked under one arm. When Maxim drew near I inhaled sharply and held my breath; he was so damn handsome. He regarded me from head to toe, calmly taking in every inch of me. It was suddenly hot in the room. He reached for my hand. "Hello." His voice was rich and smooth like honey melting on a warm biscuit.

"Hello." We stared at each other in the middle of my busy coffeehouse, oblivious to the Wednesday lunch crowd. I studied his striking face, and the sounds around me disappeared. I watched his full lips and suddenly, desperately, wanted to kiss him.

Maxim broke the spell when he let go of my hand and held out the scrapbook. "I'm done with this and wanted to make sure you got it back in one piece. Thanks again for letting me borrow it."

I grasped the book with both hands. "You're welcome. Come with me." I led us to the back of the building near the kitchen and set the scrapbook on top of a pile of paperwork on my desk.

Maxim glanced at my desk. "Some say a cluttered desk is the sign of a cluttered mind, and others say it's the sign of a genius." He reached for my hand and stroked my fingers with his thumb. He turned serious and moved his body against mine. "So which is it? Cluttered mind or genius?" He was so close I could smell the combination of soap, deodorant and cologne wafting off his body. It was altogether masculine and both aroused and excited me. My heart skipped a beat and my fingers tingled from his touch.

I ignored the desk and stared into his crystal blue eyes. He looked rested and refreshed. "In this case it's the sign of a busy woman who hasn't had time to sit down and go through her paperwork."

He grinned seductively. "Fair enough." Maxim leaned down and kissed me lightly on the lips. At the taste of him I pressed my body into his and the kiss soon increased in urgency. His fingers ran up and down my spine, and he pulled me into him. I was about to wrap my arms around his neck when a clanging sound brought us back to reality. We jumped and turned toward the kitchen where Sally was bending over to retrieve a metal bowl from the floor. Luckily, it had been empty. Her husband, Marv, frying chicken at the stove behind her, was oblivious to the racket.

Maxim laughed. "I guess this isn't the best place for a romantic rendezvous. They look busy."

"They are … that's Marv and Sally Anders. They come in on Wednesdays to fry chicken. Everyone loves it." I smiled and patted his chest. "Well, except for Rex the Panini Man."

Aunt Judy hurried past us into the kitchen. "I need three dinners, Sally. All dark meat."

Sally rose and dropped the metal bowl into the sink. She turned and pointed at Judy. "Coming right up, lady. They'll be ready in a few minutes." She set three plates on the counter and scooped generous servings of mashed potatoes onto each one.

Aunt Judy marched over to us, and I was suddenly aware that I was leaning against Maxim. I moved a step away and crossed my arms. Judy peeked up at Maxim and smiled demurely. "Hello, Mr. Hall. It's good to see you."

Maxim reached for her hand and squeezed it. "It's good to see you again, Judy. Call me Maxim. How are you today?"

"Busy!" She looked up at me. "I hate to rush you, honey, but the customers are lining up."

"Okay. Give me a minute and I'll be right there." Aunt Judy rushed to the front counter. I turned to Maxim. "I need to get back to work, but will I see you later?"

"I'd like that." He grabbed my hands, moved closer and stared into my eyes. "I really need to talk to you — privately. Do you think we could have some time alone today?"

I noted his serious tone and scrutinized his face; it gave away nothing. "I'm sure we can work something out." I thought for a moment. "Today is wild — Wednesdays are always wild — and it will be 3 before we get everything cleaned up."

"Why don't I come by at 3 them?"

"That would usually work, but there's an emergency Waconda City Council meeting this afternoon — they scheduled it at 3 so I could be there."

"Oh." Maxim looked down and furrowed his brow.

I rushed ahead. "They didn't tell me what it's about, but special meetings usually don't take longer than an hour. Why don't I call you when the meeting's over?"

Maxim shook his head. "I have a conference call with my publisher at 4 and it could take a couple of hours. We have several things to iron out, and they're still not happy with me about the tour dates I cancelled." He looked into my eyes. "Let's get together this evening."

I glanced at the front counter where Aunt Judy was writing down an order and five people were waiting in line. I felt my blood pressure rise, this time not from Maxim. "That won't work, either. I'm going to my nephews' music program at 7 and then I promised I'd stop by their house afterward for dessert."

"Oh."

I noted the sudden tension in Maxim's body, the disappointment written on his face. "But you're welcome to come to the concert."

"I'll think about it. You said it's at 7?"

I nodded. "Yes, in the school gymnasium. There's a stage at one end. Just walk in the main entrance and the signs will lead you there."

"Okay. I'm not sure whether I'll be there. It will just depend on how the call with my publisher goes." He raised my hands to his lips and leaned to within an inch of my face. "I really hope we can find some time to be alone. It's kind of important." He paused and stared into my eyes. "You'd better get going before Judy has a mental breakdown." He bent down and kissed my cheek. "I'm going to find somewhere to sit, and when you're caught up would you bring me a chicken dinner? Dark meat?"

I let go of his hands and patted his back. "I'd be happy to. Anything to drink?"

He thought for a moment. "How about some iced tea?"

"No problem. Anything else?"

He smiled and caught my eye. "A piece of cherry pie … and you. Do you think you'd have time to eat with me?"

I shook my head. "I wish I could, but like I said, Wednesdays are crazy. I won't have time to sit down until I lock the door at 2."

"Okay. I guess I'll just have to admire you from a distance."

I leaned forward and straightened the collar on his button-down shirt. "Good thing I wore my tight jeans, then."

A devilish smile lit up his face. "You can bet I'll be watching those jeans and the beautiful woman in them." Maxim headed for an empty table at the front of the building.

Chapter 26

Maxim settled into the seat beside me at 7 pm sharp as the lights dimmed for the Waconda Grade School's Winter Concert. He slipped his hand into mine and leaned toward my ear. "How was the emergency City Council meeting?"

"Boring. How was the conference call with your publisher?"

"Boring."

We glanced at each other and burst into laughter. Caitlin draped her tiny body across mine and extended her hand toward Maxim. "Hello, Mr. Hall."

He shook her hand. "Hello, Caitlin."

"Thank you for coming. I hope you won't be bored."

He feigned a shocked look. "At a grade school music program? I don't believe that's possible." He graced her with one of his charming smiles, dimples and all. "I'm sure it will be great … maybe it will even get me in the Christmas spirit."

Caitlin released her hand and held a finger to her lips. "Shhh. You can't say the word Christmas in a public school. This is the winter program." She raised her fingers in dramatic air quotes when she said the word winter.

Maxim laughed. "So noted. I'll be more careful what I say in a public school."

She gave him the thumbs-up sign, grinned in delight and sat back in her seat. Brice, next to Caitlin, leaned forward and waved at Maxim who waved back.

The curtain lifted and two spotlights illuminated the stage that was filled with enormous boxes wrapped in brightly-colored paper; a huge bow graced the top of each present. The music teacher walked to the piano near the stage, sat down and started playing. Four measures into the upbeat song the lids on the boxes suddenly popped up, revealing the kindergarten students peeking out with the lids as their hats. The crowd gasped in surprise and immediately quieted to hear the children sing about the gifts of winter, which I soon learned were snow, presents, cookies and love.

I scanned the boxes and spotted my nephews on opposite sides of the stage singing their hearts out, Nate in a blue box with yellow bow and Matt in a green box with a red bow. The students sang the first verse, the chorus and then disappeared from sight into their boxes.

The audience was caught up in the performance and I sat forward with them, excited to watch my nephews the next time they appeared. When the second verse began the kindergartners popped up again, huge smiles on their faces. The song continued for several verses, and when it was over the children stepped from their boxes and, still wearing the lids fastened under their chins, walked to the front of the stage and bowed dramatically. The audience erupted into enthusiastic applause. Caitlin lifted her phone and snapped several pictures.

As the kindergartners raced off the stage I grabbed Caitlin's arm. "Did you know that was going to happen?"

Her face was glowing. "Nate let it slip that they were going to be presents, but I had no idea they were actually going to be presents in boxes. I thought it was a figure of speech."

The first graders ran onto the stage wearing red noses and antlers for their rendition of Rudolph the Red-Nosed Reindeer, and we settled back in our chairs and watched the rest of the concert. Maxim held my hand the entire time, and when I peeked at him he was grinning at the on-stage antics. As the third graders sang about the joys of a snow day, he leaned close to my ear. "This reminds me of my boys' music programs. God, I miss those days." He was lost in thought for a moment. "It seems like yesterday." I noted the melancholy tone in his voice.

The show concluded with the kindergarten- through sixth-grade classes singing a rousing rendition of Jingle Bells, and afterward we paraded with the crowd to the cafeteria where a refreshment table loaded with cookies and red punch sat along one wall. I was nibbling on a snowman-shaped sugar cookie when Nate and Matt ran into the room and made a beeline for our little group.

Caitlin bent down and drew them in for big hugs. "You guys were great." She kissed them each on the cheek. "You were the stars of the show!"

Brice tousled their hair and agreed. "That was amazing, guys."

Nate stared up at his dad. "Were you surprised?"

Brice grabbed Nate and pulled him close. "Are you kidding? Yes, I was surprised. I jumped in my seat. No joke, I almost hit the ceiling when you popped out of that box." Nate beamed.

Matt poked my leg. "Were you surprised, Aunt Bree?"

I crouched down and hugged him tightly. "Yes, I was totally surprised. I almost hit the ceiling, I was so surprised!"

Matt pulled back and grinned from ear to ear. "Mrs. Evans said everyone in the audience was going to be really surprised when we jumped out of the boxes." He stretched to his full height, clearly pleased with himself.

Nate suddenly noticed Maxim standing next to me, planted his hands on his hips and didn't mince words. "Who are you?"

I rushed to explain. "This is my friend, Maxim." I linked my arm through Maxim's and gestured to the boys. "Maxim, these are my twin nephews, Nate and Matt."

Nate pointed to himself. "I'm Nate."

Matt ran over and poked himself in the stomach. "And I'm Matt. We're 'dentical twins."

Maxim smiled warmly, bent down and shook their little hands with his big one. "I can see that. I loved your concert. Just so you know, I was surprised too." He rose up and placed an arm around my waist.

Nate watched Maxim's actions with interest and tilted his head. "Are you Aunt Bree's boyfriend?"

Maxim's eyebrows shot up and my cheeks grew warm. Caitlin swiftly pulled Nate to her side. "It's not polite to ask such a personal question."

Maxim was unconcerned. "That's okay, Caitlin. He's just curious." Maxim crouched down and regarded Nate. "To tell you the truth, I'm not sure yet, but your Aunt Bree is a very special lady, isn't she?"

Nate moved next to me and grabbed my hand. "She's the best aunt ever." My heart melted and I squeezed his little hand.

Maxim nodded and smiled at him. "I agree."

Satisfied with Maxim's answer, Nate turned to his mom. "Can we get a cookie? Please?"

Matt hopped up and down. "We want cookies." He suddenly remembered his manners and stopped jumping. "Pretty please?"

Caitlin relented. "Sure, but just two each. There's dessert waiting at home." The boys raced off toward the refreshment table, and Caitlin turned her attention to Maxim. She smiled up at him. "We would love to have you join us at our home. School's out for Christmas break, and to celebrate I've made the boys' favorite dessert, chocolate lava cake. The adults are going to open a bottle of wine." She nudged me and giggled. "Or two. Or three."

Brice stepped forward. "Yes, you're welcome to come over. A few other friends will be there, but it won't be a huge crowd."

Maxim smiled but shook his head. "Thanks for the gracious invitation, but I'm going to say no. It's been a long day." He checked the time on his phone. "In fact, I'd better get going now." He leaned forward and shook Caitlin's hand, then Brice's. "Thanks again. It was a pleasure meeting both of you ... and your boys are adorable. I have two boys — grown now — and watching yours brings back lots of great memories." He turned and eyed the refreshment table where Nate and Matt were stacking a pile of cookies on a plate.

Caitlin reached for his arm. "I wish you would reconsider. Our get-togethers are kind of famous around here."

He regarded her with kindness. "Your persistence is very nice, but I think I'll head back to Lucy's and get some sleep." He smiled at Caitlin and Brice. "Have a great evening, okay?" They nodded and turned to talk with the other parents gathered at the reception.

I pulled Maxim aside. "You mentioned earlier that you wanted to talk ... would you like to get together later? I could make an appearance at Brice's and then beg out for the evening."

Maxim was shaking his head before I was even done talking. "No, I'm suddenly exhausted. Can I call you tomorrow?"

I thought ahead to the next day, and a heaviness settled in my heart. "Sure, I'll be around. I'm taking the day off from the coffee shop, but I'm not leaving town."

Maxim stared at the floor and frowned. "I see." He rocked back on his heels. "I'm leaving tomorrow or Friday — I haven't decided yet. My boys will be home on Christmas Eve, and I want to be there when they arrive."

"Of course." I reached for his hand and held it lightly. A melancholy settled over me, and I sensed the same was happening to Maxim. We studied each other and I could feel a sadness between us, no doubt about it.

Maxim reached up and touched my chin. "Thanks again for the invitation to the program tonight. It was fun." He glanced over at Brice and Caitlin, who were laughing with friends, then back at me. His eyes were heavy, but he managed to smile. "Enjoy your family. They're great. You're very lucky." He dropped his hand and turned to go. "I'll call you in the morning."

I could barely find my voice. "Okay. Talk to you then." Maxim stepped to the door of the cafeteria, into the hallway and I watched him until he was out of sight.

A chill swept through me, and I suddenly felt empty. I wondered if my newfound happiness had left with Maxim Hall.

Chapter 27

It was almost midnight when I sank onto the couch in my doughnut-patterned pajamas and reached for my Kindle. Reading always relaxed me at the end of a long day, and I decided to dive into Maxim's book before attempting to sleep. I tapped on the Kindle's home screen until I reached Maxim's book, but instead of loading the page I'd bookmarked, the Table of Contents page appeared. I scrolled down, searching for the chapter I'd been reading last, when I saw "Author's Note" at the bottom of the list. Curious, I tapped the heading and read Maxim's words:

"The Chair is dedicated to the most courageous person I've ever met, a beautiful woman who lived in a wheelchair for over five years and who taught me the true meaning of bravery. My wife lost the use of her legs, and also her speaking voice, in a car accident, but she never once complained, never once felt sorry for herself, never asked 'Why me?' Jacqueline Green, or Jackie, as she preferred to be called…"

I suddenly stopped reading and sat perfectly still, staring at the words "Jacqueline Green, or Jackie" until the letters blurred and were unrecognizable. My heart raced like a horse in the Kentucky Derby, my breathing faltered, and it felt like I'd been slammed into a cement wall. The color drained from my face. The Kindle slipped out of my hands and landed with a thunk on the floor, but I didn't really notice. My eyes glazed over and I stared at nothing for several long, agonizing moments until realization and understanding hit me like a freight train pulling 50 cars. Jackie Green, the woman who killed my Danny … Jackie Green was Maxim Hall's wife.

Oh. My. God. Oh my God. Holy mother in heaven, Jesus, Mary and Joseph. I fell to my knees on the floor and dropped my head into my hands as my stomach clenched in a spasm of nausea. I ran fingers through my hair and gripped it at the roots. My mind raced and the pieces fell into place in an instant. The vagueness about his wife's death. The avoidance of certain topics. The silences in conversations that stretched for minutes at a time. The questions he didn't ask. The seemingly sympathetic looks when I talked about Danny. The general moodiness. The panic when I told him I was reading The Chair.

A throbbing headache rooted into my skull, my stomach convulsed again, and I raced to the bathroom where I threw up until there was nothing left in me, then I retched some more. When I was finally empty I rinsed my mouth in the sink, splashed cold water on my face and returned to the living room where I paced like a caged animal.

The son of a bitch! The total son of a bitch! I clenched my fists. My right arm ached like a fresh wound. Maxim must think I'm a God-damned fool. He sat there as I poured my heart out to him about Danny, and he didn't say a thing. Not one God-damned word. *By the way, Bree, the woman who killed your fiancé? That was my wife, Jackie. Now get on over here and kiss me.* I clenched my jaw and shook my head. What a fucking liar ... a God-damned fucking liar.

I'd kissed him. I stopped moving and covered my mouth with both hands. The thought turned my stomach and I thought I might throw up again, but the feeling passed. I'd almost slept with him ... the man who lied to me and befriended me under false pretenses and acted like he was my friend. I'd even thought I was falling in love with him, that we could have a future together. What kind of idiot was I, anyway?

I dropped into a chair and buried my face in my hands. Why had he come here? Was it to humiliate me? Gain my love and then dash it to pieces? Toy with my heart like some fucking game and then destroy me? What was the purpose of his visit? I sat up as I realized he had no real interest in Waconda Springs ... it was all a ruse to get to me. But why? What did he want from me? His wife had already taken everything that mattered.

I stood and paced again. Tomorrow was the ten-year anniversary of Danny's death. Is that why Maxim had come to Waconda? It seemed too much of a coincidence that he was here now, of all times. There was definitely a connection between this significant date and his arrival in my life. Was he on some kind of Mission of Redemption for his wife? He said she was the most courageous person he'd ever met, the true face of bravery.

I shook my head in disbelief. So Jackie Green was Maxim Hall's wife. How convenient for the bastard that she didn't take his last name, or his little game would have been impossible to pull off. And because I'd never cared enough to dive into Jackie's background, and I forbid my family from doing the same, I knew nothing about her including the most important fact of all ... that she was married to a famous American novelist.

In the age of the internet, how could this have escaped me? How had I missed it? How had we all missed it — Dad and Mother and Brice and Caitlin and Aunt Judy? Was Maxim famous at the time of the accident or did that come later? Why in the hell did I not know that Jacqueline, aka Jackie, Green was Maxim Hall's wife? I rested my hands on my head and stared at Rosie the Riveter on my wall. I can't do it, Rosie. I just can't.

I pressed my lips together and muttered under my breath. It was doubtful that Maxim Hall, out of the blue, just happened to waltz into my coffee shop last week and...

I stopped suddenly and stared at nothing. Oh. My. God. Oh my God. The son of a bitch. My stomach lurched and I raced to the bathroom where I threw up nothing but bile; I was completely empty inside. When I was done I sat against the cold tiles in the corner of the bathroom and that's when the crying began. Within seconds my body was heaving in agony and I sobbed and screamed obscenities until I was weak from the effort.

I'd come to another realization, this one almost as bad as the first. A few months after the car accident Jackie Green had sent me $100,000 — money I used to buy and remodel my coffee shop. Jackie Green was a paraplegic who most likely didn't have a steady income after she was paralyzed, and the medical bills must have been exorbitant. I should have known it. No, Jackie Green didn't buy this building for me.

Maxim Hall did.

I leaned forward and dry heaved, then I crumped onto the cool floor and cried until I fell into a fitful sleep where I was frozen at the bottom of Waconda Springs with the peaceful Native American princess, Waconda.

This time I didn't struggle to reach the surface.

This time I didn't care.

THURSDAY, DECEMBER 21, 2017

Chapter 28

The bleak day matched my mood with its overcast skies, desolate landscape and biting cold temperatures. Snow was in the forecast, but so far none had fallen. I pulled my stocking cap lower on my forehead and stared out across Lake Waconda, its icy surface stark and exposed. The 10-degree temperature couldn't match the chill that had settled in my heart after last night's revelation, and I shivered when I thought about his utter betrayal. What a fool I'd been.

Ten years … I turned my face skyward and marveled that ten years could take forever and, at the same time, fly by. I relived the moment of Danny's death … his body lurching sideways as Jackie Green's SUV slammed into his car, the life sucked from him in an instant. I'd spent ten years missing him, my heart shrinking with each breath, ten years of forcing myself to live because I knew that's what he'd want me to do, ten years of wondering how I could spend another day on Earth without him.

The sound of a vehicle drew my attention, and I wasn't surprised to see a black Lexus pull into the parking space next to my old F-150. I willed myself to be a statue, and I stared at the lake as he stepped out of his vehicle, slammed the door, trudged through the deep snow and up the slope to where I sat on a bench next to the Waconda Springs replica. I tensed as he drew near but remained still otherwise; I wondered if I'd be able to look at him.

"Hey, Bree."

Even out here in the open, with the air bitter and raw, I could smell his cologne. The scent that once buckled my knees now settled in my stomach and soured. Out of the corner of my eye I saw him sit down on the bench opposite me. He also stared at the lake, seemingly lost in thought.

After a few minutes he turned to me. "I've been looking for you … when you didn't answer my calls or texts I was worried." I didn't respond to his words, didn't rush to explain. "I went by the coffee shop and asked your Aunt Judy where

I might find you, and she said you would be here." Silence stretched between us for several moments. "There's something I need to tell you."

I turned and eyed him then, my face pale and blank as I assessed the man who, just yesterday, had seemed thoughtful and loving but overnight had morphed into Judas himself. My voice was faint from exhaustion and heartache, and it almost disappeared in the thin air. "You're too late."

Maxim studied my face with the intensity of a judge, and as he comprehended the truth in my eyes he shivered visibly and clenched his jaw. His shoulders slumped and he looked at the ground. "You know."

I returned my gaze to the lake. "Yes. I know."

Dead air hung in the ten feet that separated us. Maxim was at a loss for words, and I wondered if he was going to say anything. I peeked at him and noted the trembling chin and the furrowed brow. He studied the lake as if looking for direction.

My voice was flat and resigned. "What are you doing here?"

He looked at me then, a lone tear running down his cheek. "I was concerned about you. I know it's the ten-year anniversary of the ... accident ... and I wanted to tell you about Jackie."

I snorted and rubbed my forehead. Was this guy for real? "I already know about Jackie. I read about her last night in the book you dedicated to her ... the book you knew I was reading. You're a smart guy ... you must have realized I'd eventually figure it out. Now I know why you were sweating bullets when you found out I was reading the book. I can't believe that no one mentioned your paraplegic wife at the book signing ... especially since she was the inspiration for the book. That certainly worked out well for you." Emotion snuck in and my voice quivered. "What I mean is, why did you come to Waconda?"

He wasn't wearing gloves, of course, and he ran his fingers through his hair and turned his face to the sky as if searching for an answer to the question. He finally returned his eyes to me and shrugged his shoulders. "To bring you the letters."

I sat up straight. "What letters?"

More tears coursed down his cheeks. "The letters Jackie wrote you."

My mouth went dry. "Jackie wrote me letters?"

Maxim jumped up and walked over to me. He indicated the bench where I was sitting. "May I?"

I scooted to the far end and made myself as small as possible, which isn't easy when you're 6'1" and 150 pounds. "Okay. But stay on your side."

He sat down and faced me but didn't speak right away. He scratched his forehead as he formulated his thoughts. "I told you that my son, Henry, went to college in August." I nodded but remained quiet. "It was the first time I'd been alone since before Jackie and I were married, and I didn't know what to do with myself. It was so quiet without the boys. Jackie had died four years earlier, and I'd been so busy taking care of Will and Henry that I hadn't gotten around to going through her things."

He paused and rubbed his eyes. "Jackie spent most of her time reading and writing in the sitting room of our apartment." He stared past me and continued. "She filled dozens of notebooks with her thoughts, short stories, vignettes ... she lost her speaking voice in the accident ... and so I decided to sort through all of it. That's when I found the letters."

My curiosity got the better of me. "How do you know they're for me?"

He focused his blue eyes on my face. "Because your name is written on the envelopes."

This wasn't what I expected. "What do the letters say?"

"I don't know. Each one is sealed, and your name's written on the front. There are five of them."

I was blown away by this revelation, and my brain, already fried from last night, struggled to piece it all together. We sat in silence for what seemed like an hour but was actually just a few minutes.

Finally I spoke. "If you came here to deliver Jackie's letters, why didn't you tell me right away who you were and why you were here?" Tears streamed down my face and a sob escaped my throat.

Maxim leaned toward me, anguish written all over his face. "That was my plan. Honest, it was. When I arrived at the coffee shop that first day the letters were in my coat pocket. I was going to walk up to the counter, introduce myself, explain our connection and hand you the letters."

"Then why didn't you?"

He leaned back and covered his eyes with his hands. "When I saw you — and I know this is going to sound crazy — you took my breath away." He dropped his hands and turned to me; there was torment in his eyes. "You were one of the most beautiful women I'd ever seen, and I was suddenly terrified of telling you why I was here in Waconda. I chickened out that first day, and when I left the coffeehouse I drove around. That's when I discovered the Legend of Waconda and Waconda Springs. As a writer I was totally intrigued."

"So you used my interest in the spring to get close to me."

Maxim waved his hands in protest. "No, that was not my intention. I mean yes, I went to the City Office and asked for more information, but when the lady told me you were the local expert I was absolutely stunned. I couldn't believe it." He shook his head. "I saw it as a way to get to know you better, and when I did that I thought I'd be able to tell you about Jackie."

I wiped the tears from my face with my pink gloves. "And yet you didn't."

"No." He buried his head in his hands.

I stared at the ground and noted the shoe patterns in the snow. My voice trembled. "Why did you string me along? Do you think I'm an idiot? I feel like such a fool. My God … you flew me to Denver. It never occurred to you to tell me that Jackie Green was your wife?"

He jumped up and walked to the metal railing surrounding the Waconda Springs replica. He leaned against it. "That's all I've thought about since the moment I met you." He studied me over his shoulder. "Please believe me. I tried to get myself to say something every time we were together."

The air rushed from my lungs. "But you didn't." My voice cracked and I cried openly.

"No, I didn't." He stared at the sky. "After I met you I couldn't get myself to face what I was really here to do. I knew that the moment I told you Jackie Green was my wife, you would reject me. That's why I was afraid to tell you the truth. I was embarrassed and ashamed." He turned to me then. "We both know that Jackie caused the accident that killed your fiancé — she ran a red light and hit his car."

I nodded as more tears rushed down my face.

Maxim pointed to himself and continued. "But what you don't know is that I'm the reason Jackie was speeding that day. If I hadn't screwed up, the accident never would have happened."

I gasped and my mouth fell open. "You mean the story is even worse than I originally thought?"

He walked over to me and bent down just inches from my face. "You need to know that I'm as much to blame for Danny's death as she is. I'll always regret my part in the accident."

I was stunned into silence. I stared at the lake but registered nothing; the tears made everything before me a blur. There were questions I needed to ask Maxim, but my brain was so jumbled that I couldn't formulate them. The past twelve hours had been such a shock, and I couldn't have imagined there was anything more to tell. I was wrong.

Maxim reached into his coat, pulled out a stack of thick envelopes held together with a rubber band and placed them on my lap. He sat next to me on the bench but this time I didn't draw back from him; I was too numb to move.

"I'm sorry for everything I've done to you. What I did was unforgivable. I know that. I didn't mean to hurt you. That was never my intention." He stared off into the distance. "I should have told you right away why I came to Waconda, but here's the truth … I fell in love with you."

At his words I snapped out of my reverie and regarded him. His eyes were pools of misery, but he managed to smile. "I know it's not fair of me, after what I've done to you, but it's true. I didn't come here to deceive you or betray you. When I first saw you I fell hard … harder than I've ever fallen for a woman." He rose abruptly and put his hands in his coat pockets. "I just wanted you to know that I'm leaving town now, and although I regret not telling you the truth right away, I'll never regret meeting you and spending time with you." His voice was filled with tenderness. "You're a remarkable woman, Bree Somers."

His smile was heartbreaking; he turned slowly and trudged back through the snow to his high-end Lexus, backed up and sped off. When he was gone I stared at the ice on the lake and tried to piece together the information from our conversation, but my brain was a tangle of words and emotions. I was too numb to process what had just happened between us. The man said he was in love with me. How was I supposed to deal with that?

In a daze, I picked up the stack of letters and inspected them. My name was written in elegant, looping handwriting on the front of each envelope: Breanne Somers. What did Jackie need to tell me?

Suddenly I had to know.

Chapter 29

I slumped in a chair at a large table in my coffee shop, the five envelopes spread out before me. Alone in the huge space, I scrutinized the handwriting that was beautiful enough to be its own font. I glanced up, stared out the window at the empty street and wondered if I could do this, if I could handle reading letters written to me by Jackie Green. I chewed on a fingernail and rubbed my right elbow.

I knew if I was going to do this I'd have to do it fast, like pulling off a Band-Aid in one fell swoop instead of easing it off gently. It would hurt less to get it over with quickly.

Since the envelopes weren't dated I decided to open all of them and hoped she'd written the dates on the letters; I preferred to read them in order. I slipped a finger under the seal of the nearest envelope and tore it away. With shaking hands I pulled out the letter and unfolded it. The date at the top read, December 21, 2010. I stared at the numbers — so she'd written this letter three years after the accident. I opened the four other envelopes and laid the letters side-by-side on the table: Jackie Green had written to me each year on the anniversary of the accident.

I picked up the first letter and began reading:

December 21, 2008
Breanne,
I'm sure I'm the last person you want to hear from, but my therapist said it would be helpful if I wrote my feelings to you on paper, even if you never read it. She says it's part of the healing process, whatever that means. It's difficult for me to write this letter, but I doubt that I will ever mail it, so I'll just pour out my heart and see if I feel better. You'll notice I didn't write "Dear" Breanne because I knew you wouldn't like me using an endearing term before your name.

Healing. It's been one year since the accident and my body has healed as much as it ever will, but not my heart. It's forever broken. I'm a mess, but it can't compare to what you've been going through. What I did is unforgivable.

Danny O'Neill. That name will be forever etched into my brain, but especially onto my heart. I killed someone. Me ... a 5'2" 120-pound woman killed a man. A wonderful man, I've come to learn. An Assistant Principal at a grade school, for God's sake! I took him away from the children at Prairie View Elementary and, most importantly, I took him away from you. I don't know that I'll ever be able to forgive myself. Why should I?

I wonder what you've been doing since the accident, and if you're still in Olathe. A friend told me that you resigned as music teacher at the school where you and Danny worked together. (Her kids go to school there.) That's understandable. I truly hope you're teaching somewhere else. My friend said you were a gifted and creative music teacher ... too bad my boys didn't attend the school where you taught. I've Googled your name, but I can't find anything recent, and you're not on social media. I've looked. I so worry about you. That's not fair of me since I took your love away, but still I do. Every day I ask God to look out for you.

I'll never forgive myself for what I did. The events of that day, December 21, 2007, play over and over in my head. I need to tell you what happened, and my therapist agrees it would be helpful for me to unburden myself. This in no way forgives what I did, but please keep reading because I need to explain. (I just realized I asked you to keep reading a letter I'm never going to mail. Oh well.)

Let me give you a little background. Three years before the accident Maxim inherited quite a bit of money after his mother's death, and he decided to take a leave of absence from his job as an attorney in a law firm to fulfill his dream of writing a novel. At the time I encouraged him and thought it was worth the gamble. I'm ashamed to say I didn't believe he'd actually get published. I thought he'd write a mediocre book, get rejected 25 times and then go back to work as a lawyer.

The book, a tender romance story with a surprise ending, was picked up quickly by an agent, and before I could turn around, was published. A second one followed, and while they didn't land at the top of the New York Times Bestsellers List, they did well, and the money started to roll in as well as calls for speaking engagements and book signings. I'm sad to say the success went to his head. Maxim had been a family man who couldn't get enough of me and the boys, but *after he was a published author he slowly became arrogant and selfish — there's no other way to put it. He spent his days in the basement office typing away and his nights out with new writing friends. When he wasn't writing and playing he was traveling to promote his books. The boys and I missed him desperately. I just couldn't hold his attention, and I wondered what had changed. I decided to be patient because I loved him. I figured he'd grow up eventually.*

Maxim and I had been college sweethearts, and maybe we got married too young. I fell in love with Maxim the first time I saw him. He was beautiful with his dark looks and vibrant smile. I was at a frat party, and I walked right up to him and said, "Hey, gorgeous!" He looked down at me and there was instant chemistry. We've been together ever since. I never wanted anyone else. I was willing to work to save our marriage, and I suggested couples counseling, but he wouldn't go.

One year ago I was working as an interior designer. I'd started my own business and it was going well. I was super busy and happy with my work. Two of Maxim's novels had been published, and he was often away promoting his books, but the day of the accident he was home.

That morning I told Maxim to pick up the boys from school at 3:30, and he agreed. I wouldn't be home until at least 6:00 but said I'd bring Chinese takeout for supper. It was a typical day. I dropped the boys off at school and headed to my first job, a brand new 6,000-square-foot home along a golf course. I'd been meeting with the couple for two months selecting and coordinating furniture, draperies and accessories. We were almost done, and I was thrilled with the results.

The second job site that day was the newly-remodeled waiting room of a neurosurgeon. I arrived after lunch and planned to spend the rest of the afternoon there. At 3:40 my cell phone rang. It was the school calling to tell me that Maxim hadn't picked up the boys. I hung up the phone and immediately dialed Maxim's cell phone. He didn't answer. I called back the school and told the secretary I'd be there in 20 minutes. I told my client that I had a family emergency, gathered my things and rushed out of there.

There's no doubt that I was driving much too fast and not paying attention to the road. I was angry and distracted. My cell phone rang, and I just knew it was Maxim. I reached into my purse and couldn't find the damn phone, so I grabbed the bag, set it on my lap and dug around in my purse. I only looked down for a few seconds, Breanne, I swear. But that's all it took. I didn't see the red light. I didn't see Danny's car. I remember the crash, glass flying into my face and then my body lifting from the seat. It was all in slow motion. Then there was blackness, total blackness until I woke up in the hospital a week later. I hadn't buckled my seatbelt, so my body was thrown around as the car spun, and that's how my back was broken. Instant paraplegic.

I want you to know that I'm glad I'm paralyzed. I deserved to die for taking Danny's life, but I think it was better that I lived and suffered. My recovery has been long and agonizing. Even now, one year later, I'm sitting in a wheelchair with too many medical problems to list. My vocal cords were also paralyzed so I'll never speak again, and I've been told that I could die of complications at any time. I deserve it.

As for Maxim, he's been trying to make up for his part in the accident. He was at a casino that afternoon with his so-called friends. The call I was trying to answer when I ran the red light? It was Maxim calling me from the casino, telling me he was on his way to the school. Can you believe it? He'd been drinking, as he often did back then. After he called me (and I didn't answer because I was in a car accident) the idiot walked out the front doors of the casino, stumbled over the curb, fell into a lamp post and cut open his forehead. One of his buddies drove him to the nearest ER where they stitched him up. He left his phone in the car, like he always did. It was evening before my dad reached him and told him I'd been in an accident and to come to the hospital. I can't get over the fact that we were in different ERs at the same time.

The accident snapped Maxim back to reality. Today he's the man I married, and he's been with me every step of the way. He's very supportive. I don't think I could have endured the physical therapy without him. Yes, I'm angry with him and feel that he's partly to blame for Danny's death. But is he 100% to blame for the accident? No, he's not. I knew it was dangerous to be driving that fast, and I'd read about distracted driving. I knew that a car could be a weapon. I should have pulled over to answer my phone. I'm the one who killed Danny, and I accept responsibility for the accident. Maxim feels a great amount of guilt, and he apologizes often. He blames himself for Danny's death, your loss, my injuries — everything.

It's complicated, as life often is. I've always tried to be a good person, to do the right thing. I was raised by Christian parents who were truly kind people. They taught me to forgive, and I believe in forgiveness. I've forgiven Maxim for his part in the events of that day, and he opened up to me in a way he'd never done before. I don't know if he'll ever be able to forgive himself, but he's trying.

I don't know what's going to happen to Maxim and me in the future, but today I have my husband back and I'm able to watch Will and Henry grow up. That's all I need. This daily prison is worth living in as punishment for what I did to Danny, his family ... and most especially to you.

Sincerely,

Jackie Green

I set the letter on the table and stared out the window. Tears coursed down my cheeks, but I barely noticed them. Now I knew what Maxim meant when he said he was to blame for the accident. It was worse than I ever could have imagined.

I was in desperate need of caffeine and food, so I made myself a double espresso and grabbed a chocolate doughnut out of the display case. I walked to the window and stared at the snow resting in huge clumps on the evergreen trees in the park as I gulped the espresso and devoured the doughnut in three huge bites. I returned to the display case for another chocolate doughnut and refilled my coffee cup. Back at the table I sat down and picked up the next letter:

December 21, 2009

Dear Bree,

Please forgive me for using a term of endearment before your name but I've been praying for you so often that I think of you as a friend. As if you would ever be friends with the likes of me. I know that's not possible, but the thought somehow keeps me sane. It's been two years since the accident that took Danny's life and my heart still hurts, but it's somehow not as sharp.

I can't imagine how you're feeling, and I wouldn't dare to guess. Is each day better than the last or are you still struggling with every breath? I was excited to find you on Facebook. I see that you prefer to be called Bree, not Breanne, so I'm correcting that in this letter. You're a beautiful woman, and from the photos of you and your family I can tell that you're tall! Some snooping around online revealed that you played volleyball at K-State and were a standout hitter. No surprise there.

You look just like your father as you share his dark hair and eyes, plus you're both so tall. Your mother is a blonde beauty. Your brother is also tall, while your mother is just plain short. Please forgive me for stalking you on Facebook. I created an account using a fake name and generic profile picture, and I'll be honest ... I did this just to look for you.

Your coffeeshop in Waconda looks like one I'd love to walk into (or rather roll into) and order a shot of espresso. From the pictures on the shop's Facebook page I can tell that you're busy and you look happy, although I know better than anyone that looks can be deceiving. I know that under the happy facade lies sadness and heartache. I admire you for doing something positive with your life.

Maxim has been my rock since the accident. In March he moved our family from Olathe to New York City just a few blocks from his book publisher so he wouldn't have to travel and be away from me and the boys. We live in a high-rise apartment overlooking Central Park. We're fortunate that his third book is a best-seller since my medical care is super expensive and health insurance doesn't cover everything.

He hired a medical company that provides top-notch health care, and all of my needs are being met. A nurse comes in every morning to help me get ready for the day, and another one arrives in the evening for the bedtime routine. Our apartment is handicap-accessible so I'm able to cook some meals and do laundry. We eat a lot of carry-out, and New York City has plenty of restaurants that deliver. Maxim does more than his share of the household chores, which blows me away because before the accident he didn't know how to run any of the appliances in the house except the microwave! A service comes in once a week to do the deep cleaning, but it's good therapy for me to do the day-to-day cleaning.

My health is okay, although paraplegics are at risk of a variety of problems, the most dangerous being infections and pneumonia. This past summer I developed a bed sore that became infected, and I ended up in the hospital on a strong dose of antibiotics. I'm carefully monitored by my doctor and home health nurses. I don't focus on how much time I have; I focus on my boys and consider myself lucky to be able to watch them grow up. I still can't talk, and it appears I never will, so I write everything down. Conversations are interesting. I'll never walk again, but that's a small price to pay for what I did.

Our boys were reluctant to move to the city, but once they got settled into school they've come to love it here. Maxim has dedicated his life to us. He arranges special outings for us and is determined that a wheelchair will not stop us from living our lives in the city. I tire easily, and many times I'd rather stay home, so he and the boys go on fun excursions and then share all the details when they arrive home.

I'm telling you this because I want you to know that Maxim is trying so hard to make amends for his part in Danny's death. He shows me this in his actions and he tells me this with his words. He actually talks to me now. We pray together and that never happened before the accident. Our faith in God has grown strong and we strive to be good people and loving parents. We're teaching our boys how to love and care for other people.

I know that none of this excuses the events of that day two years ago. Maxim messed up and so did I. In our couples therapy sessions we share equally in the blame, and this has been healing. We could easily blame each other for the course our lives took that day — him for letting us down and me for driving recklessly. But we've chosen not to do that. It's only by the grace of God that we're able to do so.

Bree, I'm so sorry we took away your fiancé, the love of your life and a wonderful man. I pray that you will find love again. When you do, hold on tight and don't let go.

Sincerely,

Jackie Green

P.S. I probably won't mail this letter, either.

I laid the letter on the table, shivered and sank back in the chair. Jackie Green was totally open and honest in these letters, and she accepted complete responsibility for her actions. She didn't make excuses, and I found this refreshing in a world where blame was passed around like the flu.

I suddenly wondered what she looked like. Maybe I could find her picture online. I stared at the letter. She spoke again about Maxim's part in the accident and their decision to share in the blame, which fascinated me. I wasn't sure how I felt about that, but she seemed sincere.

And she prayed for me. Somehow, that was most touching of all.

I picked up the third letter and read:

December 21, 2010

Dear Bree,

I can't believe it's been three years since the car accident. My heart still hurts, and you'll be glad to know that I'm still in this wheelchair. I want to tell you again how sorry I am. The guilt never leaves me, and that's a good thing. I think about Danny every day. You too. I still watch you on Facebook, and I'm thrilled when I see a picture of you smiling. I hope you really are happy and not faking it.

I wanted to share something exciting with you, even though I'm not going to mail this letter. If I did mail it, though, I think you'd be pleased. At least I hope you would be. I read about a wonderful program in the city that buys musical instruments for schools whose music programs have experienced budget cuts. I thought of you immediately and talked to Maxim about it.

We decided to donate $50,000, and they asked us if we'd like to deliver instruments to one of the schools, so we did. The day we showed up with a truck full of musical instruments and supplies was one of the happiest days in my life. We did it in honor of you, Bree, and I hope you like the idea. The music teacher almost fainted, and the students were thrilled beyond words. We took lots of pictures. It was an amazing day, and we plan to give more money next year.

Will and Henry are thriving. They're playing basketball this winter, and I go to most of the games. They're not very good, but they're learning. I don't really like basketball that much, but I enjoy watching them have fun. They're doing well in school, and they're happy and healthy. What more could a mother ask?

Maxim just published his fourth book. It's another amazing one. I don't know where he gets his ideas, but they're inspired. I think God is talking to him. When he's not writing he's taking care of me and the boys. He's grown up in the last three years, and I'm really proud of the man he has become.

We pray for you every night, Bree, and for all the people we hurt that day. And we'll keep on praying ... every day until our last breaths.

Take care,

Jackie Green

I was touched by the donation of musical instruments in my honor. Through these letters I was coming to understand that Jackie Green was a kind woman, and I probably would have liked her under different circumstances. She was a human being, which meant she was fallible like the rest of us.

The $50,000 donation reminded me of the money I'd received from Jackie that I'd used to rebuild my life. In the heat of the moment I'd forgotten to ask Maxim about it. I frowned and drummed my fingers on the table. I needed to know where that money came from. If Maxim had paid for my coffee shop I wasn't sure I could stay here. I looked around the building that had saved my life, and I shivered.

I picked up the fourth letter:

December 21, 2011

Dear Bree,

It's been four years since the car accident. Have I told you how sorry I am? I don't think I've ever asked how your arm healed. We were told they had to put your upper arm and elbow back together and that a rod and several pins were involved. That's my fault too. I feel the guilt every day. It will never go away. I hope you're okay and able to enjoy life. I still look at your pictures on Facebook. It appears that you're doing well, but everyone's happy on Facebook.

This is my fourth letter to you. They're piling up in a hidden spot in the credenza by my writing/reading chair. Each letter is sealed in its own envelope with your name and address in Waconda written on the front and a stamp in the corner. I'm not sure why I did that since I never plan to mail them. I've always been a gal who likes to complete her projects, and I guess it helps me feel organized. Maxim doesn't know about the letters. I wonder if I'll ever tell him.

I'm writing to you from my beautiful sitting room in our apartment. I have a fabulous view of the city. It snowed a few days ago, and the ugly world is covered in pure white. The room has a cozy recliner that I sit in and a large end table next to the window. Bookshelves line the walls, and there's a huge L-shaped couch in here for the boys. They often sit with me in the evenings and do their homework. They bring me so much joy. I spend most of my time reading and writing. I've filled notebooks with thoughts and short stories, and I'm proud to say that I've read every book on the shelves.

I still can't talk, but we learned sign language as a family this year. It was tiresome to write down everything I needed. With the sign language I can communicate simple things with my hands, and this has made it easier for everyone. So if I'm thirsty, I just sign that I'd like some water. I can sign when I'm hungry, when I'd like a hug, even questions about the boys' days. We're still learning, but it's made life much simpler.

Maxim continues to take exceptional care of us. He's working on his fifth novel, and whenever he has an engagement in the city he takes me along, which is no easy fete. Paraplegics have a lot of baggage, literally and figuratively.

We still pray for you, Bree. Maxim and I have a nightly prayer ritual. We ask God to take care of you, to heal your heart and to look after your needs. I keep hoping to see a man in your life in some of the pictures on Facebook, but you must not be ready. Maybe you never will be. When the right man comes along, you'll know it in your heart, like I did with Maxim. When you find that man, hold onto him. You deserve to be loved again.

Sincerely,

Jackie Green

After I read the last few sentences I rolled my eyes, tossed the letter on the table and rubbed my forehead. This headache was getting worse with every letter I read. If Jackie only knew that I'd thought the right man had come along when Maxim showed up in town, but I was totally wrong. Obviously. I opened my heart to him … and he betrayed me. What a fool I'd been. I'm obviously a terrible judge of character.

I pulled the ponytail out of my hair and shook it free. She was right about one thing: I deserved to be loved again, but how could I trust another man after such utter betrayal? One thing you learn as you get older is that betrayal is devastating and hard to overcome.

I re-read the last few paragraphs of the letter. It surprised me that Maxim was a man of faith. He'd never mentioned God or prayer during any of our conversations. Why not?

I picked up the fifth, and last, letter:

December 21, 2012

Dear Bree,

I was so sorry to read the news of your father's death in October. I saw the notes of sympathy posted on your Facebook page, and I searched for his obituary — that's when I learned about the farm accident that took his life. You must be heartbroken, Bree. I could tell by the photos I'd seen that you two were very close. He always had his arm around you, and you were both grinning from ear to ear. I could tell the smiles were genuine. I'm sure he was a great support after Danny's death.

It's been five years since the accident, and I'm sure your father's death brought back all of the pain and grief from Danny's death. I can't imagine the added strain on your heart. I pray that you're okay. Maxim and I still pray for you every night. I wonder what you would think if you knew that. Maybe you don't want our prayers. I wouldn't blame you if you didn't. But I believe prayer is a powerful force. It's certainly helped as I've learned to live in a wheelchair. I feel God's presence in my life. Maxim said he feels it too. It's a great comfort.

Oh Bree, I'm so sorry for the loss you've endured at such a young age, and my part in your grief. Nothing I could say or do would ever make it better for you. I know that. I think of you every day and I hope you're finding some sort of happiness. But now with your father's death I fear that you're filled with grief once again, and only five years after you lost Danny. I care about you, Bree, and I pray that God is showing you the way to peace.

We're fine here in New York City. The boys are growing, and Maxim continues to take wonderful care of us. I've been hospitalized several times for complications related to my paralysis. This is common, we're told. So far I've been able to recover and come back home. My only wish is to live long enough to see my sons as grown men.

Every so often I search your Facebook page for updates, and I'll be honest — I'm hoping to see some photos of you with a special man, but so far there's been nothing. I have no idea what this means, of course. Maybe you're dating someone and choose to keep it private. I respect that. Maybe you simply haven't met the right person. That's entirely possible. But my gut feeling is that men have approached you but you're not ready for another commitment. Maybe you're afraid if you hand your heart to someone, you'll lose it again.

Fear is powerful, and it often keeps us from happiness. I know I'm not the one to lecture, but I've learned so much since the accident. I've learned that, with God's help, we can push past the fear, take risks and live again. I pray that someday soon you'll be able to move on and find a man to share your life with. When that happens, hold on to him tightly.

Love is worth the risk. It's worth everything.

Until next year,

Jackie Green

Tears streamed down my face, and I laid my head on the table and gave in to the rush of emotions coursing through me. I was spent, emotionally and physically, and I wasn't sure how much more I could take. I clutched Jackie's final letter as I sobbed, my shoulders shaking with the effort. Time stopped, and I had no idea how long I stayed there thinking about Danny and Maxim and Jackie, and what a total mess my life was.

When the crying finally abated I sat up and wiped my face with the sleeve of my shirt. I laid the letter with the others on the table, rose unsteadily to my feet and walked to the window. Darkness was descending on Waconda, and the Christmas lights flickered on across the street in the city park. The colorful lights sparkled against the pristine white snow, and I gazed at the huge evergreen tree that seemed illuminated from within. I turned and stumbled back to the table where I stacked Jackie's letters in order, laid the envelopes on top of the pile and dropped into a chair.

I studied the inside of my coffee shop. I'd been reborn here … maybe that sounds a bit dramatic, but this building had been the beginning of a new life, one that had been good until Maxim came to town. Was it perfect? No. Like any life, it had its ups and downs, but I trudged along, minded my own business, made coffee for the people of Waconda and enjoyed a few laughs along the way. Why did he have to show up and ruin it all? I pounded my fist on the table. Damn him!

My head was dizzy with what I'd learned in the last 24 hours. No, it hadn't even been 24 hours, I realized. I figured it up — 18 hours ago I found out Jackie Green was Maxim's dead wife. I knew firsthand that life could change in an instant, so I shouldn't have been surprised that 18 hours was enough time to turn my world upside down.

I sat back and stared at the limestone wall. What was I going to do now?

I pulled the phone out of my back pocket, hit the home button and tapped the screen twice. I held it to my ear and listened: she answered on the third ring. My words were a quiet plea for help. "Caitlin, I need you." A sob escaped my throat.

She snapped to attention. "Where are you?"

"Coffee shop."

"I'll be right there, honey. Hold on, okay?"

"Okay."

I tapped the End Call button, rested my head on the table and fell asleep.

SUNDAY, DECEMBER 24, 2017

Chapter 30

The choir sang "Silent Night" in four-part harmony, and as I accompanied them on the piano their voices rose and fell with the angelic melody, and I allowed it to enter my soul. "Sleep in heavenly peace" … how I'd longed for peace the past few days as I absorbed the extent of Maxim's involvement in my past. I was determined to follow through on my commitments — the Christmas Eve service was one of them — but it was all an act. Inside I was aching, troubled and completely adrift.

The song ended and I zoned out as Pastor Olsen stepped to the pulpit and read the Christmas story from the Book of Luke. When I was a child Dad would lay beside me on my bed as darkness fell outside my window, and after entertaining me with the Legend of Waconda for the umpteenth time because I begged him to, we'd say a bedtime prayer. The nightly ritual was a soothing one, and we'd ask God to heal a sick kitten, send rain for the wheat, feed the hungry of the world, keep Tanner Griffin away from me at recess — whatever I deemed most important at the time.

We were a church-going family and attended the Methodist Church in Waconda every Sunday morning, come hell or high water, as Mother put it. But aside from the weekly church service and nightly prayer we didn't talk about God or pray as a family. We dubbed ourselves Christians but there was no mention of Christ. When I complained about a problem Mother's attitude was, "Get over it," and Dad's attitude was, "It will all work out."

After his life conversion at the age of 25, Danny believed in the power of prayer. The first words he uttered whenever a problem arose was, "Let's pray about it." I was soon praying on my own for a long future with Danny, continued health and happiness for both of us and direction for a fulfilling life.

The day Danny died I quit praying; God hadn't listened to my prayers, and I was angry and resentful. At the start of my new life in Waconda I returned to the

Methodist Church because I missed making music. I volunteered to play the piano and was eventually named Music Director, but I'm sure the congregation would have been surprised to know I didn't believe in prayer.

I'm not sure how or why it happened, but the day Maxim left town I fell to my knees in prayer for the first time in ten years. I was lost and tormented, and I asked God to help me navigate through this mess; I had nowhere else to turn. I caught myself praying for guidance while making a cappuccino, washing my hair, playing with Nate and Matt, whatever I happened to be doing. I didn't know if it was working, but at least God and I were on speaking terms again.

When Pastor Olsen asked the congregation to stand for the closing hymn I switched the digital piano to the organ feature, turned up the volume and filled the church with the opening notes of "Joy to the World." As the congregants sang the verses at the top of their lungs, I marveled that the roof didn't lift right off the building. Filled with the Christmas spirit and eager for food and presents, the exuberant crowd filed out of the pews and into the brisk evening air. I played through the song two more times until the church was almost empty.

I had just lifted my fingers from the keyboard when Nate and Matt appeared at the piano, buttoned up in their matching blue coats, stocking caps pulled down over their ears.

"You're coming to our house now ... right?" Matt placed his gloved hand on my arm and patted it lightly.

I nodded. "Yes, I am."

Nate peeked over his shoulder at the wooden manger filled with straw in front of the altar. He returned his gaze to me and grinned. "How did we do as Wise Men?" Matt scooted closer to his brother and watched for my reaction.

I'd been forcing smiles for everyone else, but my nephews inspired a real one. "You two were the best Wise Men I've ever seen ... and I've seen a lot, I can tell you that." I leaned in for hugs and gathered strength from their innocence and love.

Nate pulled away and frowned. "I can't believe Susie dropped baby Jesus on the floor. She ruined the whole play."

I shook my head and laughed. "It was just an accident. She picked him up and put him in the manger."

Matt's brow was furrowed. "It's a good thing baby Jesus was a doll and not a person."

"I agree." The serious look on his face brought another genuine smile to mine.

Nate pointed to the front door of the church. "We'd better get going. Mom and Dad are waiting outside. Grandma and Hank are too."

Matt nodded his head vigorously. "Yeah, Mom just wanted to make sure you were still coming to our house."

"Tell her I'll be there, okay? I just need to put away my music, and I'll leave as soon as I can."

Nate crossed his arms and regarded me with a sober look. "Mom said we can't open presents until everyone's there, so hurry, okay?"

I squeezed Nate's shoulder. "I promise I will. You'd better get going."

They said goodbye and raced off toward the front doors. I called after them using my inside teacher's voice. "And no running in church." The boys slowed down barely enough to notice, then sped up again after a few seconds.

I gathered the music that was scattered on the piano and in a nearby chair, shuffled it into a neat pile and slid it into my music bag. I turned off the digital piano and heard movement behind me. At first I thought the boys had returned to nudge me along, but when I looked over my shoulder there was Mother standing a few feet away, a polite look on her face.

"The music was very nice, Breanne." Mother's blonde-from-a-bottle hair was perfectly coiffed in a neat bob, and her gray wool coat was buttoned to the chin with a silk floral scarf peeking from the neckline. She wore black pantyhose and heels even though it was close to zero degrees outside, and her hands were covered in leather gloves.

I turned to face her. "Thank you." An uncomfortable silence settled around us. "When did you get home?"

"Around 10 last night." She offered no more and didn't move an inch.

I crossed my arms and studied her face. "Congratulations on your engagement."

Her stoic face softened into a smile. "Thank you."

"When's the big day?"

"We're thinking Valentine's Day."

My eyebrows shot up. "That's pretty soon."

She shrugged. "At our age there's no time to lose."

"I guess that's true."

I knew Mother hadn't sought me out for small talk, and she got to the point in her usual blunt style. "Brice told me about Maxim Hall's appearance in town."

I deflated and sat on the piano bench. "I wish he hadn't."

"He was right to tell me. I'm your mother and I need to know what's going on with you." Her lips were pursed, and she stretched to her full height.

I stared at her shoes that were perfectly polished and buffed. "You have a point. So what's on your mind?"

She sat down in the front pew and folded her hands. "I want to apologize."

My head jerked up and my mouth dropped open. I studied her face, but it was void of emotion. "You want to apologize? For what?"

She leaned forward, and her green eyes were full of fire. "If I'd looked into Jackie Green's background right after the accident this never would have happened."

"But I asked everyone to leave it alone. It was my decision."

"Oh, I know that, but as your mother I have a duty to protect my children from harm." She bit her lip and pointed at her chest. "I should have ignored your wishes and hired a private investigator. We really needed to know more about that woman."

I slumped on the piano bench. "It's too late for that now. The damage is done."

"I know, and I can't imagine how traumatic this must be for you."

This was one of the longest conversations I'd had with her in years, and certainly the most personal. "It's been … difficult … but I'll get by. I always do." I wondered where this was going.

Her voice turned quiet, tender even. "Yes, you manage your life very well. You're a strong person. I've known that since you were born." When I didn't say anything she continued. "Listen, I know it's been hard for you since your father died. You two were very close and he would know what to say to make you feel better. I've never been very good at this sort of thing."

I almost said "Really?" in a sarcastic tone of voice, but held it in.

She folded her hands and wrung them together. "This Maxim Hall … Brice said he brought you some letters that his wife, Jackie Green, had written to you?"

Tears threatened to fall. "Yes."

"I see." She lifted her chin. "I won't pry into the content of the letters, but I want you to know how sorry I am that he deceived you and dumped the whole mess at your feet. It was a rotten thing to do."

I agreed but said nothing. I didn't know how to respond to a supportive mother.

She jumped up and paced back and forth in front of the pew. "I wish your father was here to handle the situation. He would know exactly what to do about Maxim Hall. He was always good in a crisis."

I felt a headache forming in my right temple. I rubbed the spot and closed my eyes.

She stared at the carpet as she moved. "Your father was excellent with children, and he loved you so much." She crossed her arms and continued pacing. She stopped and regarded me. "I never knew what to do with children ... how to talk to them, interact with them."

She sat down in the pew and folded her hands. "I'm sorry I wasn't a better mother to you."

I looked at her face and spotted the beginning of a tear in the corner of one eye. I stared, dumbfounded, at my mother — Ice-T, The Ice Queen, Mrs. Glacier — and decided that since I was praying again, I'd might as well believe in Christmas miracles.

I stumbled for the right words. "You were strict at times, but we always had everything we needed..."

She held up a hand. "Don't bother. I knew from the beginning that I wasn't doing a very good job with you and Brice. Your father took to parenting so naturally and I just ... didn't. There's no other way to explain it, really."

I crossed my legs and leaned forward. "This is a surprising turn of events, Mother."

She held out her hands. "I know. When the twins were born I was determined to do a better job with them than I did with you. I saw a chance to redeem myself." She sat up straight and puffed out her chest.

I had to hand it to her — she was laying it all out on the table. "I think you've done it. I've seen how good you are with the boys — Brice has also mentioned it — and I know Nate and Matt love you a lot."

When I mentioned the boys her face lit up, and the sight tugged at my heart. It was unusual to see an authentic smile on Mother's face. Her heart was thawing in front of my eyes.

Mother rose to her feet and smoothed the front of her coat. She folded her hands together. "Well, Hank is waiting for me in the car. I'd better get going."

I pulled on my coat and gloves. "Are you going to Brice's?"

She didn't hesitate. "Of course. I bought the boys some fun gifts on our cruise. They're going to love them."

I picked up my bag. "Sounds great. I'm right behind you."

She started to leave but paused and turned to me. "All day I've been thinking about this whole Maxim Hall mess and wondering what your father would tell you."

My voice trembled. "Me too."

She walked over to me, leaned close and looked up into my eyes. "You know what he would say." I stayed quiet, locked onto her words. "He would say, 'It will all work out, Bree. Trust. Have faith. You're a strong woman, and there's nothing you can't overcome.'" She reached up, placed her hand on my shoulder and stared into my eyes. "And you know what? I totally agree with him."

Tears ran down my face and, wordlessly, I stepped toward my mother and lowered my head onto her shoulder. She enveloped me in her arms and held me tightly. We stayed like that for I don't know how long, and I felt warmth and comfort spread throughout my body. In that instant, for the first time in my life, I knew that my mother loved me.

When my tears abated I pulled back and we regarded each other, both perfectly still and basking in the uniqueness of the moment. She reached up and squeezed my arms, then turned and walked down the aisle to leave the church. When she reached the front doors she peeked over her shoulder, smiled at me and walked into the cold night.

When she was gone I gazed at the cross hanging over the altar. I could barely speak, but I knew he heard me. "Thank you."

THURSDAY, DECEMBER 28, 2017

.

Chapter 31

I tossed my work clothes in the hamper and slipped on black leggings and my favorite ratty old K-State sweatshirt. In the bathroom I freed my hair from the ponytail holder, brushed through the stubborn knots and studied myself in the mirror: dark circles peered back, evidence of a rough week, and my red-rimmed eyes were weary, exhausted and spent. I headed to the refrigerator, grabbed a Coke, opened the tab and returned to the living room where I dropped to the couch and rested my aching feet on the coffee table.

A deep sigh escaped my lips and I sipped the fizzy drink, relieved to be alone with my troubled thoughts. It had been another drawn-out day of standing at the espresso machine, contemplating my mess of a life, while Aunt Judy fussed over me and told jokes in attempt to cheer me up. But even she had finally conceded defeat; there was simply no cheering me … not in my current funk, anyway.

When I wasn't thinking of Danny I was thinking of Maxim, and I had to admit that I missed him. The pain of deception was still fresh in my mind, but as the days passed I considered his last words to me: I fell in love with you.

Did he really love me, though?

If his story was to be believed, Maxim drove to Waconda with one simple mission: to deliver the letters from Jackie. He planned to tell me who he was, hand over the letters and then be on his way. How I wish he'd done that. During our time together the opportunities for full disclosure were there, but he'd ignored them. It was difficult to wrap my mind around his choice to remain quiet.

I ran fingers through my hair and stared at Rosie the Riveter. Sure, Maxim's revelation would have been a shock to my system, but his honesty from the very beginning would have spared me from the roller coaster of emotions I'd been riding the past week.

While Maxim's deception wounded me deeply, there was another huge problem that plagued me day and night ... a problem I was reluctant to admit but knew was true: while Maxim was falling for me, I was falling for him.

I was in love with Maxim Hall.

This detail posed an enormous complication. Yes, his deceit had been like a punch to the gut, but it didn't erase my feelings for him. In spite of what he'd done, he was an incredible man. Jackie's letters were a testament to this, and in my heart I knew it was true. Maxim found Jackie's letters and chose to personally deliver them. I saw the honor in his intent ... it was his actions after meeting me, however, that were on trial in my mind. He didn't lie overtly but lies of omission are still lies.

I once read a quote that said, "A word of truth that hurts for a while is better than a lie that lasts a lifetime." I believed it.

An added complication was Maxim's role in Danny's death, and this one really tore me up. If Maxim had been a responsible parent that day instead of a selfish prick, I'd be married to Danny, driving our children in the carpool and teaching music at an elementary school. Danny would be sharing his love and humor with the world, and I wouldn't have suffered for the past ten years without him. Maxim's role in his death wasn't something to be ignored. He was complicit because his failure to pick up his children set forth a series of events that ultimately killed my Danny.

I might be able to look past the deception in Waconda, but how could I disregard Maxim's part in that awful day?

I sipped at the drink and let my head sink into the cushions of the couch. Why did life have to be so damn complicated? I'd fallen in love with Maxim and had even contemplated a future with him; I'd been clueless, of course, that he was already part of my past.

I needed a distraction. I picked up the remote control and turned the television to a rerun of Grey's Anatomy and hit the mute button. I drained the rest of the Coke, set the empty can on the coffee table and laid down on the couch with a quilt pulled up under my chin. In minutes the images on the screen blurred, and I nodded off into a fitful sleep where I was frozen at the bottom of Waconda Springs as Danny and Maxim reached in the water to save me.

I heard a knocking sound which at first I thought was part of my dream, but when the knock repeated I woke up and realized someone was at the door. The clock on the wall said 4:50. I'd been asleep for over an hour. I tossed aside the quilt, stumbled to my feet and padded to the door where the blind was closed. I pulled apart the slats and peeked through the inch of space. At that moment my heart almost stopped beating.

I jumped as if bitten and covered my mouth with both hands. Dear mother of Jesus! I pulled apart the slats again and it was true: he was still there, standing in profile on the other side of my apartment door, staring at the alley.

It was Maxim Hall.

My hand dropped from the blind like it was on fire. I stepped back and froze in place. Maxim knocked again and spoke this time. "Bree, it's me. I know you don't want to see me, but I really need to talk to you." Several seconds passed in silence. "Please?"

My mind reeled. What was Maxim doing here? Did he plan to explain his actions? Offer an apology? Beg forgiveness? Why didn't he call first? Immediately I realized the absurdity of the question … he knew I wouldn't answer.

"I'm pretty sure you're here. I talked to your Aunt Judy, and she said you'd be home." If he knew the door was unlocked, would he have walked in? I decided no, he was too civilized for that. "The coffee shop is closed, and I looked through the window … you're not in there. And your pickup is here, so you must be inside."

I didn't move a millimeter; in fact, I barely breathed.

He continued. "Okay, if you won't let me in then I guess I'll just talk out here." I pictured his breath in the icy air, his lips a rosy pink, his ungloved hands in his pockets. "I'm losing my mind. You're all I think about." His voice cracked. "I can't sleep. I can't eat. I'm going nuts without you."

He sounded miserable and I wondered if he was crying. "The boys went on a skiing trip with friends, and I just couldn't stay away. I didn't even pack anything. I just drove to the airport and took the first flight I could find to Kansas City." He paused and then continued. "I just needed to see you." The silence stretched for several minutes and his next sentence was so quiet I almost didn't hear it. "I love you."

My heart melted at his words, and I ached to see him again. His voice was deep and rich, and the sound of it brought back everything I'd felt for him before I knew who he really was. I closed my eyes and my pulse quickened. I knew exactly what would happen if I let him in, and yet I knew I couldn't send him away.

I loved him too.

I reached for the handle and opened the door. Maxim turned his face to mine and his look was cautious, yet hopeful. I understood because I felt the same. "Come in."

He stepped inside, and the cold came with him. I shut the door and we were both perfectly still, studying each other with a depth that usually made me uncomfortable but seemed natural somehow. Dark circles under his eyes proved his fatigue, but he was the same beautiful man I'd met two weeks ago who swept me off my feet, a gorgeous specimen with crystal blue eyes, a strong jaw and thick, black hair.

Neither one of us smiled as we tried to read each other's thoughts. He closed his eyes and a lone tear streamed down his cheek. My heart warmed at the sight, and I stepped forward and lightly kissed it away. He opened his eyes in surprise and started to speak. "I just want to tell you…."

"Shhh." I placed my hand over his mouth to stop his words. "Don't say anything. Please."

I dropped my hand from his mouth and replaced it with my lips. The kiss was gentle at first, and as he responded to my touch he wrapped his arms around me and pulled my body to his. Maxim's lips were still cold from the outdoors, but they were soft and supple. I opened my mouth as he devoured my lips and offered his tongue.

We kissed with the urgency of our night in Denver, and I could taste his desperation and heartache … and love. Heat welled in my stomach, spread through my limbs, and I felt a scorching desire to be as close as possible to this incredible man.

I unzipped his coat and let it drop to the floor. Maxim kicked off his shoes, turned me around and held me against the wall. His mouth first went for my lips and then moved to my neck while his hands explored the curves of my body. He moaned when I wrapped my arms around his waist and pulled him closer. With his body pressing me into the wall, he ran his teeth along my jaw line and licked my ear. His voice was a ragged whisper edged with desire. "I want you."

I reached for his hand and led him across the apartment to my bed. Standing just inches from him — our eyes locked onto each other — I pulled off my clothes, one by one, and dropped them in a pile at my feet.

Maxim stared. "My God! You are so damn beautiful." He reached for me and ran his hands up and down my skin, inspecting every inch with conscious delight, and his touch was like lightening sending bolts of electricity through me. I grasped his hair and gave in to the pleasure he was offering.

He moaned, and his voice was gravelly. "If there's a heaven, this is it."

I reached under his shirt and felt his firm, toned muscles, the fine hair covering his chest; the man was driving me insane with need. He tore off his sweater and wrapped me in his arms; our naked chests melted together and we kissed again, his tongue trailing down my neck. I ran my fingernails up and down his back and moved my hands to unbuckle his jeans. He stood perfectly still, his eyes boring into mine as I unzipped his jeans and pushed them down, along with his boxers. His eyes were wild with excitement as I kissed his neck and bit at his earlobe.

In one smooth movement Maxim pushed me onto the bed and lowered himself on top of me; I reveled in the weight of him and his exhilarating scent. I pulled his face to mine, and as our lips came together, we made tender and urgent love … love that sent my heart racing and soaring at the same time. If a heart could explode, I didn't care. I gave in to every feeling, every emotion, and surrendered to the waves of pleasure rippling through my body as time drifted away and we gave each other the release we both desperately needed.

We laid there for several minutes afterward, holding each other as he whispered words of affection and then complete awe and wonder at our love making. Without warning I started to cry, softly at first, and then the tears poured out of me like a broken faucet. Maxim ran his fingers through my hair, kissed away my tears and somehow knew that no words were necessary. When my tears finally slowed, he walked to the bathroom and returned with a tissue. As I blew my nose and dabbed at my eyes, he sat next to me on the bed and traced my belly button with a finger.

I looked up at him. "You're the first man I've been with in ten years."

Maxim didn't meet my eyes. "I know."

"I thought maybe I'd forgotten how."

He looked at me then and laughed. "You definitely haven't forgotten a thing. That was … it was … incredible." He stared into my eyes for a few moments and dropped his head. "I haven't been with anyone since before the accident. Jackie…." He peered at me to see my reaction. "Jackie and I … our marriage wasn't that great before. Maybe she wrote about it. Anyway, after the accident she couldn't have sex, and with all that had happened I simply lost interest. It's been a long time for me too."

I thought about how our lives had crossed in such a dramatic way ten years ago without even meeting each other. I'd fallen in love with Maxim before I knew who he really was, and yet I still loved him in spite of what I'd learned.

He smiled and leaned down for a gentle kiss, and then his eyes lit up. "Hey … why don't you fly back to New York with me for New Year's Eve?" He grinned like a little kid and reached for my hands. "The Big Apple is the best place in the world to celebrate the new year." His beautiful face was full of expectation and he rushed ahead excitedly. "Then we could fly back here, and I could hang out with you until my book tour starts again mid-January."

I froze in place for a moment, surprised by his suggestion. I didn't know how to respond; I was at a total loss for words which was unusual for me. After what seemed like forever but was only a moment, I gave him a tight hug and kissed him on the cheek, then I rolled off the bed, grabbed my clothes and ran into the bathroom where I cleaned myself up and got dressed.

When I emerged from the bathroom Maxim had pulled on his jeans and was buttoning his shirt, a pensive look on his face. Wordlessly he followed me to the kitchen where I grabbed two beers from the refrigerator, handed him one and sat down at the table. He settled in across from me. We popped the tops and drank, each in our own thoughts. I studied the scar above his right eyebrow, and the knowledge that it played a role in Danny's death set a shiver down my spine.

Maxim set down his beer, folded his hands on the table and studied my face with a sincerity that unnerved me. We sat like that for several minutes, neither one of us smiling or saying a word, until his face blanched and his eyes grew moist. "Wow. I am such an idiot. This isn't going to happen, is it?"

I sat perfectly still. He seemed to be reading my thoughts. I held the beer in both hands and stared at the label. "No."

He dropped his head into his hands and tears fell to the table. "Is there anything I can do to change your mind?"

My throat choked up and I was slow in answering. "No."

He lifted his head and his eyes were filled with pleading. "But I love you."

"I love you too."

He reached for my hand. "If you love me there must be a way we can work this out. You'll never know how sorry I am for Danny's death … and then for lying to you. But can't I make it up to you? There's got to be a way … I need you." His pained expression tore my heart in two, but there was no future here.

I felt for the pendant hanging at my throat and rubbed my fingers over the stones. "There's nothing you can do, Maxim. It would never work between us, and deep in your heart you know that. Every time I look at you I think of Danny." My voice was hushed, and I stared at the table. "You were part of his death. I forgive you, but I can never forget."

He cried openly and gestured to the bed in the corner. "Then what was that?"

"It was goodbye."

He dropped his head and rubbed his face with both hands. When he finally returned his attention to me there was an emptiness in his eyes that came directly from his soul. He sat back in the chair and stared past me at the wall.

I leaned forward and rested my elbows on the table. "I want to thank you for bringing me the letters. They were hard to read, but they helped me to see Jackie as a real person. I'd always pictured her as a monster, but I can tell she was a wonderful woman." Maxim returned his gaze to me but said nothing. "She was distracted and made a mistake. It was an accident … and I forgive her." I sipped at the beer and sat back in my chair.

Maxim found his voice, and it trembled slightly. "She was a wonderful woman … better than I deserved, I'll tell you that. Why she stayed with me is a mystery. She just never gave up on me. That's why I couldn't give up on her after the accident."

I reached for his hand. "Jackie said you took excellent care of her. She explained what happened the day of the accident and how you supported her in the years after. She really loved you."

Maxim's tortured face softened. "She said good things about me?"

"Yes."

He exhaled and ran his fingers through his hair. "I really did try. It just never seemed to be enough."

"She also said you prayed together, and that you prayed for me."

He stroked my fingers. "That's right. Every night we prayed for you."

My heart swelled in my chest. "That means a lot."

He shrugged. "Jackie was the one with faith, and I truly admired her for it. I kind of went along for the ride because I knew how much it meant to her."

"So you're not a man of prayer?"

He shook his head. "No, I still pray. In fact, I've been praying an awful lot this past week." He dropped his head. "Of course, those were mostly selfish prayers that you'd forgive me, and we could be together."

I'd been thinking about something. "Do you have a picture of Jackie?"

Maxim brightened. "Yes." He rose and walked to his coat that was on the floor by the door, picked it up and pulled his phone out of a pocket. He tossed the coat on the bench and returned to the table. With a few swipes he handed me the phone. "There are several photos of her, some when she was younger, a few of us as a family, others after the accident."

I held the phone and saw Jackie Green for the first time, a striking redhead sitting in the grass with two small boys. Her smile was vibrant, and the boys had their arms wrapped around her waist. They couldn't have been any closer. The next photo was Maxim and Jackie on their wedding day. So he'd always been handsome. Their smiles were genuine as they posed on the altar in a charming church.

I swiped again and saw Jackie in her wheelchair, gaunt and pale, sweat glistening on her forehead as she held a small weight in each hand. A lump formed in my throat. Physical therapy. The next photo showed Jackie in her wheelchair with Maxim and their boys kneeling next to her in what must have been the sitting room. She looked happy and content.

I handed the phone back to Maxim. "Thank you. It means a lot to know what she looked like. She was beautiful."

Maxim nodded, turned off the phone and slid it in a back pocket. We sat there, enveloped in silence, unsure where to go from here.

There was something else I needed to know. "Did you send me the $100,000?"

He didn't waste time answering. "No."

"So it wasn't your money that paid for my coffee shop?"

He was shocked by my question. "No, that was Jackie's idea. It was her money … she had a successful interior design business and some savings. She really wanted you to have it."

"I used the money to buy this building, remodel it and purchase supplies." I thought about the irony of the situation. "So in effect, the woman who messed up my first life helped me start my second one."

Maxim studied my face. "Life is funny that way, I guess."

I leaned forward and folded my hands. "It may sound strange, but in a way this whole situation has forced me to confront the feelings I buried ten years ago. It's been agonizing, but I think it will be easier to get on with my life."

Maxim nodded but his face conveyed nothing but sadness and resignation. "I'm glad to hear that. You deserve to be happy. It's all I want for you." He stood up. "I think I'd better be going." He walked to the door and pulled on his coat and shoes.

I followed him and gently placed my hand on his back. He turned to me and we held each other for a long time and finally touched our lips together in a tender goodbye kiss.

He reluctantly let go and backed to the door. His eyes were misty, and his voice trembled. "I love you, Bree."

My hand moved to cover my heart. "I love you, Maxim." I wiped at a tear and stared into those cerulean eyes for the last time.

We gazed at each other for several moments, and he let himself out. I pulled up the blind and watched him walk down the steps to his rental car, back up and drive away. I stayed there for a long time, staring at the icy parking lot and the alley beyond, and even though it was cold outside I felt my heart thawing from a long winter. Spring would be here in a few months, and that meant new life and new possibilities.

Anything could happen … even love.

I turned and walked to the nightstand next to my bed. I reached behind my neck and unhooked Danny's necklace, removed the diamond earrings and gently laid them in the heart-shaped jewelry box. Without the weight of the necklace and earrings I somehow felt freer, lighter … I knew Danny would approve.

It was time to move on.

EPILOGUE

The night Maxim left I dreamed of Waconda again. Like the hundreds of times before, she was suspended in midair over the silent water as if in flight, arms out at her sides like the wings of an airplane. Her lustrous dark hair flowed in a gentle breeze, and she smiled right before she fell into the spring, its waters icy cold. She didn't flail about or fight to save herself. Her dark brown eyes remained open and she exuded peace as she floated gently downward. When she reached the bottom her hands fell together over her heart and her eyes closed.

I was in the water with Waconda again but this time, instead of freezing alongside her, I pushed off the bottom and swam upward, gaining strength and momentum as I rose. I exploded through the surface, floated to the edge and pulled myself out of the water. When I collapsed on the bank of Waconda Springs I was chilled to the bone but laughed in delight. I was alive!

The next morning when my stupid alarm chimed at 5, I sat up and observed a new sensation in my body; I was rested and refreshed for the first time in ten years. I stretched my arms over my head and reveled in the contentment of a good night's sleep.

Waconda no longer haunts my dreams, although I think of her often when I'm awake. She's a daily presence in my life — the spring was named after her, then the town and the lake. According to the legend, Waconda threw herself into the spring to be with her lover, but I've managed to survive — thrive, even — without mine. I have no doubt Waconda would have survived if she'd given herself the chance to grieve, heal and move on.

I wasn't sure I would be a survivor but I'm glad I allowed myself the chance. Maxim Hall's appearance in town, although traumatic and heart-rending, was the push I needed to close one chapter in my life and begin another. Like steel forged in fire, I'm stronger for having gone through the flames. I sound like an inspirational poster, don't I?

I took a day and drove to Olathe where I visited Danny's grave for the first time since the funeral. I sat in the grass at his headstone for several hours … there was so much to say … and before I left I told him I was finally moving on, that I had decided to take a chance on love if it happened to come along.

As I walked through the cemetery to my pickup I watched for a sign that Danny had heard my words and approved, but no cosmic revelation appeared. It felt like a weight had lifted from my shoulders, though, and I smiled as I jumped in the pickup and drove away.

In February my phone rang, and it was Maxim; after hesitating for a moment, I answered. His voice was friendly and animated, and he was excited to share the news that he'd started writing a novel about Waconda Springs. He'd been researching his Cheyenne background and had convinced his publisher to let him write a historical novel centered around the Legend of Waconda. Our discussion was light and easy, and I told him to call any time; he said the same.

Spring did arrive in Waconda, and in the middle of April an attractive man I'd never seen walked into my coffee shop and ordered a double espresso and two glazed doughnuts. He introduced himself as Clay Miller, the new manager at Waconda Grain Company, and our conversation was fun and flirtatious. He was a little younger and a little shorter than me, but quite the looker with blond hair, blue eyes and the sweetest smile I'd ever seen. After repeated trips for coffee and doughnuts, with both of us too shy to make the first move, I finally worked up the nerve and asked him out.

He said yes.

We met in the park.

I wore flats.

THE END

LARA KETTER is a native Kansan and the author of several books. She grew up in a newspaper family and graduated from Kansas State University in 1993 with a degree in communications. She currently serves as Assistant Editor for the quarterly newspaper in her small town. She lives with her husband and three children on a farm near Tipton, Kansas. Like her main character, Bree, she is addicted to coffee and heartily agrees with the following saying: "First I drink the coffee, then I do the things."

This is her first novel. Please visit her on the Web at www.LaraKetter.com.

Made in United States
North Haven, CT
10 July 2022

21170289R00176